After
Goodlake's

After Goodlake's

TERENCE YOUNG

RAINCOAST BOOKS

Vancouver

Raincoast Books acknowledges the ongoing financial support of the Government of Canada through The Canada Council for the Arts and the Book Publishing Industry Development Program (BPIDP); and the Government of British Columbia through the BC Arts Council.

Editor: Lynn Henry
Cover design: Ingrid Paulson
Text design: Teresa Bubela

CANADIAN CATALOGUING IN PUBLICATION DATA

Young, Terence
    After Goodlakes / Terence Young.
ISBN 1-55192-683-0
    I. Title.
PS8597.O72A74 2004   C813'.54   C2003-906960-5

LIBRARY OF CONGRESS CONTROL NUMBER: 2004091805

Raincoast Books
9050 Shaughnessy Street
Vancouver, British Columbia
Canada, V6P 6E5
www.raincoast.com

At Raincoast Books we are committed to protecting the environment and to the responsible use of natural resources. We are acting on this commitment by working with suppliers and printers to phase out our use of paper produced from ancient forests. This book is one step towards that goal. It is printed on 100% ancient-forest-free paper (100% post-consumer recycled), processed chlorine- and acid-free. It is printed with vegetable-based inks. For further information, visit our website at www.raincoast.com. We are working with Markets Initiative (www.oldgrowthfree.com) on this project.

Printed in Canada by AGMV Marquis Imprimeur
10 9 8 7 6 5 4 3 2 1

For Patricia,
who knew all those years ago
that where "we could have been
and should have been" is
"exactly where we are."

[Contents]

PROLOGUE

Hours of Operation

[Hours of Operation]

A business is a promise. It's a promise that what was there in the
evening will be there the next morning. A marriage offers the same
promise, and some businesses, like some people, are better at keeping
their word than others. One of the best was Goodlake's Delicatessen. It
occupied the same address for over seventy years, a lifetime, and most of
its customers assumed it would last forever.

The delicatessen — Goodlake's to most — opened every day except
Sunday at eight-thirty, a few minutes after the last of the dayliner's many
whistles broke the morning air. On this particular morning, a Saturday in
late April, the air was a mix of sea and city, the growing light a taste of summer to come. It was the kind of morning on which the people of Victoria
finally forgot to congratulate themselves for having dodged yet another
cold winter, and began to worry that this sample of hot weather was just a
teaser, a false taste of blue sky and sun that would lead to a disappointing
June and July. They were used to suffering for their mild Decembers, for
their early flowers and cheap heating, just as they were used to watching
the city they knew change into something different, larger, less familiar.
Even the air had changed over the years. The whiff of pulp, the scent of
seaweed and wood smoke had given way to the aroma of downtowns
everywhere: a mixture of traffic, urine and cigarettes. Since 1922, Goodlake's
had opened its doors on all of it, and this morning was no exception.

Three hours earlier — just after five o'clock most days — before a
single cinnamon bun graced a plate or a single coffee bean gave up its

caffeine, the deli's owner, Fergus Goodlake, had tethered his Raleigh ten-speed to the gas meter on the deli's south side where the brick walls of Goodlake's and what was these days a second-hand sporting goods store formed a nasty little alley. On days when rain looked likely, Fergus wrapped a plastic bag around his bicycle seat and secured it with a rubber band, both of which he carried in a fanny pack. In this fanny pack, Fergus also kept two bicycle clips, one for each of his pant legs. Though he really needed only one for the pant leg that threatened to become tangled in the drive-chain, Fergus wore both of them because two clips had come with the package when he bought it. But there was no rain in the forecast today, and Fergus had walked around to the front door where he was obliged to stoop and collect two newspapers, one local and one national, before slipping his key into the Stanley deadbolt he had been convinced to buy when his son — nicknamed Helios because of an awful joke — at age thirteen demonstrated the ease with which a modern credit card could defeat the lock Fergus' father had installed just after the war. Before that, only a simple skeleton key prevented the public from pilfering the store's contents, a skeleton key which Fergus still kept in a drawer by the cash register and which he would occasionally bring out to the amazement of younger customers who had only read of such things. The deadbolt he'd installed gave him some comfort each morning he opened the shop, but he knew, too, from police visits and Chamber of Commerce bulletins, that security in this day and age was an illusion. People drove trucks through solid walls of concrete to get at ATMs, for Christ's sake. If somebody wanted in, they got in.

Still, Fergus made an effort. Today, as on each day he opened the deli, a bell sounded, triggered by the door's breaking a beam of infra-red light, a device that later in the day summoned Doris to the front counter, or the new girl, Marina, or Fergus himself if things were busy. In the early dawn, the electronic tone struck Fergus as ominous, as though he'd just triggered the launch button to an atomic warhead, and death was now winging its way through the air. In the light of a working afternoon, the sound was a little annoying and a little comforting, like the melody of a popular song on the radio where repetition also means more money. Part of the week, Fergus' wife Annie might be in the shop to answer its call, too, or she might not. Other concerns filled her hours — the demands of the catering side to the business, demands that compelled her into traffic much of the time and kept her on the road more than she liked. Some of her day was spent at home answering the phone on the separate line they'd set up especially for this purpose, confirming rentals, dealing with suppliers, keeping the books — in particular, all the bills the accountant would need to prepare their taxes. Not a single expense escaped her eye: tapes and CDs for the shop stereo, cleaning supplies, extension cords, light bulbs, spare keys, pens for the customers to sign their Visa slips, tacks for posters on the walls. If Annie could have claimed the European mints she chewed non-stop, she would have. At least once every couple of months, she rifled Fergus' wallet for the stubs and receipts that had accumulated over the weeks. Sometimes it was crammed to the point that Fergus could barely fold it in half. He would look at it in his hand — a bloated, mutant thing, quite unrecognizable from the sleek, thin billfold he remembered purchasing — and think how much it mirrored the life of its owner.

"Fergus," Annie would say, presenting him with a wad of papers. "Sit down and label these for me. I need to know where you've been."

And Fergus would sit, pencil in hand, surprised to discover all the places he'd visited and forgotten: the kitchen shop, the framing store, the hardware on Store Street. "These are as good as a diary," he thought once, "without all that meaningless weather."

Annie's duties were varied, and she came and went as the whims of Goodlake's clientele demanded. Hers was a freedom that had developed naturally, a kind of groping for light some trees will undertake because it is their business to occupy space, to fill a chunk of sky. She did not think her work superior to Fergus', or that her marriage was any better for the fact that she had liberated herself from the home. She moved through life as most of the people she knew did, instinctually, almost unconsciously, responding to the dictates of mortgage payments, cost of living, the wisdom of GICs versus mutual funds. Only recently had she felt any unease at all, but the distractions of work prevented her from articulating exactly what this unease signified. She continued to spread herself across the working day, driving into the quiet private homes of Oak Bay or Gordon Head to discuss place settings, linen, the cost of plastic compared to stainless steel.

Fergus, on the other hand, was a constant, a fixture, an indispensable component — certainly during the deli's early hours before drill-sergeant Doris arrived. Doris came in at eight, well after Fergus had worked his magic in the kitchen. After Doris walked in, chairs assumed their places, counters glistened, awnings unfolded onto the day, and the tip jar — emptied the night before — rattled with the sound of a few quarters and dollar coins that she dropped in to shame the clientele into following suit.

The smell of the deli on this morning, as on all mornings, was a blend of many things: last evening's mop-down; the metallic air breathed out by the fans of three coolers, two double-sized fridges and one 32-cubic-foot freezer; traces of natural gas from the pilots of Goodlake's' six-burner industrial range; a hint of yeast from the three breads Fergus would have left to rise overnight: focaccia, multi-grain-olive and Italian baguette; and underneath all these, the remnant odour of an infestation of rats that had plagued the store for over six months. Once Fergus started to prepare the day's main dishes — salads and soups and pasta selections, braised fillets of salmon, heartbreaking medallions of veal — the spices and sauces and oils he used to prepare them took over. Their aromas billowed out through exhaust fans into the street and pulled in customers in a way that reminded Fergus of something he'd read in the doctor's office — Fergus had been reading quite a few articles there recently, now that his prostate had loomed into view — an article about carnivorous plants and the cloying perfume some of them produced to attract their victims.

Fergus was not the first businessman to think of his customers in this way — as victims, prey with pockets — but recently he'd begun to understand the comparison from a slightly more sinister angle.

Goodlake's consumed people all right, but not those who came through its front door and left a few moments later, packages in hand, nor those who sat at one of the glass-topped iron tables and sipped from a cup of soup or poked at a Greek salad for the fifteen minutes or half hour their employer allowed them for lunch. No, Goodlake's ate the people who worked for it, smothered them like the juices of the Venus flytrap, dissolving them slowly, consuming the one thing each of them valued most in their lives: their time.

DORIS HAD BEEN WORKING at Goodlake's for over ten years, almost as long as Fergus had been working there himself since he'd taken over the place from his father in the mid-eighties. She'd walked in during one of Annie's fits of renovation and placed her résumé into Fergus' hand as he turned to grab the cup of coffee he'd placed on a stepladder. She stood before him in gear that was a cross between punk, gothic and grunge. There were sweaters. There were combat pants. There was lipstick. The shoes reminded Fergus of something he used to call "desert boots," but surely they didn't make those things anymore.

"I worked retail before this," she'd said. "Le Chateau. It's all in there."

"Oh," Fergus had said.

"I'm good with people. You'll see."

"We're not hiring right now."

Fergus had looked around for Annie. He heard the sounds of a wall or counter coming apart back where the kitchen exited onto a square of trash-strewn dirt that would later become the parking lot and partial outdoor patio for the deli. It was an angry sound, a do-not-disturb sound, and, though this was not the first occasion Fergus had felt torn between the disapproval of two women — Annie and Fergus' mother, while she was alive, were always competing for control — the weight of this woman's eyes upon him now filled him with such dread that he made himself search out his wife, no matter what she was doing.

Annie hired Doris on the spot.

"I told you I was good with people," Doris had said as she left.

In the years she'd worked for Fergus, Doris had revealed very little of herself. She lived somewhere across the blue bridge — Fergus often recognized her angular shoulders and leggy lope on the boarded walkway as he biked past the bridge on his way home — and she never spoke of her family. No mention of brothers or sisters. She couldn't have been more than twenty when she first applied to work at Goodlake's, and the years between had seen her grow from a girl into a woman. Yet, no mention of a husband or boyfriend. When Fergus started his affair with Caroline, he found it hard to look at Doris, who was only two years older. He kept thinking he could be having sex with an employee — sometimes in dreams believed he was — and counted himself lucky he didn't have a daughter that age. Fergus couldn't even say with any certainty what part of the country Doris was from. She might be an American for all he knew. There was something about the way she emphasized certain syllables in her speech that made him think she was from Ontario, a habit she had of pronouncing contractions almost as though they were two separate words: would-dint, could-dint, should-dint. She also managed to leave the "t" out of the word Saturday. Fergus had never been to Ontario, but he imagined these were characteristics of the English spoken there.

At the same time, Doris hid nothing. It was clear to Fergus from the moment he met her that Doris' personality was apparent in every action she took. The way she reached for a bottle of Brio from the shelf behind her, without looking, certain of distance and speed. The ease with which she bypassed a customer who had stepped into the middle of the queue, the kind of customer who feigned ignorance about what had happened, as though it was unclear where the line began and ended. A single look from Doris made it perfectly clear to the man — rarely — or the woman that what he or she had done was not only a breach of etiquette, but also an insight into the person's long and ugly history of petty betrayals and frauds. Occasionally, Fergus would come upon her writing something down on a piece of paper, something clearly unrelated to the business of running a delicatessen, and when he asked her once what she was writing, she said only that what he didn't know couldn't hurt him. Doris was a scary person. Fergus believed she had always been a scary person, that she always would be. It had long ago occurred to Fergus that he had somehow surrounded himself with this kind of woman all his life, the type who held a man to account for everything he did, drew attention to his inconsistencies, each little act of self-interest. At first he had imagined, particularly with Annie, that he was somehow compensating for some huge imbalance in the world, but after years of this way of looking at himself, he had decided he was wrong, that he was just easily pushed around and some people were attracted to that, even people like Annie who loved him. He was hoping Caroline was a chance at breaking this pattern, that an affair was some way of asserting himself. If lying all the time and worrying about getting caught were signs of self-affirmation, then his experiment in extra-marital relations was a huge success.

A DAY AT THE DELI was a journey toward exhaustion. This was true in two senses. It was necessary to exhaust the resources devoted to the day — the fresh vegetables, the dairy, the meat — and it was also a depletion of the patience, goodwill and manners of the people who worked there. By day's end, the contempt was palpable — especially for the last person who lingered over the three varieties of pesto in the cooler: cilantro, spinach, sun-dried tomato. Or for the person who tore into the store at the last minute, the one who pleaded with Fergus to look in the back to see if there was any fresh basil left, and then proceeded to search frantically in each section of the display case for salads, curried rices, anything they could use to cobble together a dinner for five. There was an arc — several arcs, in fact — as coffee breaks came and went in downtown government offices, lunch hours disgorged workers in staggered lots that lasted from eleven until one, and then came the final push to closing. Most days, Goodlake's could make it on what Fergus produced in the morning, but sometimes it became obvious they would need another batch of pizza bread, another kilo of vermicelli.

There was a larger arc, too, the arc in the life of the store's proprietors. Fergus had the example of his father and his grandfather, both of whom had run the deli until they either died or passed it on. Lately, Fergus had been wondering which would come first in his case.

In the last few years, Goodlake's had made some enemies. Until 1997, Fergus had allowed customers to smoke while they drank their coffees and ate their croissants. He had a good ventilation system. These people kept sales up. Fergus had nothing against cigarettes. But in anticipation of the district-wide ban that was coming into effect the next year, Fergus believed customers would be attracted to the idea of cleaner air, and he announced in the fall that Goodlake's was now a smoke-free environment. People who had once asked him how his day was going now sat outside at one of the store's tables, their bag lunches in plain view, their thermoses of coffee standing like upraised middle fingers, daring him to come out and tell them they couldn't sit there. Sales dropped. Each night Fergus had to sweep up the butts and sandwich wrappings they left behind. Small acts of vandalism surfaced: scratches in the thick enamel paint of the chairs, burn marks on the window ledges. The storm lasted almost two years, even after the ban came into effect for all businesses, but in the recent downsizing of government personnel, many of these people had moved away or given up or forgotten, and Goodlake's was returning to normal.

It was hard to say what effect a store had on a town. Goodlake's had been around long enough that it would probably be missed were it to close. Despite the changes Annie had wrought, the business maintained a loyal following of customers who went back almost to Fergus' grandfather's time. Many of Victoria's families had grown up as Eaton's department store people or Hudson's Bay people. It was a town of old grudges and long memories, and even the children fell into line once they'd had their fling with Sears or K-Mart. A person's buying habits were set in concrete. One bought Beaumark or one bought Viking. These allegiances were mysterious, aligned along a set of incomprehensible political principles, and when Eaton's finally collapsed, it was as though the country had been reduced to a single party system. One result was that people clung even more tenaciously to the institutions that were left: the City News; Murchie's — gaudy and bright though it was; Morris Tobacconists; and Goodlake's. Fergus grew to recognize the "old squad" early on in his tenure at the store. They came in to place their order for a Christmas turkey, a ham for Easter. They bought a few slices of cold roast beef, some havarti cheese, a jar of French mustard. A few stayed for coffee and a slice of one of Annie's homemade pies. One of the older ones, a man Fergus knew only as Ron, had been a regular as long as he could remember. More than three decades. Over the years, the old man had dropped off the odd gift, usually around Fergus' birthday, and after one such gift — a pen and pencil desk set with replaceable calendar on Fergus' nineteenth birthday — Fergus had asked his father what connection this man had with their family.

"Never seen the guy before he stepped into this shop," Fergus' father had said.

The gifts kept coming — there'd even been a card on each of Fergus and Annie's wedding anniversaries — and during the last thirteen years of Fergus' tenure as proprietor, he had always gone up to Ron and offered a quick thank you, a cup of coffee on the house. The man was ninety at least, but his behaviour had never seemed confusing to Fergus. After the war, Fergus' own father refused to buy anything German or Japanese — cars, appliances, electronics, even oranges — and Ron's loyalties did not seem out of place.

Fergus saw the impact streetscape had on the mood of a city. Fergus' mother would often talk about a soda shop called Terry's that she used to go to when she was young, the kind of place that sold lemon Cokes and floats and glazed donuts. A business like that can define a decade — Fergus himself remembered the cafeteria at the old YMCA on Blanshard Street, its cheap hamburgers, the u-shaped counter. In the sixties he'd eaten at a place called The Vegetable, also on Blanshard, where hippies came for lentil soups and nut burgers and squash stews. And now, even on a morning as beautiful and full of hope as this April morning was, Fergus looked around at the brick walls of Goodlake's' tired and barely serviceable kitchen — he couldn't help thinking about his prostate at moments like this — and wondered about the life of a thing, its arc. How to tell where it started to decline, what to do when you knew. It was a bleak thought, one that had been coming to him more often in the last few months, and not even the prospect of a Sunday away from work could dispel his misgivings.

PART I

While They Were Talking

[I]

Fergus Goodlake sat in the living room of his arts-and-crafts bungalow reading about current diet trends. Saturday had come and gone. Sunday, too, almost, the evening falling down around him, and he was scanning an article without really reading it, his mind flipping instead through a slideshow of the hour he'd squeezed in with Caroline today. Was this another form of pornography? To revisit again and again each move, each small journey of the hand, the mouth? He watched himself slip up behind her at the sink, felt her press against him, followed the chain of signals that led them onto the couch, the floor. These actions were so predictable, so bland in their earnestness, that he wondered for a moment if he might not be growing more simple-minded. He mechanically turned a page of the newspaper, and as he shook the whole mass of the weekend edition into place, he had the sudden feeling his happiness was about to end. The feeling was precise, quite different from the flutter he'd experienced at age five when a dream about elephants surfaced during a conversation the very next morning. And it wasn't anything like the dread he felt every couple of months, the kind that built as one thing after another went wrong on what had started out as an ordinary day — the key that twists off in the ignition to the car, the taxi driver who won't take Visa, the coffee that spills everywhere. No, this feeling was as clear as a wrong answer whispered during a high-school mathematics exam, and it came from the stereo. Fergus wasn't having an auditory hallucination. This wasn't some visit from the dead. This was

Sunday, a day off from the family business, and on Sundays the stereo blared from the moment Fergus' wife Annie rose in the morning until the two of them pulled the plug on the day and went to bed. The NAD, multi-function CD, tape player and FM receiver and its four bass-reflex, wall-mounted speakers had cost them enough money to buy half a BMW, and though it had never done so, Fergus knew from his fingernails to the nerves of his teeth that if it ever stopped spewing forth whatever music Annie had chosen to listen to over and over again — which in this case happened to be a compilation of songs by another aging whiz-kid from the sixties, Eric Clapton — there would follow from out of his wife's mouth a phrase such as "I've been thinking," or "I've been giving it some thought," or "You know what I think?" to which Fergus would answer in his best ready-for-a-ruckus drawl, "Really," or "What's that?" or "Tell me, sweetheart."

So, this evening, when the guitar solo stuttered like a cat clubbed to death in the middle of a fight, Fergus steeled himself for the worst. He put down the now-crumpled style section of the newspaper with its photo-heavy article about the expanding girth of the nation's middle class and grimaced as silence bargained its way into the house around him, a change that might actually have been a relief if it weren't for the queasiness in his stomach. What was she up to? She might as well have opened a window in the middle of a snowstorm, or taken a machete to the rose bushes: the impact on Fergus was the same. His heart went on a tear, he couldn't breathe, every car that drove by the house tightened another notch in this belt that had suddenly appeared around his throat. He mistrusted this moment the way he mistrusted every one of his now innumerable visits to the doctor. What would come up this time? What clues had he failed to see? Why could he not predict the next curve in the road?

JUST AFTER THE MUSIC stopped, Fergus heard the door of the freezer open, the rush of air as the vacuum released, followed by the clink of ice on glass and the even fainter sound of liquid pouring into itself.

These gave way to footsteps that zeroed in on the living room from the front hall until, at last, Fergus' wife of twenty-five years crossed the expanse of polished, edge-grain, tongue-in-groove flooring, sat herself in the loveseat opposite, the coffee table between them, and placed two gin and tonics complete with lemon wedges onto the twin coasters she had also brought with her.

"Pedro," she said.

A few nicknames had survived the years, Pedro being the most popular, followed by "husband" and "my Renaissance man." Annie employed these endearments unaware of how square they sounded. "Square" was Fergus' word, as were "golly" and "gosh," dated terms he'd taken a shine to from watching black and white movies. His favourite word was "joint," which he used to describe almost any building, but especially their house. Isn't it about time we painted the joint? he had the habit of saying every few years. "Square" he reserved for Annie. Nobody, in Fergus' mind, was more artless than his wife. She was like a student whose first day of school had never ended, giddy about every little thing, happy as a dog to see her teachers, dressed all wrong, no idea of the spectacle she was making of herself. Not infantile. Not some pouting starlet who wanted a different colour for her new car. But a child, the kid who couldn't be cool because coolness for Annie was an absence, a negation. The times he'd tried to talk to her about it were the times they'd nearly come to blows.

"So I embarrass you?" she'd say. "Is that what you mean?"

And before Fergus could swallow his own spit, he found himself standing on the edge of a big one, the kind of fight that would have lasted his parents a week, where words were slivers of glass and looks were automobiles heavy enough to crush a person, where there was blood in every breath and the ground buckled with each door that closed. Whenever he and Annie walked into this terrain, Fergus headed for the hills. Some people could fight in the morning and eat dinner together the same day, but not Fergus. One mean face from her and he could feel the marriage on the chopping block.

Fergus examined the drink on its coaster.

"Light of my life. How lovely! You have brought me a drink!"

"Stop it." Annie seemed to fix her eyes on a point beyond the room, beyond the street, the town, beyond even the mountains of the Olympic peninsula hunkered down across the strait like rugby players in a scrum. Then she turned.

"Do you think you will ever have an affair?"

Fergus' hand did not pause. It did not falter once on its way to the now sweating glass that teased him from the middle of the coffee table. He wouldn't allow a single sign of hesitation to show. It didn't matter how fast thirst withered his tongue, dried up his mouth as though someone had crammed into it a fistful of Saltines. What did he care what his wife had said? How had she said it? Did he *think* he would ever have an affair? No, that wasn't it. Did he think *he* would ever have an affair? Closer. Did he think he would *ever* have an affair? Possibly, yes, definitely. This way made sense. Just like Annie, too, her ass-backward way of pointing out how long they'd avoided the pitfalls of other marriages, what a marvelous couple they must be to still lie together under the same roof, the same sheets for lo these thousands of years. He imagined a series of biography specials on A&E: "They Mate For Life." Paul Newman and Joanne Woodward. Mark Twain and what was her name? He mustn't be cocky about it, though. Didn't he know it was suicide to pooh-pooh his wife's revelations?

"Hmmm." Fergus rubbed his chin in a manner he had adopted from Jimmy Stewart, an actor he liked for his ability to inspire trust. Hadn't he married only once, too? Probably. He rubbed his chin again, and then, as though he were rendering a verdict in a murder trial, he said, "No, I don't believe so. I truly don't. One can never tell about these things, of course. Why do you ask?"

"I've been thinking."

He allowed himself a breath.

"And?" he said.

Fergus' wife awoke from her brown study. For some reason she'd decided the occasion merited jewelry, and her neck and wrists were overflowing with turquoise and Mexican silver. A dress, too, for heaven's sake! One of those long sheer jobs she had picked up at that new Balinese boutique in the mall. She seemed to look across at Fergus as though noticing him for the first time, as though she were Lewis and he Clark on the evening their great adventure had suggested itself. Annie was a woman whose weight hadn't altered a hair since her adolescence. Still just a hundred and fourteen pounds, she was one of those people who could feasibly wear her graduation gown had she kept it. At forty-six, she had taken on a feline angularity that seemed to Fergus vastly more beautiful than the fuzziness of younger women. It was as though age had brought her into focus. She was crisp. She was clear.

"You're still a very attractive man, you know."

"Thank you."

"You still have all your hair and you're not fat."

Fergus began to fiddle with his drink.

"What I mean is, there are women out there — I've seen some of them, believe me — there are women who would consider themselves lucky to spend a night or two, even an hour in the company of a man in your shape."

"You flatter me, sweetheart."

"It's not flattery. It's true."

"Maybe so, but why would I want them when I have you?"

Fergus knew Annie filtered out his facile answers. They didn't register, almost as though he hadn't spoken at all. He provided background noise, and as long as he didn't say anything too contemptible, too egregiously stupid, their little chat would reach its predictable end without incident.

"Let me ask you this."

Okay, thought Fergus. *Bring it on.*

"Do you think we've stopped growing?"

"I certainly hope so." He patted his stomach.

"You know what I mean, goofball. Be serious for once. I mean it. The last few months, I don't know, it's like we're stale. No, stale's not the word. It feels like we've learned all we're going to learn about each other. We've hit a wall. Isn't that what they say? A wall? That's what it is. A big brick wall. And it makes me sad, I guess. I'm always feeling sad these days."

"Hold on a minute ..."

"And don't try to make it go away." Fergus' wife sat up in the love seat. She placed both hands on the coffee table and leaned toward him. "You always do that. You turn it into a comedy act, something to do with the weather or the stock market. You make a joke out of it and I hate it. And you know I hate it, so don't. Just don't this time, okay?"

Fergus looked down into his lap. Annie was capable of anything. Fergus had known her to stand up in the middle of a vacation — he had in mind their trip to Palm Springs — and declare she was leaving. The town, she'd said, was unbearable, a tawdry little homage to money and consumerism and racist homophobes. Fergus could do what he wanted, but she would not suffer another second breathing this contaminated air. They had driven all the way to Red Bluff in a single day. There was never any warning. Annie never gave any indication she was about to pop. She might just as easily have turned to him in her poolside chair at Place in the Sun and said she was having the time of her life and that she loved him very very much.

"Listen, Pedro. Anything's good for a while. But then one day it's not. It's like Christmas at home. The first ones we took pictures. Now we don't bother. Do you remember any of those days? I don't. I can't tell one from the next. There is nothing to tell them apart. Christmas is a big jumble of flatness in my head. I don't know how people manage to live through it without shooting themselves. Honestly, I don't. Do you know what I mean? Pedro?"

"Yes. You're always suicidal at Christmas."

"Idiot. I'm not really, you know."

"No?"

"No, but I should be. Oh, sure. One year we put the tree in the den, didn't we? I remember the pipes froze once, too. We melted snow or something. What milestones! I don't think I'm stupid, or easily bored, but these days I'm missing the point. I'm really missing the point, well, and I know what you'd say, Mr. Existential, Mr. God-has-no-place-in-the-mind-of-civilized-person, that I'm wrong thinking there's a point in the first place, but you can't really mean that. Nobody really means that."

Fergus suspected there were lots of people who really meant it, though the only name that came to mind was Albert Camus, and he could see that Annie wasn't really looking for a debate about God. He put his hands together, pressed them as though in prayer. "So?" he said.

"So, I'm saying help me out here. Is this marriage thing working for you?"

"Marriage thing? Working? You mean is it boring?"

"No, I don't mean boring. Boredom happens to people with no imagination. I mean is our marriage meaningless? Is that what happens to married people? I'm hoping it doesn't have to be. But that's what I'm feeling. You know what I think? I think people are lazy. People are just lazy, that's all. They don't have the time. They get into ruts."

"I'm not in a rut."

"Settle down. It's not your fault." She waved her hand in front of him as though she were wiping clean a bathroom mirror. "I'm not saying any-one's to blame here. Don't get me wrong. If anything, we're both to blame. Life's to blame."

"Ah. Yes. Life."

A pause followed as they both considered the implications of this final revelation. Fergus, too, was not stupid. He was beginning to see the drift of Annie's current complaint, a complaint that differed little from all her others. She was incapable of joie de vivre. After all, he thought, what's a change in diet, a change in wallpaper, a change in vacation venues if not a declaration that you are dissatisfied with the status of things as they are? Fergus, on the other hand, was a master of joie de vivre. Happiness was his forte.

At least it used to be.

He allowed a slight grimace to pass across his face, a wisp of distaste he hoped Annie would fail to notice in her present state. Just the gin, he'd say, should she ask. Bitter lemon. Bitter something, and he knew exactly what it was. Today's *felicitus interruptus* — the abrupt banishment of music, Annie's new complaint — was really just another in a recent spate of wild deviations from the contented flatline of his life, a series of developments that, were he Annie, he would probably try to interpret, give a name to, something with the word crisis in it, or pathology. He was, he supposed, unhappy, too, and had been for some time. What a miserable little word! Unhappy, like a child who cannot think of anything to do, despite the sun, the acres of uncharted backyard jungle, the toys forgotten under the bed. Such a selfish word. I'm unhappy! Boo hoo!

Unlike Annie, though, Fergus had been putting up a fight. He had been trying to maintain equilibrium, imposing on his days the template of his character, a character he had perfected over years of practise. Who was Fergus Goodlake? He was a man who preferred the status quo. He was a fan of uninterrupted familiarity. He loved Christmas at home, for example, and the way in spring the cherry blossoms on the boulevard outside their house gave way to leaves. He liked how precisely the rhododendrons bloomed every year on his birthday and he liked to read the Sunday paper in bed with coffee. Before the deli, he used to dream of running a farm, something small with an apple orchard and a few cows. Nothing more regular than the life of a farmer. Routine's the ticket. Routine keeps a person sane. If it were up to Fergus, he and Annie would eat at the same restaurant twice in a row, three times if he could convince her. He drank India pale ale and only India pale ale. For Fergus, there was no more honorable chore than mowing the lawn on the exact day.

Could he say, then, that he even loved the regularity of his affair? Could he embrace as part of himself this recent dalliance? Annie had shown true prescience in her question, a chilling kind of knowledge of him that unnerved Fergus. But this was a dalliance that had begun, not as an attempt to dispel boredom, but as an accident, a truly unforeseeable event which Fergus had tried to incorporate smoothly into his life — he imagined a potter adding more clay to the pot on his wheel — without detection certainly, but also without disturbing the order of his days or hers. Could he say that he loved this? Yes, he could, after a fashion. He loved the heady days of anticipation before a tryst, his nerves taut like a greyhound's in the gate, and the slow days of decompression afterwards when his every move became an act of contrition. These were the events that generated a fog of comfort around a person and helped obscure the ugly randomness of life: the Jack Russell that runs under the wheels of a car, the three lovely turn-of-the-century clapboard homes, each with a Mansard roof, that are torn down to make way for another block of condominiums. Who could deny that change — and by change Fergus meant all that had occurred in urban planning, entertainment, and fast food in the past fifty years — was really only the efforts of limited minds to stimulate themselves in less and less time? More roads, faster cars, louder movies, bigger hamburgers. Nothing satisfied anymore because people had lost the art of joie de vivre. In Fergus' mind, his wife's continual shifting and rearranging of their lives was a similar kind of disease, though he would never say as much to her, and to be fair, he would be the first to admit that on one level, such furious caprice was what had attracted him to her in the first place. She had charmed him on their first date by suggesting a walk along the causeway at midnight. At midnight! And half the town asleep!

Annie coughed.

"I have noticed," she said, "among our friends, some of our friends, a kind of thing that happens when they're threatened, or when their marriage is threatened."

"The Jensens ..."

"Exactly, but not only the Jensens. There are others. More than you know, Fergus."

"Excuse me, sweetheart."

"Yes, Pedro?"

Fergus looked at his wife. She was truly lovely, even more so perhaps because of the current urgency he saw lurking around her eyes, the need he had come to recognize in her, the need to pursue some form of perfection she felt she lacked, that she perpetually lacked. He wanted to tell her how life with her was adequate, that it was sufficient, that it was enough, but these were words she refused to allow in their house, and besides, they weren't as true as they used to be.

"I have to pee."

"Of course you do." Annie nodded her acknowledgment like a cashier giving change, her eyes vacant, her mind elsewhere. "I'll wait here."

[II]

The scenic route in Victoria runs along the ocean. Uplands, Beach Drive, Dallas Road. Something's always happening out on the water, and even when there isn't, people go to look. At Ross Bay there's the cemetery. Death with a view, Fergus' father calls it. Still life. In 1911, the city constructed a cement seawall in front of it. There'd been stories about coffins breaking loose in storms, kids playing with bones on the beach the next day. Fergus is only twelve, but he has heard these stories, too. Knick-knack, paddy-whack. Resurrection time. The seawall follows the curve of the bay, a sloping bulkhead designed to redirect the force of winter swells that roll in from the Pacific. These waves carry stumps and logs broken loose from booms, which the wind picks up and uses as battering rams. After a southeast gale, repair crews mend sections of the wall's wooden railings torn loose from their mooring. Sometimes the broken beams end up in the trees across the strip of paved road that forms the southern boundary of the cemetery. On stormy days, it's impossible to walk anywhere near the beach, but there are always a few drivers who like to take chances. They navigate their cars over the sidewalk at the seawall's eastern end, past the flashing barriers placed there by the police. The distance is less than a mile, but before they've gone a hundred yards, a wall of saltwater falls on these cars and stalls their motors, leaving the drivers stranded inside while bits of bark and chunks of driftwood pummel the roof and windshield. Cars that suffer a drenching don't last long. The saltwater penetrates every inch of the car's chassis and body, and in a few years it's nothing but rust.

Today, the weather is good. March is near its end. *Out like a lamb*, Fergus' mother said this morning. Wisps of high cloud barricade the spring sun every few moments, but it's warm. Fergus Goodlake is taking his time walking the length of the bay. The tide is full and he has to stick to the area above the beach of pebbles, an awkward place to walk because of the seawall's sloping sides. One foot is always lower than the other, and by the end of the bay, Fergus feels out of kilter. *I'm a real McCoy*, he thinks, imagines himself Walter Brennan lurching up to the tractor. It seems to him the only way to put himself right again is to turn around and walk back, something he will have to do anyway unless he chooses to leave the shore and make his way home through the cemetery. But Fergus doesn't want to think about home just now.

On the road above, cars pass in either direction. There are people on bicycles, singly and in groups. Fallout from their conversations drifts into Fergus' ears as he walks.

... from my own pocket. A week at least ...

... in one door and out another...

Some cars, convertibles, probably, with their radios at full volume, rumble by. They make a noise like broadcast stations coming in and out of range, a meaningless soundtrack that spreads in their wakes.

IT'S MARCH 27TH, 1964, Good Friday. Tomorrow is the first day of the Easter long weekend. Three days off school. Fergus is three-quarters through grade seven, his best year yet, thanks to Mr. Stringer. For the past six grades, Fergus' teachers have been women who were widowed during the war and who have spent the last twenty years working toward a pension, something to supplement the veteran's benefits they are entitled to as long as they don't remarry. These women teach the same material to the grade two's as they do to the grade sixes. Artwork on the walls of their classrooms reproduces itself perfectly year after year. Their students sing the same songs. They sing about wandering along a mountain track.

They sing about a knapsack. They sing about the days of yore when Wolfe the dauntless hero came, and planted firm Britannia's flag on Canada's fair domain. On Fridays, they sing about Jesus, about meeting him in the garden where he walks with them and talks with them and tells them they are his own. Their teachers want the words "The End" printed on the last page of every composition and they check each child's desk to make sure that the scribblers are on the left, the *Winston Canadian Dictionary for Schools* on the right. They speak like mothers, but most of them have never had children.

In Mr. Stringer's class, Fergus studies Latin for the first time. The students in this class also sing songs, but these songs have a purpose. They sing: *Cum, sine, ab, ex, de. Corum, tenus, pro, pre.* Mr. Stringer says he will give five dollars to the student who can recite these prepositions to him ten years from now. When he says this to the class, Fergus imagines himself at the front door of Mr. Stringer's house, a taller version of himself at least, his hand out, his lips mouthing the little song he has learned to help his memory. Because he is also learning how to solve for *x*, he calculates the sum of his allowance over the next ten years — were he not to spend a nickel — and adds it to his prize. *I'll be twenty-two,* he thinks. *I'll be rich!*

Mr. Stringer brings in his short-wave radio and lets the class listen to "The Voice of America" and "Radio Moscow," which he says isn't really in Moscow but in Kiev, a city in the Ukraine. He tells them he discovered this truth through the marvels of triangulation and spends an hour explaining geometry to them. He pulls down a map of Europe to show them where each city is located. The Russians are a secretive people, he says. They have things to hide.

Fergus has things to hide, too. For weeks now, months if he includes the scene at Christmas dinner, his parents have been fighting. No evening passes without a loud exchange of voices, and the tension between his mother and father is obvious even when they don't open their mouths. From what Fergus can gather, the problem is money. His father runs a delicatessen downtown, a place Fergus has seen only a handful of times in his life. It used to belong to Fergus' grandfather, but he died. Fergus has been told the story of the delicatessen many times, how his grandfather started it with only a dime in his pocket and built the place into a successful business over the years. Every time Fergus hears the story, he can see the shining outline of the Bluenose in his grandfather's pocket, even though he knows there actually was no dime. After the war, Fergus' father worked at many jobs: night watchman at Bapco Paints; apprentice welder at Victoria Machinery Depot. For a few years he was an usher at the Capitol Theatre and worked under a mean, high-voiced man his father called "Squeaky." When Fergus' grandfather died of a stroke, none of the sons wanted to have anything to do with family business. They all had good jobs in other towns, all of them except Fergus' father who said he would take the place on only until a buyer could be found. That was six years ago. Now, at the end of every month Fergus' father sits in the dining room going through the cheques Fergus' mother has written, and every so often he will ask her to come in and explain a bill or a notice of credit or a purchase he takes issue with. He isn't looking for someone to blame so much as he wants to include another person in the misery he has settled for. On these evenings of furious accusation, Fergus will watch his father from the living room through the space once occupied by a pair of sliding doors that no longer close. His father sits at the table, still wearing his tie from work, his white shirt and a pair of black suspenders. He hunches over the stack of canceled cheques and utilities' statements like the dwarfish king in one of Fergus' favourite fairy tales.

"What's this one from Eaton's?" he will say, or "When did the oil company come? I don't remember them coming."

In her defense, Fergus' mother will yell back to him that she is in the middle of the dishes or folding laundry. Fergus can't see her from the living room, but he knows she is in her apron, standing at the sink or hovering over the ironing board she has carried up from the basement. She will be in her gray dress and low heels, looking like Donna Reed or Harriet Nelson, except for the cigarette that is probably sitting in an ashtray somewhere close by. Fergus thinks his mother is beautiful, the closest thing in his life to a movie star, and he hates to hear her get mad at his father. His mother knows this about Fergus, that the tension between her and her husband is a wearisome thing for him to carry around, but she is tired and burdened herself, and there is very little she can do about it. She steels herself for these spats with Fergus' father, refuses his demand to capitulate.

"If you want to ask me something," she will shout, "you can bloody well come through and ask in person because I'm sure as hell not going to jump to attention every time you don't understand something."

From there, things build into a silence that one of them will break by leaving out the back door for a walk or by rummaging in every drawer of the house for a cigarette or by noisily fixing a Tom Collins out of the sparse collection of bottles that sit on the top shelf of the built-in cupboard beside the dining-room fireplace. On these evenings Fergus slips away to his bedroom where he plugs in the single earphone of his crystal radio and listens to CJVI or CKDA, local stations that play Dean Martin hits and selections from Broadway musicals. Sometimes he falls asleep with the earplug still in his ear, and he'll wake up the next morning with strange words in his head, snatches of melodies that he doesn't remember hearing.

"Out in the west Texas town of El Paso ..." he sang once at the breakfast table and then stopped, unable to go on.

The only real radio in the house is an old tube model that occupies half the counter in the kitchen and can't pull in Vancouver or Seattle anyway. At school, some students have portable transistor radios tuned to KJR and CKLG that play The Dave Clarke Five and The Beatles. Fergus didn't see the Ed Sullivan show when the Beatles played to America because their television set had no rooftop antenna at the time, but he really hasn't any idea what kind of music he prefers, anyway. If he thought about it, he'd say that the songs he hears outside his home have no place in his family. If he could express himself perfectly, he'd say that most music suggests a jubilance and lack of restraint that is entirely out of character with the feeling he gets when he opens the front door after coming home from school. In that one moment, he can tell from the air in the front hallway whether he should go up the stairs to his room or risk a moment or two looking into the fridge for something to eat.

Even when his father isn't finding fault with his mother's accounting, he's usually unhappy about something. The house they're living in is over fifty years old and its wiring and plumbing are antiquated. Fuses blow, the hot water tank barely holds enough for a single bath. The basement floods in heavy rain, so badly that nothing down there can run the risk of sitting directly on the floor. Each box and piece of furniture is elevated off the cement by blocks of wood that are discoloured and permanently wet. The upstairs is drafty and cold all winter long. The wood sash windows leak air in the slightest breeze, moving the curtains in time to each gust that blows in from the strait. There are never any apples on the three trees in the backyard and there are always too many leaves to rake. The oil furnace is not a real oil furnace but a conversion from the previous wood-burning monster that still sends more heat up the chimney than into the house. The front lawn is a gravel pit where water disappears upon contact.

Fergus' father feels the weight of every flaw, every shortcoming, every outdated electrical plug, and in his desperation he sinks the family farther into debt by seeking quick remedies. Siding salesmen once convinced him to cover the aging cedar shingles with a cleaner, more modern tile made of asbestos that turned out to be so brittle it would break if Fergus simply leaned his bike against it. His father bought storm windows, new, light plastic ones for the upstairs windows. They clouded over on contact with the sun. Two out of the four burners on the brand new electrical stove stopped working after six months. For Fergus' father, each failure is a personal slight, another indication of the contempt the world holds for him, and he responds with a fury that astonishes. Whenever Fergus thinks of his father, he sees only a face twisted in frustration and anger, hears a voice that utters only curses.

"Goddamn it," he says to the lock on the back door. "This bloody thing," he screams at another fuse that blows as soon as he screws it in.

His mother and father aren't Fergus' only concern. At school he'd recently managed to make an enemy. One of the boys who failed last year has taken a dislike to Fergus and has threatened to beat him up. This boy's hair is tight and curly like a dog's, and his skin is a sickly white, as though he has been kept in a closet most of his life. Fergus knows nothing about fighting. Physically, he is tall but very thin, with an undernourished look that embarrasses him every P.E. class and on every field trip to the Crystal Gardens. He knows he has no chance in a fight, not because the boy is so much stronger, but because he seems to hate Fergus so much. Fergus is certain of this. Fergus thinks the difference between himself and the rest of the people in the world is that he lacks the ability to hate or love anything. He certainly can't imagine loving Jesus the way he is asked to by his teacher. He doesn't believe in God, though he is a server at the local Anglican church. No, loving Jesus is absolutely out of the question. He's certainly not convinced he loves his parents. For Fergus, love really isn't even the issue. It has more to do with caring. Fergus has decided he just doesn't care about anything. On the soccer field, he will yield to anyone who wants the ball more than he does. Most of the day, he hardly says a word because he sees nothing important enough to comment on. He hasn't had to speak to his relatives in years. His parents answer all their questions for him.

"He's always down in the basement working on that bike of his."

"Lawns and garden beds mostly. But he'll do anything for fifty cents an hour."

People like his father care about things. So does his mother. It seems to Fergus that the duty of those who don't care is to defer to those who do. Or avoid them. The bully at school cares very much. Fergus doesn't hate the bully, but he's smart enough to be afraid of him. Every recess and lunch, Fergus hides in the library or a classroom to avoid a fight. His parents and the bully are angry people, and their anger confuses Fergus. If he had the time, he might wonder what it's like to be so angry, but he doesn't have the time. He spends most of his energy finding a place where he can be safe. His search isn't always successful. Twice he has turned corners and been ambushed.

The first time it happened, he was walking by the park on his way home from the store when he found himself surrounded. There were several girls in the group, gum-chewing girls in short skirts and turtle-neck sweaters who laughed each time the bully pushed Fergus and chanted his name into the cool evening air. It seemed natural to Fergus that these girls would associate themselves with the bully and his gang, though he couldn't say why. There was something terrifying and attractive in the way they hung onto each other and paused to add more make-up while the bully rammed Fergus into a tree and spat on him. The effect of their presence was to make him feel both humiliated and heroic all at once, a feeling that, in combination with the dwindling light and the near-silhouettes all around him, lent the whole experience the tone of a surreal and frightening dream. During the encounter, the boy tapped one index finger continually on Fergus' forehead, asking him questions that Fergus couldn't answer, and turning to snigger with the others behind him. Fergus believed at one point he was going to die. That someone walking a dog would find his body the next morning, broken and lifeless at the base of the tree. He was looking beyond the bully's head into the darkening ridge of fir trees that lined the park, the grey-tinted clouds above them, trying to imagine his own death, the absence that such an event entailed, his skull reeling inside each time the boy's finger descended on a point just below his hairline, until he was so consumed with fear that he must have stopped breathing, stopped seeing, stopped existing. He felt he was dead, dying at the least, and the bully must have sensed it, too, because at that moment he backed off and left Fergus standing there. Just left him, like a wind that all at once abated, and Fergus went home.

The second time, he saw the bully first, alone, no gang to egg him on. Fergus climbed a fence into someone's backyard where he hid under the back steps of the house, unsure if the bully had seen him. He held his breath as the boy passed by, and was surprised to hear him singing quietly to himself. It was a song Fergus knew well, one he sang, too, a silly camping song about gopher guts and mutilated monkey meat. Perhaps he had been wrong, too hasty in his fear of being caught again. Maybe this wasn't the bully. Fergus pulled himself out of hiding and went to the fence to see, but there was no mistaking the boy's hair, his ragged jeans. He was using a pocketknife to slash away at a stick as he walked, and the song drifted out into the air around him. Fergus waited a while and then took another route home.

The bully has circumscribed Fergus' life. He has made the choices very clear: Fergus no longer goes to the park on weekends or after school, and the entire eastern portion of his neighbourhood is a minefield of possible encounters. He might be able to relax at home, but his mother is always telling him to get out of the house and do something. So, he comes down to the beach and walks along the seawall.

At the end of the bay, Fergus climbs up to the roadway where he sits down on one of the green benches that mark the beginning of the oceanfront park's property. He feels as though he may have to sit here forever. If this were a regular weekday, Fergus might see his father's car coming home from the deli. He might stand up and wave and get a ride home. But it's not a regular weekday. It's Good Friday, and his father is at home where he has been all day, washing the car or burning the week's newspapers in the 45 gallon drum out back or combing the front and back lawns for weeds which he kills with a kettle of boiling water. His mother will be inside scrubbing potatoes for tonight's dinner. Or maybe she's sitting on the back porch with a drink, a cigarette, too, watching Fergus' father. Maybe this is one of their good days and they'll have a nice dinner together and talk about the weekend, what they will do for a treat on Sunday after church. Easter Sunday usually means a visit to Fergus' grandmother outside of town. She is his father's mother, and Fergus likes her. He would like her more if she wouldn't fuss over him so much, the kind of worried attention that suggests his parents aren't doing a good job of raising him. Her concern puts him in an awkward position. He enjoys the visits, but the ride home afterwards is invariably sour and full of sarcastic remarks from his father.

"She should mind her own business," Fergus' father will say.

Or: "I don't remember her all that choked up when my father hit me."

They don't always go. Once they went up island to stay overnight in a motel by the sea. Another time they went for a day of fishing on the Saanich Inlet. The day isn't really a tradition, but almost, and Fergus is aware that he has been both dreading the day and looking forward to it. If only he knew what mood they'll be in.

He looks at his watch. Just past 5:30. Time to start walking. Across the strait in the States, a line of smoke rises from the pulp mill in the town of Port Angeles. It spreads along the coast until it thins into a haze. For a moment Fergus has the strange feeling that the horizon is tilting slightly or that the bench he is sitting on is about to pitch forward down the slope. And then the scene reasserts itself and everything is back to normal. Above him, the electrical wires are swaying noticeably between the poles, as though a wind has come up, but there is no wind. Some slight shift has taken place, a taste of the real displacement to come two hours from now when the floor of the ocean falls away and water rushes in to fill the space it has left, when whole houses in a place called Alaska slip neatly into cracks in the earth and disappear. Fergus is aware of none of this, at least not yet, and after a moment, he gets up and walks home.

[III]

While his parents sipped their gin and talked about brick walls, Helios Goodlake poked away at the fret board of his knock-off Rickenbacker. His explorations ended in a final aimless solo that skidded on its face, lurched into the air above the stage and stopped on a single, improbable collection of notes that would never be mistaken for a chord in any composition class anywhere on the planet.

"Eat the armadillo!" someone in the outer darkness yelled.

Helios bowed low, hair brushing the floor. Then he turned to his ailing Fender amp and ripped out leads from jacks as though he were weeding a garden. No applause followed, just a few half-hearted whistles and a clap or two from friends who had come with their complimentary tickets to scope girls or drink beer at half the price of the downtown bars. The other two members of the band had already given up on the crowd and were busying themselves with their instruments, unscrewing high hats, unplugging fuzz boxes, making way for the featured band, a Californian reggae/Cajun hybrid.

"Fuck this shit," Helios spat to no one in particular.

Helios wasn't referring to the audience or to the venue or even to the vaunted calibre of the musicians gathering in the wings. What Helios was objecting to was a certain hollowness he had never felt before, a malaise that had seeped into his arms and legs and poisoned any satisfaction he might have entertained about the performance of his band. Helios had no pretensions about being an artist. He didn't attribute this feeling to the pangs of alienation or the despondency of thwarted creative genius. It was something bad, a rottenness he had sensed in the delivery of each note he had played, a fatigue of the spirit, perhaps, and it soured his mood, which even at the best of times was leagues removed from sweet.

His arms laden with wires and guitars, Helios picked up a plastic beer glass between his teeth and leaned back until the remaining beer emptied into his mouth, onto his face and down the front of his shirt. These shirts were for sale at the back of the Union Hall and bore a reproduction of a 19th century woodcut of Christ standing at a door, his hand raised to knock and his head turned slightly as though he were listening for a response from within. The original title of the work was "Christ Frappant à la Porte," but Helios had substituted the band's name, Bad Men Who Love Jesus, in bold Gothic script.

"PRAISE THE LORD," Helios intoned, his face dripping. Time to go to work. He was speaking to himself again because by this time the drummer and bass guitarist had already left. Left for good — good as in forever. This was the last night Helios could convince them to play together. They both performed with other bands around town — bands that paid — the bassist with a jazz group that had steady work at a local hotel and the drummer in a pub foursome that played golden oldies. Helios' rock dream was mostly in his own head, and, now at twenty-five, he knew it the way some people finally understand that they have waited too long to get married or have children or finish their degree. The thought made him growl, a low, guttural clearing of his throat that he maintained for the duration of each of the three trips it took to carry the stage gear out to his 1963 International Travel-All in the Union Hall lot. On his last trip he swung by the T-shirt table. A girl no older than sixteen was guarding the cash box. She was wearing a toque over her ratty blonde hair, and a hooded sweatshirt with a Counter Culture logo. Her boyfriend's probably. She must have been baking in all that gear.

"No sales tonight," the girl said.

Helios wondered briefly if she was stating a fact or threatening him.

He tried to think of some response: *How about you?* or *Fuck off, then,* but decided he was too tired to care. Besides, she was a volunteer. No mileage in pissing off someone who had done him a favour. Or too much mileage. She placed a cardboard box onto the pre-amp he was carrying, and he turned and left for work.

HELIOS WORKED PART-TIME on the midnight shift at the local Canada Post Sortation and Distribution Centre where he spent seven and a half hours flinging parcels and letters into large, wheeled canvas-and-steel chariots that looked like hospital laundry carts. It was the kind of work that made Helios feel churlish, like a bit of a lout, and he liked that about it. The people he worked with had a ruined and desperate look to them, the way most people look when they have agreed to set their sights on a pension, as though they have already accepted that they are old and will die soon. Helios liked to listen to them as they talked of time-shares they had bought on their two-week vacation in Mexico, the free dinners they had been treated to by the real estate agent. Their voices were as rough and inhuman as the building they worked in, a gigantic box of stucco and steel that was a rude imposition on the farmland around it. The work itself was a challenge only in the way staying awake was a challenge after three or four martinis. It had taken Helios a single shift to learn to interpret postal addresses, and now he read them with the same speed a computer programmer deciphers lines of hexadecimal code. When Helios was not helping to deliver the nation's mail, he sat the night desk at the Mainsail Motel where he had learned to read a different kind of language: the faces of men and women whose vacations had devolved into endurance tests, and the practised tone of the alcoholics who phoned down at all hours of the morning to ask — in voices that were hopeless in their precision — for another bucket of ice.

Nights for Helios meant a day's wage, and days meant sleep and time to practise his music, such as it was. Helios had always wanted to lead a return to the simple sound of a garage-band, the uncluttered combination of guitar, drum and bass. He despised technical frippery, the sophistry of overdubbing, all the computer hocus-pocus of sound engineers. Helios wrote lyrics, ground away at the complexities of rhythm and lead, and, whenever possible, brought his efforts to the attention of the world, most recently this evening at the Union Hall where he had agreed to play for beer and a few comps. And now, as he closed the door of his car and walked into work, he felt his foul mood skulking behind him like a sick Mexican dog.

Mailbags from Chile, Australia, India, Germany and a dozen other countries hung like high school sports banners from the girdered ceiling of the sortation centre. Helios juggled a stack of envelopes, scanning and flipping each piece as he walked, the Johnny Appleseed of correspondence, planting messages that would find fertile soil and grow, or fall on barren ground and die. In twenty minutes, he would leave the floor and take his break in a cramped cement-walled room that felt more like a bunker than a staff coffee lounge. Its one window looked not outside, but onto the work floor, and its walls were covered in job postings from other parts of the country, union notices, and several photographs of summer cabins for rent, the times available and prices per week listed below. One piece of paper stood out among the others, a bold alert in large script that advised employees of the current state of contract negotiations, the deadlines for talks and the procedures to follow in the event of a work stoppage. Above all of these, someone had taped a computer banner that bore the words, "Return to Sender ... Address Unknown," and in smaller letters underneath, "Elvis Presley."

"No such zone," Helios murmured as he encountered a postal code that could not possibly exist. He examined the return address: a poetry magazine from somewhere in Manitoba. How the item had made it this far was hard to say. One mistake like this in a bulk mail-out would cost the magazine dearly. Canada Post made its clients work for their subsidies and screw-ups meant money. But maybe because Helios' sour disposition had aroused in him a perverse generosity, or perhaps to counter the doom he sensed hovering above his head, he took a pen and corrected the code to something that would match the destination, a correction that took him all the way to coffee break. He also took down the address of the poetry magazine.

"You never know," he told himself, and walked off.

Many of the postal workers smoked. These people spent their breaks outside at one of the picnic tables the company had provided for them or, when it rained, in one of the docking bays. Often, Helios found himself the only one in the lounge, but today there was a new addition to the graveyard shift.

"Hey," Helios grunted. The new worker was Jayne, his most recent girlfriend — most recent in Helios' world meant a hiatus of over three years. The dry period had lasted so long, a friend had accused him of intentional celibacy, and his mother had openly mused about his being gay. Jayne was a woman in her early twenties, multiple earrings, baseball cap. She had gotten the job on her own merit, but when, during the interview, she informed management that she and Helios were an item — Jayne believed in being honest — they told her not to make a production on the shop floor. No exhibitions. Keep it business, they said. She told Helios they could make it a game.

"I'm Jayne," she said.

Helios looked across at her. She sat upright in her chair, her mouth a grim line, completely devoted to her role. *Let's play work,* her eyes said. *Ready? Go.*

"Helios," he said. He sat down and propped his feet on the chipped arborite seminar table that occupied the centre of the room.

"How do you spell that?"

Helios spelled his name for her.

"It's a nickname," he said. "My father thought he was being clever. It means sun." He paused, and then added, "As in …"

"I get it," Jayne said and then her face cracked into a broad smile. She crossed the few feet between them, twirled a little, and plunked herself in Helios' lap.

"Oof!"

"That was fun."

"You think you'll ever grow up?" he asked her. As he spoke, he could feel his spirits lifting, effortlessly, even a little reluctantly, his obstinate heart still rejecting the idea that one person could have this much effect on his mood.

"I didn't know your name was your dad's idea. He's a funny man."

"A name is only funny once," Helios said.

"Still, it's creative."

"Yeah, well, the joker thinks he's got prostate cancer now."

"That doesn't sound good."

"His doctor wants to do a biopsy. Dad says he's not having any operation, even if the biopsy comes up positive. I think he's worried he won't be able to get it up if he does."

"Oh."

"The man's nearly fifty. What's he worrying about? There's nothing left to get it up for, anyway."

"Don't be so mean."

Helios felt the meanness of his words as soon as he'd spoken them, knew, too, that Jayne would call him on it. Right now, he enjoyed provoking her, even this mildly, but he couldn't help wondering if one day he might care enough about her to stop. He raised his head to look at her face and saw that she was staring at his shirt. "What?" he said.

"Is the smell part of your act?"

Helios shrugged. He still reeked of beer. He hadn't bothered to change after the performance at the Union Hall. If he were working days, there would be questions, threats, some penance exacted, but the night shift demanded less of its employees: losing his life was penance enough.

"I keep telling you my father's a musician, too," Jayne said.

"You do."

"You never ask me what he plays."

"Ah." Helios saw the mock disappointment on her face, the playful indignation that almost drew Jayne's mouth into a pout. Instantly, he wanted her smile to return, realized he'd work hard to put it there. Was this how it started? Is this the way a person learned to think of someone other than himself? Conditioning? Rewards? "Okay," he said. "What does he play?"

"He plays the mandolin."

"Great." Helios' spirits sank. The thing he could bear least in life was Celtic music. He hated the jigs and reels, the violin-toting, ballad-belting hoards that sprang up at folk festivals and house parties to tap their feet and churn out verse after boring verse of Irish sea shanties. He hated how they weren't content to stop until the few guests still left on their feet after hours of uninterrupted renditions of Chieftain classics and lofty plaintive solos in the manner of Enya or Loreena McKennitt were hurling themselves arm in arm around the living room or the back deck or the basement lounge chanting each refrain at the top of their lungs.

"He plays in a Klesmer band. Jewish weddings and bar mitzvahs mostly."

Wrong again, Helios told himself. There was always something worse. "You never said you were Jewish."

"My father only," Jayne said.

"What's that supposed to mean?"

"It means I'm not Jewish."

The shop steward, a lean-faced man with a moustache, entered the lounge and threw his cap on the table next to Helios' feet. The odour of burnt tobacco hung about him. His name was Andrew but nobody called him that. He was known throughout the night shift as "Half-Sack" because of the six beer he brought to every staff softball game and beach picnic.

"It's going to come down," he said.

"The strike?"

"That, too. I was talking about the rain. I can smell it."

Helios and Jayne placed their mugs in the sink and moved back out onto the plant floor where they sorted for another hour and then moved down a level to load the postal trucks for their morning routes.

Actually, Helios had wangled the job for Jayne through a friend. The posting never made it onto paper, a sleight of hand in personnel, but he had been warned not to be stupid about it. No holding hands. Never kiss on the job. It would be better if they ignored each other. They were a few months old already, so Helios promised they'd pull it off. They'd met at an outdoor concert. Jayne had an interest in music. She had never picked up an instrument herself, not since a few piano lessons when she was ten. Her teacher had begun each one by forcing Jayne to mould her hand to a plaster cast of what he told her was Beethoven's own right hand. Jayne put up with the exercise until one day the teacher broke Jayne's middle finger. The lessons stopped. For a while her parents looked for a new teacher, but Jayne told them she didn't want to continue, not even after the injury healed. She liked listening, she said. She was good at it.

"I'll listen to you if you want," she had said to Helios.

THE FRIDAY BEFORE Jayne's first shift, Helios had sat beside his father in the oncologist's office. He had come because his mother had asked him to give his father support. She wasn't supposed to know anything about this visit, but she knew everything. The office was on the third floor of the medical building where Helios had recently gone to have polyps removed from his throat, small nodular growths that had sprung up on his larynx after a year of singing in the band. He'd thought they were going to operate on him in the hospital, but they told him that wasn't the way it was done anymore. Then they gassed him.

The office was different from those Helios had seen at his GP's. This wasn't one of six identical cubicles. There wasn't any tuning fork to play with, no scale. They didn't cut off warts here. They didn't listen to your chest, squeeze your balls. This was an office with a desk. The walls were papered. There was a bookshelf. This place meant business.

The oncologist was explaining the particulars.

"Most men can live with a bit of cancer in their prostate. It's a slow disease and there's a good chance they'll live with it until they die of something else."

"I'm for that," Helios' father said.

Helios heard his father's forced humour. Always with the jokes. He recognized the bravado, the eyebrows rising into a question: *Did I say something wrong?* His father, Fergus Goodlake. Mr. Delicatessen. More cartoon character than real person. All Victoria was like a comic strip, Helios thought. No, not a comic strip. The set of a Saturday morning children's show. Mr. Deli wakes up to a new day. Mr. Deli has trouble peeing. Gets sick. Mrs. Deli asks their son to take Mr. Deli to see Mr. Oncologist. On the way home, they visit Mr. Baker for a nice cup of coffee and a treat. Everybody hopes Mr. Deli won't have to make an appointment with Mr. Surgeon. Helios broke into a broad grin at the thought of Miss Nurse and Mr. Priest visiting Mr. Delicatessen at his bedside. He almost laughed aloud, but managed a cough to hide his mirth. He looked over to where his father sat like a boy who'd been summoned to the principal's office. Funny how you can see a person and not really see them, Helios thought. There were creases on the man's face he'd never noticed. The broken nose seemed more twisted than usual, too. Hands showed the bones under the skin the way they never had before. Had he shaved today? Put him in a police lineup and Helios might not pick him out. Not that his father had ever been a super-hero. He walked like a spastic duck after a few beers. The power cord to the lawnmower had more cuts in it than a breadboard, and only a complete fool would ever ask him to sing. But he'd never been old. Not like this.

"I hope we have the option, Fergus," the doctor was saying. "This may be simple enlargement, if we're lucky. We may only be dealing with BHP here."

Why was it, Helios wondered, doctors always looked worse than their patients? He could see the veins in the man's nose. His hair was yellow, not blond, as though somebody had coloured it with a pencil crayon. A collar that tight could kill a person, the flesh squeezing out from under it like plumber's putty around a drain. Did they all have to wear grey flannel pants?

"Please," Fergus said, waving his hand toward Helios.

"I'm sorry." The doctor turned to Helios. "Normally, as men get older ..."

Fergus interrupted. "No! I mean could you please cut the double talk. He doesn't want to hear all this. You can scare him later when he's my age."

The doctor went on. He described what happened when cancer metastasized. Prostate cancer usually moved to the lower spine. Mobility would become progressively more difficult. Pain would increase. Treatment was less successful at that stage, sometimes pointless.

"Surgery's our best bet, if it comes to that," he said, including himself in a way that Helios felt was a little less than genuine.

"So you keep telling me," Fergus said.

"I also keep telling you nothing is certain until we get the biopsy back. But there's no harm in being prepared. You need to know what you're in for if the results aren't good. It's not that complex a procedure, but there are some side effects. We discussed the possibility before, but I'm not sure if you want to talk about this in private or ..."

Helios looked at his father. Here was a man who struggled telling an employee to check the sanitary napkin dispenser in the washroom of his own delicatessen. Why would he want his son around at a time like this? For that matter, why would his son want to be around? He stood up to leave, but Fergus waved him down again.

"I'm okay," he said. "Maybe it's a good thing he hears."

"Dad, I can get a coffee. Really."

"No, you don't. I'm going to need all the help I can get. Stay, please." Helios leaned back into his chair.

"All right, then," the doctor said. "As we discussed, these operations aren't foolproof. There's a high rate of erectile dysfunction associated with the procedure. Nearly sixty percent of men who underwent this operation in the last five years have complained of impotence."

"Those are great odds," Helios said.

"Not exactly." The doctor looked confused.

"That's what I meant," Helios said.

The doctor seemed to struggle with this idea, as though he had encountered a new symptom, one not listed in his medical books.

"Okay, then. The fact is — and this is assuming again — we won't know if the nerve bundles of the penis are compromised until we operate. I mean to say we may be worrying prematurely. As I said, nothing's for certain until we get the biopsy back. And even then we'll want to get in there and have a look around, if you know what I mean. If things are bad, there's always the possibility of a graft."

"A graft? You can graft these things?"

"Nerves, Fergus. We can graft nerves. We take them from your lower leg."

"You're going to graft my leg to my dick?"

"In a sense."

"You people are insane," Helios' father said.

"We have new techniques now. We're not cutting in the dark any longer. There's an electronic probe we use to distinguish those nerves used for erections. We stimulate them and then we cut around them."

"You mean I'm going up and down while you're rooting around inside me?"

"Dad."

"Not one word to anyone about any of this. You hear?"

Helios had to stifle a laugh. The thought of his father prone on the operating table, pointing at the ceiling again and again like a crossing guard at an intersection was almost more than he could bear.

"You won't know a thing. You'll be out, Fergus."

"Helios, I told you these people were crazy. Don't ever get old, son. This is what you have to look forward to." He got up to leave.

"There's a lot we can do in post-operative therapy. Viagra is working wonders with some of our patients."

"Now, you're making fun of me," Fergus said.

"Take some time, Fergus," the doctor said. "These are big decisions. You'll want to speak to your wife."

"That shows what you know." Fergus walked toward the door.

Helios rose, too. He shrugged his shoulders in the doctor's direction. There was nothing more he could do. He picked up his coat and followed his father into the hall. They walked around the corner to the lobby where they waited for the elevator. A woman stood with them, her small daughter at her side. On the street, Helios wouldn't have given the couple a second thought, but here in a building full of medical specialists, he couldn't help imposing some cruel and terminal disease on one of them. The daughter, he thought. It must be the daughter. The mother turned to him, almost as though she had guessed his thoughts.

"Going down?" she asked.

"We are," Helios said.

"I guess," his father said.

[IV]

A blind spot, that's what it was. Annie congratulated herself on finding the precise term for what she was feeling. Unlike Fergus, who assumed every instance of forgetfulness, each failure to retrieve a word was a precursor to complete synaptic collapse, Annie dwelt in the land of her own language like a foreigner. It was enough for her simply to approximate meaning, to come close to what she meant, the way a tourist in Paris might be content to ask for "the little metal object that opens the door" when the word for key declines to surface.

"Put the thing in the thing," she would say on more than one occasion. The knife in the drawer. The book on the shelf. This refusal to articulate her thoughts annoyed Fergus, and he made a point of telling her so, yet he continued to put the knife back in the cutlery drawer and the copy of *Life is Elsewhere* beside all the other K's, because on some level that he disliked acknowledging, he understood her.

Blind spots. Fergus had told her about them. She and he had been somewhere, a field, some party at a friend's, lying down on a blanket and looking up at the sky for meteors. A shower of meteors. Something in Latin. It began with a "p." And Fergus told her that if she looked at a single star for a few minutes, it would disappear.

"Stars don't disappear," she'd said.

But of course it had.

"Does everything go away like that?" she'd asked.

"If you look at it long enough," Fergus had said.

Annie also confused popular sayings, mixed them together to suit her purpose. She might say that she and Fergus would have to "ride this through," when loan rates rose over the course of a year. Fergus would explain to her that they could either "ride it out" or "see it through," but that "riding it through" made no sense.

"You know what I mean," she'd say.

"That doesn't matter. There's a right way to say things and a wrong way."

"It's not wrong if people can figure it out."

"But they shouldn't *have* to."

Sometimes, the conjunctions bordered on insanity. Once when the federal department of taxation audited their business, she had told Fergus they were "up the creek with their pants down." This time Fergus had said nothing to challenge her.

The blind spot she was referring to this time was her marriage. Her marriage was the thing she'd been looking at, the thing that had disappeared. Only a moment ago she'd watched Fergus get up and leave for the bathroom, but it seemed like a year. What would she feel if he left for good? So like him to retreat when the conversation became challenging. But really, a marriage was such an intangible thing. This whole business of living with someone. Such a funny custom, as though people needed another of their species close by simply to feel comfortable. For years, she and Fergus had been sitting down for dinner together, hanging laundry in the basement, standing side by side at the paint store waiting for the — what *did* they call that thing? — to stop shaking the can. It was as though she'd been walking around with a complete stranger tagging after her, a tediously picky stranger, too.

Normally, Annie would have dismissed such an ordinary little observation — the thought that married people go for years without really knowing each other — but the two or three tokes she'd taken upstairs had undermined her judgment about the merits of her ideas. Pot always did this to her. It's what she liked about it: taking nothing for granted. The gin and tonic was her way of disguising the effects, hiding them from

Fergus who disapproved of drugs. He was such a dud in some ways, but Annie loved to talk when she was a bit high and this was such an interesting revelation that had come to her. She tried to imagine Fergus taking up with someone else, the brooding talks they'd have to have each night, the anguish of wondering where he was when he wasn't home, the indignation she'd feel each time she'd phone to find the line busy. How exciting! Annie felt almost sixteen again, her mind full of adolescent intrigue and joy. For Annie, smoking pot was like entering a very familiar room, "the room of herself" she called it, where she remembered how she used to feel when she was young. It was a place she couldn't imagine when she wasn't high, and one she never wanted to leave when she was.

Fergus was taking forever in there. He was probably worried about coming back to this nutty conversation, about what he'd have to say to placate her, to pacify her sense that they'd reached some kind of impasse. She almost laughed to think of him, scheming, wringing his hands for a way out of this new plan of hers. And then there was this prostate business, too, these protracted sessions with the toilet of late. The interminable worry over his bladder. It must be confusing for men. For years the thing has worked like a charm and then one day it starts screwing up. She marveled at her insight. Yes, it was suddenly so clear to her. The way men thought of themselves was so tangled up with their anatomy that a little thing like peeing could throw them off the rails for — how long had it been now, six months? These visits to the doctor were almost as regular as church. Annie suddenly saw a connection between worship and men's reverence for their penis.

"How true," she said aloud.

She thought of her son Helios, prancing through to the bathroom when he was four or five. He'd announce that he was going to "drain his lizard" or "hang a rat." All this special language devoted to the stupid thing. It might as well be a religion.

And then Annie felt a huge surge of sorrow sweep through her body. So much time! Years of it, distilled into snapshots in her head. A boy running, a room painted, a three-day summer road trip that ends at a

Thrift Motel in Kamloops. Everything she could remember seemed suddenly dear because it had happened so long ago. Is that what marriage was? Just time? Lots of time? You nail something to a wall, a picture, a set of antlers, and if it hangs there long enough, the heart will take it in? Either that, she thought, or it will disappear.

Annie understood sliding into the maudlin, the hopelessly sweet light that shone around her whenever she brought a joint to her lips, but she was never prepared for it. She wondered what she would say to Fergus when he returned, how she would reverse this direction she'd turned them in. Sunday night, and she remembered the work she had to do the next day. So empty, this house with just the two of them. She poured some of her drink into Fergus' glass. He'd never notice. She wanted to think clearly about all this. What had Fergus said? What would he want with another woman when he had her? Such a moron! She could almost believe he was lying, just telling her what she wanted to hear. He'd better not be. Still, someone had to question all this stuff they were doing every day. All this getting up and driving around. All this handing out bills and making change. All this climbing into bed and turning out the lights.

Was that a toilet she heard flush? She hoped so. She listened to hear water running, the complaint of the aging hot water faucet, its reluctant shudder. Nothing. The man was a mystery. She could have gone upstairs and smoked herself stupid in the time he was taking. She was even getting hungry now. Maybe she should comb the fridge for snacks while she was waiting, but she was hard-pressed to think what there might be in there that she would want. She wondered about food, whether it was just her altered state, or did all people who made their living from a kitchen find less and less palatable the dishes they made for others to consume? She tried to remember what she and Fergus ate before they took over the deli, which foods excited them, the treats they made for themselves when they wanted to celebrate. At some point they discovered Mexican food, or a version of it. Beans, tortillas, guacamole, something hot. And later, a dish with lamb and anchovies. Years ago now. Helios was small, not even in school then. The span of time startled her, the shock that came with it, a glimpse into things that used to be, that endured a while and one day were no longer. Had life been better then? Or is life only good in retrospect? For the first while after taking over the deli, she and Fergus referred to time as being either Before Goodlake's or After Goodlake's. They'd look at pictures of themselves and try to place the year they were taken.

"That's Before Goodlake's," one of them would say.

"Are you sure?"

"Look at the car. No doubt about it."

Annie once asked Fergus what he wanted to do after Goodlake's. At first, he didn't understand.

"This *is* After Goodlake's," he said.

"No," she said. "I mean *after* After Goodlake's. After we stop."

"Christ," Fergus said. "After Goodlake's, I'll be dead."

He had meant it as a joke at the time, but Annie wondered now whether he really thought that way. She stood up, unsure whether she was going to the kitchen to look for food or yell to see if Fergus had passed away in the bathroom. As she opened her mouth to form his name, a cascade of water echoed in the iron stack that ran through the middle of the house. No secrets here.

[V]

Fergus stood before the toilet in the main floor washroom, a room they had added to the house very soon after moving in. Their son was a toddler then, and a single toilet on the top floor was impractical, Annie had said, even cruel. *What were people thinking when they built these old houses? A single pot to piss in? Idiots!* Annie had overseen the construction, selecting tile then rejecting it, refusing to forego a pedestal sink despite the limit of their budget. In the days after it was finished they had come upon each other sneaking in just to stand and marvel. One evening almost a year and a half after they had started, they ate their dinner in the claw foot tub. Their son had searched the whole of the first floor to find them talking over dessert, the wrap-around shower curtain drawn to form a room within a room.

He lifted the lid and released a long, thin and thoroughly unsatisfying stream of pee, noting volume and pressure as he did so. So much talk these days of the prostate. And the doctor always asking about "flow." "How are the waterworks? Plumbing okay?" Doctors should know better than to say such things. Who pays attention to pee? Fergus certainly never had. But once the idea entered Fergus' head he was a goner. Now he couldn't decide from one day to the next if he was peeing more or less than he used to. He wished he could remember, but whenever he tried, all that came to him was a single image of looking down into a urinal, as though a lifetime of voiding his bladder in hundreds of different places had simply vanished, and this one generic view was all his mind could summon. It wasn't even a specific urinal, not the third from the left at his favourite brew pub on the far side of town or even the urinal at the deli. It was a nameless, placeless vision of white enamel with his member dangling above it. There was no question that if Fergus really tried, he might have retrieved other, more vivid locations: any number of bushes from his student days with the forest service, for example, or a window once at summer camp when he was too frightened to make his way through the dark to the latrine. In Pompeii, too, he had slipped behind the wall of what was once a Roman kitchen and was overjoyed to find a hole that had been used by others before him. But these and other former pit-stops were beyond his current grasp, and as far as a real comparison between the past and the present, they wouldn't have told him what he wanted to know, anyway: How much had he peed then? How little now?

He detested his doctor's little lectures on the subject, his use of acronyms to lend his words authority. "BHP is highly treatable." If indeed that's what Fergus had. "Imagine the gland as a donut wrapped right around the urethra. Imagine it getting tighter." No wonder Fergus had to pee so often, he'd said. All that pressure backing up. Could a man explode? Fergus had not wanted to know this, but of course his doctor had felt compelled to warn him of the danger of deferring treatment. So, yes, a man could explode after a fashion. "Organs could rupture," he warned. It was a good thing Fergus had come in. "The truth is, a DRE tells us only so much, and your PSA is a little high for my liking," the doctor had gone on to say, extracting his hand from a surgical glove. "A biopsy will tell us what we really need to know." Fergus didn't say much in response, only pulled on his pants. He was still digesting a particularly unpalatable truth, the simple fact that he had arrived at an age where most medical procedures were a demeaning and revolting ordeal. Fergus knew the grim resentment Annie maintained toward her annual pap smear, and in these past few months he felt he had finally joined her revulsion of things physical, the humiliation she felt upon having to submit to probing hands, legs spread. How like the act of sex, Fergus thought, except that all the poking around was about death now, not life.

Fergus sighed. It was hard to care. A nuisance, that's what it was, nothing more. Men all over the world, several times a day, trying to find some place to get rid of the water they were carrying around, only to have their bodies turn traitor and shut off the tap. It was almost comical. And to think of them pausing to notice how much and how fast, as though it were some kind of contest. Oh, yes, Fergus had heard the stories about boys and snow, writing their names. He'd even read a book, a novel, where a girl expresses her jealousy of such boys. He didn't believe a word of it. Surely women had better things to do than to waste their time wishing for parts they weren't born with. Annie would be horrified. As for the snow, well, he didn't believe that yarn either. The only boys who'd ever do something that stupid were boys who had heard about it on the playground and were too mindless to see such stunts for the baseless popular myths they were. Of course, Fergus had forgotten an evening long ago, a rare vacation with his parents at some seaside cabin with oil stoves that blazed all July and August and electric toasters that cooked one side of a piece of bread at a time. It was after a brief summer rain and the tide was full, the water nudging logs that had washed up on the beach during the previous winter. His father had taken him down to the water's edge and thrown a rock, breaking the dark glassy surface. Bio-luminescence lit up the spot where the rock had landed, and then all too quickly the darkness had returned.

"It's better with a stick," his father had said just before he turned and left Fergus there. When his mother called him to bed, Fergus was in the middle of peeing in a wide arc, watching as the stream cut a path of light in a semi-circle in front of him. How wide was that arc? Four feet? Five? It seemed immense at the time. And his mother certainly hadn't betrayed any jealousy when she crossed the thin strip of sand to see what he was doing.

"We have to swim in that water, for crying out loud," was all she said.

FERGUS WAITED AS the last few drops dribbled into the bowl. Were drops normal? How many should there be? Men were always comparing themselves to horses, to the sheer quantity these animals expelled and the force with which they expelled it. Such a spectacle in a parade! Now he found himself in public washrooms listening, comparing the sound of other men to his own. Some were truly horse-like, but so what? Not to be like a horse, was this a sign of something? Fergus realized he had been worrying this issue to death for months. And now a biopsy. Annie's talk of an affair had upset him, too; it was a shock to his system. For a moment he had actually believed she knew. But was it really so coincidental the subject should come up? Eighteen months was a long time, after all, and it wasn't as though infidelity was so rare. On any given day there must be thousands of adulterers in the world who have to listen to a spouse's playful nagging: Do you still love me? Could you ever love someone else? Perhaps they even watch movies that are the exact mirror of their situation. Murderers must go through it all the time, come to think of it, given the number of films on the topic. At least he wasn't a murderer. Oh, well, he decided. We'll just have to wait. But the Jensens? A more ridiculous example of a marriage would be hard to find. The man was nothing but a libido. What had Helios called him? A penis with a guidance system? Something like that. He was the type of person who liked to broadcast how much sex he was having, the kind of teenager who had never grown up, thought everyone wanted to hear the details. At a barbecue once, Fergus had overheard him talking to another couple.

"I get home for lunch two or three times a week. Lunch and a nap. Don't get a lot of sleep though, do we, sweetheart?"

They're over forty, for Christ's sake? Does he really think anyone's interested? And the wife. Becky? Winking at his side. Happy as a heifer in heat. The idiot never suspected a thing, as it turned out. Not for years. There had been babysitters, tennis wives, an Avon lady. The whole block knew, but she never twigged. Not until she found him in the hammock with her own sister. And even then she refused to dump him. First it was counseling. Then it was some retreat on an island where they had to spend whole hours looking into each other's eyes or massaging each other's hands. They slept head to foot. Annie had relayed the details to him as they came in. He thought she'd seen such remedies for the cowardice they were, that the husband was doing everything he was told just to get off the hook. Who wouldn't? Sex wasn't an area where you could trust people to be honest. Fergus was sure of that.

He zipped up, ran a bit of water over his hands and returned to the living-room, but not before casting a glance in the mirror: it was true. He brushed a hand through his still mostly red hair, gave himself a good punch in the gut. Yes, Pedro, it was true.

AN HOUR LATER found them deep in food. They had broken out the Moroccan olives and a bottle of red wine. Fergus had found some of their deli's hummus in the fridge, too, and several pieces of pita. There would be no need for dinner tonight.

"You can't control these things." Fergus was on his second glass, and he believed everything he said. Growing up in the forest of his parents' anger, Fergus had developed a talent for hiding. He found it easy to play the fool while at the same time lamenting foolishness.

"I didn't say I wanted to," Annie said.

"You say I'm not allowed to fall in love. You say it's to be strictly sexual."

"Well, I'm assuming."

"Yes, but you can't just tell me to look for another woman. People look for other people when they need to, when there's something missing in their lives. I'm not missing anything."

"You don't think you are, Pedro, but sometimes we don't know when our lives are lacking. We get used to it, yes, but that doesn't mean we're healthy."

"Don't speak of us as victims, or at least not me. Perhaps you should be the one looking for someone else." Fergus regretted the tone of his words as soon as they left his mouth.

"Actually, I've thought about it. Yes, I've thought about it."

"I'm sorry," Fergus said.

They finished their wine and polished off what remained of the pita and hummus. Olive pits lay strewn on their plates, and each time Fergus looked at them, he was reminded of the rat droppings he was still finding on occasion on the deli floor.

"I'm sorry you're unhappy," he continued. "But I don't see how my having an affair can help matters. And besides, the whole idea behind affairs is that they're a secret. There's all that telephoning and meeting in hotel rooms. You can't be serious."

"Of course, I'm not serious. I'd probably kill you if you slept with another woman."

"You would?"

"Oh, I don't know what I'd do. I'm at a loss. I feel like we're standing still. An affair would shake us up a bit, don't you think?"

"So would a heart attack."

"Don't be morbid. Nobody's dying around here. Affairs aren't lethal, at least not the kind we would have."

"*We* wouldn't be having the affair. *I* would."

"But you would tell me about it."

"I don't think so."

"Yes, you would, so we could talk about how you were feeling and what it was like for me to have to deal with someone else in your life."

"Why would I do that? Nobody broadcasts that kind of news to the world."

"Not to the world, Fergus. Just to me."

"But that's just the thing." Fergus began to enumerate, a trait he knew Annie detested. "Part of having an affair demands that the injured party — in this case you — must seek consolation from friends, from sisters and brothers, from hairdressers and taxi drivers, from neighbours, the gas man, the clerk at the motor vehicle branch. Affairs are a public airing of grievance, my sweet. You must tell all who will listen of the injustice of having been wronged. How could I agree to such universal condemnation? What would our son think?"

"You mean you wouldn't tell me if you were having an affair?"

"The odds are against it."

"Fergus, you're a total shit! That's the whole point. If you don't tell me, no good can come of it." She sank deeper into the loveseat beside him.

Fergus poured more wine into her glass.

"So. I suppose if you were having an affair right now, there'd be no way for me to know that, either."

Fergus said nothing.

"You're not, are you?"

"Not what, my love?"

"Having an affair."

"Absolutely not."

"You'd better not be. I mean it, mister. That is such a shitty thing to say! You did say you wouldn't tell me if you were, didn't you?"

"Yes, I did say that."

"I never thought I was living with a liar. All these years. Okay, so tell me, am I really living with a man who would lie to me?"

Fergus placed the bowl of hummus on top of the now empty plate. He picked up both plate and bowl along with his wine glass and headed into the kitchen.

"You see?" He tossed these words over his shoulder. "Already we are leaving Christmas behind. Yesterday, I was boring old Pedro, and today I'm a mystery."

"Don't try to be funny, Fergus. It doesn't suit you."

Fergus opened the door of the dishwasher with the toe of his shoe. He searched for a place to deposit his load, realizing after a minute of staring that the dishes were clean. He frowned. Nobody in good conscience could ignore the fact that a machine full of clean plates, glasses and cutlery had to be emptied. Annie's voice seemed distant, a muted sound like water lapping around the piles of a dock.

"I beg your pardon?" he asked.

"And what do you know about hotel rooms and telephones, anyway?" Annie was saying, but Fergus sensed from her tone that she wasn't really saying it to him. He emptied, then loaded the dishwasher. He added soap, shut the door and turned the thing on. Lights blinked, a motor hummed. After a few seconds, water exploded through nozzles, a satisfying sound, the very same sound he loved to hear on his trips through the car wash, except now he was outside instead of inside. So many things are like that, Fergus thought. One day you're planting an apple tree in the backyard, and before you know it you're cutting it down and burning it. A complete flip. Is that what he was doing? A flip? His first apartment had been in a building that no longer existed, a turn-of-the-century place on lower Rockland. He had a one-bedroom then, complete with gas fire. Was that an English thing? To say "gas fire," not fireplace? Blue flames shot furiously out of white ceramic jets. Hardly relaxing, hardly the simulated log constructions he saw in homes these days. Annie and he often sat in front of it and drank tea, reading aloud to each other from books they were studying in their courses. Poetry sometimes. There was a book of love poems by Pablo Neruda. Fergus had never read much poetry before, nothing modern anyway. They had read the entire collection in one sitting. It was the first time either of them had encountered love as a vicious animal, a creature that destroyed its prey mercilessly, tearing limb from limb, thigh and breast. Fergus still remembered the phrase "murderous love," how they had both marveled at it, even imagined that was the kind of love they were experiencing. Love as killer. Love lying in wait. Not like now. Not love sneaking away. Not love the dissembler. What *was* slowly turns into what *is*. Children, too. Fergus used to bribe his own son, Helios. *Here's a buck,* he'd say. *You need to get out of the house.* An hour later Helios would be back in his room, face buried in a book. Like that for years. Now look at him. Long hair. The music. A nice girl. Nobody thinks life is ever going to change.

[VI]

Fergus had met Caroline almost a year and a half ago. She had been recommended to them by a friend of Annie's, a personal injury lawyer who owned a California Spanish replica two blocks away. Over drinks one Sunday afternoon, Annie's friend had shown them the greenhouse Caroline had built for her, the three cedar garden-benches she had made to measure.

"A good carpenter is worth more to me than a good mechanic," the woman had said. "And I have both."

Fergus and Annie's house always needed work. Caroline was there almost two months. First it was the front steps, all new stringers, shingle siding. Later the original wooden gutters needed replacing. Fergus found other jobs for her, too. He looked forward to the weekends, to seeing her Toyota in the driveway at the end of a day at work. The rest of the week Caroline rode maintenance trucks with city crews: boulevards, beach patrol, no sewer stuff. Fergus talked with her while she shifted lumber from one place to another, stocked up her nail pouch. He brought her coffee, stayed home some Saturday afternoons to give her a hand while Annie took care of things at the deli. Something about a woman swinging a hammer. Hair tied back, looped through the hole at the back of her cap. A yellow cap. The front of it said CAT.

"Think *you'd* like it?" Annie said when she saw him out in the yard one Sunday morning. "Somebody watching you all the time?"

"No, you're wrong," he said to Annie. "She likes me to help. It's good to keep an eye on these people."

The first Saturday Fergus came home early, Caroline had just finished ripping apart the front steps. Barely one o'clock. With the steps gone, Fergus could see into the dark hollow under the porch. He wondered about the creatures that lived in that gloom. Black widow spiders, he'd heard. A breeding ground for them. Caroline was holding a glass jar that contained some papers.

"What's that?" he'd asked.

"Time capsule."

"I beg your pardon?"

"The last guy who worked on these steps. He left his bills. In 1956, a piece of two-by-ten-by-twelve cost a dollar sixteen."

"Oh," Fergus said. "What's one cost now?"

He was thinking of the wad of receipts in his wallet he had to give to Annie, a hundred little purchases he'd stuffed away for her to deduct from their income. Thank God she took an interest in that sort of thing.

"You don't want to know," Caroline said.

"But I will."

"You will what?"

"Know. You're going to charge me, aren't you? Make me pay?"

"That's right," Caroline said. "Sometimes I forget."

She ruffled in her pocket and pulled out a few Visa receipts.

"I'll put 'em in this jar for the next guy," she said.

"That'll be after my time, I hope."

"I don't know," Caroline said. "You look like you're here for a while longer."

"Can I make you a coffee? Tea?"

Fergus invited her onto the deck, where he brought out two cups of coffee and a couple of muffins from the supermarket. Fergus apologized for the pedestrian fare, told her it came with the job.

"I hate cooking at home. Something about working in a kitchen all day long. I get back here and all I want is what's easiest."

"So, Goodlake's *is* your place. I thought it might be. 'Goodlake's, good food,'" she quoted.

"You've been in?"

"Lots of times."

"I don't remember seeing you," Fergus said.

"I remember you, though."

"Yeah?"

AT FIRST, FERGUS put it down to proximity. Just being in someone's company. No wonder so many affairs started in the workplace. People hang out long enough, they're bound to get ideas. Ideas came slowly to Fergus, though. He'd had no experience in this area for a very long time. What to think about all the jokes, the quickness to laugh, to urge the other person on with a story, to make Caroline feel as though what she had to say was interesting, to make himself believe what she had to say was also interesting. To be obtuse, to fail to see the inner workings of things, to hear a hint and not take it. To understand in an instant that he hadn't changed, that his first instinct was always to lie, that it always had been.

"Are we having an affair?" Caroline asked Fergus one afternoon. They had taken a break and retreated to a pub-style restaurant that offered anonymity in the form of low ceilings, dark booths.

"Is that what you think's happening here?" Fergus asked.

"What else?"

Fergus heard himself pronouncing his words as though he were listening to the script from a very bad play read out in front of him. People actually said these things! But there was something else he noticed, too, a kind of momentum that had been building between him and Caroline over the last few weeks, the momentum of sex. It was a feeling he'd almost forgotten — memories of feelings are the first things to go, he decided, before names, dates, faces — the preparations the body and the mind make, hormonal adjustments, probably, the same kind of tweaking that happens to a battalion as it undertakes to go to war. He could feel the inevitability in what he was doing, a commitment to a course of action from which he could not be deterred, not by common sense, not by loyalties long maintained, not by any moral code that could be invoked to stop him. Yes, he thought. So much like war, the great military orgasm that won't be denied, won't be shut off in mid-arousal. He was amazed at his own determination once he recognized what was going on, amazed at what he was willing to sacrifice, how little it meant to him.

"I think we need to find us a bed," Caroline said.

In a dark corner of Fergus' cluttered cellar, on the mattress from a long discarded fold-out couch, Fergus found himself stretched out naked with a woman who had only just been born when he'd started seeing Annie. It was not yet four o'clock, but Fergus' ears were alive to the sounds of the house above him, the silence of the empty rooms that seemed to be listening, too, old and inarticulate friends who would register their disappointment in him every time he entered them from now on. But what did Fergus care? It was late summer, the basement air a mixture of cut grass and old leather suitcases and dust. To shed clothes and wind the body up to a peak again like frantic party crashers looking for a space in a house, any space, any house … Fergus had no doubt in that moment that he would lie and lie again to make such a scene happen as often and for as long as he could manage.

"You always this fast?" Caroline asked.

"Sorry," Fergus said. "I was nervous. I thought I heard a car in the driveway."

"We're going to have to slow you down. That's okay for adolescents, but somebody your age …"

"Don't remind me," Fergus said. He was embarrassed now, feeling silly and juvenile to be sitting in the dark on a mattress on the cement floor of his basement. Kids playing doctor. Show me yours.

"So …"

"Please," Fergus said. "Don't ask me what I'm thinking. There are a number of things you could say right now, but I hope that won't be one of them."

"I don't need to ask, Fergus. That's what I like about you. You're as clear as glass."

"I'd better not be so easy to read," Fergus said. He tried to imagine the muscles of his face, the messages they were sending out. Unwise to yawn right now? A frown? Maybe a bit of a pucker? Something to break the signal.

"Are you all right?"

"A little shocked, I think," Fergus said.

"At me?"

"No, at me."

"You'll get used to it, Fergus. People can get used to anything."

"Yes," he said. "I think that's what I'm afraid of."

Caroline pulled him to his feet and burrowed into him with a kind of hug. It was a funny thing to do, Fergus thought, the kind of thing a kid might think of. He returned the hug, unsure what was being conveyed by the gesture, worried it might convey too much.

IN THE HOUR AFTER Caroline left and before Annie arrived, Fergus sat in the living room, staring out at the street. He'd watched Caroline's truck pull away and then waited a moment, expecting something, a phone call, a knock on the door, a tap on the shoulder. Once, when he was about eight years old, Fergus had stolen a pack of gum from the grocery store close to his house. He'd walked home and gone immediately upstairs to sit in the corner of his room where he methodically went through the package, stick by stick, until his jaw ached with fatigue from the mass of gum he'd crammed into his mouth. All at once, the door to his bedroom slammed open, and his father, in three short steps, had come directly to where Fergus crouched, snatched the gum from his mouth and given Fergus such a stunning box on the ear that he could not hear properly on that side of his head for over a month. For years afterward, Fergus simply assumed that his father, and adults in general, possessed the power to see into the hearts of children, that transgressions were as apparent to them as blemishes on the face, open wounds. He didn't discover until some time later the more plausible explanation, that the store's owner, a Mr. Allison, had simply phoned the Goodlake home to tell Fergus' father what had happened, that a few well-placed words in the ear of a parent would ensure the kind of justice he wanted. When the truth finally came to Fergus — it was a good ten years after the event, when he was in a funk about school, what to do about it, whether to bother going at all — he summoned up a picture of that bitter little shopkeeper, the mat of chalk-grey hair that lay like a field of rain-flattened grass across the top of his skull, how he doled out the penny candy, the jawbreakers, licorice pipes, dropping them into a paper bag as though they were street drugs and Fergus an addict, how he'd been betrayed by this man who was now long dead or retired and senile in some home for the elderly. And Fergus seethed thinking of him, of the lie that had been perpetrated, how he wished he could find the man and smash his hand against his head the way Fergus' father had unleashed his own hand like an attack dog against Fergus. But even after this mystery was solved and the magical mechanics of justice proven false, Fergus maintained an unarticulated faith in a kind of moral force that ruled the universe, one that would bide its time and exact revenge, compensation, amends. So, when the phone didn't ring and no knock rattled the front door, Fergus remained skeptical. Could a person shatter something and not see the pieces lying on the floor? Was it possible to sunder a bond between two people without both people feeling the break? Even when Annie came through the door, her face alight with the prospect of a restful Sunday ahead, no parties to cater, the deli put to bed until Monday, not even then did Fergus truly believe he was in the clear.

"I see she got the trim on," Annie said.

"Looks good, doesn't it? I told her about the trellis. She said she'd find a bit of one-by-two. It won't take much."

"Do we have to eat tonight?" Annie asked. "Let's just forage. Wine, that's all we need. Please say you don't care about food."

"I don't care about food," he said. "But I want a shower."

"Be my guest. Worked up a sweat, did you?"

"Sort of," Fergus said. "You know me."

Even in the shower, Fergus continued to look for signs of a change. He soaped himself all over, used a face cloth to scrub himself down. Could adultery be erased — God, he hated that word, its cheap novel sound, the Biblical overtones, Charlton Heston on a mountain, frowning, tablets in hand. He rubbed some more, tilted his head back to rinse. Could it wash off like a layer of dirt? He parted the map-of-the-world, clambered out of the old tub, to stand in front of the mirror, which he rubbed with his towel for a better view. Same squint, same pale eyebrows, same mole. Shoulders a bit saggy, perhaps, but no more than usual. Tightened his stomach, clenched his gut.

"So now what, wag? Are you pleased with yourself? Do you feel smug?"

He thought about his initial excuse — that it had happened because he and Caroline had been in the same place at the same time. Did that mean it would stop when she left? No, he told himself. It would not. This was more than just chance. He'd been thinking about this for a long time — "this" meaning a jolt, an explosion. Perhaps humans are not designed for contentment, he thought. Years of peace take a kind of toll. Years of going to work and coming home, years of paying bills regularly, taking out the garbage, dismantling the summer furniture and storing it under the deck, taking it out again. Maybe we sabotage ourselves because we need to. The adrenalin of fear, excitement, risk, is somehow therapeutic, like a vitamin we're lacking. Animals will gnaw on almost anything if their body tells them to. Are we any different? No, he could see now that he had not been passive in this. He had not simply gone along with Caroline. He'd been as active as he knew how to be, burbling in her ear about one thing and another, watching her as she worked, dispensing with the demands of the deli as quickly as he could so he could come home early. There was strategy, there was pre-meditation. He was guilty. He was guilty as hell.

But he was pleased, too.

That new perfume in his nostrils — eau de hammer? work boots? — and a craziness in his skull he hadn't felt for years. It was as though the moment Caroline first touched him, she had planted something, a thought, a new nerve, a sensation, and with all the myopic intensity of a soccer fan, Fergus cheered it on.

Two weeks later, Caroline gave him a key to her apartment, had an extra one cut just for him. Fergus took wild risks. Left even earlier in the morning for work, stopped in at Caroline's, surprised her in bed while her daughter Melissa slept in the adjoining room. Arrived late at the deli and worked like a man possessed to be ready for Doris when she came at eight. Often wasn't. He phoned Caroline at odd times. From pay booths, but sometimes from home, after a few drinks when he felt reckless, stupid with desire. Sometimes he'd drive to her place in the evening, out on an errand, not enough time to stop, but drawn to her street just the same. He'd imagine himself parking, buzzing her on the intercom, hearing her voice, the click of the door. She lived above a Chinese store, one of the few left now that Mac's and 7-11 had invaded the business. He'd sit in his car across the street and watch the bright lights above the cashier, the pitiful white buckets of flowers outside, the headlines of the major papers staring out at him. Maybe she needed milk or bread and would come down. He could pretend to be a customer, put his purchases down beside hers, give her a wink and leave. Twice he had dashed in to the store on impulse and bought a bouquet of flowers for her, and then quietly climbed the stairs to her apartment and left the flowers outside her door. No card, nothing to identify himself. That was too risky. There was even the possibility he might be seen by someone he knew, the chance encounter with a neighbour who had business in Esquimalt. Unlikely, yes, but his heart always took ages to settle down after these episodes.

Sometimes he shocked himself by thinking about what he was doing in the coarsest terms: His bit on the side. Still looking at the menu after he's ordered the main course. A spare piece of tail. After all, there was no use kidding himself at his age. Once in a while, Fergus debated spilling the beans to Annie. He understood the compulsion to be honest. It wasn't something he had grown up with, but he could recognize it in others, this need to confess.

It wasn't a long debate.

An old reflex soon kicked in. He made Annie feel she was the one coming up short, that she and he were not really a match. He tried to bait her into hating him, picked fights with her over nothing. He said she'd thrown away a dust jacket he wanted. Couldn't she put the CD back in its case just for once? Whatever she said, he would contradict it. He made her ideas seem piddling, typical. Fergus knew she was equal to a fight, but he also knew she'd make no effort to defend herself. How he knew this, he couldn't say. He just knew. Maybe he had radar. Maybe she did. He didn't know. Probably, she just wasn't used to his being mean and it threw her off. After a while he cooled out. Any fool could see she didn't suspect a thing. Could be he was just kidding himself, but he ended up deciding it was better to keep quiet. Confession aborted. No sense in stirring up a hornets' nest. Friends of theirs who'd gone down that road ended up boring everybody with all their talk. The Jensens! All they did was jabber. Like there was nothing else in the world that interested them.

[VII]

The "Seven O'Clock Show" has just finished, a special on the Comox Valley fire. Survivor stories. Moon landscapes. Stumps for miles. Then the chalkboard, the broad strokes of the weatherman sketching out frontal systems, highs and lows, the cue for Fergus' father to get up from his chair, cross the carpet to turn off the television. Only tonight, he stays where he is. The credits roll. Regional CBC music leaks out of the Viking console. The guessing game begins. Is his father inviting him to watch another show? Is he daring him to change the channel himself without permission? Everything's a setup and Fergus knows it. What the hell. Fergus takes a risk, asks to see "The Everglades." Nothing else interests him, and even this show with its thin stories about alligator poachers and high speed air-boats isn't really enough of a reason to stay in the living-room. But Fergus is twelve years old. Options are few. If he doesn't stay here with his father, he'll have to go upstairs to his room where he'll read books he has already read, or sit and worry about the open sore that has appeared in the small crevice of skin between his scrotum and his thigh. It's been three weeks and still it hasn't healed. Fergus believes he has cancer, that the sore will spread until his whole body is one bleeding wound.

"It's only seven-thirty," he says to his father. Anyway, he thinks, it's not as though he has school tomorrow.

His father says nothing. The television stays on. "Don Messer's Jubilee." Down-east fiddling with the Islanders. Marg and Charlie, too. It lasts until the first commercial break, a spot about the new unbreakable container of Prell Shampoo. A man tosses the shampoo to his wife in the shower, who drops the bottle and is surprised it doesn't shatter. She's just picking it up when the screen begins to shake. For a brief moment, Fergus thinks the movement is part of the commercial, but then he realizes that the house is moving, not the television. The wooden structure has suddenly become fluid and full of noise. The Duncan Phyfe table in the front window wobbles on its uneven legs. There is a kind of echo in the upright piano as though somebody has just run a finger across the harp. Then the shaking stops. Fergus turns to his father, who sits in his recliner in the far corner of the room. He seems small and unthreatening, the way he would if Fergus were looking at him through the wrong end of a telescope.

"That was a big one," his father says. He says this as though he now owns the earthquake, as though he has given the event meaning by labelling it. Fergus sees this happen, how with a few words something that was theirs to share has now been taken away from him. He hears his mother yell from upstairs.

"Did you feel that?"

Fergus knows that his father won't answer his mother, that answering is some kind of defeat for him, so he answers instead.

"Dad says it was a big one."

Fergus' mother comes down to the first landing and peers over the banister at them.

"What are you guys doing?"

"Watching TV," Fergus says.

"Must be nice," she says and goes back up.

Fergus' father leaves the room. A CBC announcer interrupts the program with news about a large earthquake in Alaska. Reports of heavy damage are still coming in. Viewers should catch the latest on the late news at eleven. Don Messer returns to the screen and Fergus watches until the end.

AT ELEVEN O'CLOCK, they all gather for the national news. A large earthquake near Anchorage, Alaska, has caused a lot of damage. It's been only three and a half hours since the quake, but already there are reports of buildings completely destroyed, roads that have subsided into cracks in the earth. The news station plays a recording of a radio announcer who was on the air in Anchorage at the time:

"Hey, boy!—Oh-wee, that's a good one! Hey—boy oh boy oh boy! Man, that's an earthquake! Hey, that's an earthquake for sure!— Whee-eee! Boy oh boy—this is something you'd read—doesn't come up very often up here, but I'm going through it right now! Man— everything's moving—you know, all that stuff in all the cabinets have come up loose... Who-eee! Scared the hell out of me, man! Oh boy, I wish this house would quit shaking! That damn bird cage—oooo—oh man! I've never lived through anything like this before in my life! And it hasn't even shown signs of stopping yet, either—ooooeeee—the whole place is shaking—like someone was holding—Hold it, I'd better put the television on the floor. Just a minute—Boy! Let me tell you that sure scared the hell out of me and it's still shaking, I'm telling you! I wonder if I should get outside? Oh boy! Man, I'm telling you that's the worst thing I ever lived through! You couldn't even stand up when that thing was going like that— I was falling all over the place here. I turned this thing on, and started talking just after the thing started, and man! I'm telling you, this house was shaking like a leaf! The picture frames—all the doors were opened —the dishes were falling out of the cabinets—and it's still swaying back and forth—I've got to go through and make a check to make sure that none of the water lines are ruptured or anything. Man, I hope I don't live through one of those things again ..."

While they're listening, Fergus watches his mother. Impatient, he thinks. No, fed up. She tears at the skin around her fingernails, stops a minute to smooth her dress across the top of her knees and then goes back to tearing at her skin again. There's nothing to see on the television screen. Only the single word "Earthquake" and the newscaster sitting quietly as the radio report finishes, but they all watch the set, Fergus' father leaning forward in his chair, Fergus and his mother on the couch, the curtains drawn against Good Friday night and the topsy-turvy world still reeling a couple of thousand miles to the north.

"That didn't sound real to me," Fergus' mother says.

"Be quiet," Fergus' father says when the newscaster returns with more information.

The man tells them that, worse than the earthquake, are the predicted tidal waves that may sweep down the coast and wipe out villages and towns all the way to California. The magnitude of the quake was 8.6, and because it occurred under the ocean, massive amounts of water will have been displaced, water that will form waves capable of traveling up to five hundred miles an hour. The newscaster calls these waves tsunamis, a word Fergus has never heard before. He places it alongside other words like tarantula and constrictor and embolism. He imagines the giant wave building out in the night-shrouded waters of the Pacific, as big as a mountain, curling in on itself and rolling southward towards them as they sit. He tries to compute the distance and the speed, but he has no idea how far away Alaska is. *When will it arrive?* he wonders.

His father gets up at the end of the news and shuts off the set. Then he walks over to the thermostat and turns it down to sixty-two degrees from the sixty-eight he set it to when he got up this morning. He walks around the main floor, shutting out lights, checking the taps, the back and front doors. Fergus isn't sure what's happening. It looks as though his father is preparing to go to bed, but the idea makes no sense to Fergus after what they've seen. Shouldn't they be getting into their car and leaving? Surely, his father heard the warning. He couldn't have mistaken the man's words.

"Let's call it a day," his father says.

Okay, let's, Fergus thinks. Judgement Day. Doomsday. Fergus knows his father is crazy. He looks to his mother, who has picked up a glass from the coffee table, the juice glass Fergus brought in after dinner. She is holding it up to the light, turning it a bit. Fergus wants to tell her it's not important now, that they should start filling the car with food, some clothing. *It's time to go,* he wants to say. His mother walks into the kitchen, turns on the light Fergus' father has only just shut off. Fergus can hear her running some water. He hears the glass as she drops it, rinsed, into the rack beside the sink. He hears her switch out the kitchen light again and start up the stairs to bed.

"What do you say, Fergus?" she asks from the top of the stairs.

"Oh," he says.

"Coming?"

"Coming."

Fergus makes his way to his room where he goes immediately to the window and looks out at the bay, the curved strip of road that moulds to its shape and the pale wash of streetlight that fades to nothing almost as soon as it reaches the dark chop of the water. He wonders whether the top floor of their house is higher than the wave that is coming. Even if it is, Fergus thinks, there is nothing that can stand up to a wall of water moving five hundred miles an hour. The house will be blown to pieces as surely as if a train had run into it.

He can't understand his parents' behaviour. He is tempted to walk into their room and ask them to explain themselves, to tell him why they are so unconcerned, but he knows what will happen. They will make light of his fear and laugh and remind him of the time he used to stay up night after night waiting for a fire truck to come and set their house ablaze, convinced by the name alone that this was exactly what such machines did. *If he had only asked us,* his mother always says to friends that come over. *Such an imagination!* Only Fergus could have dreamt up such a scene. *Go to bed,* they'll tell him. *Nothing's going to happen. You worry too much.* Fergus can hear them talking, their voices soft and indistinct through the useless hot air vent that feeds both their rooms. His father's is an occasional low murmur, a sullen reaction to the stream of questions that roll out of his mother until she tires of his cheap answers and yawns and lapses into silence.

It is barely eleven o'clock, but the town seems to have stopped. A car hasn't passed their street for over fifteen minutes. Not even a breeze.

Fergus looks at the Westclox alarm beside his bed, its radium-coated hands and numbers suspended against the semi-darkness of his room. He knows he won't sleep. Not while there is the chance he will wake to the sound of his windows breaking, caving inwards from the weight of tons of water against them. He listens for the rhythmic drone of his father's breathing as he sinks deeper into sleep. Soon he will start snoring, and his mother will kick him to make him turn on his side. It's not Fergus' fault they won't listen to reason. They heard the news the same as Fergus.

He throws back the covers and sits up. He steps onto the rug beside his bed. He remembers every floorboard of his room, each squeaky giveaway, and he moves quickly to dress and gather a few extra clothes that he places into the Second World War rucksack he uses to carry his books to school. The moon has been full for the last two days, and now it shines through the watery, fifty-year-old window panes of his room, casting rippled rectangles of light onto the blue walls. Fergus grabs his Ray-O-Vac flashlight and his jackknife from the dresser drawer and stuffs them into the rucksack along with his clothes.

He looks around, tries to imagine his room under water, seaweed and fish floating among his things. He worries about what will happen to his collection of bottle caps, the scale model reproduction of a British how-itzer his father had given him for his birthday. He wonders what will happen to his parents. *Probably nothing,* he tells himself. At the same time, he is too afraid to stay in the house and wait. He slips out into the hallway and navigates the worn stairs to the main floor, where he stops in the kitchen for some food. From the cupboard next to the hot water tank he takes two tins of Libby's beans, a can of apple juice, one cellophane sleeve of crackers. There is nothing in the fridge that he wants except a wedge of the deli's cheddar for the crackers. On his way to the basement, he takes his father's binoculars that hang behind the door. Fergus' supplies are too much for the rucksack alone, and he puts as much as he can into the basket of the Raleigh three-speed that leans on its kickstand beside the furnace chimney. The door to the outside has been more difficult than usual lately, trying to dig its way into the cement each time it opens, and Fergus has to lift with all his strength on the handle in order to avoid making noise, an effort he has to repeat once he has wheeled his bike outside. It's too risky to take the time to lock the basement from the inside and leave by the less reluctant kitchen door which will latch itself after him, but he feels bad, nevertheless, leaving his parents vulnerable this way, on the verge of disaster, their house unlocked. He has no clear idea where he wants to go, but higher ground lies to the north of the city, and so he heads in that direction.

PART II

Some Necessary Repairs

[1]

On a bright Friday in early May, two weeks after she had nearly lost her mind and told her husband to have an affair, Annie found herself driving back from a client who owned a house in the rocky highlands outside Victoria. The roads in that region carved nauseating curves around scrubby little hills and through forests of junk third growth or demented arbutus from which deer appeared without warning, sometimes with fawns in tow. Annie had almost wiped out an entire family on the way up, so on this return trip she was hugging the shoulder, riding the brake and leaning into the steering wheel as though she'd been caught in a snowstorm and couldn't see three feet beyond her bumper. The house Annie had visited looked like a military bunker that had been airlifted out of Iraq and bolted onto the side of a cliff to take advantage of the property's southern view, and Annie was remembering the panorama of wooded hills that seemed to roll like a green wave right up to the very edge of Georgia and Juan de Fuca straits, Mount Baker in the far distance. She was remembering, too, the conversation she'd had with the client, a woman in her sixties, her wrists and arms obscured by dozens of silver bangles, who was hosting a gathering of teachers on one of their non-instructional days coming up at the end of the month. Annie knew what non-instructional days were from the parents' side of the fence, but this was a business visit. She shut her mouth and did her job. Even when the woman told her the teachers were meeting to discuss the issue of "wellness" among members of their profession, Annie just took out her measuring tape and looked around at the textured cement walls, the rough wool tapestries, the automobile-sized pillows strewn a little too artfully about the room while the woman explained that she wasn't a teacher herself, but a kind of counselor who employed a variety of techniques to get people talking.

"People forget about themselves," she had said to Annie. "They go to work. They deal with crisis after crisis throughout the day. They make plans for the coming weeks, and then they come home exhausted."

"Sounds familiar," Annie said. She was taking a few measurements of the main living room where the food was to be served. The tape was just a prop, something to lend an air of professionalism to her visit. It allowed her to move about, shift from one side of the room to another. She could talk, she could turn away. Annie had seen at a glance where best to set up. The place was wired to code. Plugs everywhere. A kitchen off the living room. No problems here. A floor-to-ceiling window stretched for nearly thirty feet on the south side of the house, interrupted only by double doors that led out onto a multi-leveled deck.

The woman was still talking.

"And then what do they do? They have a drink, or two drinks. Some of them still have a cigarette. Then, maybe it's a nice dinner, a plate of oily pasta or a big fat piece of meat. They deserve it, they tell themselves. All their grievances are washed away in a sea of grease and alcohol and smoke."

"Perhaps you want to go over the menu with me?" But the woman didn't hear her.

"Do they take a walk? Do they discuss their frustrations from work with a loved one? Do they do something that might actually help their situation? No, they just go on day after day until an artery pops or their liver gives up."

"You paint a pretty picture."

"So many sick people! Everywhere you look. They walk around half dead from caffeine poisoning or chronic muscle spasms, terrified to take a sick day because of the work they'll come back to. And their families! Those people suffer, too. Make no mistake!"

"I hear you."

"Well, okay, then. Let's talk about that. What about yourself? Here you are, the perfect example of a successful businesswoman, pad in hand. You've dressed yourself beautifully for the job, and no doubt you give orders, tell others what to do, reward some, fire the odd one, suffer resentment. Is it worth it?"

"It's called making a living, I believe," Annie said, although some of the woman's words resonated with a percolating dissatisfaction she had only just begun to recognize.

"Yes, it is. That's exactly what it's called. Isn't that sad?"

"I'm not following you."

"It's obvious you're not happy, you know."

Annie pressed a button on her tape measure, and the metal snake coiled in on itself with a hiss and a percussive snap. Period, it said. End of sentence. She tugged at the cuffs of her blouse and adjusted her skirt, which is what she always did when she was struggling to invent a reason to remove herself. Next came the apology. She mentioned another appointment, expressed her assurance that Goodlake's would fulfill its contract obligations to the letter, grabbed her purse, her pocket organizer and a handful of notes and left. It was time she was back at the store, anyway. Fergus would be wondering. She dumped everything in the trunk, plunked herself down in the driver's seat and phoned Doris at the deli.

"This one's a nutter, Doris. We'll need at least three on."

"I'm the nutter. Who else would work for you?"

"Okay, Doris. You have the menu. Set it up. The date's on the board." Before starting off, Annie reminded herself again of the best route through town to the delicatessen. Then she backed out of the driveway.

GOODLAKE'S DELI AND CATERING sat in a part of Victoria people in the seventies used to call "Old Town." Back then, there had been spreads in

The Colonist and *The Times* announcing a new market square that was opening in "Old Town," and commentaries by local architects that talked about the rejuvenation of Victoria's core through developing "Old Town." Annie could remember thinking — she was still in high school at the time — how those words had sounded more like a description, as though they might just as easily have been "Tired Town" or "Dead Town." And besides, how could a watery little name like that add sparkle to a cluster of ugly brick buildings and alleyways where there was nothing but pawnbrokers, machinery depots, and a few curiosity shops? It was also where tourists could find the single block of stores that passed itself off as Chinatown, but even Chinatown was a place anybody would regret after a walk down one side of the street and up the other. All that neon!

The delicatessen was the hub of the Goodlake universe. It had been started by Fergus' grandfather, a man who could remember the Boer War. Fergus always made it clear to Annie that his grandfather had not actually been in the Boer War. It was enough, he said, that he could remember it. For years, Annie didn't have the heart to tell Fergus she had no idea what he was talking about, and besides, hadn't Fergus' grandfather died years ago? Fergus told her to imagine her own grandchildren and how one day they would talk about their grandparents as people who could remember the Vietnam War.

"We didn't realize it when it was happening," he said, "but those were interesting times." Fergus had a habit of looking back on his life as though he'd already lived it. When they were at university together, Annie would sit with him in the cafeteria and listen to him joke about future historians discussing the essays they were writing, the books they were reading, his relationship with Annie. He'd talk in the voice of one of his English professors and comment about himself and his circle of friends the way academics talked about the Bloomsbury group or the Paris expatriates.

Annie married Fergus in 1975. He was twenty-five, she was twenty-two, and when she married him, her name changed from Mitton to

Goodlake because that's what happened in 1975. It was automatic. It was the law. Besides, she hadn't really given the idea of keeping her own name much thought. Her family had come from Ontario to B.C. in the mid-1960s because Noranda Mining wanted to open an office on the west coast, and when it closed three years later her father jumped ship and went to work with the Ministry of Mines, which he hated almost as much. Annie had two older sisters, twins, who despised Victoria for its smallness and their father for bringing them there. The day they both graduated from high school was the day they hitchhiked back to Toronto just in time to attend the Strawberry Fields Rock Festival in Mosport, where they found all their old friends camped out in pup tents listening to Sly and the Family Stone and Jethro Tull and Jose Feliciano and Mountain. These friends had grade thirteen yet to come, which meant that a year later Annie's sisters attended a second graduation where they got drunker than they had at their own, with boyfriends they later married and divorced. Right now, Marlene was minus a husband for the second time and living in Sudbury in a house with a view of the original giant nickel and a stepson who refused to leave when his father did. Mary had abandoned Canada to go to New Zealand where she had taken a degree in dentistry. Correspondence between the sisters was non-existent, and Annie's parents had followed their daughters' lead by splitting up over ten years ago. Annie couldn't say where her father was these days, but her mother, she was sure, was still in Toronto, the city to which she had returned the moment the marriage was over. Annie didn't give them much thought, just as she hadn't given Fergus' family or their business much thought. She told people when she married that she was immune to history, a phrase she had picked up in one of her classes. She told them she and Fergus were free to choose their own future. None of this was true, she found out later. Her stupidity startled her. Every time she thought about the collection of neurotics and social misfits she had voluntarily hitched her wagon to, how for years they had tugged on the reins whenever they liked, she made a mental note to tell any girl crazy enough to marry Helios not to repeat her mistake. Her mistake. Such a harsh word, mistake. It always startled her, that she could think this way, that she had been thinking this way more and more in recent months. For years she had believed in a kind of "rightness" about the life she lived with Fergus. People meet for a reason, she'd always thought. At the one high-school reunion she'd attended, the organizers had taken a photo of the class — a ten-year update — and as the group assembled on the dais, Annie had watched with a growing sense of disappointment: these were not remarkable people, nothing bound them other than a common time, a common place. If anything, they appeared all the more ordinary and forgettable because of their urge to get together again, to celebrate the fact of themselves. She hadn't been married that long then. Helios was barely five. The revelation didn't transfer to her marriage, not immediately. Now, twenty years later, she was beginning to see her own life in a similar way. Perhaps myopia among the young was needed for the survival of the species. To see themselves as unique, a singular conjunction. Otherwise, the truth would shatter them.

THE ROAD INTO TOWN veered past another small lake. Annie glanced at a log house someone had built on the shore and tried to imagine briefly what it would be like if Helios lived there with a wife, some children, maybe. She shuddered. It was impossible to warn Helios about mistakes he hadn't made yet. That would be fortune telling. For one thing, Helios didn't listen, and for another, he wasn't living Annie's life, so any advice she thought might come in handy was completely useless. It was as though she was trying to give Helios a map to a place he'd never visit. And as much as she didn't like to admit it, Goodlake's had been — well — good for her, too. Marriage was a box she'd fallen into. Ten years falling. The deli had pulled her out of it. She thought about the house she had just visited, the years of work that had brought her there.

"Is it worth it?" the woman had asked her.

With her face pressed against the windshield, and the automatic transmission screaming in second gear as she went down yet another twisting hill, Annie forced herself to remember her quick exit, the troublesome words that had preceded it. Annie knew she wasn't a woman of the world. She knew she'd married too young. Sex makes people do stupid things, she told herself. Birth control was around then, but somehow Annie couldn't be bothered to ask the family doctor for a prescription. He'd been so moral about everything. Girls who wanted the pill before they were married were loose, and married women who wanted the pill were selfish. After all these years, Annie couldn't bring herself to say her son's real name, it sounded so awkward. Some names were just a mistake, and she and Fergus had made it. Helios never complained.

Probably, it wasn't wise to look at her life this way, she thought. Pointless childhood, pointless adolescence, pointless marriage, a pointless job in the family business. And now this woman had to open her big mouth. Women like her made a career out of ruining a person's day. What did she know? She had no special powers of vision, no insight. She was like a newspaper astrologist who made predictions that had all the weight of bumper stickers: Turn to friends this week. Avoid cash transactions. Seek true love. Maybe Annie had never meditated, self-actualized, explored her chakras, danced the Dance of Anger, or sung the body electric. Maybe the new age had passed her by the same as the old age of drugs, hitchhiking and group sex. But she was catching up with a little help from her son — it was Helios who had first introduced her to pot — and, anyway, Annie could tell a con artist when she saw one.

At a turn in the road, a motorcycle came out of nowhere, the rider leaning the bike far over, almost parallel with the pavement. He passed so close to Annie that she could see the rivets on his jean jacket, the earring that poked out from under the side of the skull cap that passed for a helmet. She was certain she was going to hit him, and when he disappeared in her rear-view mirror, Annie pulled over. She wrenched up the emergency brake of her ten-year-old Toyota and rolled down the window. Relax, she told herself. Nobody's hurt. She took a few deep breaths. The mild spring air flooded the car with the scents of long grass, wild rose and flowers she could recognize but not name. Perhaps she was a little open to suggestion after her recent encounter or perhaps she was feeling just a little shaken from her near miss.

A field stretched out toward the west, a rolling field dotted with copses of maple and Garry oak and fir. The scene reminded her of a postcard of an English vale, and Annie remarked to herself how easy it was to imagine she was somewhere else. Some days have a feeling about them. And then she forced herself to say what that feeling was. Some days feel like the end of the world. Yes, that was it. They feel like something's going to die. Okay, she corrected herself, that's a bit melodramatic. What did she know about death? She opened the car door and got out. She moved as though she were expecting something, an earthquake or a nuclear flash. Maybe a walk was in order. Some fresh air. Annie took a few steps toward a ditch that divided the road from the farmer's field beyond. She looked down and saw nothing. No deer bludgeoned to death by the fender of a speeding car. No mattresses. No McDonald's wrappers or Dairy Queen milkshakes. It was an ordinary drainage ditch with an ordinary stone culvert at one end, and for some reason it made her think of Fergus. Fergus as philanderer. She tried to imagine him reciting poetry to a faceless beauty, a model perhaps, or a flight attendant on a layover from Paris. The thought made her laugh aloud, and her voice carried for miles.

[11]

Caroline's friend Nathan had never been a practising Jew, and by "practising," as she explained to Fergus, she meant he didn't do the hat thing or all that Passover stuff that was getting such heavy press these days. Yes, he was Jewish, and thanks to the primitive conditions of a camping trip they had both taken together when they were young, she happened to know he was circumcised. But, as she pointed out with a deft movement of her free hand — the other held a cup of coffee — so was Fergus, and Fergus was … what was he, anyway? Danish? Norwegian? English! Anyway, she didn't see what there was for Fergus to fuss about. Jewish, schmewish. The fact was she had many friends who just happened to be men, and some were even more exotic than Nathan, for heaven's sake. Besides, Nathan was gay, okay? Enough said? She didn't like all this tension between her and Fergus. It was too much like somebody's marriage. Could he please relax now?

Fergus agreed he would, but added that, while he didn't pretend to be an expert on Jewish culture, most of the movies he had seen made it pretty clear that gays and orthodox Jews led mutually exclusive lifestyles.

"Are you saying I'm lying, Fergus? Is that what you're saying?"

"It's a strange mix, you have to agree." Fergus could see that she was genuinely hurt, and he regretted taking the argument this far. He'd just put away his cellphone, a quick call to Doris to see how things had been at the deli since he'd left, to buy himself a little more time with Caroline.

"Listen, Fergus," Doris had said. "I'm not going to take responsibility for what happens here when you're gone like this all the time. I'm an employee. You don't pay me to make executive decisions."

"I'm not asking you to. Things come up. I have to deal with them." Caroline had choked back a laugh at this point.

"What's wrong, Doris?" Fergus continued. "Just close the place down at five as usual. I'll be in early tomorrow."

After he'd hung up, he could feel the tension in his neck, a sense that he was being attacked. He had to force himself to relax. He had to remember that Caroline wasn't like Doris. There was no need to shoot at everything that moved.

"Fergus, he's Jewish and he's gay. It happens. More than you know. I don't think I've said anything wrong here. What I mean is I don't believe I am betraying any confidences by telling you this. The truth is Nathan's being gay isn't even relevant, so I really wish you'd just forget about it, okay?"

Fergus looked across at Caroline from his cushion on the rug. There was something familiar and even comforting in the way she dressed — by dressed, he meant the style of clothing she affected, for very little covered either her or him at the moment. Most of what Caroline had been wearing when he arrived had been cast onto the couch beside her. An eclectic assortment. It was as though some giant wheel had turned and the world had once again discovered long skirts and braids and work boots, a combination of earnest urban green mixed with Mennonite, fleece and Velcro. Maybe this was the influence of the snowboard scene and Mountain Equipment Co-op, a brand name he had spied on nearly everything Caroline owned, or maybe eclecticism was the order of the day now. Whatever the reason, it made for an arousing and protracted unveiling. He wanted to wipe a speck of food from the corner of her mouth, but he knew what she would say if he even tried. The temptation to infuriate her was hard to resist. Even so, he held back. His hands were full enough already with his most recent indiscretion, a complaint about one of her many younger friends, this one male, this one Nathan.

A warm May sun was bouncing off the windows of the industrial laundry across the street into the north-facing living room of Caroline Arnaud's apartment. She and Fergus were finishing their coffee and a half dozen Tim Horton's Bavarian Cream donuts. It was Caroline's idea to follow sex with pastry, a treat celebrated with a treat, and Fergus was still in shock — half naked on the floor of a woman's apartment, a sickly sweet confection dribbling from the corners of his mouth, cheap caffeine racing through his veins. All he needed now was a cigarette! He couldn't be happier. The thing was, Caroline looked happy, too, something that always seemed unlikely to Fergus, how a woman this young could be content with someone his age. Maybe at first, but for this long? Fergus refused to count the months. Thank God he'd always bicycled to work. Keeps a person fit, younger. At the same time, he wondered how someone of his advanced years could be this happy in the company of a woman so much his junior. Was he just pretending to find her interesting? Right now, for example. Caroline had coerced Fergus into looking at IKEA catalogues for some better dishes and a good kitchen table. Caroline adored IKEA almost as much as she adored Tim Horton's. As far as Fergus could tell, she seemed to adore almost everything. She had begged him to help her plan a trip to the Vancouver furniture outlet, an undertaking of considerable expense when one included the cost of the ferry to and from the mainland, and he had agreed, though planning wasn't an accurate description of what they were doing. For the last half hour, he and Caroline had looked at colour pictures of lamps and couches and armchairs and outrageous glassware and kitchen gadgets, ignoring the prices.

Two floors below, Caroline's five-year-old daughter Melissa was having a day away from pre-school in the apartment of Caroline's friend Donna, who helped Caroline out from time to time because she liked Melissa and because she had no children of her own. A day off — Caroline was pretending to be sick, a head cold sort of, some fever, she'd told her boss — was a rare occurrence, so she made the best of her time, sketching out what she wanted to do ultimately with the small space available to her and feasting on Bavarian Creams and asking Fergus if he wanted another cup of coffee. When she also happened to mention a project she was planning to undertake with her friend Nathan, Fergus, who was always suspicious of the men in her life, especially the younger ones, subjected her to a barrage of questions. Fergus knew Caroline tolerated his jealousy because she found it cute and non-threatening. She told him it reminded her of a small dog guarding a big bone. My life as a bone, she had said to him once, and he'd had to ask her to explain the reference. Caroline also told Fergus she liked him because he was forty-nine and married and had a twenty-five-year-old son. She believed men like Fergus were more stable than younger men, more placid and well-behaved. Fergus wanted to point out that Annie might not consider him particularly well-behaved if she knew where he was, but he hated to ruin Caroline's happy mood. Fergus loved Caroline for the countless ways happiness came to her, how often it came to her and with such intensity. He found that he had to keep a part of himself in check whenever he was with her, a hard part of himself that had set up house under his skin some time ago, and which he would just as soon took a vacation, especially when he was with Caroline. Around her he found himself consciously trying to be gentle, to be more present, to contribute. Not that Caroline pushed Fergus around. She didn't have to. His sense of how precarious this little world was made him value it all the more, that and Caroline's love of sex. Fergus had never been with somebody so eager, and he often found himself thinking about their couplings at the oddest times. Staring into the fridge. Raising a blind. Turning a tap. He thought of himself as lucky, but Caroline saw things differently. Didn't he think it was strange, she asked him, that a woman would want any other arrangement? Wasn't it better to have her daughter grow up in a stable, peaceful house where men were admitted only when it was convenient and only if they didn't carry on endlessly about cars or sports or careers? Wasn't this the kind of control women had always wanted in their lives? Fergus said he couldn't even begin to imagine what she meant by "career," and he hated both cars and sports. Caroline said if he kept talking that way she might not let him go home.

"I ain't misbehavin'," he began to sing, but Caroline kindly put her hand over his mouth to stop him.

"If you want real proof, this whole big thing with Nathan is a perfect example of why men are way more trouble than they're worth."

The truth was Fergus wasn't at all concerned about religion or money or sexual orientation, but he did worry the age gap to death. Even Annie in her quest for a more meaningful marriage wouldn't have suggested an affair with a woman this young. He was certain of it. Hadn't she said she would kill him? Yes, she had. Would she eviscerate him? No doubt whatsoever.

"Twenty years," he kept saying to Caroline, "twenty years! Imagine a thirty-year-old man with a ten-year-old girlfriend! A twenty-year-old with a seed, for Christ's sake."

"Isn't it more than twenty?"

"Stop that," Fergus said.

Caroline said he sounded like a kid in grade eight whose best friend was in grade six. She tried to explain that age didn't matter once people grew up.

"After that, it's all personality. You're like one of those teachers at university, one of the younger ones. I'm like a mature student." And besides, wasn't he even just a little amused about it all? Here he was worrying about her and another, younger man when he was off doing the same thing himself.

"My point exactly. It happens. But in your case it makes sense. You're supposed to be with someone your own age." And then, because Caroline had smiled a little too long at this comment, he had said, "Me, too, I suppose."

So, she explained it all over again.

NATHAN WAS AN OLD FRIEND, as she had already told him, and once upon a time he and Caroline had been students at the same university together. Now, Nathan was nearly through his master's on his way to being an architect, and Caroline was working for the city cutting lawns, cleaning out public washrooms, the kind of job people normally left when summer ended and college began. But she was twenty-eight years old, wasn't she? With a daughter to think of? And she and Melissa lived in this wonderful, paper-thin one-bedroom above a Chinese store — a place like a shoe-box or hadn't Fergus noticed? — and there wasn't a day went by Caroline didn't think about looking for a house of their own, even a condominium. Anyway, when she'd become pregnant, a lot of her friends had gone so far as to tell her life was over. To them, Caroline was a living example of the warnings their parents had given them, and they slipped away from Caroline as though their friendship with her carried an expiry date. Nathan was one of the few who stayed in touch. He helped make the change from student to human being a little more bearable, and as far as her life ending … well, Caroline hadn't seen things that way. In fact, most people she knew, including Fergus, had gone to university because they'd run out of ideas or because their parents expected it of them. Caroline was a good case in point and was always the first to admit it. She had never got any satisfaction from school. Spending whole days reading a textbook didn't strike her as honest work — "No, Fergus, don't try to object" — and as far as she was concerned, the art of writing essays was over-rated. So when being late finally turned into being knocked up, she told anyone who wanted to know that pregnancy was the best thing that ever happened to her — yes, she realized it was a bit of a grim thing to say — and when her foreman offered to keep her on through the winter at union wages, she couldn't refuse.

Now, after all this time, her good friend Nathan was in graduate studies. Had Fergus ever made it to graduate school? Caroline didn't think so, but she told him he should be proud of his B.A. It just wasn't her thing. Well, Nathan and a bunch of art students had a house over by the park, a rental from the twenties that someone had converted into lots and lots of bedrooms. And while she was on the subject of houses, she didn't mind saying that it still broke her heart to think of the crap a beautiful old family home had to put up with in its lifetime, the kinds of ugly cuts and additions a wood butcher will make just to squeeze some more money out of his investment. New walls nailed right into hard-wood floors, bathrooms plopped into the middle of a hallway and pipes sticking out of what used to be the dining room ceiling.

"Old houses are beautiful things, Fergus, and I hope you and Annie will remember that."

"I don't think we should be talking about my wife."

"That's where you're wrong. We should probably be talking about nothing else. You have a lot of history together."

"One tale at a time, okay?"

Caroline agreed. As Fergus knew, she could spend hours looking at the joinery on some of the staircases she'd seen. Nathan's place in particular. Newel posts like classical columns and wainscotings without a single knot. Sometimes on her lunch hour she'd drop in to poke around, just to see what she was missing now that she'd quit school. Cases of empties lined the back stairs, and most of the kitchen counter was covered in pizza boxes and dirty glasses. Some things never change.

On this one day — it was last week, Wednesday — she found Nathan sitting in the living room rolling a joint.

"You remember pot, don't you, Fergus?" Caroline said. "You're from the sixties. Hell, you guys invented the stuff!"

"Please, Caroline."

"I know. You were different." She poked him in the stomach.

"I like to think so."

"That's your problem, Fergus. Isn't that what I always say?"

"I believe you do."

"Darn right, I do." She went on. "People who complain about student financial aid — people like you, Fergus — would have a field day at Nathan's house. Every semester he uses the money from his loan to buy whole pounds of pot and sell it for a profit, with enough left over to keep him and the others in smoke for the rest of the year."

"Pity the honest wage earner," Fergus said.

Well, Caroline supposed she could be angry, too. Even at $13.50 an hour, she was having trouble making the rent, the truck payment, not to mention a hundred dollars a week for an unlicensed daycare. "But you have to respect the ingenuity of some people, don't you, Fergus?" It wasn't as though Nathan wasn't going to pay back the loan. So why should anyone care if he had the brains to beat the system? The way she figured it, if money matters to you, you'll find a way to get it. It just didn't matter that much to her.

And Nathan took pride in rolling his joints. Even Fergus could appreciate a skill like this. Nothing sloppy for Nathan. He used only a single paper and wrapped the bud so tight and even, you'd swear some machine had made it. Caroline had watched him for a bit, then sat down in the chair opposite and threw her bag lunch on the coffee table.

'Just the man I'm looking for,' he says.

'I'm not the marrying kind, Nathan,' I say.

'There's a hundred bucks in it for you,' he says.

'Money for sex,' I say. 'That's all you fags are about, isn't it?'

'It's less complicated that way,' he says to me. 'Nobody gets hurt.'

Fergus was not impressed by her account so far, but Caroline told him not to get his dick in a knot. Real people talked this way to each other, she told him, and if he got out more he'd see what she meant.

"I *am* getting out. Coming here is getting out for me."

"You make me cry when you talk like that."

As it turned out, Nathan was making a good impression in his program. One of his professors had selected him out of the whole student body to do a job for the local Catholic diocese. The cathedral was shopping around for a new look behind the altar, something upbeat — charismatic was the word Nathan had used — and they wanted someone to mock up a new cross, one that would make a statement.

'Sixteen feet?' I say when he tells me.

'Maybe bigger,' Nathan says.

'That's a big cross,' I say. 'I don't think I've seen one as big as that. If I have, I don't remember it.'

'Oh, you'd remember,' Nathan says. 'Something that big you don't forget.'

'Stop it,' I say.

The joke was Nathan couldn't hammer a nail to save his life. A lot like Fergus, now that she thought about it. Perhaps they should meet some time? No? Okay. Yes, there was a point to all this. Just listen, she told Fergus.

Nathan was an ideas man. Give him a wrench and he looked like a girl. He tried to unplug his mother's bathroom sink once to save her some money and the plumber they called after Nathan gave up said only someone who really knew what he was doing could have made such a mess. Nathan used to tell that story a lot, like he was proud of being an idiot. Which is where Caroline came in. A carpenter she wasn't, but she got the job done. Some people called it moonlighting. She called it paying the rent. Fences, decks, tool sheds, kitchen counters. That was how she'd met Fergus, or didn't he remember? Those gutters he'd wanted installed? The front steps. And Fergus should know, too, that when she finished a job, she could take a level and put it anywhere. In her book, plumb meant plumb, flush meant flush and square meant square.

'When?' I ask Nathan.

'Not this Friday, but the next one,' Nathan says. 'Meet me at the lumberyard. Better yet, I'll pick you up.'

'I'll see about a sitter,' I say.

And then they finished the joint and Caroline ate her lunch.

"THAT'S ALL THERE is to it," she told Fergus. "A simple carpentry job. Some nails, a bit of wood. No romance. Strictly a financial relationship."

"How can you get off work? You don't have Fridays free. He's asking you to give up a day's wage?"

"Flex day. They don't exist in the real world."

"If I give you a hundred dollars, will you tell him no?"

"If you give me a hundred dollars, I'll beat you over the head with this catalogue."

"I don't like the part about you smoking pot."

"Relax. You're just worried about all this stuff with your doctor."

"Not a whit. There's no stuff."

"How much time have you got?"

"Not very long, I'm afraid." He looked down at his watch.

"You're quite a freak, aren't you? Don't you feel a little strange sitting here?"

"Don't tell me you don't."

"It's my apartment. This is normal for me."

"I suppose."

Fergus was used to Caroline's kidding. She had told him once she liked to balance his fatalism with a bit of humour. She said it was as though he had never learned how to play, and whenever he tried, he felt guilty. Right now, he was thinking of the biography he'd seen the other night of Bob Crane, the American colonel from "Hogan's Heroes," how he destroyed his marriage by running off with one of the big-breasted actresses that played the German girl in the series — Sigrid? Heidi? — and how his career had fallen apart because of an addiction to pornography. He'd turned to God, only to end up dead in a motel room, beaten so badly that they had to call in specialists to identify the body. Fergus looked around Caroline's apartment, imagined forensic detectives taking samples of hair and blood, sealing them up in plastic bags and then photographing every inch of the room while what remained of Fergus lay in a heap on the floor. Someone was interviewing tenants from the adjoining apartments. Yes, they'd say. That's the guy. Every couple of weeks, like clockwork. Fergus could see another series of biography specials: Unlucky Lotharios.

"I believe people having affairs are supposed to feel guilty," Fergus said.

"That's just what I mean. You put yourself in a box. You're 'a person having an affair.' To me you're just Fergus. I met you. No labels."

"You're equivocating."

"English major."

"Classics. Anyway, you're rationalizing. You're justifying yourself."

"Nothing wrong with that. The way I see it, we're doing this because we can. Don't misunderstand me. I don't mean we're thrill seekers or anything. But people can do this. They can have more than one life. More is always better. As long as you don't hurt anybody. It's just a little weird."

"It's not as weird as you think. It's almost typical. You know what they used to call it back in the Jurassic?"

"Who are 'they,' Fergus?"

"People. Men. You know the type." He lowered his jaw until the lower palate protruded like a chimpanzee's.

"Tell me, Fergus, what did they call it?"

"They used to call it 'getting lucky.' Have you heard of that one? I suppose it meant any sex at all. Weekend's coming. Maybe I'll get lucky. Does a woman get lucky? Or does she just get laid? You would know. Are you feeling lucky, today? No, that's Clint Eastwood, isn't it? Anyway, there was a guy on one of the forestry crews I worked on once, a very senior guy. Project boss. Older than I am now, he was at the time."

"If that's possible."

"Yes. He's dead now. Well, he was being all confidential one night. Had something to drink. He started talking about his marriage, the decades he'd been with this woman. How he'd never screwed around on her in years, not for years and years. Like a monk, he said. I remember that. A fucking monk, he said. Until one day he was out on some long stretch of gravel road up north, somewhere outside Cassiar, a truly awful piece of road. Miles and miles of washboard. And he sees this woman hitchhiking. It sounds stupid I know, but he swore it was true. So, he stops and tells her to get in, but she's drunk, almost falling down, and he helps her into the back of this panel wagon. It's big and wide, and right away she falls asleep. Passes out, I guess. And he's humming and hawing and wondering what the hell's going on, and then he yells at her. Asks her if she needs anything. But she's gone, down for the count. She's drunk herself into the middle of next week, is how he puts it. Skirt up around her hips, her mouth hanging open. Probably stank, too. But that doesn't stop him. No, not this old guy — I was having a hard time listening to him, drunk as he was himself. He just drops his pants and climbs in there with her. I couldn't believe what he was telling me. I mean it must have been like having sex with a corpse, for Christ's sake! And then he tells me that was the only time in his whole marriage he ever got lucky. Can you imagine? That's how he saw himself. A lucky guy."

"It's different now, anyway."

"That's not what I was thinking," Fergus said.

"I mean sex. Getting lucky. It's more than luck these days. It's a miracle. Think of the minefield of microbes and viruses a person has to get across just for a little fun. If that happened today —that old guy and that hitchhiker — he might as well be putting a gun in his mouth. Seriously. It's hardly worth it."

"I see what you mean." Fergus sat for a minute thinking. He took a sip of cold coffee, poked at a donut.

"You don't think," he said, "that I have anything like that, do you?"

"You, Fergus? Not a chance. You're like an old toy that's never been opened. Still in the original box."

"Old toy, eh?"

"I meant unused. You have to stop thinking you're like Jack Nicholson or Warren Beatty or who's that other loser? Robert Redford?"

"I try not to think of my life as a Hollywood movie. There are better examples in books."

"Name one."

"Rochester."

Caroline looked blank.

"*Jane Eyre*."

"I hated that book, and besides, his wife was insane. From what you tell me, Annie sounds more on the ball."

"What I mean is I'm not doing anything very original here. The divorce courts are full of people like me."

"That's not quite true. Your wife isn't nuts. There's nothing falling apart to make you come over here. I wish there was sometimes, but maybe I don't, too. You're just here because you want to be. And that's what makes it even weirder."

"I don't think it's as easy for you as you say it is."

"Define easy."

Which is when Fergus' cell rang.

[111]

"He hasn't been here all afternoon," Doris said.

She was cutting lemons into wedges and tossing them into a steel bowl on the island in Goodlake's expansive kitchen.

Helios looked on for a minute. He'd never got along with Doris; something about his being the son of the boss and five years younger. Long hair didn't save him, neither did the earring. "My mother, then?"

"On a job."

Doris took a handful of the wedges, plunked them into a glass pitcher and filled the pitcher with water.

"They wanted my truck. They said they had some stuff to go to the dump. Maybe you could tell them I have to work tonight, but I can get to it tomorrow afternoon."

"If I see them."

"You don't like me, do you, Doris?"

"What makes you say that?"

"The way you talk to me. It's like I disgust you."

"I don't know you," she said. "If I knew you, then maybe I wouldn't like you. Right now, you're not important enough for me to have an opinion one way or the other."

"Can I have some pie?" Helios said.

"Sure you can have some pie."

"Apple. And some coffee, please."

Helios took his food and sat down at a table over by the front window where he could look out at the street. He wished he had a brother or a sister, someone he could gripe with about people like Doris, people like his parents. Jayne wasn't the same. She defended them, tried to see their good side.

"You're too close," she said. "Children can't see their parents objectively."

"Doris is not my parent," Helios said.

"No, she's worse. She gets paid to put up with them. You don't."

The deli was busy for a weekday. Several people had lined up along the front of the display case waiting to give their orders. Marina was wiping down the special board. Soup was all gone for the day, pasta, too. Somewhere around five, Doris would walk out into the street and give away the leftover loaves of bread to some of the street people down by the shelter. Helios knew the routine, had even helped out when he was younger. The least he could do, Fergus had said. The building had his name on it, after all. Maybe if he was a Young or a Smith and it was Young's Deli or Smith's Deli, then Helios could ignore the connection. Goodlake's, no. Kids at school would ask him if that was his dad they'd seen, his mom.

"No," he'd say. "But we're related."

"Lucky for you."

Helios turned his head to see a man enter the deli. Cane, Tilley hat, the waist of his pants up around his ears.

"Hello, Ron," Helios said.

"Well! You working here again?"

"Pie and coffee," Helios said. He made a flourish with his hands.

"Me, too," Ron said.

"You want my seat? I'm just leaving."

"It's a good one, all right."

Helios made room and carried his plates up to Doris, who had just disappeared into the walk-in cooler. Marina was out back crushing boxes and, with no one to see him, Helios took a dollar from his pocket and threw it into the tip jar. Not the kind of thing Doris would appreciate, a gratuity from the enemy. He pushed his plates forward on the counter and left the exact change for his food beside them.

"Hey, kid."

He turned to see Doris coming toward him. She was writing as she walked, a pad of paper or small notebook in one hand, her pen poised above it.

"If it helps you out, Fergus phoned earlier and said he wouldn't be in before closing."

"Did he say where he was?"

"I don't know and I don't ask."

"What's that supposed to mean?"

"Fergus is losing his grip."

"He's been acting a little strange lately."

"Lately? Fergus? But I guess just because your parents are weird doesn't mean you are."

"That's what I was thinking."

"Doesn't mean you aren't, either."

"It's true. Why do you stay on, Doris?"

"Where you are isn't important," she said. "Who you are is."

"Ron keeps coming back," he said. Helios nodded toward the window. "Must be something to the place. See you, Doris."

"Hey, kid."

Helios turned. Doris was writing in her notebook. "What now, Doris?" She didn't look up. "Thanks for the tip," she said.

OUT ON THE STREET, Helios told himself he needed a nap before work. Where was Jayne, he wondered. Maybe there was enough time to stop in at the pawn shop. He'd seen a '64 Fender Vibroverb there last week. Black face, 15″ speaker, 40 watts. The kind of thing Stevie Ray Vaughan had used. Way too much money — they were asking three grand — but there was no harm in looking. He recognized his truck as it appeared in the line of cars parked along the street ahead of him. Such a beast. Same year as the amp, almost. What was the world like then? A world with great ugly trucks and beautiful amplifiers? All those sneaky Russians, and the Beatles just hitting their stride. Atom bombs and bikinis. Elvis making an idiot out of himself. Kid Galahad. Viva Las Vegas.

And Goodlake's. Goodlake's was there. Helios' grandfather at the helm. Thought he was just running the place until they could sell it. What a sap! Twenty-eight years later … Helios shuddered. Fergus was thirty-five when he took it over. Ten years to go for me, thought Helios. Better get busy. Better get gone.

He climbed into the truck, slapped a tape into the player. Watched the green light hesitate a bit, like maybe it wouldn't play this music if it didn't like it. Just a bit of CC. Swamp music. Something to drive home to. Skip the amp for now. Too many things to buy in this world.

[IV]

Looked at from above, Fergus' neighbourhood is an area of eleven or twelve suburban blocks. The lots vary in size and configuration, bending and curving to follow the shape of the bays and headlands that make up Victoria's southern coastline. Some of the lots are vacant, the grass in them long and their fruit trees wild and unpruned. Twenty years earlier, such a lot might have cost under a thousand dollars, and in all that time the price has not changed. Elsewhere in the country, real estate is rising in value, but Vancouver Island sits in the thinning postwar fog, unaware of its own worth. Nobody thinks of getting rich quickly. There is no talk of stock trends or mutual funds. Nobody buys a house and flips it six months later. The bank is the best place for saving money. There are corner groceries and butchers and bakeries. None of them is a franchise. Coffee comes in a can, and it is still exciting to see the waitress at the A&W wheel up to a car on roller skates and hang a tray of burgers, fries and Brown Cows on the driver's window. In summer, people swim at beaches like Coles Bay or at lakes like Elk and Beaver and Thetis. In winter they pay fifty cents and throw their clothes into one of the green wooden lockers at the Crystal Gardens, an aging public pool once visited by Johnny Weismuller and where big bands occasionally play the music of Glenn Miller and Tommy Dorsey. There are no recreation centres, still only the YMCA at the corner of View and Blanshard. There is only one liquor store, and customers have to ask a clerk to fetch a bottle from the wall of shelves behind the counter. They can point, but they cannot touch.

Fergus passes the homes of his neighbours as he makes his way toward Cook Street, the major artery that will lead him north and out of town. It is barely eleven-thirty, but the roads are quiet enough to draw attention to a boy alone, his clothes and bicycle silver in the moonlight that penetrates the boulevard trees, a phantom boy intent on moving through these streets unnoticed. The chain as it passes over the teeth of the sprocket, the drive crank that strains against its bearings, the friction of the rubber tires on asphalt — all of these conspire to create a locus of sound that Fergus fears is loud enough to bring people out of their sleep. He looks into the dark windows of houses he has known all his life, the occupants in bed now, oblivious to the danger that threatens them: Mr. Brook who works as a longshoreman, his young wife, their two children; Mrs. Stockman whose dead husband built their house himself when there were only open fields and an unimpeded view of the ocean; the Franklin sisters and their brood of cats. Fergus cannot see these houses for what they are, rundown fire traps with antique wiring and leaky roofs. They are too familiar to judge, like people whose short-comings are not apparent until they are placed alongside other people. Fergus believes he is bicycling into a life without them, a place that sits in his mind like the description from a travel brochure, the landscape wholly fantastical. He may as well try to picture himself in Mexico or Disneyland, other places he has never been. He presses down on his pedals and with each revolution another face disappears. His bicycle is a machine that is wiping out dogs and cats, fathers and mothers. Whole families fall prey to it, as though Fergus is the Angel of Death, and where his watery shadow falls, things die.

When Fergus reaches his school, the moonlight is so bright he can read the chiseled inscription lodged high in the brick gable of the main building: Erected A.D. 1914. He computes the numbers in his head and marvels at the coincidental perfection of the result. Fifty years it has been since then. Both world wars have come and gone in that time. Only his grandmother is older. The slate roof of the building gleams and the darkness under its eaves is impenetrable. Fergus can see the windows of his classroom, the art the teacher has taped to each of them, outlines of the various leaves they have been studying in their science unit on trees: maple, oak, alder. The words "deciduous" and "evergreen" rise in Fergus' mind and fall away again as he turns west.

As he rides, Fergus thinks about what he will do after the big wave wipes the land clean of people. Perhaps this is the aspect of the deluge that most appeals to him, the removal of a world where people work at jobs they despise, where a new day is just another opportunity to gripe, another chance to return home defeated, the way his father returns home from the delicatessen each day, his hands on the wheel of the car, turning it into the driveway as though he were driving into his own grave. Fergus is not yet a teenager, but he senses already his days as a child are numbered. He feels like a guest in his own house, embarrassed each time his mother dusts his room, deposits clean clothes on his bed, guilty when his father makes a reference to "putting food on the table." He wonders briefly why anyone bothers to have children when they begrudge them the groceries they eat, the space they take up. Certainly, there will be no living under this roof once he is out of school, not if he isn't working and paying his way. His parents have spoken approvingly of friends who pack up their children's clothes the minute they graduate, offer them the options of rent or the front door. Fergus is relieved that he no longer has to imagine what he will do when this time comes, how he will support himself. The thought of a career has always paralyzed him. It still does. He can think only of the garbage men who visit his house once a week, the sound of the steel garbage can that they deftly tilt and roll out to the street. Could he do that? Could he drive the street sweeper that cleans the gutters? Could he be a teacher like Mr. Stringer? No, Fergus decides. He could never be a teacher.

In the wake of the tidal wave, though, all these problems will mean nothing. Life will be a question of survival. Fergus pedals through the dark streets of Victoria, streets that will soon become strewn with debris, the contents of houses and corner stores, bits of broken cars and meaningless machinery. Soon he will return here to scavenge for food and nails and tools that he will use to build himself a house. He will comb the ruins of this town the way Robinson Crusoe plundered the remains of his wrecked ship. Fergus can feel himself getting excited, just as he got excited each time Defoe's hero came upon another keg of gunpowder, a small deck gun, a telescope. He can see that he, too, will undertake to build himself a palisade, this one from trees that have been uprooted, cutting them into lengths with an axe he imagines salvaging from a hardware store. Perhaps he will be lucky enough to come upon more batteries for his flashlight, too, maybe even a radio. He doesn't believe there will be other survivors. There will be no need to share his wealth with anyone else. It does not occur to Fergus that a catastrophe of this magnitude will attract the attention of the planet. He is too busy exploring a future that is unencumbered by bank accounts, gas payments, tax forms. He feels like one of Ernest Thompson Seton's little savages, a child from Swiss Family Robinson, the rules and demands of the old world relegated to history and a new order beginning.

[V]

Annie looked back to where she had parked the car, and as she did so, she could see something pooling under the engine, a dark mass that didn't absorb quickly into the gravel shoulder. She knew Fergus had been topping up a reservoir under the hood for the last few months — he might've said steering fluid now that she thought about it — and major repair work was imminent, if not overdue. The spreading black patch would probably have meant something to anyone familiar with basic mechanics, but Annie was a user, not a fixer. What happened on the other side of the dashboard or underneath the brake and accelerator was of no interest to her. She liked point-and-shoot cameras, Macintosh computers and battery-driven watches. She liked her shiny black stereo, the little drawer that appeared on command like a dog begging for a treat, the way it retreated into its house when rewarded. How the sound traveled from the doghouse to the speakers was of no interest to her, and designers who tried to implicate the owner in the operation and maintenance of their product simply annoyed her. She had once heard a psychologist on the radio explain women's indifference to the inner workings of things as a fear of their own mortality, that they didn't want the illusion of simplicity shattered. If they saw how complex a car or a camera actually was, they would worry continually that it might break down, a fear that applied to their own bodies as well. That's why, the psychologist went on to say, all the best surgeons were men. Annie couldn't believe the arrogance of the speaker. How like a man, she'd thought.

When a woman shows no interest in his toys, he accuses her of being scared. He can never accept that his little hobbies might just be boring. So, when she first noticed the leak, she had no urge to get down on her knees, lean under the car and examine it, perhaps dip a finger and sniff it for gas, coolant, oil. The idea didn't occur to her, and if it had she would have dismissed it as a stupid one. Fluids dripping from cars did not hold for her the kind of horror they held for most men who, though no more capable than Annie, numbered among their inherited responsibilities the grief, anxiety and frustration associated with all things automotive. Annie looked at the mess, registered some annoyance, and immediately placed the blame for this annoyance at Fergus' feet. His whole family was inexplicable in its uselessness. Ex-pats. Longstockings. The town was full of them. The kind of people who believed they didn't have to do anything. As though lasting this long was a virtue in itself. Once when a repairman had come to fix the washing machine, Annie had come across the defective part lying on its side by the basement door. In big yellow letters across its case the repairman had written "NFG." Annie had asked him what the letters stood for when he returned with the new part.

"No fucking good, ma'am," he'd said without looking up.

After that Annie and Fergus had used the acronym as their own secret signal when either of them didn't like something. "NFG," Annie would say coming out of a film. "ANFG," Fergus would declare after a meal out. Absolutely no fucking good.

Now Annie wanted to take a piece of chalk and write NFG across her car and across the foreheads of every inept and useless member of Fergus' family.

ANNIE KNEW THAT the story of Fergus' grandfather was supposed to be inspiring. He'd enlisted in the 88th Regiment of the Canadian Expeditionary Force in May of 1917. On his Attestation Paper, he filled in his occupation as "farmer," his age as twenty-two and his eye colour as black, and when he came home a little over a year and a half later, he found most of the people in his hometown of Duncan wiped out, if not by the war, then by the Spanish influenza. According to newspapers from the time, bodies were stacked like cordwood outside the makeshift city morgue. At least, this was the metaphor the family used whenever they launched into the legend of their origins.

"Stacked like cordwood," Fergus' father would pronounce from his place at the head of the table. Sunday dinners at the Goodlakes, Annie had discovered soon after her marriage, were an exercise in collective dementia, where everyone inexplicably forgot that each sentence, each word that issued from their lips had come out in exactly the same order the week before. The first couple of times, Annie thought it was comical, even cute, but before long she revised her opinion. It was torture.

At forty-six, Annie could recite the grandfather's tale by heart. She'd heard it repeated by Fergus' father at the dinner table at least once a year to guests or cousins who came to Victoria for a holiday. Fergus' father had three brothers and a sister. One of the brothers, Alex, worked in the smelter in Trail. Gordon ran a backhoe and bobcat service in Terrace with Fergus' other brother, Dennis. The sister, Barbara, lived in Halifax and rarely came to visit. None of them seemed to tire of hearing about their old man, how in the mid-twenties the veteran had moved to Victoria, where he began selling a few brands of imported sliced meats and cheeses, how he brought in local products like Saltspring Island lamb on special order. How, during the Depression, he had carried hundred-pound sacks of coal to houses by night to supplement the business and had even made a few fast runs to booze-starved America out of boathouses hidden along the Victoria waterfront — at this point in the telling some family members exchanged winks and smiles: Such a naughty bunch we were! they seemed to say, as though there were a direct line between the Goodlakes and Al Capone. Annie could even see how a person like Fergus' grandfather might be a good subject for a movie or a novel, but she was so sick of hearing about him over the years that she had no urge to undertake the job herself. And besides, once the store's survival had been assured, the story ended. The formula for success had not been tampered with since.

Annie couldn't actually remember seeing the store before she met Fergus — before she met Fergus! What a thought! When he drove her past the street on one of their first dates, she told Fergus she was surprised to find out it was on a block that she believed she knew well. Annie wasn't being quite truthful. She was no more surprised to find out the place existed than she was when Fergus told her the car they were driving in was a Fairlane. Things previously invisible to her, she later admitted to herself, had probably been invisible for a good reason. The entrance was hidden in a wall of shade, and cracks in the sidewalk gave the impression the whole building was about to subside into a geological fault. If anything, she thought, Goodlake's looked more like the set of a movie than it did like a real store. How it had survived the years was beyond her under-standing, but anyone raised in Victoria also knew how the city clung to pointless institutions much longer than other cities.

They'd sat in Fergus' parents' 1963 Ford — Fergus had yet to buy a car of his own at the age of twenty-two — outside a clothing store that had named itself after one of the characters from *The Hobbit*. Annie listened to Fergus while he embellished the deli's origins. It was how she would come to hear them embellished by Fergus' father, but on that day she found her-self listening the way, as a child, she had listened to her mother read a book at bedtime. An Anglican communion service could not have been more solemn. Annie had never met someone who spoke of his family history with this kind of reverence, a respect tinged with — what? — fear? These many years later, standing on a country road beside her crippled, second-hand Japanese import, she finally wondered what impression she gave to others when she spoke of her own family. Then, she realized that she never did. Her sisters had fled Victoria the first chance they got. The parents had split up years ago. How exactly should Annie say that her mother and father had put their lives on hold for her, that they'd spent most of their married life politely waiting until she grew up so they could separate? Not much of a story there, no Goodlake dynasty to worship.

She remembered that day outside the deli, how Fergus talked and she had watched the store. Customers entered and left, but not often, brown paper packages tucked under one arm or sticking out from the top of a cloth shopping bag. Annie had imagined stopping one of these people to ask what it was about the store that kept them coming back. She was picturing testimonials of loyal, unstinting service over the years, a sense of tradition that malls and shopping centres were incapable of. She didn't picture them scratching their heads, uncertain, hard-pressed to come up with an answer. She found out only later that the deli occupied its address the way a boring friend will continue to call, unaware how dull his company is. Given enough time, a friend like this is invited to Christmas and Thanksgiving dinners, not because people are being generous or because they pity the person, but because the table would seem incomplete without them, as if it lacked a tablecloth or a butter knife. Nothing catastrophic, but wrong somehow. She found out that the kind of people who shopped at Goodlake's were the kind of people who couldn't say why they did anything at all. For these people, every move they made in life was based on vague feelings, the feeling, for example, that it would be morally wrong not to walk in at least once a week and share a few words with the store's only occupant, a man in a white apron whose job was to operate a meat slicer that sat on top of the middle of the three display cases. This man was Fergus' father, who had taken over the business from his father in 1957, after a stroke had put the old man into a nursing hospital. The stroke happened on a Saturday, and on Monday morning Fergus' father walked in and took his place. The shop didn't lose a single day of business, so the story goes. Customers remarked on the seamless transition, the flawless continuity of service.

When Annie first met Fergus, she was eighteen, working at a specialty porcelain dealer on Fort Street. The store was run by a couple of Dutchmen who traveled the world buying rare pieces of porcelain and rugs and bronze sculptures. She was on her lunch break, sitting on a bench in Pioneer Park. Across the street, joggers ran around the circular track on the roof of the Y.M.C.A. It was September, the days still warm, and Annie was living on her own in a bachelor apartment at the corner of Meares and Government. Her sisters were back east and her parents were in the process of divorce. She wasn't unhappy — just feeling a little alone — and when she saw Fergus lying on the grass reading a book — something from one of his classes, the pre-Socratics, she thought — she decided to go over and ask his name. He could not have looked more shocked had she asked him if he wanted a blow job. It was his first year of university. Latin, Greek and Roman studies, some French and English. How annoying to see now what was not obvious then: the need, the lack of purpose, as if connecting with someone gave meaning to anything. People should be forbidden to see a member of the opposite sex until they are thirty. Sometimes she wished she could go back in time and wring her ignorant neck. Fergus talked to her. They went for walks. He was easy to astonish. No teenager should have her own apartment. Opportunity is a death sentence.

Fergus had described the family business as a kind of time capsule. A person walking into Goodlake's in 1973, he'd said, would see little that wasn't there in 1960, or 1930 for that matter. He wasn't kidding. The first time Annie walked in she saw a half-dozen dusty sausages hanging from the ceiling above three cooled display cases that contained pickled herring, a few blocks of cheddar, havarti and Swiss cheeses and more rolls of sausage with their cut ends turned toward the customer like freshly amputated fingers. The interior walls of the shop were an Arctic white, marred only by the occasional splatter of flies that had been squashed over the years, their remains never removed. A manual cash register as large as a gas pump occupied the counter next to a front window where the single word "Goodlake's" had been stenciled in block red letters some time before the Second World War. There was a poster on the far wall of men and women in costumes dancing in the town square of Liechtenstein, and in front of that stood a pyramid of tins of Italian olive oil. Other than this half-hearted nod to atmosphere, there were no frills. No smiling cows bolted above the store's entrance, no blinking lights, no music ethnic or otherwise, and no real reason to hang around.

"If I cut this any thinner," Annie had heard Fergus' father say a hundred times, "you could use it for wallpaper." It might have been funny once, Annie decided, and then only if she hadn't known that it was Fergus' grandfather's joke word for word.

She couldn't say when she began to feel uneasy — the wedding was a disaster like all weddings she'd ever been to and nothing to judge the future by — but she could tell after a few months that she dreaded Fergus' family. In her mind, they seemed like a gloomy Renaissance painting, one of those portraits of merchants, their possessions all laid out in front of them with a space remaining for Fergus and her. Fergus made fun of Annie when she told him she was afraid.

"That kind of thing," he'd say, mimicking his father's line whenever a new customer asked for kippers, "you'd better go to Safeway. I don't carry it." Fergus was a little too convincing in his imitation.

SHE LOOKED AROUND HER. The dead car. The open field. The pastoral scene that had pulled her from her thoughts of business was still very pastoral, but it had acquired a meanness since her discovery of the car's flaw. What good are you now? it seemed to say. How will all your fancy ideas get you home?

Annie told herself that the car might still be drivable, but from the look of things she suspected it probably wasn't. For safety's sake, she decided to ask Fergus. The sun was moving below a line of trees circling the field, sending long shadows toward her across the grass. She could have sat in the car and phoned, but she thought how much nicer it would be to stand under the open sky, surrounded by birds and squirrels, the late afternoon breeze. *Something for myself,* she said, quoting her client. The shoes she was wearing were impractical for this kind of adventure, so she took them off and placed them on the driver's seat of her car, then climbed over a crumbling snake fence and walked out into the field. A scene came into her mind from an old black and white Italian film, the kind of thing Fergus used to take her to at the university theatre. Her skirt was not tight by any means, but it was on the short side, an inch or so above the knee, and although she had pulled out the shoulder pads from her jacket, she felt a slight resemblance to women of the fifties, and particularly to the one in the film who had left a husband or a boyfriend at a party and walked off into the Italian countryside, shoes dangling from her fingers and the Mediterranean gleaming in the distance. Perhaps it was the contrast of women's fashions with the natural surroundings, the incongruity of the two, that struck Annie. Women seemed so useless sometimes, so ill-adapted to the world. She could feel twigs and thistles tearing at her nylons. What stupid things to wear, she thought, and for what? Close to the middle of the field, she pulled her cellphone from her bag and dialed the deli.

"Hello, Doris. Can I speak to Fergus?"

"No."

"Cut it out, Doris."

Fergus was not at the deli, it turned out. He was running a few errands and had said he might not be back before closing.

"He takes a lot of breaks," Doris said.

"Fergus is seeing a doctor, Doris. He's worried about something."

"Just so you know."

"What are you trying to say? Is something bothering you?"

"I think you should give me a raise. All the work I do around here."

"Not over the phone, please, Doris. I'll tell Fergus. It's a good suggestion. Really, thanks. I'll try him on his cell." Annie couldn't imagine what errands Fergus might have dreamed up, but it was a nice day. Perhaps he had just wanted to get out into the sun. She hoped she could remember his number. Fergus hadn't wanted a cellphone, and when she had given it to him anyway as a birthday gift, he had only complained about becoming too accessible. Annie had told him that he and she were business people, that they needed to be more accessible, but she had to admit that until now she'd had no occasion to call him.

"Thank Christ you have the thing turned on." She thought she could detect some shuffling in the background, the clatter of a spoon against a saucer, another voice perhaps. Was that a zipper?

"Where are you? Doris said you were out on errands."

Fergus said that he had left the deli to visit a few kitchen stores. There was a Mexican juicer he wanted, the hand-operated kind that looked like a robot, all aluminum. He'd thought it might make a nice addition to the counter, but there were none to be had, and he had stopped for a coffee. He told her to wait a minute while he got somewhere quieter where he could talk. A door closed. Annie thought he sounded more hollow.

"Where did you stop for coffee?" she asked. She liked to think of Fergus getting out, sitting down in the sun somewhere, relaxing. He worked so hard at the deli sometimes. She had forgotten to be angry at him about the car.

"Some joint on Government Street," he told her. It was Italian, pretty expensive.

"Fergus, there's something leaking out of the car. I don't know what it is, but there's a lot of it. I think maybe you should come and get me."

"Oh, no!" he said. That is, yes — yes, he should. No, she shouldn't try to drive the thing. She should just wait where she was. And by the way, where was she? Out there, for Christ's sake! Okay, he'd forgotten she'd told him. He would go home and get his car and be there as soon as possible. No, he didn't think it was romantic. She might have been killed. Yes, he knew whose fault it was. Maybe she should sit in the car and lock the doors. He wasn't being ridiculous. No, he didn't think a picnic was a good idea. It would be dark soon. He'd bring her a sandwich. Yes, he loved her. He wasn't trying to get off the phone. He was worried about her, that's all. Yes, goodbye.

Annie slipped the cellphone back into her bag. Fergus was right. There wasn't much sun left. She shivered at the thought of the night that was coming. What would she have done if Fergus hadn't been there? A taxi, she supposed. Helios would have come, if she'd asked him, but she didn't like to. He was doing enough these days taking Fergus to his doctor's appointments. And, yes, she guessed it was true. She might have been killed.

[VI]

Fergus stood outside Caroline's door a few minutes to orient himself. Belt undone, shirt unbuttoned, standing in his bare feet. He felt winded, something he never felt in real life. When his doctor had suggested he work out a little more often, Fergus told him to suggest something else. Exercise was a stranger to him, he said. *I bicycle to work. That should be enough.* Otherwise, it was better to walk than run. Better to sit than walk. Those were his mottos. The doctor didn't say anything.

Oblique afternoon light entered the upper floor of the apartment block through a square of glass at the top of the stairwell, the kind of skylight that belonged in a factory or a warehouse, steel-framed, wire-reinforced. People fell through these in movies. The light charged the walls around him with a dull, diseased glow, and Fergus couldn't help thinking his vision was fading. Even the air was muddy, almost particulate, as though someone had taken a picture of it and enlarged it until there was nothing but dots. For a few seconds, Fergus entertained the idea of blindness. Perhaps if he were blind, people wouldn't think he was so awful when they found out about Caroline. Sure, they'd say, he's a jerk, but he has to put up with that, too. Justice. Some kind of balance. Probably could get away with murder if he were deaf as well. Fergus closed his eyes to complete the illusion. He thought about negotiating the stairs with a cane, finding his way out of the building and onto the street.

But Fergus wasn't going blind. He knew it was only the slow death of the day adding to his already low opinion of himself. I'm feeling less human, he tried telling himself. A touch of monkey, randy baboon, maybe. Cheetah. But the joke died miles before it hit his tongue. Animals would never stoop so low. Less human, in a pig's eye. He was feeling less something, but it wasn't less human. He felt less decent. Something Caroline said earlier came back to him.

"You put the 'mental' in compartmentalize," she'd said.

He hadn't wanted to check in with the delicatessen from Caroline's phone. The paranoiac in him had stayed his hand. Call display would have tweaked Doris' curiosity. Doris the underpaid. Doris the Marxist. Doris the Rock 'em, Sock 'em Robot. Just wind her up and let her go. So he'd used his cell and forgotten to turn it off. Absent-minded para-noiac. Stupid paranoiac. How easy it was for worlds to collide. The terror came back to him, hearing one ring, then another and another coming from his jacket pocket. It might be important, Caroline had said. The shock of hearing Annie's voice and Caroline's in the same room had given him such a fright. It was as though they were both standing there waiting to be introduced: Caroline, Annie. Annie, Caroline. Would such a moment really be so bad? Would Fergus, for example, be sufficiently generous and emotionally detached to shake the hand of a man who was sleeping with Annie? He almost tripped in his escape to the hall.

Fergus looked about him. He remembered how light-hearted he felt sometimes when he climbed these stairs, drawn to them the way people are drawn to mirrors that distort the way they look. *That's what I'd look like skinny. That's what I'd look like short. This is what it would be like with another life.* His kind of game. What if? Let's play house. Nothing serious. No real intention behind the thought. Intentions sug-gested a plan and Fergus had no plans. When he was a teenager, he'd sometimes go to the Empress Hotel and sit in the lobby, pretend he was an American tourist. He'd fake some terrible southern accent, a Beverly Hillbillies drawl. People would talk to him, ask where he was from, and he'd say Los Angeles or Dallas or Miami. American cities sounded so much more exotic. He'd invent a high school, a mother and father.

Going to Caroline's was almost the same thing except more convincing. Here, he knew where the coffee filters were, which switch operated the bathroom fan, how to light the pilot on the gas stove.

Fergus paused at the entrance to Caroline's apartment, unable to walk back in. His brain felt thick and sluggish, as though ideas were all at once harder to grasp, slippery like fish. Once, he was a simple person with simple problems like tax returns and plugged perimeter drains. Once, he had woken every morning with a clear conscience. Why would a person ever choose to give up that kind of easy living? Even as he cobbled the question together in his mind, he knew the answer. He remembered how Helios used to come home outraged at the treatment a friend of his received from his father. The man had married again two or three years earlier, predictably to a younger woman, and now he had a couple of kids.

"It's like his first family doesn't even exist," Helios had said at dinner one night. "Like he's almost embarrassed by them."

Annie and Fergus had commiserated with Helios, told him his friend was welcome to come on holiday with them that summer. "Some men," Annie said to Helios, "make the mistake of believing they could have a fresh start in life, that if they just turned their back on everything and everyone, the world would become new again."

"It's just kind of sad, that's all," Helios had said.

Sad, all right, Fergus thought, but now he recognized another side of the story. Caroline and her daughter, the small apartment, the kitchen table that had been painted a hundred times, the chairs that didn't match. Fergus didn't want a new start. He liked his old start just fine and had no intentions of turning his back on anybody. What he wanted was to remember what starting felt like again, which wasn't the same thing. He never knew he was starting while it was happening. He made soup, took an extra job at the liquor store, drove on bald tires with a bald spare in the trunk, and he didn't once tell himself what a lousy start he was having. Or a great start. Twenty-five years later Fergus was lucky if he managed even a dream of those days, a dream that let him talk to his friend who died young or climb the staircase to their son's old bedroom. The best photographs were still only photographs. What Fergus wanted was to walk around in the past, sit down and spend some time talking to it. He wouldn't be in such a hurry this time. Caroline was as close as he could get. Maybe this whole affair was just an exercise in make-believe, but what wasn't? The real question was whether he'd like Annie doing the same thing.

FERGUS OPENED THE DOOR and returned to Caroline's living room. She was still flipping through the pages of the catalogue.

"I have to go," he told her. "My car's broken down." He was careful not to say "Annie's car." It was a strategy he'd developed. If he didn't say Annie's name, it was easier to believe she didn't exist. My house, my car. My bedroom. A lot of married men he'd met talked this way.

"You're a good person, Fergus." Caroline was still looking down.

"I can't stay much longer anyway. The deli closes in half an hour and you know what that means."

"Home again, home again, jiggity-jig."

"What time are you leaving tomorrow?"

"The early ferry."

"Should I phone you later?"

"There are no shoulds, Fergus. Phone me because you want to."

"It isn't my fault. Cars break down."

"Yes, they do."

"I really should go."

"Should is your middle name. Did you know that?"

Fergus stood in the doorway. For all Caroline's brave words, Fergus knew she didn't like the lack of control she was forced to accept. Not one bit. She didn't like running her life around his schedule. Often she wouldn't. Any pleasure they took from this arrangement — he couldn't call it a relationship; people who met once every couple of weeks for an hour didn't have a relationship — relied on pretense. They pretended they didn't want to go out to eat, that it was much better to prepare a dinner together, just the two of them. A dinner at four o'clock in the afternoon. On a Saturday, too. And Fergus always had to go home and eat again at seven. They talked about different parks as though one day they might actually go for a walk in one of them, arm in arm. Caroline spoke of friends such as Nathan, his sense of humour, his similar taste in books, movies, art and how much he and Fergus would hit it off when they finally got a chance to meet. "I'll call you. I will."

"I know you will," Caroline said.

As Fergus closed the door behind him, he tried smiling back at Caroline, the kind of smile that suggested a complicity, a mutual frustration with "things," but she wasn't looking. He headed downstairs, mulling over the day's events. Annie had had no idea what she was saying when she had told him to go out and have an affair. As if you could turn these things off and on like a light! Once things were set in motion, they were hard to stop. Nothing about an affair was spontaneous, except maybe the first kiss. After that it was a board game: Annie has a meeting that will keep her late. Fergus takes the afternoon off. There are chores that need doing — a trip to the wholesaler for lettuce, olive oil, flour — but they don't have to take that long. Fergus learns how to exploit his wife's gullibility and to invent alibis. He learns how to disappoint Caroline at least once a month.

You can't have your cake and eat it too. He'd never understood that stupid phrase until now. What was that supposed to mean? What idiot would pass the cake on without taking a bite? Was that supposed to be noble? Now he knew: cake comes at such a cost, most people lose their appetite just trying to get some. Now, every time he opened his mouth, he was lying, and the stress of keeping track of the lies was beginning to show. Helios thought he was out of his mind, a complete mental case. Would he feel any better if he just said, "God, you have no idea, Helios. This business of cheating on your mother is awfully tiring. My nerves are a mess!"? The thought that he could actually move his lips and say such a thing filled him with horror, as though his hand were reaching uncontrollably toward a fire alarm.

Outside, the streetlights were coming on. Fergus had a fair bicycle ride in front of him. He briefly entertained flagging down a taxi, but this was Victoria, not New York. Would they take a bicycle? He might wait hours. And besides, he had very little cash, and credit card companies sent statements at the end of the month. *A taxi, Fergus? You never take taxis.* He started biking toward home. A half hour at least, he calculated, and then another forty-five minutes to find Annie. It would be very dark. He took out the cellphone and punched in his son's number. Then he turned the power on and punched it in again.

[VII]

Helios was watching television in the living room of his basement apartment, guitar draped across his lap and a pencil and a pad of paper on the cushion beside him. He had a few hours before the Friday shift on night desk at the motel. Somewhere around eight o'clock, he would rouse himself and pack some instant noodles, two carrots, a Ziploc of roasted almonds that came from the bulk bins he liked so much at the supermarket. He was reaching for the remote when his father called.

"I need you to pick me up," Fergus said.

Helios heard the control in his father's voice, the panic beneath the words. He knew that Fergus' jaw was tight, his mouth a line of bared teeth. "Okay," he said. "Mind telling me why?"

"It's your mother. Her car's on the fritz. She's stranded."

"What about yours?" Helios knew a question like this would only make his father angry. It was hard not to obey Fergus' alarm bell immediately, not to jump up and address whatever problem he'd decided to elevate to a crisis. But Helios was tired, and he would rather spend this time before work relaxing.

"That'll take too long. I'd have to bike home first. This will be quicker."

"You know I have to work tonight."

"It's getting dark, for Christ's sake! She's out there alone. It won't take long."

"All right. Calm down. I'll pick you up at the store in a few minutes."

"I'm not at the store."

"So then I'll pick you up where you are." Helios was starting to wonder if his father was the one who needed help, not his mother. He listened as his father explained where Helios could find him.

"In ten," he told his father. Then he hung up.

He walked around the apartment grabbing what he needed for work in case he was longer than a couple of hours. Maybe this was what happened when your parents got older. They got quirky. They talked nonsense. His grandfather had died over fifteen years ago, but Helios could still remember some of the antics his parents had had to put up with.

He shifted some papers on the kitchen table, and a bulletin from the CUPW drifted to the floor. *Strike vote next week. Hundred percent membership turnout required. Be there.* Helios picked up the bulletin, crumpled it and took aim at the recycle box on the far side of the room. Unions took themselves so seriously. Another club, more rules. Order, order. But Helios would attend. He would vote. He might not be Billy Bragg, but he had his head on right. There is power in a union. He walked over and picked up the union pamphlet from where it had landed on the floor and dropped it in the box.

The exhaust manifold on Helios' truck was cracked and had been ever since he'd bought it. The noise was almost unbearable for the first five minutes, but after the engine had generated some heat, the crack closed down to nothing. *Like a lot of people I know,* the guy selling it had told him. Seventy-five bucks and a case of beer. Just the right price for a cornbinder. Helios waited a few moments to let the oil circulate, help the truck's old bones get used to moving again. Let the neighbours fume, he thought. And then he headed off to Esquimalt on the other side of town where his father had said to meet him. What he was doing so far from the store was anybody's guess, but Helios didn't want to know. The last thing he needed to hear was that his father was cracking up.

When Helios was ten, his grandmother and grandfather had moved from their three-storey home near the water to a bungalow closer to town. Movers had taken care of everything, and all Helios' grandfather had to do was drive the car from the old house to the new one, six blocks at the most. He'd insisted it was no problem and had walked back by himself to the empty old house once all the furniture and clothes were in their new home. Helios remembered standing, his mother and father and uncles beside him, his grandmother watching from the front window, waiting for the car to arrive. There'd been a few incidents in the previous months, a crumpled fender, corners taken a little too sharply. Helios' grandfather had got lost once coming home from the store. He'd had to phone Helios' grandmother from a pay booth outside of town.

Helios was the first to see his grandfather as he turned the corner onto the street. Signal flashing, the old man turned the wheel hand-over-hand as though everything was normal, except he'd driven the whole distance on the sidewalk, the wheels of the Ford Cortina straddling the cement strip like a giant car, too big for the road. He came to a stop in front of the house and got out, slammed the car door behind him and locked it. Key in pants pocket again. Job well done. Turned and faced the crowd. *What? What?* Then, Helios' father going over to him.

"Jesus," Fergus said.

Nobody else breathed. Helios never saw his grandfather in the driver's seat again. Six months later the old man was dead. The retirement vacation. Barbados. Walked off the path to look at the view. Or maybe just to walk off the path.

HELIOS SPOTTED FERGUS waiting for him outside the public library. Even at this distance, he knew what his father was thinking: the rattle-trap of a truck, the way Helios drove it. He opened the rear, slid his father's bicycle into the back and slammed the door three times until the latch finally engaged. He walked around to the passenger door — still hanging ajar after Fergus' feeble attempt to close it — and repeated the procedure, his father's face grimacing on the other side of the glass only a few inches away, the kind of ghost Helios imagined lurked behind the mirror each time he looked into it, his hidden self, all this man's peculiarities, foibles, eccentricities ripening like cancerous cells, waiting for Helios' immune system to weaken so that they could assert themselves and take over. He shuddered at the thought, walked around the front of the truck and threw himself into the driver's seat with uncharacteristic force.

Helios should take the highway north, Fergus said. They'd turn off before the overpass. Helios knew the Travel-All's bench seat didn't allow for much comfort, and he glanced over at Fergus. His father sat bolt upright like a child, the lap belt connected loosely around his hips. Clouds were coming in from the west. Helios watched them roll over the town in the last of the fading light.

"I hope your wipers are working this time," Fergus said.

"They work."

"I'm just saying."

Helios could feel his father looking at his long hair, tied back now in a ponytail. It occurred to him that he hadn't even shaved.

"Who's this?" Fergus asked.

Helios was surprised Fergus had detected the music over the noise of the engine. He was so oblivious most of the time. He knew his father probably didn't really want to know the name of the artist; this was just his attempt at conversation.

"The Winkle Pickers."

"Ah," Fergus said. "Like the shoe."

Another band his father had never heard of. Like the shoe? What was wrong with the man? The sixties was his time, not Helios'. It was as though he had been asleep all those years. His mother was no better. All she ever bought were "best of's." Best of Fleetwood Mac. Best of Van Morrison. Best of Emmy Lou Harris.

"I told you to get that power steering looked at," he said.

"Who says it's the power steering?"

"I'm guessing."

"You're probably right. I can never get your mother to stop driving long enough for me to take it to the shop. And those guys … did I tell you what they told me the last time?"

"Don't take it there."

"The nail was just sitting in the tread!"

"You told me."

"I pulled it out with my fingers, for Christ's sake. With my fingers!"

They drove on. Friday night. Dinner traffic from out of town streaming in, but Fergus and Helios were headed the other way. Number ten exit coming up fast. Fergus nudged Helios and they headed off into the Highlands.

"You should call her," Helios said. "Let her know we're on our way."

Helios pulled over and watched as Fergus pulled the cell from his pocket. In the dim light of the passing traffic his father couldn't make out where the power button was. He punched at several likely candidates until he was eventually rewarded with a soft green glow.

"You're supposed to keep the power on," Helios told him. "People can't get through if you don't."

"That should tell you something, shouldn't it?" Fergus said.

It soon became apparent that Fergus didn't know Annie's number.

"I've never phoned her before. Doris takes care of all that."

"Maybe she'll call us," Helios suggested.

"Yes, that's right. She can call us now. If she's worried, she can call us. Good thinking. The power's on." Fergus placed the phone on the seat between them, face up, an oracle with nothing to say, at least not yet.

Streetlights dwindled to one every half mile, and then to none at all. Centre lines disappeared. The world shrank to the small patch of road lit up by the truck's headlights. High beams switched from high to low and back to high. Helios shifted down and down again as each new hill appeared.

"You seem a little rattled tonight," Helios said. "I mean you don't seem yourself."

"It's nothing. A long day."

"Did you hear back from the doctor yet?"

"Not a peep."

"That looks like the car there." Helios pointed up ahead where a Camry sat off to the side of the road on the gravel shoulder.

"He's supposed to phone this week," muttered Fergus.

"She could have left her flashers on." Helios slowed his approach almost to a dead stop as both he and his father peered at the car in front of them.

"Sure looks like her car," Fergus said.

"Are you worried?"

"She'll be fine."

"About the doctor."

"Not until he tells me I should be."

They crossed the road and pulled up to Annie's car, bumper to bumper, about ten feet apart. Helios got out immediately, leaving the truck's lights on, but Fergus stayed where he was. The beams of light cut through the dark, lighting up the gravel and revealing a first few drops of rain. Helios felt as though he were in a National Geographic documentary, the kind in which a submersible picks out a sunken wreck on the bottom of the sea. He didn't like the feeling. He felt even worse when he discovered that his mother wasn't in the car.

WHEN HELIOS CAME BACK with the news that Annie wasn't sitting in the driver's seat waiting for them, his father said nothing. It was as though Fergus had been expecting her not to be there. Helios watched him climb out of the truck and stand looking off into the dark field beside the road, Helios turning to look, too, his sense of dread rising. The two of them moved tentatively away from the lights of the truck and into the dark, open expanse of grass. They circled the field, Helios calling out, "Mom! Can you hear me!" His father seemed stunned, shouting "Hello!" and "We're here!" poking his head into bushes and yelling again. To look at him, Helios thought, you'd think he was in a game of hide and seek and had given up. The clouds they'd seen on the way there had massed into one solid band that stretched from horizon to horizon, and when the rain started to come, it fell in weighty, large drops, as though someone were taking liberal handfuls from a bucket and hurling them in their direction. By the time they reached the truck, they were soaked through.

"What a nuisance," Helios' father said. "I told her to wait in the car. I even told her to lock herself in, it for Christ's sake. What does she think she's doing, wandering off like this?" He stared at his cellphone. Helios imagined he was daring it to ring.

"We should wait a few minutes," Helios said. "She might have walked to a house for some reason."

"Why would she do that? She knew we were coming."

"Maybe she got scared. We were awhile getting here."

The rain fell on the steel roof of the truck. The noise was so loud, it might as well have been hail. Helios began to worry. He was also angry with his father. The man wasn't helpful. Blaming her because she wasn't there. What good was that supposed to do?

Helios sat for several minutes before he realized he was waiting for his father to suggest some course of action, a plan. It was a familiar situation, and he was surprised how quickly he had fallen back into being a child again. It was as if he'd always been waiting for his father to make up his mind about one thing or another. The thought was unsettling, but he understood where it came from. Helios had discovered that most people didn't strike him as strange until he had a chance to step back from them. He had spent years living with this man. Familiarity was the problem. He'd passed him on the stairs, sat at dinner with him, gone on hikes. His parents were like wallpaper. He hadn't really noticed them after the first look. Everyone discovered sooner or later their parents weren't perfect, that they made mistakes. But what if his father was a complete idiot?

Helios wiped condensation from the turquoise metal dash. He toyed with the heavy Bakelite shifter knob, unscrewing it and screwing it back on. He began to put another tape in the player and then thought better of it.

"I should make sure the car's locked for the night," he said. "You won't want to tow it until tomorrow."

"Sure. You go ahead."

When Helios opened the door of the Camry to press the power locks, he saw the note on the driver's seat. He and his father had been there nearly forty minutes, and neither of them had thought to look. Maybe they were both idiots. He glanced briefly at his mother's loopy script, then brought the note back to the truck, keeping it dry under his jacket. He slammed the door as he got in and thrust the note into his father's lap.

"There you go."

"What's this?"

"Read it."

I got cold waiting for you. (WHY DON'T YOU KEEP YOUR CELL PHONE ON?!!!) A car stopped to see if I was okay, so I grabbed a ride into town. CALL ME WHEN YOU GET THIS.
Annie

"You see?" Helios said. "She's okay. Probably sitting down with a glass of wine as we speak. Give her a call and tell her where we are."

Fergus slumped against the back of the seat. "These fucking phones will be the death of me."

HELIOS MADE IT to work on time, and his father had the car towed to a garage the next day. It wasn't until his mother called nearly a week later that Helios knew life wasn't back to normal. He had just finished his shower. The ceilings in his suite were so low he had to tilt the nozzle almost horizontal to get his hair wet. The bathroom reeked like a sewer vent. People brought exterminators in to buildings that smelled half as bad. He was using the hair dryer to clear the bathroom mirror when he heard the phone. Sometimes he let the machine get it, sometimes he didn't. This time, he answered. His mother didn't seem upset, just curious.

"Did your dad say anything to you the other night?"

"About what?" He'd brought the phone into the bathroom and was wiping down the mirror with a towel.

"Me, maybe?"

"He was mad at you for not staying with the car, I suppose, but I think he was just worried."

"Nothing about me and someone else?"

"Absolutely not. What's up?" Helios worked through his long hair with a brush, a much easier task since Jayne had introduced him to conditioner.

"A little while back, we were relaxing. I'd had some of your pot, just a little. Weeks ago. It was a Sunday. I was starting to feel like we weren't really in touch with each other. The usual stuff. You know me. The store. Business. So I made a bit of a joke."

"You? A joke? What was it?"

"I told him he should have an affair."

"You're a lunatic, mother." Shaving was an unattractive thought, but he needed a distraction, something to occupy him while his mother filled his head with stuff he didn't really want to hear. He prepared to lather up anyway. Brush, mug between his knees. The one-armed barber.

"It was a joke. I'd had a few puffs. I didn't mean it."

Helios closed his eyes. He'd always told himself he might regret selling to his mother one day. What possible good can come from turning your own mother onto weed? "So, what's the problem?" he asked, though he thought it should be clear to anyone listening that he had no real desire to know.

"So, now he thinks *I'm* having one."

"I don't follow." Helios watched himself apply lather to one half of his face. A mirror was so much like television. He wondered if there had been a commotion when they were first invented. People losing themselves for hours, making faces, staying up late, unable to tear themselves away. The medieval church posting warnings. He dragged the razor down his right cheek. This could be a comedy act. How to shave and talk on the phone at the same time.

"He thinks I was trying to hide my own affair by telling him to have one."

"That makes no sense."

"He thinks whoever I'm having the affair with drove me into town the other night when the car broke down."

"He says this?"

"You know how he is. He says he's only making fun. But I can tell. It's all to do with this prostate business. Like he has to prove he's a man. You know he's been running for a month now? I hate people who run."

"Me, too." Helios wiped a face cloth across the smooth half of his face and switched the phone to the other ear.

"Have you seen the chin-up bar?"

"Don't tell me any more. What're you going to do?"

"I was thinking you could help."

"You want me to talk to him?"

"He'd know I'd been talking to you. No, I want you to wait until he brings it up with you."

"What if he doesn't?" Helios gave up shaving. This way he'd only slit his throat, which is what he felt like doing if this silly conversation went on any longer.

"He will. Your father's not one to suffer in silence."

"And then?"

"Then, you offer to spy on me."

"This is getting freakish."

"You don't *really* spy, you just tell him you are. When he hears you saw nothing, he'll stop all this nonsense."

"How do you dream up stuff like this?"

"Will you do it?"

"Give me a day to think."

[VIII]

Fergus reaches down to adjust the Lucifer. When his light's working right, its beam will spread almost twenty feet in front of his bicycle, enough for him to see the type of sewer grate that once sent him over his handlebars onto his face. No stitches that time, but the following week his teacher tried to persuade him to sit out the class picture. *Plenty more years of those,* she said. *Looks like a moustache,* his mother said when the scab formed.

The roads are dry. Moon and streetlight make his lamp almost unnecessary. *Knock, knock,* Fergus asks himself. He flicks the St. Christopher bell clamped to his handlebars. *Isobel who?* he asks. The Lucifer spins with the turning tire, its high-pitched hum like a siren, varying in pitch as Fergus speeds up, slows down. Full moon, every power pole throwing out wattage for miles. If it weren't for the police, Fergus would ride in silence. They might stop him if he shuts off the light, so he keeps it on. They might stop him anyway. He rehearses a speech he'll recite if they do. He'll say his cousin asked him over for dinner earlier in the day and on his way home he got a flat, which took him a long time to fix. Fergus will point to the pump secured on the frame of the bike. He'll take out the tire repair kit from the tool bag that hangs below his bicycle seat. He'll show them the glue, the irregular patches of rubber, the three tire irons that came with the kit. *It's okay,* he'll say. *My parents know. I phoned them.* He practises the speech until he knows exactly what he had for dinner, what time he left, the name of his cousin, the street and number where his cousin lives, the type of car his father drives. He rehearses it until he can answer all their questions. *Isobel upon a bike,* he says.

He pedals up Cook Street and turns before the hill and the orphanage that sits on top of it. He angles west toward the Island Highway and the Malahat Drive. He is thinking of Mount Finlayson, a craggy rock in Goldstream Park that rises over a thousand feet above sea level, more than high enough to avoid the wave that's coming. Fergus plans to climb to the top and watch his home disappear, the homes of all his friends. It's too late to save anyone now. Any minute he expects to hear the rush of water behind him, and he pedals faster into the dark early hours of morning. The police don't stop him.

Fergus is not surprised to see people out on the street at this time. Like him, they're running away, though they seem in no hurry. Just past the Roundabout, two men yell at him from the parking lot of the Colony Motor Inn.

"Hey, kid," one shouts. "Come over here."

"Let me try your bike," the other says.

Fergus has been expecting them, these people who will try to come after him, the ones that will want to steal his bicycle so they can escape more quickly, and he pedals away from them until his legs hurt. When he looks in his side mirror, he sees no one's following. *Good thing I'm so fast,* Fergus tells himself. *Soon enough those two will drown. The water will wash over them both, over everyone in this city, even the dead. This is one wave the seawall won't stop.* Fergus sees coffins rising up from their graves once again, bones littering the beach.

When an RCMP officer passes him going the other way, Fergus panics and leaves the highway at the Colquitz overpass. He scrambles down a gravel embankment and follows a road he hopes runs parallel to the highway. He's not sure exactly where he is but he continues to head west toward the hills. Sidewalks disappear. The space between houses grows. Under a streetlight, he looks at his watch. Nearly three-thirty. If he were a paperboy, he wouldn't have long to sleep before his morning route.

Fergus is proud of his bicycle. It has never covered so much ground on a single trip. He feels independent, as though he could live a life of his own, a life without his bickering parents, their patch-quilt days of tiffs and silences.

The ground rises and falls. Sometimes he rides through a hollow where the mist of the morning has gathered, and the cool air cuts through his jacket and makes him shiver. He can smell cow dung and wood smoke. In a few of the houses he passes, there's a light on. Somebody up early, making tea, probably, the way his mother will sometimes when she can't sleep. On his way to the bathroom, Fergus has seen her sitting at the kitchen table, her head bent over a cup, a book open before her.

WHENEVER THE ROAD veers away from the hills he believes are only a few miles ahead of him, he adjusts his route. He turns down one street. Then another. After another hour of riding, Fergus is prepared to admit he is lost. He has no idea where the highway is or whether he is still heading west, but when he stops to look behind him he is able to tell that he has been climbing steadily for some time. The lights of the city are visible; even the thin strip of civilization across the strait in Port Angeles has risen into view, a beaded necklace of red and white and yellow under the moping dark mountains. In the light of his torch, Fergus' watch reads just after five. Another hour to sunrise, at least another half hour until black yields to grey and grey to the blue Fergus knows will be coming, when shapes turn into what they really are: fence, stump, parked car.

On a normal Saturday, Fergus is up by six-thirty, downstairs in front of the TV, watching the Farm News, even Wunda Wunda for a while, biding his time until the morning's real cartoons start: Funorama, Rocky and Bullwinkle, Quick Draw McGraw. These are the hours he won't be disturbed, his parents sleeping, having a lie-in, buying their late morning with unlimited access to stations one through twelve. The deli won't open until noon today, if it opens at all, and on Saturdays Fergus has complete control of the airwaves. He can still feel the heavy dial of the Viking console TV. The satisfying weight of it, clunking into position as it rolls through the channels like the cylinder of his replica Colt '45. For nearly four hours, while his parents sleep, have their showers, prepare their eggs and toast and coffee, read their Saturday paper and smoke the first cigarettes of the weekend, Fergus lies on his stomach and forgets what he can about the bully who will be waiting for him at school on Monday. About his father's war against everything that's wrong with his life. His mother's brooding sadness. Finally, after repeated announcements, he will heed the call for breakfast, or one of his parents will storm in to shut off the TV, as though they didn't want him watching it in the first place, and while the TV screen is dwindling to a single white dot, they'll open the living-room curtains to reveal the dull day, which Fergus will scuttle to avoid, first in his room and later down at the bay among the latest crop of beached boom logs where he will light a fire and tend it until evening. Fergus thinks even if there hadn't been a tidal wave, he might have hit upon the idea of taking off like this. Such an easy thing, to run away.

Fergus continues on up into the hills. There are almost no houses now, or if there are, they sit at the end of long driveways behind stretches of maple and alder, only a mailbox to mark their presence. He passes open fields, crosses bridges over streams full with the heavy runoff of a wet March. The light is growing stronger, and Fergus is beginning to feel the effects of lack of sleep. His pack feels heavier, and the steep roads have forced him more than once to walk. In a last effort to put himself as high above the wave as possible, he turns onto a dirt road that leads up into a stand of fir. The road is partly overgrown, but about a half mile in, Fergus sees a structure off to one side, something not quite natural, but emerging from the ground as though it has grown there. When he moves closer, he sees it's a large mound, maybe fifteen feet high, made of bricks, and there's a kind of tunnel that leads to a central chimney, its view of the sky obscured by young cedars. They've taken hold along the sloping sides and some of them are quite big. Fergus leaves his bike against a tree and crawls into the very centre of the mound where he sits on a carpet of moss and looks up. Day filters down through the cedar branches, a muted glow that throws the brick walls of the chimney into relief. Fergus has the feeling no one's visited this place in a very long time, and leaning his head against his pack, he falls fast asleep.

PART III

Not Exactly a Crucifixion

[I]

The night Annie's car had broken down, the night she decided not to wait for Fergus, a young man on his way to town had seen her standing by the car waving her arms. He'd stopped to help, waited for her in his Volvo while she scribbled an explanation. She'd left the note, a scrap of paper she'd torn from her day-planner, on the front seat where she knew Fergus would find it and where the breeze and rain wouldn't destroy it. To write the truth — that she wasn't cold but scared — would only have upset Fergus. She told herself she'd explain everything to him later. But she never had.

Scared was probably not the right word for what she'd felt, but Annie didn't say things like "weirded out." When she'd hung up from talking to Fergus, the clouds hadn't yet completely covered the sky, and some of the sunset was finding its way to the field where she was standing. Arbutus trees further up the hill caught the light, red trunks ablaze and leaves doubtfully green, as though someone had hand-tinted a black and white picture of them. Fergus' concern had left her a little unsettled — he'd been insistent, almost angry with her — but she forgot him in a minute, taken by the play of colours around her, cedar branches almost tropical, grass like glacial runoff, the effect confirming her suspicion that this was a special moment. Instead of walking back to the car and locking herself in as Fergus had instructed her, she moved toward a break in the trees at the field's edge. The field was just a field. It wasn't a pasture. No cows anywhere. No sheep. She might have been in a park for all she knew, but she wasn't. She stepped into a ring of mushrooms, didn't notice it until she was nearly out. Then stopped. She'd heard of them but had never seen one: a real crop circle. The circumference, she guessed, must have been eight feet in diameter. At once, she could hear a younger Helios lecturing her in her head. *Two metres, mother.* A fairy ring. Her skin prickled at the thought.

Once, Helios had left a plate of pot cookies in the fridge to cool. He'd spent the afternoon making them with a friend and then had gone out. Annie had eaten a few by mistake, hungry from having worked in the garden for the afternoon. After an hour, she believed she was going insane. If Helios hadn't called and discovered her mistake, she might have done something drastic.

Now, as she stepped out of the ring, she felt a similar terror rising. She told herself to get a grip, turned her back on the mushrooms and walked into the forest a little ways, the break in the trees now obviously a dirt road, its twin tracks visible but almost obliterated by salal and ferns. She walked on, forced herself to, a dare of sorts, the light nearly gone now and shapes looming under the branches, inexplicable, indecipherable. Stump? Boulder? A bird flew through the upper canopy, large cousin to the crow, its wings the sound of a person breathing hard. She might have been walking on the ocean floor, fish swimming above her, branches moving like kelp in the current. The thought made her gasp for air. Her experiment with bravery had gone far enough. She turned to find the field again, but dusk had settled and the old logging road had transformed into bush. Fergus was on his way, she reminded herself. Words without comfort. There was at least an hour to wait before he arrived. Finally, fear made her run. Before she broke out into the clearing, she fell twice, scratching her hands when she put them out to save herself. Her cellphone slipped from her pocket and was lost in the undergrowth. Even in the open, terror did not slacken its grip, and she flagged down the first car, this young guy. Young? He was in his thirties. When had that become young? He had a cabin, he said. On a lake. Said he was taking a rest from work for a while.

"Nice idea, if you can afford it," Annie said.

"You don't need that much."

"Cars are handy," she said. She didn't want to sound ungrateful, but really. She'd just left one nut, and now this economics genius!

"It's a friend's. I give her a massage every once in a while. She lets me use it for groceries."

"I see."

"You're pretty skeptical, aren't you?"

"I'm just thinking what I have to trade."

"Listen, it's taken me some time, but now I spend next to nothing. Ten years ago I worked in the bush ..."

"When you were fifteen?"

"I'm thirty-seven."

"Really?"

"I was a pilot. Otters, Beavers. I flew rich Americans into fishing lodges. Company geologists used me to get up into the backcountry. Fire season was nuts. I took my money and bought the cabin and a house in town. Rent pays the mortgage and then some. I use the library, buy in bulk, heat my place with wood I scavenge from the hydro lines. What I can't make, I trade for with massage. Haircuts, a little dental. The cashless society. The government hates people like me. My time's my own and I don't have to hustle."

Annie was quiet for a while. She was conscious of her clothes, her briefcase, her useless shoes. She was conscious, too, of how much she liked this person. There was something solid about him, a sense that he knew what he wanted. She found herself wondering what kind of a woman would attract his attention.

"So," he said. "Tempted?"

"I beg your pardon?"

"Want to quit your job?"

"Like I said. I'm thinking what I have to trade."

He dropped her off at the deli, a stupid decision, but for some reason she didn't want him to see where she lived. As though bringing him there would be a kind of infidelity. Silly word, that. Unfaithful. And faithful means what? Fergus would give her the Latin origin, a lecture, too. But she could imagine for the first time what it would be like to step outside herself for a moment, talk freely to someone like this pilot monk, want to tell him about her life, what was on her mind these days. He didn't seem the type to make a joke out of everything. Or at least that's how she imagined him now that he was gone. Easy now to turn him into whatever she wanted. She remembered something Fergus had said. Perhaps she should be the one looking for someone else.

She unlocked the front door and walked over to the phone. Would she be able to remember where she dropped her cell? She hoped so. Her day planner flipped right to Fergus' number.

"Where are you?" she said.

NOW, A WEEK LATER, Annie watched Fergus shut the front door behind him. The sun was almost up, a big morning ahead of them both. She had to be at the deli by eight. Doris would already have the place open for deliveries, but she needed Annie to set up today's catering job. Normally, Annie slept while Fergus prepped the kitchen for the day, but these days she was sleeping badly. She heard him cross the porch and descend the steps two at a time. She heard the soft slap of his new runners against the sidewalk as he began his morning run, a five-kilometre route that took him out to the waterfront and through the park. He'd been at it for several weeks now. The first time, he had come home a mess after an hour. Wheezing, coughing. His hiccups had lasted into the afternoon.

"Maybe you should try walking a bit. Build up to it."

"This is normal, believe me. Everybody suffers a little at first. You should see some of those guys out there. They look like they're gonna die."

"So do you."

Now, he'd be gone for twenty-five minutes, maybe thirty, only a little ruddy-faced at the end. Annie could see he'd managed to fit another ritual into his life. She opened the front door. On the landing, two litres of one percent and a jug of orange juice. The bill, too. Annie would still drink whole milk if it weren't for Fergus. Sometimes she bought a litre for herself, poured half of it over a big bowl of Raisin Bran and brought it to bed with her just before going to sleep. She picked up the morning paper. All these early people! Newspaper boys, milkmen. A whole world at work. She unfolded the daily, the face of some killer leering out at her from the front page. This was the one she'd seen on the news last night. He'd taken a two-by-four to his former girlfriend and the man she was with. On a suburban boulevard of all places. A crowd of people had watched. Some had tried to argue with the killer, but he'd threatened them with his big stick and they'd backed off. By the time the police arrived, it was all over. There'd been warning signs. An apartment block broken into. Some nasty phone messages. But the police had said they couldn't arrest him unless he actually did something. Now they could. The kettle whistled to her from the kitchen, and she went through to make a pot of Earl Grey.

Try as she would, she couldn't imagine Fergus as a murderous, jealous lover. This was a good thing, she told herself. Unless he was a slow fuse, the most she had to complain about was his running gear stinking up the house and a few stupid phone calls. The headlines in her mind weren't too intimidating: "Suspicious husband starts jogging." "Man calls wife more than he used to." She should never have put the idea of an affair in his head in the first place. What had she been thinking? A woman was dead because she'd tried to escape her boyfriend, a redneck stick-man breaking his toys so nobody else could play with them. Fleeing contentment — a good house, decent man — just wasn't in the same league. Besides, it had backfired. All this physical fitness. And now Fergus had started phoning her from the deli, something he'd never done before.

"Hey, sweetheart. How are you?"

"Fergus, you don't need to check on me."

"Can't a fellow phone his wife when he wants to?"

"I feel like I'm under surveillance, for Christ's sake. You've got to give me some breathing room. For the last time, I'm not seeing anybody. Nobody. Not a soul. I promise."

"I know that, Annie. I just have this urge to call, okay?"

"Do me a favour. Fight it."

"So, where are you anyway?"

"I'm hanging up now, Fergus."

"I'll call you later, okay?"

Click.

Had she been oblivious all these years? What signs had she missed? Nobody jumps the tracks because of a single, dumb suggestion. Maybe there were people who would tell her later they'd seen it coming for a long time. "That Fergus. A bomb waiting to go off."

Annie tried to imagine Fergus touching another woman the way he touched her. Perhaps that was the real betrayal. To use the same gestures, the same signals of affection he reserved for her. He'd have to. Things like that are second nature. She knew instinctively she would reach out for another man in exactly the same way she reached for Fergus.

ANNIE'S WORST FEAR when she'd married Fergus was that they'd end up running the deli, and that had happened over fifteen years ago. Annie couldn't believe it at the time. Just after they had moved in together, Fergus had turned a summer job with the federal forest service into a full-time position. Much of the first year, he was away, monitoring plots of trees that were long-term experiments in thinning and fertilization. He liked working with trees.

"My office is a nursery," he said. "Think of it."

His contract was renewed. The next year the same, and the next. Nobody saying anything about the deli, about what would happen when Fergus' father retired. Helios was nearly four, they had a house to renovate. They weren't rich, but nobody they knew was rich.

Then came the eighties.

In 1982, government trucks at the Federal Forest Research Centre stopped moving. Gas allowances ceased, projects operating for years were mothballed. Technicians like Fergus had their hours reduced.

He spent most of one whole field season on the end of a hose, washing Fords and Internationals and GMCs that weren't even dirty. Mortgage rates climbed to fifteen percent, then to seventeen in 1984. In 1985, Fergus caved in. Those were Annie's words for what happened. Nobody in his right mind could seriously want to take over such a dull and pathetic little business, could he? Tradition was a fine thing. Family loyalty was also something to be respected. But this ... this was unfair. Fergus' father was a lunatic to expect anything of the sort. Hadn't she and Fergus joked between themselves about what a sad little life his parents had had, the mom-and-pop saga of Western Canada? They'd made fun of these people, for Christ's sake! Fergus would stand behind the kitchen island with a dishcloth tucked into his pants for an apron — did anybody wear aprons anymore? Where would a person buy such a thing? — and imitate his father making a sale. Annie had cracked up. Fergus had cracked up. Didn't he remember?

"Why you? What about selling the place? Don't they own the property?"

"Exactly. Selling now would be a mistake. Somebody's got to keep the place going until things turn around."

"But you could do anything you want! You could go back to school. You wanted to start an orchard. Remember? Grow fruit? You like being outside."

"When I'm outside. I like inside too."

"You need to ask yourself what you want, Fergus. If you want this, fine. But it has to be what you want. There's still time. You could register for next semester."

"No. It's too late for school. I'm just a Technician Four and sciences scare me. I didn't know what I was doing in a classroom, and I still wouldn't. This will solve that little problem."

Annie nearly threw up her breakfast.

God, she thought. I must be queen of the stupids! I've wasted ten years of my life on a misfit, for Christ's sake! And now he's glad someone has finally solved his "little problem." How many thousands of men like Fergus were there? Men who'd be a lot happier just being told what to do instead of having to dream up some scheme, some career they'd probably hate anyway. She wanted to take his sacred homemade bottles of beer and pour them down the sink right in front of him. She wanted to run a knife across every one of his dumb records, put them back in their sleeves and laugh at him when he tried to play them.

Instead, she told him she wanted in.

"We're doing this together, pal," she said. "This is a team effort. I hope you understand that."

"You'll be bored."

"Nothing new there."

So, Fergus put on a smock and took his father's place behind the counter. Clients said almost nothing.

"Looks good on you," one said.

"You ought to be ashamed, Bill," another said. "Dyeing your hair like that."

Annie studied the books. She discovered things. She discovered that people never stop buying food. They give up books or clothes or music, but they never deny themselves their favourite dishes. It was a good thing to know, but it wasn't enough. Annie looked around. British Welding had closed up shop. International Harvester had moved. The ship chandlers was now a restaurant. There were boutiques. There were brewpubs and condominiums. Old Town was finally starting to happen. She saw office workers on the prowl for a good lunch. The nineties gleamed at her from the horizon.

"What we need is a make-over," she told Fergus one day.

"You think? I'd say the place is kind of retro already."

"Retro? Like what? You mean like a butter churn? Like garter belts? Do you mean useless?"

"Don't be so snippy. I mean it already has a kind of charm. So few things stay the same for this long."

"I know what you mean."

"You do?"

"Yes, I really do."

"You don't sound like you do."

"I don't, do I?"

She'd never admitted this to Fergus, but she tipped a beer and drained it when Fergus' father died on vacation. The fights she'd imagined with him over the renovations — the Sunday dinner arguments — were gone the moment he stepped off that cliff. Annie was astonished by her luck. Giddy, really. She found it hard to stop smiling at the funeral. During the reception, she thanked Fergus' uncles several times for coming. She filled sherry glasses the second they were empty. Somewhere, a pump had been primed just for her. All she had to do was flick a switch.

The white walls of the delicatessen faded to faux-marble; Mexican quarry tile swallowed the black and white linoleum. Fergus' mother only shrugged her shoulders when Fergus brought her down to see the changes.

"It was always a terrible place," she said. "I thank God it's out of my hands now."

There was the new canvas awning out front. There was the brand-new sidewalk Annie had sued the city to install. There were the four wrought-iron tables and chairs she put on it. More tables lined one of the shop's inside walls.

There was Fergus' way with food. How he played chef when Helios was young, money scarce and dinners out scarcer. Mister Master, he called himself. He liked to show off with a frying pan, get frisky on the business end of a whisk.

"Mister Master will now separate an egg with his bare hands!"

"Mister Master calls upon the water of life to burn! Burn, I say!"

There was Fergus' bag of tricks. There was Annie who exploited it. Pasta salads shoved aside tubs of pickled herring. Greek salads, black bean salads, selections of roasted vegetables. Italian baguettes and loaves of multi-grain. Homemade dolmades and tapenade. Linguine and fettuccini fresh every day, and soups with lentils and roasted peppers. Three kinds of coffee. Annie brought home-baked berry pies to serve as the store's dessert selection. When a woman asked whether the deli could make up a spread for the party she was giving, Annie hired a couple of university students, dressed them in white shirts, ties and black skirts and drove them in a rented van, along with an evening's worth of hors d'oeuvres and canapés, to the woman's house. She bought hot plates and steam tables and coolers, and when she needed to, she rented a barbecue the size of a small car to prepare Portobello mushrooms and salmon fillets.

"You know what you are," Fergus said to her after their first year. "You're a victim of your own success." He meant it as a compliment.

She liked the phrase — irony almost always eluded her — but saw things differently. Yes, the increased business was both a blessing and a curse. Annie worked much harder once the deli started doing well. Yes, business was good only when it created more business, and, yes, creating more business was a job in itself. After the renovations and the move into catering, Annie spent much of her time in her car driving to people's houses, municipal community halls, writing up bids for contracts, organizing rentals. Cutlery, plates, glassware. Fergus looked after the store, Annie made small talk with customers. The food flowed, the cleanup went without a hitch. Most of the time these were evening affairs, and Annie wouldn't arrive home until after one in the morning. She never complained. She was her own boss, no one to answer to but herself — and Fergus, she supposed, but not really. What she didn't say to Fergus was that marriage and a child had cost her something. Time mostly, years of it. She felt like a victim who had turned herself into a success, into someone who had wrestled some control back into her own hands. It was a good feeling.

NOW, FROM THE KITCHEN, Annie heard Fergus return and head to the shower on the second floor. The water ran, the fan kicked in. She opened her day planner. *Teachers' in-service* underlined, a copy of the menu attached. Fare for a non-instructional day: twenty litres of curried pumpkin soup. Sixty smoked salmon wraps. Arugula salad with lime dressing. Ten loaves of focaccia. Two steam tables filled with Mexican

rice, pasta carbonara and lasagna. Annie had been putting this together
for days. Fergus would put the finishing touches on it this morning —
plus the deli fare for the day, poor guy. Should she offer to go in? He'd
just complain. Anyway, he liked a challenge.

Annie looked at her watch. Five-twenty. *Hurry up, Fergus.* Nine
o'clock coffee and croissants; nine-thirty start. The deli's van should be
on the road by eight-fifteen at the latest. Annie would show up around
eleven. She looked out the window. A deck day if she'd ever seen one.
Star fest all the way to the horizon. Some Dean Martin song was
floating around in her head. One from a compilation she'd bought, *Best
of the Lounge Years.* Life sounded simpler the way he sang about it.

One girl, one boy.

Some grief, some joy.

Memories are made of this.

She'd even seen him sing it once on TV, remembered him at the
opening of the program, lurching about on a bar stool, cigarette in hand,
his signature song about everybody loving somebody sometime. The
chronic slur, the bad jokes and breasts, skits about a drunken Santa
Claus. Her parents' admiration. *Good old Dean. Sings like an angel,* they'd
say. Couldn't see the act for what it was: an act. Annie remembered
thinking it was like what people did with each other every day, only
Dean was getting paid for it.

[11]

Early Friday morning, Helios stood at the night desk of the Mainsail Motel. He could see the ivy clad face of the Empress Hotel, the south wall of the former customs building — now the British Wax Museum — and the squat offices of Blackball Ferries, closed for the night but still illuminated against thieves and vandals, of which there were now more than ever in Victoria. Real jobs had dried up years ago when the lumber market crashed and the salmon disappeared. All that was left were a dwindling number of government positions and the service industry that catered to the swollen ranks of the retired and the diminishing number of American tourists who could still be fooled into visiting "a little bit of Olde England." Helios had never been to Britain, so for all he knew, the comparison might be true. Most of the English people he had ever met seemed quite at home in T-shirt shops and fast food emporiums. He grimaced every time he thought of Government Street. How disappointing to spend decent money on a vacation only to find a cheap strip of crap like that. Living in Victoria, he sometimes felt, must be a lot like living in Disneyland after closing time.

He had just finished quarreling with a late arrival who complained when he found out there were no rooms for smokers.

"What the hell kind of town is this, anyway?" the man had said. He carried a briefcase and a large leather flight bag. "Do you expect me to stand outside with all those losers?"

"Not much I can do about it," Helios said. "If you want, I'll phone around. There are a few hotels with smoking floors."

But the man wanted to argue.

"Listen, you long-haired freak. If I wanted another hotel, I'd tell you that. I reserved a room. I put down a deposit. I walked all the way here from the stupid bus station and I'm not about to walk any farther." The man's goatee was wet with — perspiration? rain? — and his nose moved whenever he spoke. Like a rabbit's when it eats.

"Look. Normally, we might be able to come up with something. A room with a window that opens, something like that. But this place is sealed as tight as a drum. You light up one cigarette and everybody's breathing your smoke."

The man had asked to see the manager. Helios told him the manager had left at ten. What was the number, the man demanded. He'd phone him at home. But Helios refused to give it to him. After that, the man sat in the bar until it closed. Finally, after standing outside under a propane heat lamp with a couple of other guests for another fifteen minutes, he took a room. As he headed to the elevator, he looked back at Helios as though he wanted to kill him.

AROUND ONE·THIRTY, Jayne came by.

"Slow night?"

"No other kind. What's your excuse?"

"Can't sleep." She took off her Gore-Tex jacket and shook the rain from it onto the floor. "Insomnia's always better with company."

"Your day off, though," he said, but he was glad to see her, and the fact that he was made him smile.

"Yeah." She leaned across the desk and took a mint from the bowl.

"Have a seat in the office. I'll be in." He ran through the reservations for the night. All had arrived. He stapled the remaining Visa imprints to the room allocations and arranged them alphabetically for the morning shift to find. Another cup of Dickson's House Blend, one for Jayne. He carried them through.

"Sorry about the band." She blew on her coffee.

"Had to happen. Things weren't right."

"No."

"What do you mean, 'no'?"

"What you said. Things weren't working out."

The desk phone rang. Helios got it on the third ring.

"Hey, hippy shit," a voice said. "Guess what I'm doing."

Helios hung up. Not his problem. The next shift would total up the wet bar, assess the cleaning costs. The man would pay or he wouldn't.

"It's going to be a longer, slower night," he said to Jayne.

"Don't quit now. This may be all you have for a while."

"Oh, boy. Picket duty."

Jayne said the strike vote was eighty-seven percent in favour. The union negotiators had a strong mandate and they were going to use it. Rotating at first. Things would escalate. Strike pay only for those on the line.

"That's fair," Helios said.

But he was worried. Two part-time jobs barely kept him alive. Lose one and he'd be strapped, fucked, up against it. He'd never make the rent on his basement suite now. Or should he say his "ground-level" apartment.

"Is there a schedule up yet?"

"Tomorrow," Jayne said. "I asked if we could work our duty at the same time. No promises, but Half-Sack said he'd do what he could."

"You know what they say."

"They say a lot of things."

"Nobody wins in a strike."

"And winning means?"

"You can have a Danish for that." Helios headed to the kitchen. The prospect of walking a picket line depressed him. In one sense it was a good thing to stand up to the corporation, but in another it was just avoiding the issue. More money wasn't going to get him a more meaningful life.

People were just selling their days for cash, an hour at a time, and the union's job was to see they got the highest price. He thought about what would happen if he lost his apartment. No pity on that front. Business was business. This wasn't a society that encouraged people to help one another. The pursuit of individual happiness was a selfish kind of code, he decided. It turned people into a bunch of grubby little groundhogs, digging their own holes and stuffing them with all their groundhog things. He thought of the people he rented from: yuppie man and his yuppie wife looking down the cellar stairs and seeing dollar signs. Something to help with the mortgage, they told themselves. A little Sheetrock. Some pot lamps. A second-hand stove. Never mind the beams at eye level. Never mind the mould and the spiders, the hot air pipes running through the bathroom. Kids running around upstairs bouncing their balls, throwing their boots off against the front door. Half the city was living off the troglodytes underneath their dining room, and Helios' landlord had the nerve to ask if he would mind splitting the cable costs. The man was stealing it in the first place, and then wanted money for what he'd stolen! There was something about the middle class Helios didn't like. No, he was wrong. There were a lot of things he didn't like. If only they didn't think of themselves so much. It hadn't been much different when he had a room downtown with the junkies and the winos. They thought a lot about themselves, too, their next drink, their next fix. But at least they didn't pretend to be anything more than what they were. He could almost miss them for that, although he didn't miss the needles. Didn't miss the smell. Blood on the sidewalk. Trouble was, Helios had nowhere else to go. He hated sharing a house. All that stress over food and dishes, and somebody always had a cat. If worse came to outright bottom of the barrel, he might have to move home for a while. He hated the thought. People his age shouldn't even think of it as an option. Besides, his parents were getting more eccentric by the day.

He set down a selection of pastries on the table for Jayne to choose from.

"Are we driving tonight?" Jayne asked.

"Sure we are. More coffee?"

AN HOUR LATER, Helios went to the desk and made a call. There was a wait of about five minutes until one of the other night staff — a chambermaid right out of high school — knocked on the office door. Helios told her he'd be gone for a couple hours on an errand for the manager.

"The manager wants me to drive her car," he said. "Keep the valves clean. Rotate the tires. You know."

He told her she was to mind the desk, take messages, ward off the forces of darkness. She looked uncertain, as if Helios was playing some kind of a joke on her, more uncertain when he handed her a set of keys and made her write down his cell number on a piece of hotel stationery.

"You can do this, luv," he said to her in a British accent. "Fink of it as a kind of test you have to pass." Then he and Jayne went to the basement garage.

THE COAST ROAD at night in a '67 Jaguar XKE. Top down, the smell of the ocean filling the car. Traces of wood smoke from beach fires. It was the time of year when late spring becomes confused with early summer, close to the end of school, the weather mild. Teenagers who couldn't get away from their parents fast enough looked for a strip of sand and logs, some matches, a case of beer. Helios wound through the four-speed gearbox as though he were James Bond on a mission to save the world. A world of toggle switches and knock-off wheel hubs.

"It feels like we're lying in a coffin for two."

"What?" Jayne yelled back over the noise of the wind and the engine. "Did you ask me something?"

Helios pulled over. "Still a bit cold for this shit." He got out to release the ragtop.

"What's happening with your dad?"

"Good question."

"Seriously. What does the doctor say?"

"Biopsy's good. The GP was thinking cancer on the left side of the prostate, but he was wrong. It's benign enlargement. The old man's running all over town buying up Brazil nuts. I counted five bottles of selenium supplements in the kitchen last time I was there."

"That's a relief for him."

"Him, yes. My mother, no."

"Must be hard. I can't imagine."

"She's happy he's not sick, but he's driving her nuts. He runs every day. There's a chin-up bar in the downstairs hallway. Doris has been making strange noises about him, too."

"I have to meet this Doris some day. What's her complaint?"

"The shop. She's doing the lion's share of the work these days. Fergus is out and about a lot, she says, and it's not right. I see her point."

"And your mother? What does she say to him?"

"There's nothing she can say. He's convinced she's having an affair."

They were heading east, now, back towards town. Sky getting light, only about a half hour before sunrise. The car low on gas. Helios drove into an all-night Chevron on the outskirts of downtown. Techron Supreme, jet fuel. Highest octane money could buy. He grabbed an additive from the trunk. Early Jaguars liked a lot of lead. A shotglass-full should do it. He shoved in the nozzle and counted the litres until he hit fifty.

"You don't have to pay, I hope."

"We have an understanding. I keep the receipts, she trades me a little extra cash I don't have to declare."

"All this for a car."

"Please. This isn't a car. It's an investment. The manager wants the engine clear of carbon and the carpets clean. Comes with the job."

"Still."

"I know. Tired yet?"

"When's breakfast?"

HELIOS AND JAYNE pulled into the motel shortly after sunrise. Staff were rolling back the pool cover. Steam rose into the May morning. The traffic along Belleville took the place of the ocean surf. Helios stretched the car cover from bumper to bumper. People and their toys. Helios supposed his truck was a kind of toy. A better one. He took the distributor cap he'd removed after parking and brought it with him to the office. The chambermaid seemed relieved to see him.

"So?"

"Some guy kept phoning for you."

"I'm not surprised. What did you tell him?"

"I didn't tell him anything. I said you weren't here."

"My shift's over in five minutes. After that I won't be."

An hour later, Helios and Jayne were finishing their coffee at a booth in the motel's restaurant. The table was strewn with sections of the morning paper and the remnants of a pancake breakfast, the plates sticky with syrup and sausage grease, garnishes of parsley and thin slices of orange uneaten.

"You're not rock and roll," Jayne was saying. "That's for sure."

"I love you, too."

Jayne blew him a kiss.

"Take a look at the name you chose. If that doesn't convince you, nothing will."

"I told you already. It's a nickname. Don't ask for the real one."

"I mean the band. 'Bad Men Who Love Jesus.'"

"You don't need to tell me. I have a stack of Bibles at home from all the nuts who thought we were born again. They packed a bar one night to check us out, said they were Mormons and I guess they were because the owner was getting mad at them for not buying any beer. And I thought university students were bad. Did you know the Mormons baptize the dead?"

"That's not what I meant."

"No?"

"It's the idea. The loveable jerk. The good-hearted woman in love with the good-timing man."

"I don't think I'm going to like this."

"Exactly. You're country."

"And you're sick." He ruffled the pages of the paper as though he were preparing to leave. "I bet you'd never say something like that to your father."

"My father wouldn't listen if I did. You're nicer than he is."

"I'm trying, but it isn't easy."

"You see? That's all country is. Bad men trying to be good. Women loving them even though they're bad. Your music's full of that stuff. You just need a different presentation."

"Boy, am I sleepy all of a sudden."

"I'm thinking Gram Parsons or Jerry Jeff Walker. Steve Earle, maybe."

"Is that what you're thinking?"

[111]

Friday morning was double everything. Two root vegetable pies. Four vegetarian pizza breads. Two tubs of Tunisian salad. Twice the fusilli, twice the penne, twice the vermicelli. Two stock pots on the go at once. The new girl — Fergus struggled to come up with her name, something foreign, sounded like a boat, Marina! — had to grind as much coffee in one morning as she did for the rest of the week. Today had been three times as bad as usual with Annie's group of teachers. Luckily there were people he could call, part-timers who could come in for a morning when needed. They'd packed the van and sent it off a couple of hours ago. Saturday would be a relief after this. June weather in May — even this late in May — didn't help. Everybody thinking they wanted to get out for a walk, take in some place like Goodlake's for lunch, maybe sit outside and read the *Globe*. Fergus felt guilty leaving the store this early in the day. Doris wouldn't like it at all. How much longer could he pull off these little excursions? He could see things heading downhill. Little things. There was grease on the overhead fan. The double sink looked like it belonged in a gas station. And wasn't that an ugly look Doris gave him when he told her? Worse than the time he'd made fun of Ani DiFranco.

"Then why doesn't she spell it that way?" he'd asked. "Maybe A-W-N-I or A-H-N-I. Something that makes sense."

"It's her own name," Doris had said. "I think she should get to say how she wants it pronounced."

"What's wrong with Annie? I like Annie."

"Funny man, but it's not her name. Her name's Ani."

"And, anyway, isn't she a bit young for you, Doris?"

"She's my age. We were born on the same day. Besides, look who's talking."

"What?" Fergus felt his muscles stiffen, his limbs tense, ready for an attack.

But Doris had only pointed down towards his feet, to the skate shoes he had put on this morning in a hurry to get out the door. They were an old pair of Helios' he'd found comfortable, easy to slip on. "DC Shoes" written across the back.

"Oh," he said. "They're not mine."

"What did you think I meant?"

Fergus had made some excuse, something about the Shania Twain tape he kept for the deli sound system. At least music like that was understandable, he'd said. All these kids running around like they just got out of British public school. Isn't Ahni wonderful? Don't you just love Nirvahna? My ahnt's in town for the hols. She's simply sooper. Doris had never really forgiven him.

FERGUS HUNG HIS APRON beside the door to the kitchen, slipped on his jacket and pulled at the sleeves. He adjusted his collar. From his inside pocket, he pulled out a dry cleaning bill and examined it, brows furrowed. He was trying to mix an air of purpose with a touch of annoyance, as though he'd been put on the spot.

"Hold the fort, will you, Doris?"

"Are you asking me?"

Fergus knew better than to engage Doris, and he left the store quickly, turning back only once to see Doris scribbling angrily into the palm of one hand. Whoever was on the receiving end of that bill would not be pleased, he told himself, and then made his way toward Blanshard Street. He walked quickly, stepping off the curb on occasion to pass weekend shoppers who paused to talk or change direction. Caroline had said eleven and he was already three minutes late. Not that she was expecting him. *Just passing by,* he'd say. *In the neighbourhood.*

Annie was off up into the hills again. Amazing how she got to roam about. Couldn't risk phoning her again. It would put her in such a snit. Sometimes he thought he was losing it. Running up town to check on Caroline. Phoning Annie to see if she was all right. Wouldn't it be typical, though? Worrying himself to death about getting caught with Caroline, and then Annie telling him she's the one who wants out. Out! He had never said anything about wanting out. That wasn't the issue. "Out" wasn't part of the equation. He felt like one of those novelty acts he'd watched on the Ed Sullivan show when he was a kid, a guy who spun plates on top of long sticks, two plates, then three, adding another each time, running back to the first one when it started to wobble, the audience waiting for the whole thing to collapse. What a relief if it had collapsed! Such a glorious mess! Each vertebra of Fergus' spine sang at the thought.

That's what it was all about, wasn't it? Keeping it up. The male thing to do. Chipmunk with multiple stashes of nuts, worried someone was going to find one. People with nothing to hide had nothing to worry about. He tried to remember what that was like. Free mind, clear conscience. He shook his head. It was as though he had stepped behind the scenery on some movie set. He'd seen the false doors, the phony dormers. There was no making the leap of faith back again. What bothered him was how everyone wanted to believe life was different from what it was. Even Annie. If Fergus said he had a few errands to take care of, why would she doubt him? The world was easy pickings for a liar.

It was all Annie's fault, anyway. Her and her friend with the perfect carpenter, the great mechanic. Annie, who had said she was tired of asking Fergus to do something about the steps, the two long gutters that hadn't held water in years. The friend who had said Caroline did good work, didn't charge much and could use the money.

"This is usurpation!" he'd said to Annie. "You've taken over my domain."

"I wouldn't have to if you looked after it."

"A woman, too. That's low. If this was a play, it would be a tragedy. The downfall of a good man who couldn't see the writing on the wall."

"Cheer up, Macbeth. She's no witch. In fact, she's kind of cute. You should see her daughter."

Fergus wondered if he'd have the nerve to point this out to Annie when the time came. "Hey," he'd say. "You told me I should."

ST. ANDREW'S STOOD on the corner of View and Blanshard. It was the Catholic cathedral. Fergus had never been inside. He thought of churches as theme parks. Once you'd been to one ... He walked up the alley to the back of the church. A yellow Datsun stood parked in a visitor's slot, the roof sagging a bit from the weight of the wood it carried. Fergus saw Caroline and Nathan sitting on a bench in the cathedral garden. They were looking at a sheet of paper; then, they were looking at him.

"So?" Caroline said.

"Fergus," he said, extending a hand.

"I know," said Nathan. "Caroline told me you might drop by."

She did? Was he that transparent? What else had Caroline said?

"Make yourself useful, Fergus," Caroline said. She pointed to the car. She wasn't exactly shaking her head, but something about her was saying "No."

It was hot. There was no one else around. The back door of a Greek restaurant opened onto the lot, and garbage cans of rotting kitchen scraps were starting to bake in the morning sun. The flies were going nuts.

"Is there some magic formula?" Fergus asked Nathan. He was ripping away at the plastic twine the yard boys had used to tie down the wood.

"A knife would help."

"I mean the cross. Is there an ideal ratio? Something that appeals to the eye because it's perfect?"

Nathan stopped untying the wood and turned to Fergus.

"Hold out your arms," he said, and Fergus put them out the way he would if he were going to dive into a pool.

"No, like this."

"Oh. That makes sense."

"Except it's crap. Christians are full of crap like that."

They dumped the lumber next to a wrought iron fence. On the other side was the cathedral garden. Fergus hadn't taken a good look the first time, but now he saw there were little paths that zigzagged between beds of roses and stone benches where people could sit and get away from the city traffic. Two big cedars kept the place in shade. A monk was sweeping the flagstones and the steps that led up into the rectory. Fergus had seen him before. He lived in a house a few blocks away with several other Franciscans. They made quite a sight walking through the city streets in their long brown robes and hoods. To look at them, Fergus thought, you'd swear you were in Italy maybe, or France. He turned back to see Nathan and Caroline talking together. There was nothing intimate in the way they stood. They weren't intentionally excluding him. Nevertheless, he felt as though he wasn't even there. There was a better word than "excluded" to describe what Fergus was feeling, a word that carried nowhere near the moral overtone of a word like "unnatural," a word Fergus often used to describe his relationship with Caroline (who openly made fun of him every time he used it). The word that came to Fergus' mind on this occasion was "anachronistic." He felt anachronistic, the way someone would feel if he were transported to the time of Dickens or Shakespeare. This was as close to time travel as he would ever get, Fergus realized. Whatever connection a person thought he had with someone from another generation, it was false. You could talk to them, send them letters. Even sit and have a drink with them. At the end of the day, people born twenty years apart, even ten years apart ... they might as well be different species.

Fergus looked at Nathan. How much older than Helios was he, a year? Two years? He certainly didn't look gay. Harder to believe was Fergus himself, a man nearly twice Nathan's age, acting like a teenager. Was it just him, or had there been a soupçon of rivalry while they were unloading the lumber. "Christians are full of crap." Was that a test?

In the forest service, everyone had been older than Fergus, even the lowly field technicians who would never rise in the ranks without a degree. Fergus was in university then. They'd probably hated him, a know-it-all who brought books like *Crime and Punishment* to read at lunch. What a prig! And even though Fergus had no natural aptitude for machines like chainsaws — a simple axe had proved beyond him — he'd walked about like the project director. Now, Fergus felt like one of those men he remembered seeing in pubs downtown in the days when he and Annie still went to pubs, the men who tried to ingratiate themselves with a table of young people, convinced they were still current, that they could still hold their own.

Caroline put on her tool belt. Nathan said something about this cross being only a prototype, something to give the congregation the effect without the expense. If they liked it, he said, there'd be something more permanent built, out of ferrous cement, possibly, with lights.

"I pull this off," Nathan said, "they'll let me submit a proposal for a chapel they want built. Baptismal font, marble floors, the whole nine yards. I could go crazy."

The cross had to look solid, at least. Nathan gave instructions and Caroline did what she could to follow them.

"Nothing fancy," he told her. "Bend the nails over if you have to. This isn't Chartres."

"Why's it crap?" Fergus asked Nathan.

"Why is what crap?"

"The proportions of the cross. What you said about my arms. The cross. You said it was crap."

"It is."

"So, there aren't any rules?"

"No, there are rules. Lots of them."

Caroline had told him Nathan could be a pain in the ass sometimes, but she also said if a person was patient he could usually learn something.

"But ..."

"But they're crap."

"Because ..."

"Because there's no cross. There never was."

At this point Fergus heard the monk start sweeping the path near the fence. Fergus made a face at Nathan. The cross lay at their feet, half-built, spread out across three parking spaces. Nathan gave it a kick.

"Think about it. What empire is going to waste its time hammering two pieces of wood together when one will do? The man died on a stick, if he ever lived at all."

Caroline took out a handful of nails from her belt and knocked the last few boards into position. It was a big cross. Eighteen feet from top to bottom. Hollow, but from a distance no one would guess. Nathan took out a pocketknife and scratched in some letters on the bottom.

"Your name?" Fergus asked.

"That would be crass."

Fergus looked closer. His classics degree was failing him. "What's that supposed to mean?" he said.

"Jesus of Nazareth, King of the Jews. It's Latin."

"Ah. Another rule?"

"Another rule."

Fergus checked his watch: nearly one.

"Let's get this puppy vertical," Nathan said.

He hoisted the cross up and over one shoulder. Fergus picked up the bottom end so it wouldn't drag on the pavement. Caroline took the middle. They made their way over to the side entrance. Caroline said something Fergus didn't quite catch. "Nice day for a crucifixion," it sounded like. Then he heard a gate clang shut and some footsteps coming up behind him. A hand settled on Fergus' back. He put his end down and turned around. It was the monk.

"Excuse me," the monk said.

Fergus didn't know what to say. He had never spoken to a monk before. He'd always imagined they were under a vow of silence. He was thinking the man must have been offended by what they'd been saying, that maybe he was so angry he'd blown forty years of Christian obedience just to tell them off. There was some gray stubble on his chin and Fergus could see lines around his eyes. The rope that held his robe together hung at his side, nearly touching the ground.

"May I help you?" the monk said.

"What's the hold up back there?" Nathan said.

Caroline turned to see what the fuss was about. She looked at Fergus and the monk like they were a couple of bowling pins.

"Nothing," Fergus said, and the monk and Fergus picked up his end together. Nathan made his way up the three steps, but there was no chance the cross would fit through the side door. They tried twisting it one way and then another, but any fool could do the math. Nathan turned and headed down the alley toward the main entrance at the front of the church. The monk, Fergus and Caroline followed.

Saturday traffic rolled by. Passengers stared out their windows as the quartet turned onto the sidewalk. Tourists coming the other way walked around them. One group of Japanese stopped to take pictures of Nathan all hunched over.

"A little late in the year for a passion play," Caroline said.

Fergus winced. What was going through the monk's head? He didn't seem angry, but Fergus worried they'd offended him. Fergus wasn't a religious person. Neither was Annie. But the list of things Fergus didn't know was still a lot longer than the list of the things he did. A man puts on a monkey suit and spends his days with a broom, he must have his reasons.

The middle door of the three arched openings to the church was as wide as a goal post and a good twenty feet tall. On either side as they entered were two clamshells the size of kitchen sinks, the kind Fergus remembered seeing in Tarzan movies where the native gets his foot stuck and Tarzan comes to his rescue. Each was full of water. A man in front of Nathan dipped his fingers in and crossed himself as he walked up the centre aisle. Nathan reached out with one hand as he passed and followed his example. Caroline put her hand in, too. She wiped her brow. Fergus watched the monk and copied him. Inside, there weren't many people, a few oldsters up near the front holding rosaries and kneeling, their lips moving and the beads twisting between their fingers. They didn't even look up. It was a tight squeeze getting around the altar, but they made it without hitting any of the big candlesticks or vases of flowers. They leaned the cross up against a wall.

"Fergus Goodlake." Fergus offered the monk his hand.

"Bob Emerson."

Fergus wasn't expecting such a normal name. Brother Something, maybe, or Father, but not Bob. And the grip was a disappointment, too, nothing like the "Onward Christian Soldiers" thing Fergus had going in his head. The monk turned to Nathan and Caroline.

"Nathan … Nathan Cohen."

"I know," the monk said. "The bishop told me."

"I'm the carpenter. Caroline."

They all stood around looking at the cross. Fergus could hear some of the people in the front pews whispering their prayers. Outside, a police car was shoving its noisy way through the streets. Ideas began to pop into Fergus' head. He couldn't help it; he'd always had a nervous reaction to silence, to the kind of serious air churches held. He thought about what Nathan had said about there being no such thing as a cross. He was trying to imagine how a big outfit like the Catholic Church could make such a mistake. Or had they done it on purpose? Maybe it was an aesthetics thing. After all, there wasn't a lot of artistic appeal to a stake in the ground. Fergus started thinking about what cemeteries would be like without crosses. What would people hang around their necks? Logos for international aid agencies? And then a really stupid phrase started repeating itself over and over like a bumper sticker on a car: "Walk tall and carry a big stick." He worried he might blurt it out by accident.

"You have some nice stained glass," Nathan was saying to the monk.

"From other churches, most of it."

Fergus turned to look.

The whole of the south side of the church was lit up like a strip mall.

One scene had a group of monks turning a grape press, but instead of grapes, they were pressing the body of Christ, and his blood was flowing out into freshly tilled furrows of soil. Underneath it, a line of Gothic script said, "In Memory of Thomas Fullerton. Donated by his Executors."

"Imagine that," Caroline said.

"What?" Nathan asked.

"They killed the guy, and then they put up a window in his memory."

The monk looked at Nathan. Nathan shrugged. And Fergus knew he had to get out of there. The stand Caroline had made to hold the cross upright was still back in the parking lot. Fergus left the others to talk while he went to get it. He arrived at the car just as a parking attendant was writing out a ticket.

"This is a private lot," Fergus said.

"I don't need you to tell me that. Clean up this mess before I charge you with littering, too." The attendant walked away.

Fergus left the ticket where it was and picked up the stand. He really should get back to the deli, he reminded himself. In the church, Bob and Nathan were whispering as loud as two people can whisper and still be whispering.

"Who cares?" Nathan was saying. "What does it matter?"

Bob was waving his arms behind him.

"*They* do," he said.

Fergus decided to ignore them. He gave the stand to Caroline and walked over to the altar to look at the censers. Behind him Caroline took out her hammer and started to drive a couple of nails into the stand to get it ready for the cross. She might as well have fired a gun. The mumbling in the front pew stopped. A few gray heads looked up. Bob turned.

"Okay," the monk said. "This is too much. You people have to go."

[I V]

Fergus Goodlake is sleeping in a lime kiln. Before he was born and before his father was born — even before his grandfather hit upon the idea of opening a delicatessen — a family that has now all but disappeared from the local phone directories found it easier to make their own quicklime than buy the cement manufactured by Robert Butchart in his quarry a few miles up the Saanich Peninsula. The kiln is not much more than a large, squat chimney, rising like a cone out of the ground with an access at the bottom for hauling out ash and lime. Trees have grown up around and through the brick structure, their roots splitting it in several places. It sits at the end of what was once a logging road. Large stumps of Douglas fir and red cedar dot the mongrel second growth around the kiln, a few of them with springboard marks still visible. Close to the road as the kiln is — there is barely a half-mile between it and the asphalt — few people know it exists, and those who do are now quite old.

Fergus dreams through the morning. He dreams he's standing on a wharf at a lakeside resort. There are cattails and reeds along the shore. A large powerboat passes close to the wharf, and someone on board throws out a rope to Fergus, but Fergus knows the rope is a trick, that the moment he grabs hold of it, the boat will speed up and pull him in. People play that game all the time. He's seen it done before. And then he's standing at the wheel of the boat, looking back at the wharf, the slack in the rope tightening until he sees himself pulled from the dock into the water. He dreams his father is in one of the resort cabins looking for a can of coffee. His father is opening every cupboard and slamming it angrily even though there are cans of coffee unopened in each cupboard he searches. Fergus wants to point out to his father the cans he has overlooked, but he knows what his father will say, that none of them is the can he's looking for.

Morning passes. The weak spring sun seeps obliquely into the shaft of the limekiln, but the woods around it remain damp and cold. Occasionally, Fergus wakes, thinking of the flood he has been running from. Then, he falls back asleep, dreaming of the people he left behind, their faces as they struggle to stay afloat among the cars and furniture and animals swirling in the rising tide that swallows houses by the dozen. As the cold morning works its way through his jacket and the sweater underneath, he shivers and curls into himself, anxious and fitful, until he falls below the level of dreams and sleeps deeply right through to mid-afternoon.

WHAT FERGUS DOES not know is that about the time he decided to walk home from his afternoon along the Ross Bay seawall — a good five hours before he hopped on his bicycle and headed for the hills — the 10,000-ton Liberty ship S.S. *Chena* had just docked at the end of the long main pier of Valdez, Alaska, a town of about 1,100 people on Prince William Sound. It was bringing fruit and supplies — the boat's first visit after a long winter — and people had gathered to greet the crew, some of whom were throwing oranges down to children, while a few others had already disembarked and were shaking hands with the stevedores working to get the ship unloaded. Just after five-thirty, those on board felt the hull shudder a little, as though some of the cargo gear had collapsed on deck; then their ears caught the sound of fir trees snapping in half along the shore. They turned to see houses swaying on their foundations, and then, very gracefully, the town's waterfront collapsed as the sea floor gave way and slipped into the depths of the sound. In the surge wave that followed the earthquake, the pier went under, in the words of one onlooker, as quickly as "a bobber on a fish line when a big one hits." Nearly ninety metres in length, the structure was far too long for any of the people on it to make it back to the beach, and sailors looking down from the decks of the *Chena* saw children sucked under the surface, still holding the oranges they had caught minutes earlier.

At the same moment, just outside Anchorage, Alaska, in a subdivision known as Turnagain Heights, Mrs. Lowell Thomas gathered up her two children, aged six and eight, and herded them outside along with the family dog, Bozie, an aging German shepherd. Mrs. Thomas had heard a rumble not unlike the sound of artillery practise from the local army base, but something told her this sound was different, and she hurried her children to a safe distance from the house, even refusing her youngest time to get a pair of shoes. They had barely turned to look behind them when the ground heaved, the house split in two, and the bluff on which the house was standing sank to sea level, taking Mrs. Thomas and her two children with it. Had they stayed in the house they most certainly would have been killed, as were two of the neighbour's children, but the Thomases rode the collapsing earth to a standstill beside the wreckage of their home. It now lay at the foot of a new cliff formed by the capricious logic of the buckling earth.

The town of Anchorage itself sustained nearly three-hundred million dollars damage in the four to six minutes that the tremor lasted, though the death toll didn't rise above the improbably low number of nine thanks to the timing of the earthquake — schools were out and most of the downtown shoppers had gone home to enjoy the Easter long weekend. Penney's Department Store was the most recent addition to Anchorage's downtown, and in the course of its destruction, the building lost most of its cement façade, whole sections of which fell to the sidewalk, killing two people and crushing a parked car into an eighteen-inch pancake of steel. The brand-new Four Seasons apartment house collapsed into a pile of broken lumber only a week before the tenants were due to move in. Some parts of city blocks dropped as much as three metres, taking streetfront buildings with them. The marquee of the Denali Theatre dropped to ground level without breaking a single bulb.

Within the hour, as Fergus sat down to eat dinner with his mother and father, the Aleut villages of Kagyuat and Chenega were washed out of existence by a series of three waves. The houses in Chenega sat on wooden pilings, and after the third wave, only the pilings remained, dozens of them standing in a kind of order that at first glance a person might easily mistake for an empty outdoor movie theatre were it not for the wreckage of the homes strewn among them. At Kagyuat, the villagers evacuated to a nearby hill, but some, thinking the worst over, returned to their houses too soon, forgetting the tribe's history. In their distant past, a similar event had destroyed the village, and a warning had persisted in local legends that the third wave was the worst. Those killed at Kagyuat were killed on the third wave.

Most of the waves that swept through Prince William Sound were generated by underwater slides, and they varied in intensity. The wave that struck Valdez reached a height of sixty-seven metres, while the one that wiped out Kagyuat was much smaller, only nine metres. On a larger scale, though, tsunamis began to spread out from the epicentre, heading south and west. In two-and-a-half hours, the first of six large waves reached the Queen Charlotte Islands. In three and a half hours, it started down the mouth of the Alberni Inlet on Vancouver Island, where it reduced its speed by half and would not reach the towns of Alberni and Port Alberni until just after midnight. Four hours after the first shock, it swept the coasts of Oregon and California. Fergus was reluctantly climbing the stairs for bed, still developing his plan of escape, well after four children on an Easter camp-out in Newport, Oregon, had been plucked from the beach and drowned. He was struggling to close the basement door behind him when the townspeople of Crescent City, California, saw the fourth and largest wave roll in to their pretty little bay. There was a full moon. A good number of boats lay at anchor, many more occupied berths at one of the marinas. The first three waves had been like tidal surges. They rolled over Front Street, flooding businesses, carrying a few light boats up into the town and tossing cars up against buildings. This damage attracted gawkers to the waterfront, people with no knowledge of the cumulative effect of tsunamis. The fourth wave to hit was about six metres high. Just before its arrival, the waters of the harbour retreated in a rush that capsized several boats and left others sitting on the sea bottom. It also drew a few amazed onlookers out into the now-empty bay. When the water returned, it carried with it a large amount of debris — automobile tires, car chassis, broken beams and beach logs — which accounted for most of the thirty blocks of devastation and the seven and a half million dollars' worth of destruction, as well as the eleven dead, two of whom were children.

By the time Fergus set out on his long journey to the hills outside Victoria, most of the danger from the tsunami had already rolled by. Before he had even reached the city's outskirts, Alberni and Port Alberni were awash from the first wave. Alerted by the evening news, the residents were already busy moving people to higher ground. The second wave rolled into their town at two-hundred-and-forty miles an hour about the time Fergus first discovered he had lost his way. And Fergus was falling asleep shortly before the last wave, just over a metre tall, lapped over the ruined waterside homes and tossed the last bits of flood detritus onto the mud-covered streets.

FERGUS OPENS HIS EYES on Saturday, March 28, knowing there has been no tsunami. It's as though someone whispers the truth in his ear the second he wakes up. If he were asked right now whether he ever really believed a tidal wave would destroy his town, he'd answer no. He feels the same now as he does after a night of worrying about dying of cancer — a little foolish, incredulous that he ever entertained seriously such a possibility. But he knows he's capable of believing almost anything as soon as the sun goes down, and part of him marvels at how much the world alters in the light of day. The transformation is a kind of magic, like the way an oar seems to bend on entering the water or how his left hand becomes his right in the mirror. He can look at these things a hundred times, hear his father explain the reasons behind the mystery, and still not tear himself away. He is almost willing to accept the terror of the dark, the minutes that telescope into hours, the gruesome creatures that lurk beside his dresser, in the eaves outside his window, if it means that he gets to feel the miraculous relief that comes with the dawn.

He pulls himself upright, stiff from the cold. Above him the sky moves in and out of view with the movement of the trees. The chimney isn't tall — it's only about the height of his father's aluminum extension ladder. Fergus remembers how it appeared when he first came upon it in the early morning, like the lair of some animal. He's amazed he had the courage to enter. He has no idea what the place is, thinks it might have been part of a house that burned down. Perhaps people died in the fire. He brushes off the moss and twigs that have stuck to his jeans and runs his hands through his hair. The air smells clean, if a bit musty from the carpet of decomposing needles that makes up the forest floor. He crawls back out the short tunnel to look for his bike. Right where he left it. Instantly, he is ravenous. He pulls at the straps of his rucksack to find the cheese and crackers he put there the night before, but everything is in a lump from hours of using the rucksack as a pillow. He opens the can of juice and takes a long drink, picks at the broken crackers, the misshapen piece of cheddar. Sunlight fills a space further up the hill and Fergus goes to see what there is to see and to warm himself up in the open.

From a patch of rock that looks south, Fergus can see Victoria, bright and sharp, lit up by the sun against a backdrop of sea and mountains. There's the breakwater, and the dome of the Parliament Buildings. There's Mt. Tolmie and the islands off Oak Bay. He can even see the Empress Hotel. At least that's where it should be. He's surprised to feel a little disappointed by what he sees. The city is the same as it was yesterday. For a second he'd let himself believe everything would be different, that he would be looking down upon a new world like an explorer who crests a hill to stare out at an undiscovered ocean. The thought excited him, even though he knew it couldn't be true, and now that the scene has resolved itself into the familiar, he realizes how much he'd been looking forward to a change. He sits down, tilts the tin of apple juice against his lips, and thinks about what to do next.

[V]

"**I**sn't that your father?"

After breakfast at the hotel, Helios and Jayne had started walking up Blanshard to a second-hand music store. Jayne had talked Helios into venturing beyond the shelter of his musical niche, his almost exclusive preoccupation with obscure bands like The Knickerbockers, The Remains, The Hombres and Count Five. "You can at least listen," she had said.

Helios knew he was a bit blinkered in his taste, lost in the past. Music wasn't music if the band hadn't broken up before he was born. But, he told Jayne, that didn't mean he had to put up with U2 or Radiohead, either.

"None of that," she'd said. "Why would you? Why would anybody?" They were nearing View Street when Jayne pointed out a man turning into an alley at the side of the cathedral on the corner of View and Blanshard. The man was in a hurry, almost running as he got closer to the building.

"Jesus," Helios said.

"I'm pretty sure that's him. You never told me he was Catholic."

"He's not."

They stood for a minute looking at the church. Its copper-covered spire soared to a point above a superstructure of red brick and buttresses and hideous embellishments that reminded Helios of the various debates he'd had with Saturday morning Jehovah Witnesses, all their cant about Armageddon and the Whore of Babylon. He suspected they hadn't been talking about architectural excess, but there was no denying the place was ugly. Jayne nudged him with her elbow.

"Well?"

The "Don't Walk" light was flashing. Jayne tugged him across the street toward the church, her hand on his collar like a mother with her oversized son. The music store lay in the opposite direction.

"Come on. You know you're curious."

They walked down View until they came to the rear of the cathedral, but they could see nothing. Helios headed toward the parkade across the street, and from the top level, it was easy enough to spot his father. But who were those other two people? Jayne and Helios watched his father hold out his arms and then drop them again, as though he were playing a game of Simon Says.

"I used to skateboard in this parkade," Helios said. "We called the exit ramp 'the corkscrew.'"

"You get a good view from up here," Jayne said.

Flat roofs stretched away from them in all directions, thousands of square metres of sloping, tar-covered textbook illustrations of plane geometry, their surfaces littered with bits of two by four, beer bottles bleached by the sun and patches of volunteer grasses that had been blown there by the wind.

"I could tolerate downtown if I had a place up here," Jayne said. "Think what you could grow in all this sun."

"My mother would go crazy. It would be a jungle."

"I wonder why people don't."

"It's Victoria," Helios said. "We just don't."

They settled in, leaned over the wall of the parkade and let the sun warm their necks, their backs. They looked on as one of Fergus' friends, a woman about their age, knocked together a large, rough cross from lumber that Helios' father helped the other person, a man and also young, remove from the roof of a car. They saw a monk sweeping the paths of the church garden behind the rectory. They watched the monk hover within earshot of the three in the parking lot, and then they saw him take up the end of the cross with Fergus as the three carried it up the alley and out of sight.

"Okay," Jayne said, when the show disappeared from view.

"I told you he was getting strange," Helios said. He remembered what his mother has asked him, to pretend to spy on her. And now here he was spying on Fergus. *A better idea,* he thought, *one that makes sense.*

They ran down the stairwell and out to the street just in time to catch the tail end of the cross as it entered the main doors of St. Andrew's. Jayne started to follow, but Helios held her back from entering. He made a show of approaching the entrance stealthily, flattening himself to the wall of the church, looking first one way, then the other. One finger to his pursed lips, he silenced Jayne and reached into his pocket with his free hand to pull out a dollar coin which he pinched between two fingers and carried over to a panhandler sitting on the front steps of the cathedral. The man's right arm was bent in a most unnatural way, and he had lost all his teeth. His lips were moving as if in conversation, but they curled outwards on occasion, almost reaching the man's chin. Helios dropped the coin into a yogurt container the man had placed on the cement in front of him, and as Helios' money joined the quarters, pennies and dimes, the man's face broadened into a grotesque smile that occupied almost half his face. Helios bowed and said nothing. Then he turned back to Jayne, who had watched his performance from under the shade of a large cedar tree on the south side of the church.

"What's next, Sherlock?" she asked as he came over to her.

"We could wait."

Helios could see Jayne was perplexed. She wanted to continue the chase. "A church is a serious house on serious ground," he said to Jayne a minute later.

"Who told you that?"

"I read it somewhere."

"What's your point?"

"There should be some place on the earth where a person can go and not worry about people spying on him."

"And you think a church is it?"

"What I think isn't important. It's what *they* think."

"And who would that be?"

"The people who go to church."

"I see."

Helios was worried about his father. He didn't know why Fergus had come to St. Andrew's, and he didn't understand what had been going on with the lumber and the cross and the monk. The woman was familiar, but Helios couldn't place her. He also knew it was none of his business. He told Jayne they should go to the music store. She should show him what she wanted him to see. Maybe they'd come back this way to get his truck. Maybe they'd bump into his father. That wasn't spying, Helios said. That was chance.

They walked up to Yates and turned west. For the past few years the city had been trying to make the street over. There were new wrought iron benches and stumpy little trees in planters. Some of the sidewalk had been replaced with paving stones, and the major businesses had hired painters to spruce up their storefronts in what the paint people were calling heritage colours. Helios' landlord had put out a bundle the year before on the same combinations, showing off the fish-scale shakes on his gables, the clapboard siding. It had taken him months. People would pass by on their walks and the landlord would stop what he was doing and talk to them about the features of his house, telling them it was Queen Anne Eclectic and the date it had been built. Helios had to close his window just to shut out the man's voice. His landlord was like everybody else in this town, trying to turn the clock back and forward at the same time.

Helios dodged a pile of french fries. Outside a coffee house the breeze was blowing paper cups and plastic lids all over. A desert was more friendly, he told Jayne.

"A desert at night," she said.

OVER BREAKFAST THAT morning, Jayne had been telling Helios his lyrics were good. Most musicians could play well enough, she said, but they had crap for brains when it came to writing a decent line of poetry. Almost every song she'd ever read on the page was embarrassing, the kind of simple-minded verse kids wrote in high school when they found out their teachers weren't telling them the truth. A few people managed to be playful without being offensive, and even fewer had something to say.

"'Genghis Khan,'" she'd quoted, "'he could not keep, all his kings supplied with sleep. We'll climb that hill no matter how steep, when we get up to it.'"

"I know this one," Helios had said. He didn't really, but what he knew or didn't know wasn't important at the time.

"The thing about Dylan is he never sings the same song twice." Jayne started to get excited. "He likes to mix it up. You know? On one version he thumbs his nose at Roger McGuinn because he got the lyrics backwards when he was with The Byrds. 'Pack up your money, pull up your tent, McGuinn,' he says. And then McGuinn gets him back later with the Nitty Gritty Dirt Band. 'Pack up your money,' he says, 'pick up your tent, Dylan.' They're having fun with each other and the writing is good. At least it's not painful."

"No," Helios had said.

Helios had let Jayne lecture him about music. She was good at it. Names flew out of her mouth. She hummed bits of songs. It was like giving a microphone to a birdwatcher. She couldn't believe her luck: someone wanted to listen. Helios had never heard of most of the people she talked about. He couldn't really believe someone called Eric von Schmidt had ever really existed, but apparently he had. Jayne had some of the man's cover art at home as well as two of the collaborations he'd done with Geoff Muldaur, whoever he was. It used to be Helios was the one stabbing and pointing his finger in other people's faces. This was a nice change.

"You should have your own copies," she'd said finally. "This stuff takes a lot of listening."

"Can't I just borrow yours?"

"I never lend music."

NOW, HELIOS WAS flipping through stacks of CDs without really seeing any of them. *This used to be fun,* he thought. Now it was hard to take seriously. Jayne had once said that the words "music industry" were oxymoronic.

"You got the moron part right," he'd said, uncertain what she meant.

Up at the front of the store, Jayne had collected a handful of empty jewel cases and was asking the clerk to retrieve the disks from behind the counter. She signaled Helios to join her. He pulled out his wallet as he walked, but Jayne made him put it away.

"Consider this my investment."

Out of the store, as they traced their way back towards Helios' truck at the hotel, Jayne suggested they both get some sleep. Helios had another shift on desk that evening, and she was barely standing. Helios felt her lean into his jacket. It turned out he didn't mind her doing so, and they walked a long way like that.

"You can say no, if you want," she said after a block or two.

"No to what?"

"My father's playing at the synagogue. It's a bar mitzvah."

"He invited us?"

"Does it matter?"

"I guess not."

"The food is unbelievable."

They turned in the direction of the cathedral. Helios could see that a crowd of people had gathered around the front steps and when he and Jane got a little closer, they saw an ambulance had pulled right up onto the sidewalk.

[VI]

Annie walked through the arched front door of the client's house into a semi-circular foyer. The floor was a seamless slab of black granite and the walls were faced with rock as well, although what kind, Annie couldn't say. She passed a row of display tables on which sat neat piles of handouts and brochures, along with posters of smiling people in various exotic locations, their bodies radiating good health and happiness. Above and behind the tables, taped to the rock wall, hung a half-dozen banners. They carried words Annie had never seen before — "Jin Shin Do," "Reiki" — and others that seemed English but held no meaning: "Reflexology," "Craniosacral Therapy," "Iridology." Another banner over the door reminded registered workshop participants to please turn off their cellphones. According to the banner, this was a "no stress zone." Annie reached into her purse and pressed the appropriate button. She walked through to the living room where she found two of the deli staff setting up steam tables and plugging in urns of coffee.

"Where are the teachers?"

One of the girls responded by angling her head toward the window and the deck. Annie followed with her eyes. In chairs, on cushions, leaning up against railings, several dozen women and a few men sat like kindergarten students playing a game, their eyes closed, hands folded neatly on their knees.

"What's going on?" Annie asked.

"They're just finishing," the girl said.

"Finishing what?"

"I was in the kitchen. I haven't been keeping track."

"They're visualizing a spiritual guide," a voice explained behind her.

Annie turned to see the house's owner emerge from an office off the living-room, her wrists still heavy with the silver bracelets Annie had seen the first time she'd come here.

"It's an exercise they can take away with them. They create a place in their mind where they feel safe," the woman said.

"Hmmm," Annie replied. She directed her attention to a forest of coffee cups arrayed in rows next to the burbling urns. Some questions shouldn't have answers, she decided.

"It might be a beach or a house in the country. It can be anywhere."

Annie moved cups into alignment with other cups. White cups on a white tablecloth. If she closed her eyes slightly, they almost disappeared.

"After that, it's just a matter of waiting."

"I see."

Annie told herself if she weren't in business, she wouldn't be having this conversation. She wouldn't have to listen to a single word this woman was saying. All at once, she hated the deli. How had she managed to put up with it all these years?

"Yes," the woman said. "It doesn't take long. Pretty soon someone will appear. That's the spiritual guide."

"Like an imaginary friend."

"Good comparison. Children know a lot more than adults about the world outside the senses."

"So, have you had a chance to look things over?"

The door to the deck slid open and a couple of teachers walked in. Annie wished she hadn't asked about them. Now they looked like two teenagers who had just finished playing spin the bottle, silly smirks on their faces, self-conscious. They walked over to one of the steam tables and lifted the lid.

"Oooh," they said together, and then giggled at the coincidence.

Their host walked over to them. Annie left for the kitchen where she helped arrange wraps on platters. She shouldn't allow herself to get so angry. This was a day off for the teachers. What did it matter to Annie if they sat around with their eyes closed talking to people who weren't there? Anything was probably better than a day in front of a bunch of kids. That was what non-instructional days were for, weren't they? A chance to get away from the drudgery of the job? And who was she to say a little mindless relaxation was out of line? No, Annie could see on this return visit that she should be concerned more about herself than about the antics of a group of overworked and anxiety-ridden educators. Her automatic skepticism troubled her. Even the words "spiritual guide" triggered a deep and almost undeniable urge to put some distance between her and the person who had spoken them. Maybe it was the Anglican in her. She'd stopped going to church almost as soon as she was confirmed, but no doubt the damage had already been done. She couldn't remember a time when she hadn't been completely intolerant of people who made a great display of their love of God. She found it especially distressing when the world around her decided it was okay to hug instead of saying hello or goodbye. What was wrong with shaking hands? If she were honest about it, though, she'd have to say she was attracted as well as repulsed by the way some people so easily abandoned their dignity. The few actors she'd known over the years, for example. There was something enviable in how quickly they could summon anger or joy or sorrow. Not that Annie ever trusted them. Who knew when they were telling the truth? Did *they*? She looked down at the plate in front of her. It was full.

"Put these out with the salads," Annie said. The girl helping her hefted the laden platter to her shoulder and bore it away.

ANNIE LEFT THE KITCHEN and walked among the teachers already standing, their plates full, a cup of soup in hand. A lineup had formed along the sides of the buffet tables, and Annie looked automatically for napkins, a supply of cutlery, the carefully placed cards carrying the name Goodlake's, the store's phone number and fax. Some of the teachers had moved out into the foyer where representatives of the various alternative medicines were explaining the attributes of their products. One woman lay face down on a mat on the floor while the therapist rolled two steel balls up and down her spine.

"I'm aligning your nervous system with one of the magnetic meridians that run right through this island."

The woman said nothing.

Participants wore a peel-and-stick tag somewhere on their person: Hello! My name is _____. Annie noticed several people glance at her chest as she walked by. She found the experience unnerving, just as she found this whole congregation of hucksters and charlatans unsettling and wearisome. She looked about her. The girls had things well in hand. Lunch was proceeding nicely. More coffee and pastry in the afternoon, a bit of cleanup. There was no need for her to stay much longer. She opened the front door and retrieved her cellphone from her bag. She wouldn't disturb anyone out here. Two men leaned against the porch banister smoking. Annie excused herself as she walked past them.

"No smoking, no phones," she said. "What else?"

"No sex," one of the men said. He wore a Scottish rugby jersey.

"No liquor," said the other.

Annie stopped and turned.

"So, why did you come?"

"You're not a teacher, are you?" said the one with the jersey.

"It's that obvious?"

The man tapped at his name tag: Roger.

"Right," she said, remembering. "I must stand out."

The other, whose tag said Tony, turned away from the breeze to light himself another cigarette.

"And anyway," he said, "if you were a teacher, you'd know how these things work."

"My name's Annie." She took a step closer.

"Organizers send around a list of all the workshops," Roger said. "Teachers choose one. When the day comes, it's always full. You take what's left."

"I thought you two looked a little out of place."

"It's that obvious?" Roger said. He was smiling.

"Speak for yourself," Tony said. "You should see my spiritual guide." He carved an hourglass in the air.

Whether it was because they were the only men among thirty women, or because their attitude flew in the face of all the serious health-mongers, Annie couldn't say — she knew only that she liked them.

"What do you think of the food?" she asked them.

"Best part of the day," Roger said.

"The soup," Tony said.

Annie drew a couple of cards from her pocket.

"Fans get a free coffee. Just off Store Street. Look for the awnings."

Roger jammed his cigarette into one corner of his mouth and took the card, which he held at a distance to read. Failing that, he groped in his breast pocket for a pair of reading glasses. Annie took pity on him.

"Goodlake's," she said. "We've been around forever."

"I knew that," Roger said. He offered Annie his hand. "You're not leaving, are you? We're going to need someone to keep us in line this afternoon."

"Sorry," Annie said. "Nice to meet you, Roger."

"I'm Tony," he said. He tore off his name tag and handed it to "Tony," who relinquished his in turn. "We switched. Someone has to keep that woman on her toes."

"You're awful." Annie turned away. She almost regretted leaving. Wellness was a crock, but a good laugh was hard to resist. Those two were heading for trouble. Their students probably loved them. She dialed the answering service, walked down the driveway with the cell to her ear and listened to her messages: Doris wanted to know when she was coming in because she was on her own again, or didn't she know, and would Annie be locking up tonight? A distributor called to say he had lost her order. The third was from Helios. Everybody was okay, he said, but she should come to the emergency ward at Jubilee Hospital. Fergus had just been admitted.

FRIDAY TRAFFIC INTO TOWN was bad, even at two o'clock. Annie was convinced on three separate occasions she was going to die. Distracted for most of the trip, she tried deciphering Helios' message. At first she thought Fergus might have caught his hand in one of the meat slicers at the deli, but when she phoned for more information, Doris said he hadn't been in the shop since before lunch.

"I don't know where he goes," she said. "And I don't want to. You two need to talk more, get your signals synchronized or something. Are you serious about this deli or aren't you? Things are going to pot here."

Wherever Fergus' phone was, nobody was answering. Annie could feel herself getting angry. Some part of her knew that Fergus had brought this on himself. He'd been acting so odd lately.

Helios had been born at the Jubilee Hospital. Whenever she visited someone there, she felt a sense of ownership the moment she walked into the building, as though she expected the staff to recognize her despite the nearly twenty-six years that had passed since Helios' birth. When the administration made the move to pay parking in the eighties, she wrote a letter to the paper, calling the decision an outrage. She wrote that "people should not be penalized for their compassion," and the editorial the next day used her very words in its own attack, quoting her in full and giving her credit. Now, as she drove into the lot, she wasn't sure if it was her displeasure at having to plug a machine that was upsetting her or the fact that she was about to see a side of her husband she'd always suspected was there. More and more, Fergus was starting to turn into his father.

Helios was waiting for her in the emergency lounge. The new girl, Jayne, was there, too. Such a busy place and this just an ordinary weekday! Accidents must be happening all the time, she guessed. Annie wondered what the ward would look like after something big, an earthquake or a volcano like Mount St. Helen's.

"Where's Fergus?"

"A bed just came up," Helios said. "They'll get to him as soon as they can. It's not a big deal. I should have told you to stay at home."

"You know I wouldn't have done that. Hi, Jayne. You and Helios don't have to stay. They take hours here. I can wait now."

"We were just walking by," Jayne said. "It was a total coincidence."

"Okay," Annie said, "tell me."

"We don't know a lot," Helios said.

"We saw an ambulance," Jayne said. "Outside the cathedral, the one by the beer and wine store. They brought a stretcher out and Fergus was on it. So we got the truck and followed."

"He was at a church?" Annie asked.

Helios said he didn't know anything about that. Annie could always tell when her son was lying, and she knew he was lying now. But this wasn't the time to call him on it. Not now, not in front of Jayne who was probably in on whatever they were hiding.

"What did he say?"

"He has a concussion," Helios said. "The nurses said they had him sitting up but he wasn't making much sense. I think they wanted to close the cut, so we didn't get a chance to speak to him."

Annie sat down. Jayne brought her a coffee. There wasn't much she could say to Helios. Something wasn't right, she could feel it, and if nobody was going to tell her about it, there wasn't a whole lot she could do to make them. She'd have to wait until she saw Fergus. Still, it was strange. Not only had her husband been taken to hospital suffering from a concussion and some sort of wound that involved stitches, he had apparently received his injuries at a church, a Catholic church at that. These facts would require some explaining.

Across from Annie, a girl much younger than Jayne cradled the head of her boyfriend in her arms. The boy's face was covered in sweat and every once in a while he convulsed, as though someone had prodded him with something sharp. The girl's lips were moving, repeating several words, the same phrase over and over again, consolation possibly or encouragement, Annie couldn't hear exactly, but she was drawn more to the girl's face than to her words, the singular expression of what Annie could only imagine as the girl's love for this boy, her determination to hold onto him, to keep him alive. The moment was never-ending for the girl, as though she'd entered a trance, and, though she felt a voyeur, Annie couldn't tear her eyes away. For a moment, Annie believed she was fascinated with the pair because of her own circumstances, Fergus hurt and she powerless to help him, but she saw almost immediately that the opposite was true. There was nothing similar at all.

A nurse came into the lounge.

"Philips?" she asked.

The girl whispered something in the boy's ear. She helped him to his feet, and half doubled over, he leaned on her all the way to the admitting desk where he slumped into a chair to answer questions.

[VII]

This is what Fergus remembered later.

The monk who had introduced himself as Bob had lost his temper. Somewhere between Fergus' going to the car and his return, Nathan had said something to upset the man, no doubt some reference to his theory of the fraudulent cross and the fallacious underpinnings of the Catholic church, just the kind of contentious information a young guy like Nathan couldn't refrain from making public. Fergus was surprised to detect within himself a growing sense of anticipation as the disagreement gained in volume, and he noted as well an undeniable sympathy for the monk, who probably didn't need some cocky post-graduate architecture student lecturing him on the history of Christianity. Wisely, and despite his own bias, Fergus decided to stay out of the fray and busied himself with examining the altar, an imposing but sparsely decked piece of real estate that sat on its own, surrounded by a sea of choir stalls.

Fergus remembered thinking that the last time he had been anywhere near an altar was twenty-five years ago when he had married Annie, and this thought made him reflect a little on the nature of time and on his own strangely selective memory. More precisely, he started to think about the garden in front of his house. He could picture quite easily the three large flowering currants, now all but finished, their new foliage drooping under its own weight. He didn't even have to close his eyes to see the insanely prolific camellia that dropped its blossoms along the side path. Only last week, Fergus had watched from behind the living-room curtains as the garbage man stooped to retrieve one, pausing long enough to tuck its stem through a buttonhole in his overalls. And these days it was the broom they were both agog over, the hybrids Annie had placed in a row along one bed, each plant a different color: cinnamon orange, firebrick red, vermilion, goldenrod. The remarkable thing was that every year Fergus forgot completely which plant produced what bloom, even forgetting that some of them bloomed at all, and the effect was almost as though he had forgotten his own birthday, or more startling yet, Christmas (despite Annie's complaints about the day's homogeneous blandness). The truth was that all of spring came as a total surprise to him, and he never failed to mention his shock to Annie who would say only that he forgot every year because none of it was his doing, not a single bulb. The garden, she reminded him, was her creation. And so it was.

He looked up at the candlesticks on the altar. Weren't they supposed to represent something. The epistle? The gospel? He used to know this. Why did it seem so often these days that even the most common piece of knowledge had abandoned him? It came to him at that moment that he must be suffering from some kind of madness, and that now, in this church, he had been granted a moment of clarity, a vision of sorts. The vision was more an idea than anything, nothing outrageous, just the thought that the best thing he could do for all concerned was to walk out of this place, retrace his steps, put on an apron and get back to work. What, after all, did he think he was doing? He looked around. Bob was pointing his finger at Nathan, and Nathan was making some sweeping gesture that included the whole building. Caroline was ignoring all of them, using her hammer to drown out the argument. The air of the church thundered with each blow as she drove nails into the stand that was to hold the experimental cross perpendicular. The very last thing he could remember was spotting what looked like a tiddly wink on the floor, a white tiddly wink. How funny. To think the priest and the altar boys might have been crouching down on the floor here playing a child's game. He was just bending down to pick it up when a huge weight struck him on the back of his head.

None of these memories was accessible until many hours later, and even then they didn't return all at once. The time immediately following the accident was especially confusing, a little like the afternoon his mother had spent searching for him at the fairgrounds when he was six. Fergus had had no idea he was lost. He'd just turned left when she'd turned right. Before he knew it, a crowd of people were looking down at him, talking to him, their hands grabbing his jacket to lead him somewhere, and with each tug on his arm Fergus had the unmistakable feeling that he'd done something terribly wrong. In the present case, Fergus hadn't even known he'd passed out until the doctor told him, but he wasn't surprised to hear the event had escaped his notice. He had no idea what losing consciousness was like for other people, but on the few occasions it had happened to him, the experience had been unexceptional, much the same, in Fergus' mind, as going under a general anaesthetic. The anaesthetist tells the patient to count backwards from one hundred. The next thing he knows, he's in a semi-private, his bladder the size of a football and a terrible taste at the back of his throat. Indeed, Fergus' entire understanding of death derived from the times he'd been knocked out and from the three operations he'd undergone in his life: appendix, wisdom teeth, and adenoids. Death, like unconsciousness, was a blank tape, a skip in the record, a page missing from a book.

Laid out on the floor of the cathedral and slowly regaining control of his mind, Fergus thought first about the deli. He assumed this was, in fact, where he was. Why would he be anywhere else? He had spent so much of his life at the shop that sometimes when he and Annie were driving out to a friend's or to a show, he mindlessly started driving downtown instead. He didn't remember anything about a cross. He had no memory of a monk named Bob or the cruel methods by which the Roman Empire economized on executions. He certainly had no idea he was bleeding, or that someone had placed under his head a wad of paper towels from the church washroom to soak up the growing puddle of blood that had gathered on the floor beneath him. He wasn't even certain what he was looking at, and it wasn't until a face popped into view that he realized he was staring at a church's vaulted ceiling, a revelation that confused him more than anything. And finally, not in his wildest imaginings would he have guessed that the ten minutes he would never recollect, as well as the cupful of blood he had lost through a cut that required twelve stitches to close, were due to an eighteen-foot wooden cross pitching forward from its precarious perch against a pillar and landing directly on the top of his skull.

AS THE AMBULANCE whined and cajoled its way up Fort Street to the hospital, Fergus was terrified to discover Caroline sitting beside him. *What was she doing here?* He was so terrified he didn't speak a word to her for the entire trip, even closed his eyes to avoid her, all the while flipping through the Rolodex of his mind for clues as to what had happened to him. Had he been shot? Where was Annie? Had Annie shot him? He was dying to ask, hoping perhaps that Caroline might blurt out the truth, but Caroline said nothing, only held his hand, a display of affection that made Fergus shrink out of fear that the paramedics would convey this detail to Annie, wherever she was, in handcuffs, behind bars, the guilty weapon in a plastic bag down in a police laboratory while officers waited for the doctors to dig a matching bullet out of his skull so they could convict her.

Fergus sensed someone behind him, an ambulance attendant, probably, stanching the wound. He wondered if his skull was broken. Maybe this was how Kennedy felt in Dallas after the shooting, his brain fading out like a song, the young president's last thoughts dodging around his cranium in a panic over the metal slug that had decided to crash their party. Weren't they of an age now, he and old JFK? Close, certainly. Fergus had been sick the day Kennedy had died, home from school with a cold. His mother brought him the news with a glass of orange juice. Now he felt a kinship with the man from Camelot, as though all those years ago, sitting up in bed and sipping from his glass, Fergus had been listening to a prophecy about himself. *Poor kid,* he thought, unsure now whether he might not actually be the philandering

Bostonian himself who'd had a premonition about his assassination as a boy. Could it be?

At the hospital, the attendants wheeled Fergus past reception and directly into the ward, where they transferred him to a stretcher that stood on its own in the hall. A nurse came up and loomed over him.

"Sir? Mr. Goodlake? Can you hear me? You wife will be here in a few minutes. She's just talking to admitting. We'll get you a bed as soon as we can, okay? Mr. Goodlake? Don't move your head for a while, all right? We've stopped the bleeding for now, but you shouldn't move."

Then she was gone. Fergus stared up at the recessed fluorescent light above his head. Two flies lay on the inside of the plastic ceiling panel, and Fergus watched them for a while until he realized they were dead. Something the nurse had said was bothering him. She'd said something about Annie. Around him, Fergus could hear the murmuring conversations of visitors who were trying to keep their voices low. To Fergus they sounded like the congregants of a church where the service was about to begin. Church? The word resonated strongly for some reason. Was this a Sunday? Had he and Annie been at church? A wedding maybe? A funeral?

"Hey," Caroline said. She was pulling up a chair and speaking into his ear. "That was quite a knock you took."

"Yes, it was," Fergus said. A knock! "I'm not supposed to move my head."

"The nurse said to make sure you didn't fall asleep, either, so do me a favour and keep those peepers open, okay?"

"Yes. Quite a knock, indeed."

"Nathan says hello. He had to stay and straighten things out with Bob."

"Of course." Nathan? Bob?

"Listen. I got a bit freaked out when the ambulance came. I didn't know what to tell them, so I said I was your wife."

"So that's what the nurse meant."

"I even used her name."

"Good move."

"Except it's not. Think about it."

"I have a headache."

"Annie will want to see you when she hears what happened. Imagine what she'll say when she finds out it's her second visit."

Fergus didn't feel up to this. There were too many plates in the air. He couldn't catch them all this time. The pain in his head was starting to scare him, too. He wanted to close his eyes, but Caroline would just tell him to open them again.

"Caroline. There are a couple of things ..."

"Excuse me?" a nurse said. "Mrs. Goodlake? Your son and his girlfriend are here. They're asking after your husband. Should I send them in?"

"Christ, no!" Caroline said, and then to Fergus, "I'll tell them about your headache, sweetheart. They'll understand."

"Thanks."

A minute later, an intern wheeled him out of the hall and into a small room a few doors down. The sounds of the ward vanished the moment the door closed, and in the face of the storm that was threatening to break over him, Fergus found himself grateful for the illusion of calm, no matter how short-lived it would prove to be. He listened dutifully as a deep voice explained the administration of a local anaesthetic, the need to shave the scalp around the cut, how he might want to invest in a good hat for the next while, and finally the number of stitches they were estimating, somewhere between ten and fifteen. Did Fergus remember much of the accident?

"Not really."

Perhaps he might like to answer a few questions, then? What day of the week was it? What year? Who was the current prime minister? Fergus couldn't muster a single correct response, but his lack of success didn't bother him. He had the feeling that as long as he allowed this soft, conciliatory and soothing voice to speak to him, everything would be all right. What a marvel these health workers were! So unperturbed by the sight of a man's flesh peeled back, the tender carapace of his brain revealed!

Whatever the government was paying them wasn't enough. Imagine! Here they were, at all hours, like good parents who waited at the bottom of the playground slide just in case something went wrong. He was almost in tears thinking about these selfless people. How petty his life seemed in comparison. Sliced meats and Greek salads! Thermal carafes of Mocha Java!

Fergus couldn't feel the thread or the needle, but imagined he could hear them as the intern tugged his way from one side of the cut to the other, the rough reluctance of cotton against skin that Fergus remembered from the many times he had dressed the Christmas turkey, the way the hole closed a little more with each stitch, leaving a puckered, bulging mouth that grinned back at him as he slid the bird whole into the oven. Fergus wondered if these thoughts ever came to the man working on him. Did he ever think of the people he'd sewed back together as he laboured over his own holiday bird?

"You're going to be just fine," the intern said.

"I know."

"Just a little funny-looking for a while."

"Small price," Fergus said.

"Head injuries are tricky things. We had a guy once — this is quite a few months ago now — they brought him in around midnight. A motorcycle accident. Pretty messy. We operated right away. A lot of fluid, let me tell you. Six hours, but we pulled him out of the fire. Anyway, the next day he disappears from his bed. The janitors found him three weeks later in a ventilation shaft."

"Oh," Fergus said.

"Just wandered off."

"I see."

"You've gotta wonder what was going through his head."

"Sure do."

"There was hell to pay over that one."

[VIII]

Fergus believes it's possible his parents haven't noticed his absence. They may have passed their long morning thinking he'd gone down to the beach. Perhaps one of them would have thought to check his room, and, finding him gone, might have descended the basement stairs to see whether his bike was still there. Then, it would become clear: he'd arranged a meeting with a friend, perhaps a trek to Beacon Hill Park, or maybe further afield, out to Willows or even Cadboro Bay. They would be concerned he hadn't told them, of course, and the unlocked basement door would be certain to cause a scene. If it were his mother who found it, she would slip the bolt back into the hasp so his father wouldn't stew.

Fergus likes his mother, but he feels sorry for her, too. She never seems to enjoy what she is doing, as though there's some other life for which she is better suited, that of a secretary like Della Street or a teacher like Our Miss Brooks. Fergus' mother is tall, but most of the time he doesn't notice her height. Only on parent/teacher days. Then he's struck by the way she towers over the other mothers, elegant in her white coat, waiting her turn to speak to the teacher and, later, bending down to cast a look into the hastily arranged order of Fergus' desk. Like most children, Fergus has learned the meaning of defeat long before anyone has taught it to him. He's learned it through the stories that are not told, but alluded to. A farm his father could have bought but didn't. The war years his mother spent living with a mother-in-law who bullied, and a father-in-law who took no notice because he was afraid. He's learned it through the few pieces of jewelry his mother keeps in a plain wooden box on her dresser, and through the nearly opaque blue bottle of Evening in Paris that sits on the top shelf of the medicine chest, things that are not sad in themselves, but which become sad the moment they are valued. Fergus has only to think of his mother to understand the meaning of disappointment.

He looks out from his rocky vantage. In this weather, his mother would certainly have taken her coffee out on the back porch to catch the sun before it passed over the house. She spends a lot of her mornings there, mostly because she has to hang the laundry on the line that stretches across to the pear tree, but sometimes she just leans over the back railing with a cigarette and stares out into the neighborhood. By now, his father has been at work for nearly three hours, his apron tied in a neat bow right in the middle of his stomach. Fergus has mimicked his father in front of the mirror, taking a clean apron from the laundry and wrapping the long strings around his body — in Fergus' case, twice — and parading back and forth in front of his reflection, the apron's hem almost at his feet like a full-length skirt. He is not interested in what his father does for a living so much as in the accessories associated with the trade: the slicers, the knives, the great rolls of brown wrapping paper that would run the length of Fergus' street if only his father would let him try. He can see it unrolling now, along the streets of southern Fairfield where the cherry trees are gathering steam, their buds working toward an explosion that will last almost three weeks. Even this high up, Fergus can feel the winds off the Georgia Strait. They carry the warm, southern air of the "pineapple express," and the sun is already hot enough for a T-shirt. The sounds of the city encroach a little, but there is none of the relentless river of sound that Fergus remembers from his one trip to Vancouver. There, the night was unending with its sirens and heavy trucks. From where he sits, he can just see the road that led him here, and in the whole time he has been watching, not a single car has passed. Is anybody looking for him?

It's a long weekend. Easter Monday means he doesn't have to worry about school until Tuesday. He imagines what it would be like not to worry at all. Not to stand across the street in the shadow of the corner store and watch the playground like an antelope waiting to drink from a communal watering hole. At the end of the school day, not to linger behind the Venetian blinds of his classroom to see which bicycles remain in the covered rack by the annex. To take his time on the way home, stop at the park the way he used to, buy some licorice whips. Fergus is not surprised to discover he'd been looking forward to this flood more than he'd realized. It is exactly the kind of miracle he's been waiting for, just like the ones he's gone to sleep thinking about every night for years: earthquake, volcano, even a door he can walk through to find himself in a different time. This is his favourite fantasy, that somehow he could be transported to the early days of Victoria before his house or the others around it were built, where a forest grows instead, and instead of roads there are deer paths that lead down to the bay, a bay without a seawall or a cemetery or storm drains that cloud the water after every rain. Fergus spends hours living in this world. He builds himself a cabin with a front porch that looks out over the sea and makes friends with the Indians who come down to dig clams at low tide. He takes long walks through what will be his neighborhood, carves his name on the trunks of trees he believes will still be there a hundred years later, imagines himself look-ing for these trees when he steps back through the door. And now he adds the very spot he's sitting on to the list of sights he would visit, the pilgrimages he would make in what he feels must have been a better time. He squints his eyes, tries to obliterate the city from the land, to see the southern tip of Vancouver Island the way it appeared to Cook or Juan de Fuca. Fergus believes he could survive in such a land, make a life for himself, a better life than any he could make in this one.

He walks back into the woods, and retraces his way down to the lime kiln. From this angle, his refuge looks like an entrance into the ground, the kind of inviting hole he remembers from watching *The Time Machine* and *Journey to the Center of the Earth*. But this is a hole that leads nowhere. Fergus crawls back in and sits in the shaft of forest-green light, wishing the inexplicable mound of bricks and mortar would perform the same magical transformations he has seen in film and read about in books. It's the same weak hope he sometimes summons rounding the final corner on his way to school, wishing it to disappear, to leave nothing but a vacant field behind. He waits, holds his breath. *Listen,* he tells himself.

There is no sudden wind, no flash of light. The bricks beside him remain damp and cold, and Fergus understands very clearly that he cannot stay here any longer. Another night is out of the question. There's no protection from the rain, should it come, and his food supplies are inadequate. He would like to step outside and be anywhere but where he is, in this town on an ordinary spring day in the middle of the 20th century with nowhere to go but back to his house, where his parents have probably not even realized their son has been gone the entire day. In the same way that he once was forced to acknowledge that his house contains no secret passages and no hidden rooms, he now understands that there is only one method of time travel, the one he is using at this very moment, and that in its slow and predictable fashion, it will take him all the way to the end of the century where he will be just as unhappy as he is now.

Fergus looks at his watch. The afternoon light will begin to fade soon, and he's still not sure exactly where he is. If he starts now, he may make it home by dark. He returns to his bicycle and walks it back down to the rough logging road and out to the pavement. He's stiff from his cramped sleep, and as he raises his right leg over the bar, something in him protests. It's bad enough he has to straddle the Spartan leather contours of his Brooks saddle so soon after a long ride; worse for Fergus is the thought that his adventure has been cut short and that his efforts will only take him home.

His sense of failure vanishes with the first hill, however, and for the next fifteen minutes his descent is quick, even exhilarating. He recognizes nothing from his ride here the previous night. Once he leaves

the hills behind, the countryside is almost English, or at least it approx-
imates the image Fergus has built up of England from looking at
Rupert anthologies and from reading his collection of *Secret Seven*
stories. Fields rise and fall like waves, divided by hedges and, on occasion,
a stream. At an intersection, he stops to look at the street signs and
realizes he has somehow ended up on Helmcken Road, a name he
knows from the trips his parents make at least every two weeks to see
Fergus' grandmother. She doesn't live on this road, but the look of
the houses and the sight of a familiar corner store tells him she's not far.
This is his father's mother, who has been living alone in the house she
and Fergus' grandfather shared until he died of a stroke seven years ago.
Fergus remembers very little of his grandfather, though one of the
stories about him is that he was so excited at the birth of a grandson
that he left his store unattended to drive to the hospital and see the new
"bull moose." Even now, whenever Fergus' father has a drink or two,
he starts calling Fergus "the bull moose," and tries to wrestle him.
These fights usually end with Fergus getting hurt and his mother
telling his father to "leave the kid alone."

Fergus thinks his grandmother is a likeable person, but even he can
tell she is happiest on her own. Whenever he and his parents visit her,
she makes a plateful of sandwiches that she cuts into four and places on
a three-tiered tea caddy, along with pieces of shortbread. There's always
a bottle of ginger ale for Fergus while everyone else sips sherry from
small crystal glasses. After a decent interval, he's allowed to explore
the property behind her house, a triangular piece of land that borders the
right-of-way for the Esquimalt and Nanaimo Railway. Fergus has often
stood above the tracks and watched flatcars of lumber from up-island
mills as well as passenger coaches pass through Victoria's outskirts, the
engine's whistle blowing at each crossing on its way into town. In the
wake of his journey's failure, the idea of a visit today seems like a good
one to Fergus, a welcome postponement of his return home. If he can
find his way there, she will give him something to eat, and he will have
prolonged his adventure. She may even let him stay the night, though

this last hope is unlikely because of tomorrow's Easter service. His parents won't allow him to miss it. But even a faint hope is enough to revive Fergus' sense of mission.

Fergus crosses the road and stops at the corner store he remembers. He's thirsty, despite having drunk a whole can of apple juice. In front of the store, Fergus slides his bike into a steel rack that advertises 7-UP. He locks his bike to the rack and brings his rucksack into the store. The floorboards of the store are unpainted and worn smooth, so much so that in some places nails have appeared, their heads polished bright from the passage of many feet. A freezer sits to the right of the front counter full of Fudgsicles and Mr. Freeze and Drumsticks, and Fergus looks in his wallet, even though he knows to a penny how much money he put in it the night before. A stack of *Victoria Times* newspapers sits near the door, the front page covered with pictures of the devastation caused by the earthquake. Fergus reads the headlines.

"Did you feel it?" the store's owner asks him.

"I was watching TV," Fergus says.

"This old store shook for a bit," the man says. "We live upstairs, and you could tell something was going on."

"My father said it was a big one."

"Plenty of us were saying the same thing."

"But no tidal wave," Fergus says. "The news said one was coming down."

"Not here, there wasn't. But Port Alberni got hit. People's houses washed right off the ground."

"I didn't know that," Fergus says.

"They're saying ten million dollars at least. It's all in the paper."

Fergus buys the newspaper for fourteen cents and then digs out another twelve cents for a bottle of Fanta with a straw. He walks outside and sits on the steps of the store to read about the biggest natural disaster to hit the west coast in a hundred years. The headlines are large: ALASKA RIPPED BY EARTHQUAKE, and beneath that one, TIDAL WAVE FLOODS PORT ALBERNI. A map of Alaska shows the cities of

Anchorage, Valdez and Seward, and beneath it is a photograph of a house in Crescent City, California. The house lies on its side, surrounded by broken timbers and bits of furnishings. He reads on another page how the seismograph at the Dominion Astrophysical Observatory just outside Victoria made an initial attempt to record the tremor and then gave out, overloaded by the size of the jolt. On the same page, he learns that the tidal waves bypassed Victoria completely. There are pictures of boats sunk in Port Alberni and a long shot of the main street of Anchorage. Fergus reads every word about the disaster. He flips back and forth from section to section, scanning the bylines for the slightest information about the aftereffects of the tsunami and the quake. Alaska's neighbour Siberia escapes completely, but a world away in the Gulf of Mexico, the shifting plates generate a six-foot wave that travels four hundred miles along the coast of Louisiana and Texas. In Tacoma, Washington, the birds and animals in Point Defiance Park Zoo send up an alarming din at the moment the tremor hits.

"First it was the ducks and the geese," a zoo attendant is quoted as saying. "Then the lions, coyotes and all the rest joined in. The noise was deafening."

A party of fifty teenagers at Pachena Beach on the west coast of Vancouver Island became stranded when one of a series of waves knocked out the road leading to the point where they had set up camp.

With each article, Fergus grows a little more angry. He feels the stories on these pages should really be his, that he's been robbed, the way he was two years ago when his father refused to take him to the Seattle World's Fair.

"On what I make, kid," his father had said, "you're lucky you get bus fare."

While everybody else was riding the monorail and taking the elevator up the Space Needle, Fergus and his family spent his father's two-week holiday in a beach cabin at The Park Sands Motor Hotel in Parksville, B.C. Fergus ate beans on toast for breakfast, lunch and dinner, dug for clams and ran after the golf balls Fergus' father hit from one end of the long stretch of sand to the other. But Fergus hadn't wanted a holiday, not in Parksville and not even in Seattle. What Fergus wanted then, and what he wants now, is to be a part of something important, an event that people will look back on the way they do the Second World War.

Fergus is starting to close the newspaper when his eye is caught by a story about a circus girl, a British aerialist by the name of Ann Mombray, who fell forty feet to a packed dirt floor in front of three thousand people. He reads that the Hamid Morton circus was performing in the State Fair Park livestock museum in Dallas, Texas, and Miss Mombray, swinging by a neck collar suspended from her partner's teeth, plunged brilliantly, breaking both ankles, several ribs and one shoulder. Onlookers say one of her feet may have brushed a guy wire during her act, causing her to lose her grip. Fergus doesn't believe it. He's certain her fall was a result of the quake. There's no picture of the girl, but Fergus can see her anyway, in a leotard of sequins, high above the crowd, spotlights focused on her as she spins beneath the roof of a circus tent. He sees the poles of the tent shudder hideously as thousands of miles to the north, the land under Alaska collapses. He sees the girl jerk like a fish on a line and then break loose to fall out of the beams of light, through darkness to the ground below. He hears the hush of the audience as they realize what has happened, watches the lights find their quarry again while circus workers rush towards the girl. Fergus is amazed. It's as though a hand had reached all the way from Alaska to Texas and plucked the girl out of the air, cut the thread she dangled from, and dropped her.

[IX]

Helios and Jayne arrived at the hospital a half hour after the ambulance that delivered Fergus. It had taken them thirty minutes to walk back to the motel and coax Helios' truck into motion. Even so, they'd have been at the hospital sooner if they hadn't run into Helios' friend from the night before. He was sitting in the patio of the motel eating a burger. There was a cigarette in the ashtray on the table and two empty Heinekens beside it. He was working on a third.

"I'm going to have your job, asshole."

"You won't like it," Helios said.

The man stood up and grabbed Helios by the arm.

"Smart-ass little shit. You're coming with me." He started dragging Helios toward the main entrance. "Let's see what your boss says."

Helios wrenched himself free and turned to face the man. He placed his hands on the man's chest and gave him a solid shove backwards into the landscaped bed that bordered the restaurant. The man tried to get up, but he was tangled in a dense arrangement of rosebushes and every time he attempted to pull himself out, he made things worse for himself. A crowd gathered at the windows of the restaurant, Helios' manager among them. There were witnesses, Helios consoled himself. Even if there weren't. He turned and walked toward the parking lot.

"I'm off duty," he said over his shoulder to no one in particular.

THE NURSE AT RECEPTION told Helios his father was still a bit light-headed, which was understandable, she said, under the circumstances. Helios interrupted her to ask if she thought his father's condition had been building for a while. The nurse looked puzzled.

"It was a pretty good whack on the head," she said, "if that's what you mean."

She told him again that Fergus was disoriented, confused. Until a doctor had a look at him and stitched him up, she couldn't say much more. For now, one visitor at a time was probably all he could handle.

"Someone's already here?"

"His wife was with him in the ambulance. She's there now."

"My mother?"

"I'll see how he's coming along, okay?" The nurse turned and walked back into the ward.

Helios had left a message for his mother from the motel payphone before he left, but he guessed it was possible she might have got here ahead of him. He didn't remember seeing her in the crowd of people in front of the cathedral, but she might have found out about Fergus some other way.

He and Jayne sat down to wait for the nurse to return. He noticed there were only a few chairs vacant, and it wasn't even two o'clock. The pair across from them seemed in a bad way. The girl was in tears holding her boyfriend's head in her lap, and he looked completely out of it, his face bathed in sweat and his mouth moving or twitching every few minutes. Helios thought he might have overdosed until he saw the short sleeves and the skateboard. Not the type, he decided. The shoes were two hundred at least. The kid probably bailed somewhere, hit his head. Maybe he had the flu. He hoped it wasn't another one with meningitis. What would that make it now? Four? Helios bent his neck forward to his chest. No pain. He felt the glands in his neck. Christ, he was acting like his father! He looked around to see if anyone had been watching. Jayne was leafing through a *National Geographic* she'd found among the stacks of *Chatelaine* and *People*.

"I didn't know this," she said.

Helios waited. He knew enough about Jayne now to know his side of the conversation wasn't always necessary. Besides, he was tired. He'd been up all night at the hotel. Sleep was starting to sneak up on him.

"Look at this guy. He's sitting in a big bowl of mercury."

Helios looked up to see the nurse from reception and another woman talking. Helios recognized the woman, or at least he knew where he'd seen her before. She was the person he and Jayne had watched from the top of the parkade, the one who'd been hammering the cross together in the back lot of the church. Now she was standing at the entrance to the waiting room of the emergency ward, looking around as if she expected to see someone she knew. She was older than Jayne, but not by much. The overalls she wore suited her. So did the pencil behind her ear.

"Right through a tire," Jayne said. "You gotta look at this."

Helios nudged her and pointed out the woman.

"What's she doing here?"

The woman turned toward them. She raised her hand and gave a little wave. Then she pointed at her watch, shrugged her shoulders and left through the automatic doors.

"This is a weird day," Jayne said.

HELIOS' MOTHER DIDN'T walk into the lounge until another twenty minutes had passed, and from the way she spoke, Helios could tell this wasn't her second visit. Her face was drawn. She spoke like a machine. This wasn't a good time to bring up the carpenter, he told himself. He played dumb about the church, too. Was it a bad sign, he wondered, if a person spent a lot of time worrying about his parents? Things had been no different when he was younger. Not better at all.

Helios' mother sat next to Jayne, and together they waited for the nurse to give them an update on Fergus. Helios had a hard time keeping himself from falling asleep. He was thinking about his parents' house, about his room on the top floor at the back. The sun always rose in his window first. It was a good room, a little small, but big enough for him. He remembered how he had fought his mother, refused to let her strip the walls, sand the floors, paint the trim the way she had painted the trim and altered the look of every other room in the house over the years. If he had memories of growing up, they were the smells of turpentine and Polystripper, the air thick with fumes and dust from sanding and the damp pasty odour that leaked from fresh wallpaper for weeks afterwards. She tried to tempt him with swatches from catalogues, thinking she could bring him on side, but she never realized he was in a constant state of mourning for each of the spaces she had changed beyond recognition in her search for the kind of perfection he believed the house already had attained just by being the house in which he lived. He wasn't a son, he was an obstacle, and when she finally bribed him into the basement with promises of a private entrance and his own personal kitchen — *two floors between us*, she kept telling him, *can you imagine?* — she set upon his old room like a rebel army that had taken possession of their country's capital city after years of struggle. Within weeks it was unrecognizable, the windows valenced and hung with thick damask curtains, the floors glowing from five coats of satin Varathane, and a new name: the guest room. As she had done in the living room, the kitchen, the dining room and the master bedroom, Annie installed a noisy dimmer switch. These she sometimes used for effect in the evening to make the entire house more muted and soft, to the point that Helios often felt as though he was wandering around in a diorama at a museum. That feeling disappeared as soon as he descended the ten stairs into the basement where, in his new room, he became the household pet that had to be quarantined because of a bad habit. His room was dark. The windows were small. Spiders were everywhere. There were floods. He could feel every earthquake — creaks and groans like the house was coming down on his head all the time. The smell of gas. It was an awful place to bring his friends. Like the damp hull of a boat, rife with mould.

"You're snoring," Jayne said.

"Go," his mother said to both of them. She promised she would call later, good news or bad. "Get some sleep," she told Helios, and he didn't disagree.

HELIOS LEANED HIS HEAD against the passenger window while Jayne struggled with the International's sloppy stick shift. He listened to her search for third, then reached over and guided her hand into place. "How come you're so perky?"

"Sleep is for wimps."

"I think my father is losing his mind."

At Helios' apartment, Jayne slipped a CD into the stereo, and joined Helios under the covers.

"Who's this?"

"Listen first. If you like it, I'll tell you later. Knowing too much ruins a thing."

A thin but not unpleasant female voice filled the room, supported by a trio of acoustical instruments.

"Did she just say Robson Street?"

"That's what she said."

Above their heads, Helios' landlords walked from room to room. Sometimes they closed a door, ran for a phone. The springs of a sofa strained against someone's weight. A microwave timer drew children from their bedrooms on the third floor. Other sounds were harder to interpret, but over time Helios had cracked the codes. A reluctant drawer in the hall armoire. The bag of white flour being dragged from its home in the pantry closet. Helios kept track of the family's movements the same way he'd kept track of his parents as they trooped across the main floor of the house he had grown up in. Once, when he was sixteen, he'd smoked a joint under the back deck, and in the hours that followed in the darkness of his bedroom, he couldn't stop thinking he was listening to the passage of thoughts in his own mind. All the sub-routines of his brain were chatting around him, flushing toilets, turning out lights, adjusting thermostats. The sensation was a pleasant one. And now, despite this apartment's limitations — low ceilings, the unpredictable heat, a tricky sewer connection — Helios felt at home.

HE WOKE IN the dark. Jayne was pinching his nose, and the dream she'd hauled him out of — something to do with drowning or being buried alive — pedaled out of sight like a paperboy. When he looked at it, the bedside clock struck him as utterly incomprehensible.

"It's time," Jayne said, "to walk the line."

"You can't be serious."

"I've never been on strike before. This is exciting. Don't you think this is exciting? I hope we get some scabs. Some real low-lifes I can shout at and call names."

"Like 'scab'?"

"Among other things." She threw back the covers and stepped out of the bed. Her underwear had become twisted, and Helios watched in the muted streetlight as she wrenched her boxers around to the front again.

"How many times in your life," she asked him, "have you had a real cause?"

"I remember the Peace Marches."

"Please. Don't give me any airy-fairy shit about nuclear bombs and climate change. That's called having nothing better to do. This is different."

"Because it's about money?"

"Money is our language. It's what gives us power. They try to limit cost of living increases? They tell us they want to contract out the jobs we do? What they're saying is 'shut up.'"

"I've never thought of it like that."

"Nobody tells me to shut up," Jayne said.

"Except your father."

Jayne glared at him. Helios walked into the bathroom. He needed a shower badly. At this time of the evening the competition wasn't so bad. He opened both taps wide and waited with one finger under the faucet while the hot water made its long journey from the tank on the far side of the basement through whatever illegal maze of copper elbows and second-hand piping his landlord had jerry-rigged during the construction of Helios' apartment. Helios imagined a path that traveled first to the top floor and then to the kitchen on the main before descending back to the cellar where the water was easily half the temperature it started out at. He'd timed it once: an unbelievable ninety-seven seconds before there was any discernible change from the usual glacial cold despite the fact that he was no more than twenty feet from its source.

As he waited, Helios mused that over the past few weeks Jayne had made herself at home among his few possessions. The lower two drawers of his dresser were now full of her clothes. Pharmaceuticals he had never heard of stood in rows along the back of the bathroom vanity. There were three different types of shampoo. A pair of slippers seemed always to be perfectly placed on her side of the bed, half-hidden, the toes pointing under the box spring. There was different reading material, too. The *TLS*. *Harper's*.

"You don't have a computer," she had said on her first visit. Her words had sounded more like a declaration, a statement of behavioral fact, than a question, so he said nothing. After that, she brought a laptop, which she plugged into his phone jack.

"I have a local server," she said.

"Oh."

These thoughts were new to him. Helios had never fallen into the habit of assessment. Life didn't appear to him as a series of bar graphs the way it did to his mother, each year competing with the last. Perhaps that's what filling out tax forms did to a person — the yearly tabulation of income and expenses, the documentation of good years and bad. Helios wouldn't know. When information of this nature arrived in the mail — T4s, bank statements — he set it aside in a pile until the deadline for submission passed. Then he threw it out. He believed the hours he had saved not sweating the numbers were worth a lot more than whatever future punishment the government might inflict. So, now he didn't ask himself whether his life was better now that Jayne was in it, or whether he considered the pleasure they took in each other's company an indication of something significant. If there was a question in his mind, it concerned the undeniable effect that a diet of steady sex — and "steady" in Helios' world meant more than once in two years — was having upon his mood.

He stood with the shower nozzle spraying him full in the face, trying to imagine what it would be like to carry a picket. After a few seconds he stopped, as he always did when he found himself speculating about the future. In a few hours he would know everything there was to know about pickets, strike coordinators, public abuse. Until then, there were other things that deserved his attention. For one, his mother hadn't phoned yet. No word about Helios' father. Was this good or bad? Should he phone her?

"Hey," Jayne shouted outside the shower curtain.

"Shit."

"You don't have to swear."

"I was thinking."

"My turn." She stepped into the tub behind him and pushed him out.

To have to think about sex had always been a burden to Helios. He couldn't shut it off the way he shut off other thoughts, however much he tried, and he resented it. From the day he'd turned twelve, biology was an imposition, a problem that needed a solution. So, these days, when the solution walked in and tossed him out of his shower, he felt enormously relieved. And when it came out of the bathroom a few minutes later and asked him what kind of a limp-wristed strike he thought he was going to in foot gear as useless as a pair of running shoes, he was speechless.

"Shit-kickers," Jayne said, pointing down at her own worn Daytons. "That's what you need."

[X]

"**N**one of this makes any sense."

Annie had just finished pulling back the covers of their bed so Fergus could lie down. Before they'd left the emergency ward, the intern who had treated Fergus told her to stay with him, maybe keep him awake for a couple of hours. Annie realized she must have looked annoyed or impatient because the intern had talked to her as though he suspected she might not want to spend a lot of time playing nurse. She was even more annoyed to acknowledge that he was right; she didn't have a lot of patience. Not for Fergus, not these days. She dragged in a chair from the den, set it just inside the door and dimmed the lights.

"It doesn't make any sense at all," she said again.

"You're right," Fergus said.

"Stop that. Stop agreeing with me."

"But what if I do?"

She looked over at him. The intern had shaved a circular area on the top of Fergus' skull in order to stitch up the wound. From this distance, he looked medieval, like the friar in the story of Robin Hood, except not so fat. He looked ridiculous.

"It's not helpful. I'm the one in the dark here. I'm not supposed to know what's going on. You are."

Fergus pointed at his head and shrugged his shoulders.

"NFG," he said.

"How convenient. Well, let me tell you something, then. The nurse at reception made me feel just a little stupid this afternoon."

"I'm sorry."

"Stupid and humiliated. Not only does she refuse to let me see you after your mysterious ordeal, but she calls the police over to ask me some questions. I have to show them identification. I have to give them names and addresses. I have to write my signature on a piece of paper, which they take and compare to the signatures on my VISA card and my driver's licence. They tell me there's been another woman claiming she's your wife and they need to be sure who they're dealing with."

"Whom," Fergus said.

"I beg your pardon?"

"It's whom," he said. "Whom they're dealing with. With whom, actually."

"Yeah? Well, I want to know the person *with whom* I'm dealing, Fergus. All right? Would that be okay? These people made me feel like a fool. They want to know if you're some kind of bigamist. Impossible, I say. You'd be surprised, they say. It happens all the time. And then they tell me she brought you in from a church. A cathedral, they say. They haven't got all the details yet, but there was something about a cross falling on you. Lots of blood, apparently. Those head wounds, they say. Very messy. Am I ringing a bell?"

The overhead incandescent, running at half the wattage it was used to, hummed like an obsessive mosquito. From her chair by the door, Annie watched as Fergus' eyes blinked rapidly several times. He seemed almost to look through her to something happening out in the hall, and the effect was so unnerving that she turned her head briefly to look.

"That was Caroline."

Annie said nothing.

"She worked on our house. The front steps? Remember?"

"Caroline the carpenter? With the little girl?"

"Yes."

Annie wasn't quite sure what Fergus was saying. Was he hallucinating? Was this part of the concussion?

"I guess I was out of the shop. Some dumb errand. You know me. I can stay in harness only so long. Just a short walk, some coffee. And I bumped into her. She was with her new boyfriend, I think she called him Nathan. He's a student. Wants to be an architect. They needed a hand with a project he was working on. Some kind of contract with the Catholics. He was building them a new cross for the church and it was a little heavy so I helped carry it."

"Why didn't you say?"

"You just reminded me. When you told me about the cross, all the blood. It came back. The doctor said this might happen."

"So, it fell?"

"Must have."

"Why would she say she was your wife?"

"The ambulance. Family only, I guess. I don't know. I think she was feeling a little guilty after asking me to help. She probably wanted to see I'd be okay."

"So she should."

"Hey, you know what a klutz I am. It was probably all my fault."

"I should phone her."

"What?"

"And thank her. Who knows? Maybe she saved your life."

"Let me do that."

"You lie down. I think a little sleep would be good for you now." Annie shut out the light and then went over to the bed. She pulled the covers up around Fergus' neck and took away one of his pillows.

"Twenty-five years and you're still an idiot."

"That's my job."

"No more errands. You stay put, okay? I'll check on you later."

"You bet."

Annie walked away from the bed and then turned.

"You don't really believe I'm having an affair, do you?" But Fergus' eyes were already closed.

Annie shut the door behind her and walked down the stairs to the front hall. It had been years, but all at once she wanted a cigarette. She wanted to stand and smoke and crack jokes like those teachers she'd met this morning. A couple of characters, those two. The one guy — Tony? — she could see he liked her. If he wasn't flirting, she was the Queen of England. Funny the way people didn't forget how. It wasn't as though natural selection was being well served at their age. Why the hell would Nature want a couple of middle-aged strangers to get it on? No doubt about it, evolution would be better off if some human attributes just atrophied and died. But they didn't. What was even funnier, Annie wouldn't have given those two a second look at sixteen. Yuck, she'd have said. Old perverts. Maybe Nature was kinder than Annie thought. Maybe it rewarded people for making it past youth by giving them a pair of eyes that changed with the years. After all, she didn't find Fergus ugly, did she? Goofy with that bald patch maybe, but not ugly.

She poured herself a glass of wine from the bottle in the fridge. The answering machine by the pantry cupboard was blinking, and Annie went over to check the messages. Doris sounded a little angry no one had called her back. "No worries," she said. "I'll close." One of the girls from the catered lunch was wondering when they'd be paid. And a message from Caroline the carpenter. It was for both of them. She was sorry about the accident. She called it a freak accident, and she hoped Fergus was okay. Maybe he could call when he was feeling better just to let her know how he was doing.

Annie played the messages again, remembering how religious Fergus used to be about checking their first answering machine. He'd walk straight to it whenever they returned from somewhere. Even if they'd only gone to the store, he'd run and look, and no matter how banal the call, he'd listen right through to the end. Perhaps that was the appeal of such devices, they made people feel important. *You have three messages.*

Annie wasn't surprised when she first saw them showing up in movies. Before long, every film she saw had a scene of the tape rewinding furiously and then a series of non-sequiturs separated by beeps. She remembered one where the wife listens to a message her husband left just before he was killed in some kind of gruesome accident, a plane probably. Or was it suicide? Oh, how everybody gushed over that scene. *So true*, her friend had said. *Just like life*. And then there were the ironies. The lover leaving a message, the husband discovering the awful truth. Hollywood had been using this stuff for years.

Annie debated calling Caroline. It would be good to know exactly what had happened. Their GP would want the details, and Fergus still seemed a bit foggy about the accident. What was her last name? Annie couldn't remember. There might be a receipt lying around from the time she'd worked on the stairs, but where to start looking now? Strange how she'd left a message and not her home number. Did she think they'd still have it after … what was it … a year? Two? She shouldn't forget to call Helios. Maybe after another glass of wine.

Annie moved to the living room, where she placed her glass on the coffee table and lay down on the couch. She remembered stupidly that it was Saturday tomorrow. For some reason, she'd thought the weekend had already come. Fergus would be no help. A gloom began to spread over her, the prospect of another day in the trenches with all its competing smells of basil and vinegar and Mop & Glow and countless pounds of used coffee grounds piling up in the garbage, the whine of exhaust fans, Doris' inevitable sour mood, that annoying chime each customer triggered every time the infra-red beam was broken. It was more than she could bear right now, and she closed her eyes against the looming sneer of morning.

Immediately, the sounds of the house began to settle around her. She heard the furnace kick in, and a few moments later the fan as it flooded the main floor with warm air. The fridge made a loud clunk at one point and was silent thereafter. She even heard the motion detector on the outside wall as the spotlight registered another passing cat.

Floorboards flexed, gravity tugged at the ceiling fixtures, window glass deflected a spring breeze. Annie relaxed into the cushions that held her. Automatically and unbeckoned, as sometimes happened when Annie allowed herself to drift, a cross-section of the house appeared in her mind, and she saw Fergus lying in the room above her and herself laid out on the couch. When Helios was living here, she'd put him in the picture, too. Everybody safe, tucked in. The image helped her sleep. Now, though, she couldn't help seeing Fergus' shaved skull, the line of stitches that ran across it. Something like that must have really hurt. She felt her own head, imagined a heavy weight striking it. She shuddered. There was some irony in all of this. After all, it was a cross that had wounded Fergus. He used to tell her how much he'd hated going to church with his parents, and except for a few weddings and funerals, he hadn't attended a service since leaving home. Maybe God was getting back at him. She thought of a petty old man nudging that cross with one of his big invisible fingers, sending it down on the back of Fergus' head. Probably does it all the time, she thought. Wasn't there a story about a medieval thief bludgeoning some rich Christian to death with the big silver crucifix he had stolen? Or was it a priest and a candlestick? Anyway, the old guy had a sense of humour. Still, she thought, a god might come in handy sometimes. Someone to talk to. She remembered watching all the teachers out on her client's deck, thinking themselves into a pleasant landscape, waiting for their spiritual guides. *Somewhere you feel comfortable,* the woman had said. *Secure.* A beach is what Annie would choose, one of those sandy stretches on Savary Island, rimmed with logs to lean against, the tide in, sun about an hour away from setting. There would be a blanket, a green plaid steamer blanket like the one her parents always kept in the back seat of their car. And a thermos of tea. She'd pour herself a cup and then she'd watch the ocean and wait. Annie could feel herself getting a little excited. It was the same way she felt in the days before taking a flight — incredulous that radical change could happen. Part of her never really believed the day would arrive, that there were such things as planes. It was a leap of faith she held off taking until the very last minute, a reluctance she attributed to her limited imagination. She and those teachers couldn't be more different, she decided. What had they thought they'd see? And what would a spiritual guide look like anyway? She was sure hers would be a man, if one ever showed itself. She'd never trust a woman. Certainly not a woman like her client this morning. There was something about her.

WHEN ANNIE OPENED her eyes, it was dark. She was surprised to see she had forgotten to draw the curtains, and now the streetlight shone into the room with its watery rays. It coloured the Japanese plum trees on the boulevard, too, their purple leaves now silver and shaking in the breeze from passing cars. Annie was cold but that wasn't why she had woken. In the kitchen, the answering machine was repeating the messages she had listened to earlier.

"What on earth …?" Her legs seemed unwilling to bend, frozen almost, as if to move them would be to break them. With effort, she sat up and then pulled herself to her feet. She found Fergus in his robe, standing next to the answering machine. He was laughing.

"Fergus?"

"Jesus! I'm sorry. I didn't mean to wake you. I saw you sleeping on the couch and came in here."

"Are you all right?"

"Probably not. My prostate's the size of a golf ball, and I'm peeing fifteen times a night. I look like someone who's been on the wrong end of a baseball bat."

"And that's funny?"

"It is, kind of. Don't you think so?"

Annie watched her husband. There were tears in his eyes, and he used the sleeve of his robe to wipe them away. "She didn't leave her number," Annie said.

Fergus walked over to the fridge and opened it. He pushed aside a few jars, bent to his knees to peer closer. "There was a bottle of wine in here yesterday."

"Open another one. You can top me up while you're at it."

Even as they left her lips, Annie could feel the impact of her words on Fergus, on his bones, his muscles. His whole frame slackened visibly. What effect permission — any permission — had on a person! Open another bottle of wine. Take a day off work. She remembered the cigarette she'd wanted so badly earlier. There were none in the house — hadn't been any for years — but Annie still had some pot upstairs. Now was a good time to light up, if there ever was one. Fergus looked shattered enough to accept anything right now. Is that what it took for him to loosen up? Collapse? She watched him rise and make his way to the liquor cabinet, saw him grope in the drawer for a corkscrew. For the first time, Annie seriously wondered about this marriage of hers. About all marriages, for that matter. Did people really know what they were agreeing to?

PART IV

Another Last Supper

[I]

One day stretched into two. Then into a week. And still Fergus refused to go to the deli. His head hurt, he told Annie. He looked funny. People would ask questions.

"Other people have medical plans," he said. "They get to take days off sick."

"We have a medical plan, too." Annie said. "We just don't have a spare Fergus. I'll do what I can in there. I wish you'd write more of this stuff down. One of the part-time people is going to have to give me a hand. This is going to cost us, Fergus. Do me a favour and get better, soon, okay?"

But Fergus didn't want to get better. He spent his days walking around the house in his robe, fiddling with loose towel racks and door-knobs, making them even looser, replacing light bulbs in rooms they rarely used, forcing strips of newspaper into gaps in the casement windows where the wind blew in. He made himself cup after cup of coffee, dripping the brew directly into a stainless-steel travel mug that he carried with him from kitchen to living room to bedroom, pausing along the way to put it down, only to walk off and spend the next fifteen minutes retracing his steps to find on which shelf, dresser, newel post or window ledge he had left it. One day Annie brought the mug to him from where she'd found it in the cupboard under the bathroom sink. Fergus had started out examining the leaky trap but had been distracted by the cupboard's contents: first-aid kits they'd never opened, bulk packs of rubber gloves, an assortment of prescription bottles, some half-full, that Fergus couldn't remember buying.

"Forget this?" she'd said, handing him the mug.

"You take Xanax?"

The hair around Fergus' cut was growing back, stubbly red whiskers mixed now — he was absolutely certain — with more grey than he'd had before the accident. He kept running his hand over the area, avoiding the stitches, which were due to come out in another week. He hadn't showered since the Friday at Emergency, only bathed, and the dull sheen of a scalp full of grease made Fergus start slightly whenever he looked in the mirror. It was the combination of robe, stitches, and limp, waxy hair that compelled him to look closer, a portrait that matched almost perfectly the description he'd developed for himself should he ever be committed for psychiatric problems. Fergus wasn't drawn so much to the possibility of going insane, as he was to looking insane, or indigent, or feeble. He'd always believed he had it in him.

"You never phoned to thank Caroline," Annie said after work on the Thursday following the accident.

"How do you know?"

"Because I did it for you. She's got an apartment above a store somewhere near the Gorge. The place looks like a crackhouse."

"You went over there? You went to Caroline's place?"

"I thought it would be a little more personal than phoning. And you weren't about to do anything."

"I'd have gotten round to it eventually."

"But I knew you wouldn't. You're funny that way. Her last name's Arnaud, just so you know. She was very nice about the whole thing. Told me it was her fault, too, but even over the phone I could tell she was too smart to let an accident like that happen. She'd need your help."

"You're a mean person. Did you know that?"

"I'm also all you've got, looking the way you do. Cheer up. I bought us some flowers from that store she lives above. They actually have a great selection. Even some Bird of Paradise and for once the salal didn't look like it had been sitting there a month. Cheap, too. I couldn't believe it."

Annie dragged out two green vases from under the kitchen sink and started to clip and arrange her purchases into bouquets.

Fergus looked on in disbelief. Was this really happening? What did she mean, "looking the way you do"? And him a sick man! He adjusted the collar on his robe and smoothed the terrycloth sleeves. He was imagining a troupe of people just like him, true friends all, standing around an oil drum, warming their hands over a fire. They'd never make fun of him. He'd tell them what Annie used to say, and they'd be horrified, shake their heads and pat him on the back.

"Anyway, I invited her to dinner." Annie was rummaging through one of the kitchen cupboards for a tin of tomatoes.

Fergus immediately found a chair and sat down. His legs had given out. He'd been doing so well, too. Almost managing to put recent events behind him. The hospital. The shock of the answering machine last Friday. The way his life had teetered for a while there, a bowling pin about to go down. This week had been blessedly quiet in comparison. Sleeping late. A little reading. A bit of a breather. Only this morning he'd been congratulating himself for pulling through, relieved just to be walking.

"Tonight?" His voice was barely a whisper.

Annie didn't seem to hear him. There was a muffled grunt, and for a second Fergus could have sworn a dog was in the room. He turned to see half of Annie disappearing into the recesses of the cupboard in her search, swallowed amid the sounds of bread tins banging against one another, the distressed complaints of cellophane packages threatening to burst. The kitchen cabinets were deep and capacious; tins and dry goods could hide for years, well beyond their expiry dates. Fergus watched as Annie extracted herself, triumphant, tin in hand.

"Did you say something?"

"You mentioned dinner."

"Yes. She wants to get a sitter. I tried telling her we still had a few toys kicking around. There's the VCR, too, if she doesn't mind her daughter watching a movie. But she said she'd relax more if she was on her own. So I suggested a week this Sunday. Almost the solstice."

"Just the three of us."

"I asked her to bring her boyfriend. You said his name was Nathan. She promised she'd ask, but I got the impression things weren't going that well between them. It must be tough when you're young like that and you've got a kid. Most men that age don't want baggage. Men! What am I saying? Boys."

"What makes you think she's so young?"

"You talked to her, Fergus. Remember?"

FERGUS' HEAD WAS hurting again, a pulsing kind of pain that made him think of small flowers blooming, one after another. He told Annie he was going to lie down upstairs. She shouldn't make dinner on his account, he said, and he left the kitchen in a hurry, bumping his shoulder on the fridge as he walked by it. At the top of the stairs, he stopped and turned and sat down on the first step. He rubbed his shoulder, which he was surprised to discover had actually taken quite a blow. Down in the kitchen, Annie was battling with the electric can opener, stopping it and starting it again and again. He could hear her talking to it, berating it. Without the proper touch — Annie did not have this with any machine — the gadget would grind away at a single spot on the tin for hours. She expected so much of everything. The deli, this house, their troubled cars. It was as though she believed the whole world had signed a contract with her to operate as advertised without interruption for the duration of her life. Even Fergus. Nobody knew better than he did how easy it was to disappoint her. Temptingly easy. Helios had made a game of it for a while. Right from the first day of school, he seemed determined not to be a typical first child. They had enrolled him in enrichment programs after teachers revealed his scores on school-wide aptitude tests, but he refused to do the work. His teacher said he lacked motivation.

"Your son's too smart for his own good," he said. "Once he sees the point of an exercise, he loses interest. It's like he's read the last chapter of a book first and sees no need to finish the rest."

Annie had always done well at school. She was willing to accept Helios might have a learning disability or difficulty understanding some of the material, but she couldn't get her head around simple boredom. She dragged him to parent/teacher interviews to explain himself, pushed him into a Waldorf school for a few months and got rid of their television. The last year of high school he'd finished on correspondence, and even then he graduated with straight C's. Living at home for another five years was just one more way to annoy her.

Fergus stood up and walked into the bedroom. When he turned on the light, he remembered what he'd been doing before Annie had come home. The bedspread was covered with photographs that he'd been placing into the sleeves of five new albums Annie had bought the day before.

"As long as you're home, you might as well make yourself useful."

There were hundreds of photos going back years, a cardboard box full of them that he and Annie had never got round to sorting. They'd shoot a roll, develop it, sit around the kitchen table looking at it for a few moments, and then throw the stack of pictures like losing lottery tickets into the box. Sometimes they'd keep a few out to send to friends, but that was rare, and more often than not, those few they'd chosen would hang around in the front hall for a few days until somebody threw them into the box just to get rid of them.

Now he had them spread out across the bed, rectangles of snapshot colour mixed with the odd black and white, overlapping to form triangles and nameless polygons in a jumbled, random mass that resembled the pattern of a patch-work quilt. Originally he had set out to organize them all by year or, failing that, by event. But the task had defeated him almost from the start, overwhelmed him, just the sight of all their earlier selves, so much clearer than he remembered them, beaming in their ignorance of the future, so caught up in a present that was now irretrievably over. It seemed to him he had read a poem about just this very feeling, about this cloying and inescapably sad yearning for what he and Annie once were. An English poet probably, someone like Hardy, only bleaker. What was his name? He'd look for him later, pull out some of his old texts from university. How stupid he'd been back then, Fergus thought. He hadn't understood a word, despite the dozens of essays he'd written. How stupid to teach poetry to the young in the first place. So caught up in themselves, their own little dramas. He didn't know which was worse, the students who studied poetry or those who wrote it. There used to be readings at lunch in the Student Union Building. Annie had taken him a few times when they first started going out, but the poets were always boring. At least those who studied it might actually remember a line or two over the years, but those who wrote it never read anything but their own narcissistic dribblings.

He looked back down at the mess in front of him. This was the obstacle that lay between him and sleep. One album sat half-complete on the bedside table. Four more to go. Annie would object the moment she saw what he had done, but there was nothing she could do about it. In desperation, Fergus had settled on a simple system: he would allot whole albums to each member of the family. One of Annie, one of Helios, and another of himself. More as they were needed. He would base his decision on whoever was most prominent in the photograph. He'd probably need a fourth category for pictures that featured none of them, landscapes, friends, the sort of useless pictures everybody takes just because they've got a camera in their hands, as though Ansel Adams or Diane Arbus were ordinary people who turned into artists the moment they had the money to buy a thirty-five-millimeter camera. Maybe he could just throw those pictures out. In thirty years, nobody was going to be able to tell one sunset from another, anyway. He'd come across a whole roll somebody'd taken of a large cedar stump that had washed up on the sand. From every conceivable angle, too. He wanted to blame Annie, but he knew his own crude artistic eye too well. There must have been a scene when these came back from the pharmacy. He tossed the whole lot into the wastebasket beside his dresser. Delete, he said to himself and pressed an imaginary button on the bedstead.

Fergus couldn't bear to put the rest of the photos away. He told himself all he needed was a short nap, and then he'd get up refreshed, ready to tackle the job in a better frame of mind. The covers were loose from the morning — he'd thrown them back when he heard Annie leave for the deli, but hadn't bothered to make the bed — and he slipped between the sheets, trying not to disturb anything. A few pictures fell to the floor. Most stayed where they were. Fergus relaxed into the mattress and pillow. He imagined he could feel the added weight, as though an extra blanket were covering him, a blanket of fixer and developer and Kodak paper on which was printed the thin film of his entire married life.

He lay on his back, motionless, looking up at the ceiling. *What seems to be the problem?* he asked himself. The bones of the house creaked around him like a counselor shifting his weight in a chair, pad in hand, waiting for an answer. Something below his bedroom window tipped the lid of their garbage can and sent it crashing onto the cement path.

"Well, doctor," Fergus said, "I've got myself in a bit of a jam."

"Define your terms, please."

"Well, okay. I mean, I'm not sure. You know how you go through life thinking you're one kind of person?"

"Go on."

"Outgoing, for example? Or neat? You've always seen yourself as a neat person. It's something you've taken pride in. At least I'm neat, you tell yourself."

"Yes."

"Well, what if you find out you're not the neat person you thought you were? What if you find out you're the complete opposite? That's my problem, you see. I'm not quite the person I thought I was."

"That's not necessarily a bad thing."

"No?"

"Nobody's the person they think they are."

"The jam is I wouldn't like anyone else to know it. They would be so disappointed in me. I'd feel like I let them down."

"You don't want to be caught by Annie."

"Especially Annie."

"How about Helios?"

"Him, too."

"What do you think would happen?"

"I'd end up living by myself in some low-rent district eating out of a frying pan and scrounging for empties in the garbage cans outside Wal-Mart."

"Would that be so awful?"

"I like it where I am."

"That's too bad because from the look of things you won't be here much longer."

Fergus shuddered at this last exchange. He knew that the significance of most things didn't hit him until the final moment. Months before a flight, the idea of buying a plane ticket always struck Fergus as an acceptable idea, one of Annie's less wearing tricks to drag him out of his stuffy routines. She pinned up brochures of their destination. They read about the place in bed. But the night before leaving, he barely closed his eyes. Everything about the house seemed dear. Coffee in the morning by the kitchen window took on the glow of a religious ritual. He mourned every familiar breath he would miss while he was gone. What had he been thinking?

FERGUS COULD SMELL onions frying, and the unmistakable aroma of freshly minced garlic. He wanted to turn on his side, but he knew he'd send the layer of photographs flying. There was no sleeping now. Hunger tugged at him to get up and go downstairs. And he had to pee again. The selenium supplements didn't seem to be working, just as Fergus had feared they wouldn't. His doctor had told him to try them for a while.

"Give them a chance. You might get lucky."

For people with bad luck, there were other options. The doctor could bake the prostate with microwaves and burn off some of that extra tissue. Or he could flood it with hot water and kill a few million cells without the side effects of radiation. Thermotherapy, he called it. And there was always surgery. Just prune it back a bit.

"You don't want to wait too long on this, Fergus. Think of someone stepping on a garden hose. That's what's happening to you. Pretty soon you won't be able to water a dandelion."

At least he hadn't given Fergus his little lecture on impotence again. The man was obsessed with the topic. Fergus was convinced if he'd come in with a cold or a broken arm his doctor would have found some connection to sex. He reminded Fergus of a customer who came into the deli sometimes, a large man who took very small steps, mincing steps that had made Fergus think the man was gay until he noticed his torso. It went on forever, unnaturally long like a birth defect, and when it finally ended, the legs that remained were as short as a boy's. Each time he came to the deli he told a new joke, always something sexual. His delivery was dreadful, a halting, mistake-ridden recitation that sabotaged any potential for humour. Fergus listened to the jokes, even laughed at them, but the experience drained him and he didn't look forward to it. Sometimes he repeated the jokes to Caroline or Annie. He thought he might do a better job, that all the joke needed was a little more life to become effective. He remembered the last one he told to Annie. They were in the car on the way to the deli.

"A woman was getting married for the fourth time," he said, "and she wanted a white wedding dress."

"Fergus, you know I don't like these."

"Just listen. She wants a white dress, but the sales clerk tells her she can't have one because she's been married three times before."

"How stupid."

"And the woman tells her it's okay. She's still a virgin, she says, but the clerk doesn't believe her. How is that possible? The woman tells the clerk her first husband was a psychiatrist, and all he did was talk about it. Her second husband was even worse. He was a gynecologist, and he just looked at it. Her third husband, though, he was a lot better. She really misses him a lot."

"What did he do?"

"He was a stamp collector."

There was a moment while they drove in silence.

"Why is that so funny?"

"He's a stamp collector, for Christ's sake! Think about it. The first one talks, the second one looks. It's obvious."

"He collects it?"

"Jesus, you're hopeless. You know that?"

"I just don't see the humour."

"What do you do with stamps? You lick them, that's what."

"Yes. But stamp collectors don't lick their stamps. They hang them on those little hinge things and put them in albums for people to look at. I know because I used to do it."

Fergus could see it was useless to argue with her, and they had driven the rest of the way to the deli without speaking.

BY NOW, MOST of the photographs had worked their way to the edge of the bed where they had fallen to the floor. Fergus threw back the quilt and stood up as the remaining few fluttered around him. He walked over to the bedroom door and opened it, inhaling deeply the aroma of whatever Annie was cooking.

"Hey," he shouted down the stairs. "Did you make enough for me?"

[11]

Fergus tears the article about the aerial gymnast from the paper, folds it neatly and slips it into a corner of his wallet. He takes the rest of the newspaper and stuffs it into his rucksack. The now empty bottle of pop is worth two cents and Fergus walks back into the store for the deposit. The sun is still bright, another couple of hours of light remain, and the air is warm. Helmcken Road crosses the highway not far from here, Fergus remembers. Then there's a school and another intersection. He's pleased with his plan. Over the phone at his grandmother's, he'll describe his day to his parents and ask his mother to let him spend the night.

FOR THE LAST SEVEN YEARS, Fergus' grandmother has lived alone in the house she and her husband bought in 1926, one of the first stucco homes built in Victoria, a three-bedroom English cottage on the city's outskirts in a tired and decaying municipality called View Royal. Like its neighbour Esquimalt, View Royal has pockets of houses that were once some of the most beautiful in the city, but that have, over the years, fallen out of favour because of their distance from Victoria's centre and because they lack the appeal of the modern subdivisions that are currently laying waste to the fertile farmland of Gordon Head around the recently established University of Victoria. View Royal's depressed real estate market has meant it has become a place for people on fixed incomes who gladly drive a few extra miles in exchange for lower taxes. They will tell anybody who asks them that their view of Esquimalt Harbour is better than anything Dallas Road has to offer. Where else can a person walk a half-mile to an Indian Reservation and eat the finest smoked salmon on the coast and watch this year's crop of young braves race their war canoes?

Fergus' grandmother's house sits on a hill in the middle of a long narrow lot, one end of which abuts what was once the island highway while the other overlooks a deep cut in the rock where rail cars pass on their way north and south. A gravel driveway follows the eastern property line and runs through a stand of fir that was overlooked during the flurry of logging in the last half of the nineteenth century, a time when loggers turned up their noses at schoolmarms and trees whose roots swelled more than they liked. The shade these survivors cast always leaves Fergus with the impression he has been visiting a park, especially in the summer when the house is ringed by hollyhocks and sweet peas and climbing roses, and the carefully terraced garden beds are full of chard and kale and three different kinds of lettuce. At the foot of the driveway and nailed to the same post that supports the mailbox is a wooden sign painted turquoise and bearing the words Wake Si Ah. The phrase means "journey's end." It is one of several phrases Fergus' grandfather learned from the Chinook-English dictionary he bought to converse with his Songhees neighbours, and it is one that, for him, was ultimately true. He died of a stroke in his bed in 1957 while Fergus' grandmother was boiling the water for their Saturday morning tea.

Fergus' grandmother, whose name is Gladys, knows she won't be able to stay in the house much longer. The wood-burning furnace uses nearly six cords of mill-ends a year, and even though she has managed to retain the Chinese houseboy whose services she first engaged over thirty years ago, he comes less frequently than he used to. The task of feeding the furnace's maw is nearly beyond her. A local mechanic maintains her '49 Austin out of a love for British cars, and at seventy-five, she is still an alert and capable driver. But traffic is faster than it was ten years ago. Many of the streets have changed. She gets confused on Fort Street now that it is one-way, and more than once she has driven against the oncoming cars for almost a whole block before realizing her mistake.

It's only a matter of time before a policeman takes her licence away.

Today, she's feeling guilty. It is Saturday of the long weekend, but still she has made no arrangements to attend Easter service at the cathedral tomorrow. It's been decades since she last missed going — was it during the war? — and she knows she should really make the effort. Lately, though, her will has been lacking. Many of the people she would have asked to go with her are dead, and she has no desire to impose on her son's one day off. If her daughter were in town, Gladys wouldn't hesitate, but she isn't and hasn't been for years.

Of greater interest to her right now is the flyer she knows is waiting for her in the mailbox. The Safeway that opened a year ago on Esquimalt Road has been delivering coupons and notices of sales for several months now, and Gladys is always astonished at the bargains. Tinned beef for twenty-nine cents last week. Canned corn nineteen cents. She's been wanting a box of Ritz crackers and some salmon paste, but these items are rarely discounted and she knows it. The thrill of lifting the lid on the mailbox is still something she looks forward to, though, and today it pulls her from the afternoon sun, the warmth its early spring rays generate through the panes of her kitchen window, and prods her to the front hall. She slips on a cardigan and heads out the front door.

The old island highway may be a secondary artery now, but Gladys can still hear lots of traffic as she walks down the driveway. Over the years, she has become fond of the noise, the way a person becomes fond of the sound of a river or a waterfall. And there are the trains, too. In a few hours the weekender will be coming into town, blowing its whistle at every crossing, not so many more people to warn now than when they first moved out here. Once she might have counted each blast of the horn, each concerned reminder, thinking about the train's progress as it made its way alongside Admirals Road past the naval base and on into town. She might have turned from what she was doing and spoken to her husband, commented on how late it was running tonight, or early, but not anymore. It's enough for her to know the rolling stock is still rolling, that she is still walking to the mailbox after more than thirty years — with a cane now, but still walking. On her right, among the ferns and grasses under the trees, snowdrops have appeared by the hundreds. Soon they'll be joined by Easter lilies and trilliums, and, later, Indian paintbrush. She supposes there are people who get to this point in life and worry every year whether this might be the last time they'll see these flowers, smell these blossoms, but not Gladys. Her religious convictions aren't strong enough to convince that another world is waiting for her, and if she wanted anything from God, it would be to stay exactly where she is; but her common sense tells her whatever's waiting in the wings for her is no different from what is waiting for everybody, and she takes some comfort from this truth. *Let's get on with it*, she finds herself thinking more and more these days.

Gladys' driveway exits onto the old highway at one of the busiest and most dangerous points in its entire length, about a hundred yards past the trestle at the bottom of Four Mile Hill. The hill itself is steep and blind at the bottom because a trestle obscures oncoming traffic and because there is a bend in the road at just that point. Gladys has been awakened on more than one evening by the sound of cars colliding, has waited in the dark for the inevitable approach of the ambulance, sometimes as long as half an hour. And walking down the next morning for the paper, she has sometimes found a hubcap, a piece of a tail lens along the shoulder of the road, and sometimes, too, a patch of gravel, stained dark with oil or gas or blood.

This afternoon, there are no signs of lives cut short, no fresh grief at the highway's edge, only the traffic, steady and purposeful and growing. She has heard nothing about an earthquake in Alaska, hasn't even turned on the radio for days and won't bother herself with the television her son bought for her last Christmas. She doesn't know about the sudden disappearance of the town of Valdez or the miraculous escape of the S.S. *Chena*, or that less than twelve hours ago in Beverly Beach, Oregon, a mother and a father lost all four of their children when a wave swept over their tent as they slept, four children who were five until six months ago when their brother died in a house fire. Gladys has no idea of the wreckage in Crescent City, California, or of the rearranged streets and sidewalks of Anchorage. Other than the ache she still feels at the absence of a man she grew to love only in the last years of his life, and the question surrounding her own departure from this world, she has little else on her mind. If she's bothered by anything, it's by the knowledge that tomorrow her son Bill will come and take her for a drive, out to Metchosin for tea perhaps, but more likely somewhere farther, a beach where he can find an excuse to pull out a bottle of Three Crown and pretend the day is an occasion. He will bring her grandson Fergus and the boy's unhappy mother, who smokes night and day and hasn't a civil word for anybody. Gladys' son will talk about the deli, the old customers who still come seven years later to ask after her, about how she's doing alone. He will talk about the suppliers and how it's harder now than ever to stay ahead, never saying exactly that he hates the place, that he wishes the earth would open and swallow every brick that holds the building together, swallow too his promise to keep the business going, the one he made a decade after his return from overseas and the war, another Goodlake with a legend to build, to pass on at more dinner tables to more children who will become sick of hearing it. It will be enough to watch him have a second drink and a third, to hear the bitterness rise in his throat, the sarcastic observations he will begin to make, the jokes he will tell that aren't jokes but just his way of letting everyone know he isn't happy, as if they didn't know that already.

Gladys lets out the long breath she didn't know she'd been holding and reaches into the mailbox. She pulls out the flyer, its pages busy with numbers and exclamation marks and pictures of tins and cuts of meat, and slips it under her arm to read later with her tea. Her back to the road, she begins her return journey up the driveway, conscious of the cars passing behind her and how she must look to the people in them, even in the brief snapshot of their passing, an old woman with a cane, bundled up in a cardigan and a scarf despite this bright spring day, as though she is cooling down slowly, from the inside out, like the furnace she has fed all winter, down to its last few pieces of fuel.

Slow as she is, it's only a few minutes before Gladys has moved back into the shade of the fir trees and has become once again invisible. She feels a little silly to have pulled herself all this way for a scrap of paper, but she's happy to have it, too, and is looking forward to the warmth of her kitchen and the cup of tea she will make when she gets there. She doesn't know she has finished her errand a little too soon, that if she'd only lingered a while longer at the gate, sat for just a minute on the bench her husband had set in concrete there and paused to look at the world going by, she might have seen something extraordinary. She might have seen her own grandson Fergus. But Gladys doesn't linger, and is almost halfway to the house when Fergus begins his descent from the top of Four Mile Hill. He is already moving fast toward her, ignorant of the history of the road he is traveling on. Fergus is simply concentrating on one of the steepest hills he has ever biked down, thrilled by the speed he is accumulating, but a little worried, too. He is moving almost as fast as the traffic that is coming up behind him, and he applies his brakes to reduce his anxiety as well as his rate of acceleration. The bicycle shudders each time he squeezes. The wire that controls his rear brake strains to keep the small blocks of rubber against the wheel. The long journey is taking its toll on the working parts of the bicycle, only a cheap bicycle to begin with, a third-hand veteran Fergus' father had bought for him at Palmer's Stove Store on Johnson Street as part of a deal for an oil space-heater he wanted for the garage. Nothing has ever been replaced on it, certainly not the rusting brake cables, and Fergus doesn't know enough about mechanics to recognize a worn cable when he sees one. Fergus is approaching the trestle at the bottom of the hill, a black iron overpass that, because of the shadow it casts at this time of day, looks like the mouth of a tunnel into which the road enters and disappears. He's swallowed in an instant, and in the second it takes for his eyes to adjust from bright sunlight to shade, he barely manages to see the road curve to his right or the scallop of gravel shoulder that signals the start of his grandmother's driveway. The maneuver is a tense one, but he leaves the pavement without incident and dismounts, pleased with himself to arrive at this house under his own steam, as though he were actually a real person in control of his own life, deciding to pay a visit to his grandmother because the idea had come to him on a whim and not because of tradition or his parents' nagging guilt. He looks up the long drive. He is giddy at the thought of his accomplishment. He feels that something has changed. Is it possible these trees are different? Has he seen them before? Is that his grandmother walking up the steps to her house? *Just me*, he'll say. *It's just me.*

AN HOUR LATER, Fergus' grandmother pours a second cup of tea for him. On the table are a plate of Peek Frean biscuits and the last half of a lemon loaf.

"It's a shame," she tells him.

"Next year will be better. He'll be in high school."

"Still. Your father should know."

Fergus reaches for another cookie. He's considering what will happen if his grandmother tells his parents about the bully. They may resent him for confiding in her. Or they may not care. His grandmother thinks he has come to her house because he needs to talk to someone about the trouble he is having. He has said nothing about the earthquake, about how he wanted the surface of the earth wiped clean, about his disappointment when it wasn't. He feels he has been unkind relegating her to the ravaging floodwaters along with his parents, all the students at his school. Perhaps she is the one person he would rather didn't die.

"Maybe we'll talk to him about it tomorrow. When you come for lunch. I could tell him if you want."

"Maybe."

"Would you like me to tell him? I could, you know. He'll listen to me."

"Okay." Fergus knows she wants to be helpful, and he agrees because he can see she wants him to. She is the only ally he has. *Your mother.* That's what he hears his mother say to his father. *We have to see your mother*, she tells Fergus' father, as though she fears the prospect of a visit.

This woman, his grandmother, has some kind of power to shield him, even just a little bit, and he will try to take advantage of it.

His tea finished, the cookies gone, Fergus reconsiders staying overnight. Something has collapsed inside him — his dream of escape — and it is a familiar feeling. He is beginning to understand that much of the world looks good from a distance, but that under scrutiny the appearance of goodness disappears. To pass an evening under the same roof as this woman is almost inconceivable now, even frightening. Instead, Fergus tells his grandmother he would like her to phone his parents after he leaves. Could she tell them about his visit, about why he's not at home? Would she do that for him? he asks. She agrees. He walks with her out the front door and feels her look on as he places two wrapped slices of lemon loaf into the box at the back of his bike. He lets her kiss him on the cheek and listens as she tells him to be careful as he prepares to ride down the driveway.

"Shouldn't you walk it?"

Fergus shakes his head and pushes off.

As he gathers speed, Fergus applies pressure to his brakes. He is well over halfway down the driveway when he hears a slight snap as the brake line gives way. He is moving too fast to think, too fast to ease the bike towards somewhere safe. He crosses the first lane just as a car passes and he moves into the westbound lane, which is completely empty of cars. Fergus knows he can still manage a controlled stop. If he pumps his front brake a little and straightens his handle bars, gravity will do the rest, but in the middle of his efforts to stay upright and keep the bike pointed into the opposite shoulder, he hazards a look to his right, a look that costs him his balance and sends him across a swath of long grass and into a chain-link fence, the posts of which are anchored in cement so firmly that when Fergus' head strikes one of them, it hardly moves at all.

At the moment of impact, when her grandson loses consciousness, Fergus' grandmother has turned onto the flagstone path that leads to the rear of her house. Already, she has forgotten to phone Fergus' parents. She pauses to look at the profusion of daffodils and, more recently, tulips that have come into bloom just in the last few days. Some of the flowers in town have already finished, but under the canopy of fir and cedar that surrounds Gladys' property, spring happens later than it does in the rest of Victoria. Or, as Gladys likes to think, it happens again.

[III]

More than a week ago, the picket captains had outlined the duties for each shift: sign in to qualify for strike pay. Keep no more than a three-foot gap between pickets. Stay moving. Courts didn't recognize blockades. This was not a protest. This was not a political demonstration. Postal workers were withdrawing services legitimately and ensuring their work wasn't performed by outsiders. Do not engage in violent acts. Speak to the press at every opportunity.

Helios and Jayne had signed up for their usual night shift, so there'd be no need to alter their sleeping habits. They had been hoping the strike wouldn't last long, but eight days later, things didn't look good. Since they were part-time employees, tonight was only their third night of picket duty, and they still felt new. The main entrance and exit of the sortation centre provided a natural bottleneck for the picketers. A group from the previous shift was trickling back and forth across the two-lane driveway, their heads down. To Helios, they looked like people who had lost something very small — the screw to a hinge from a set of eyeglasses, perhaps — and were patiently and methodically scouring the ground for it. He had grown up in a family that had little use for unions. Organized workers asked for unrealistic wages and benefits, his grandfather always said. They were hard to fire. Security made them lazy and their work shoddy. Everybody wants to retire, he said, but nobody wants to put in the time. Everybody wants to go to heaven, but nobody wants to die. Helios had soaked up the small-business credo from the age of ten, when the job of running the deli had passed to his father and mother, and he'd heard nothing but complaints about the quality of hired help ever since. They stole. They phoned in sick when they wanted to go to the beach. They ate too much. They were rude to the customers. They dressed inappropriately. They smelled.

Half-Sack was walking the line of strikers who had come to replace the afternoon shift, handing out a foam-board sign and a piece of string to each one.

"No rain in the forecast," he was saying, "but we suit up for them all, don't we?"

The signs had the number of their union local and a demand, which varied from sign to sign. Helios' read "On Strike for a Fair Contract." He looped the string through a couple of holes and put it over his head. Jayne pulled out a camera and took a picture.

"Look dissatisfied," she told him. Her sign read "Fair Work for a Fair Wage."

They started walking, Jayne in front, but after a few minutes she fell back beside Helios. One of the picketers pulled out a Discman and tuned himself out. Then another did the same thing.

"Wish I'd thought of that," Helios said.

"You're not leaving me here alone," Jayne said.

Street lamps along Glanford Avenue kept the procession bathed in light. Few cars passed. Around three, somebody in a Datsun four-wheel drive with over-size tires threw a beer bottle at the picket line. It ricocheted off a light pole and shattered against a rock. The same truck came by a few minutes later, the driver's window open and a hand extended with the middle finger raised.

"That's the third time he's been by this week," Half-Sack said.

Sometimes the curtains in the home across the road shifted slightly, as though someone was peeking out at them. The air was buoyant and carried a hint of summer mornings to come. As he walked, Helios wondered how anyone could be bothered to go to all this effort over a few clauses and some contentious contract language. Jayne objected.

"This is part of our job. It's not enough to earn a wage. We have to maintain the standards."

They'd been watching a movie the other night, a Japanese film Jayne liked. *The Seven Samurai*. Helios was disappointed with it. He didn't like the way the villagers turned their backs on the men who had saved their town.

"I'd have let them die," he said when it ended. "What a bunch of ingrates."

"Those samurai needed a union," Jayne had said.

Now, he was thinking about the film again. He saw the townspeople as small businessmen like his father, worried about profits and competition. They couldn't see past their own interests. The world needed a few visionaries to keep everybody focused on what mattered. Maybe that's what had been bothering him lately. There wasn't enough vision in his life.

"So, what kind of songs would you write," he asked Jayne, "if you wrote songs?"

"There was a songwriter in the sixties called Phil Ochs. I'd write his kind of songs."

"Sing me one."

So she sang him the "Draft Dodger Rag," every verse, and repeated the chorus each time. Her voice had a slight tremolo, and her pitch was flawless. Helios was impressed.

"Can you believe they've been on Castro's case all this time?" she said when she was finished.

"Who was Senator Dodd?"

THE NIGHT TOOK a long time to pass, but Helios found it no worse than a night at the hotel. A little better, even. He watched milk trucks pass on their routes and paperboys bicycle down the road, their carriers full. The ground he and the others were standing on had once been a farm, and the whole area around the postal centre was a kind of no-man's land between the suburbs and the country. Helios knew which side was going to win. The city needed a place for its warehouses, its discount box stores and bulk retail outlets. An "industrial park," the sign off the highway called it. Jane had pointed it out to Helios as yet another oxymoron. It hadn't occurred to him that such a place was good or bad. A person was born into his time and that's what he had to deal with. Basement suites. Part-time jobs. Bad music. He looked at Jayne walking along just ahead of him. The sky was getting light over her shoulder.

"You coming to dinner?" he asked.

"With your parents?"

"My mother was asking. It's the dinner to thank the woman who brought my father to the hospital. She said it's the least she can do."

"She's right about that. Sure, why not?"

At about six A.M., a couple of the management staff drove in through the picket line. A few of the picketers parted the line to let them in, and the driver paused for a minute to ask how things were going. Helios listened in. Their voices sounded strained, as though the civilities were a little less sincere than the ones they had exchanged a week ago; there was clearly not much love lost between those out of work and those working twice as hard as they used to. *It wouldn't take much,* Helios thought. *What if one day they didn't let the car through? What if the driver decided not to use his brakes?* Helios could see somebody taking it upon himself to put a baseball bat through the car's windshield. He could see himself being that person.

Not today, though. The shift ended without incident. Jayne and Helios fired up the truck and headed out for breakfast. Over the week of strike duty, Jayne had been adding to Helios' wardrobe with a few purchases from Value Village. She'd found a pair of cowboy boots in good shape, the stitching sound and the heels almost new. He'd liked them from the moment he put them on. They were the first things he reached for out of bed in the morning, and the last to come off before he went to sleep, those and the boot cut jeans she'd picked up cheap. Now, as they drove into town, she pulled a Mexican cowboy hat from the back seat and placed it on his head.

"Damn! I could almost like you for the way you look."

Helios twisted the rearview and inspected the addition. "My mother dressed me up like this for Hallowe'en once."

"All you need now is a good pair of sunglasses."

"And some sun."

SOMETIMES IT WAS HARD to sleep the day away. On a few occasions, Helios had come away from a shift lit up like a light bulb, his brain buzzing and unwilling to turn off. He'd allowed the sun to tempt him into staying up, thought maybe he could pull it off. In the end, it never worked and he crashed worse than ever. Now he took a pill whenever he felt like that. Jayne wasn't pleased when she found out, but soon she was taking them too. Today they slept a full eight hours.

They pulled up in front of Helios' parents' house about ten minutes late. Helios was heading for the front steps when Jayne said she wanted to spend a few minutes walking around the front yard first. She told him she needed to get the lay of the land. The lawn was freshly cut and some-body'd been at the beds recently, too. She plucked off one of the smaller rhododendron blossoms and tucked it behind one ear. She ran her hand along the box hedge.

"What was it like?"

"What was what like?"

"Living here. Growing up in this house. I can't picture you in it, for some reason. There isn't a whole lot of your personality coming through here. You don't seem to belong."

"It's just a house."

They walked up the steps.

"You say she built these?"

Helios used his key to open the door. He could hear voices coming from the kitchen, the slam of the oven door. His mother had put flowers in the hall. A candle was burning in the nook that had once held the house's original Bakelite wall phone. There was a new painting hanging to the right of the door. It was a different house every time he walked in.

Jayne was removing her shoes.

"Don't bother."

"Show me around?"

Helios shrugged. He took her upstairs, walked her through the bedrooms. He opened the wood sash window of his old room and showed her how he used to get from the porch roof to the main gable, and from there to the very top of the house.

"You can see the ocean," he told her.

"Let's go." Jayne had one leg already out the window.

They looked over the neighborhood, the neat rectangles of backyards with their fruit trees and swing sets and vegetable plots. Jayne pointed out a cat on a fence watching another cat as it walked by underneath. Some people were already convinced it was summer; their barbecues were sending smoke into the evening air along with the smells of seared chicken and beef. Children bicycled up the street and groups of strollers walked by. None of them thought to look up.

Jayne said, "I feel like god."

"Is this the longest day?" Helios asked.

"It feels like it."

Just below them, the door to the deck opened and closed. Helios' mother came into view, followed by Caroline. They carried glasses of wine. Helios' mother was pointing at something. It was difficult to hear what they were saying. After a minute, they sat down in a couple of deck chairs Helios' mother had pulled together. The two women leaned into each other and laughed about something, and pulled back to clink their glasses. Then, simultaneously, they both lowered their heads and shook them as though they couldn't believe what they'd just said. Helios took a penny from his pocket and tossed it onto the floor of the deck beside them. For a moment the appearance of the coin baffled them. They looked behind them. They got up and looked over the railings into the yard below. Helios whistled, a leering pair of notes that slid up the scale and down again. His mother looked up to the roof.

"I *thought* that was your truck out front."

THEY SAT AROUND the living room before dinner. A bottle of red breathed on the coffee table beside a block of cheese and a plate of crackers. Helios' father brought in a bowl of pistachios and passed them round.

"Where do you want the shells?" Caroline asked.

"Right."

Fergus left and came back with a bowl.

Helios' mother wanted to know how the strike was going. She'd been watching the news and there didn't seem to be much movement on either side. Helios knew his parents' views too well to feel comfortable answering, but he didn't have to.

"People always get hung up on the wage demands," Jayne said. "That's all the public hears about. Actually, it really pisses me off."

"You bet," Caroline said. "Meanwhile, they're cutting benefits behind your back."

In less than a minute, the three women had moved from the strike to universal daycare, a guaranteed minimum wage and the elimination of the five-day working week. Fergus and Helios said nothing. Helios was on his third glass of wine when his mother stood up and announced they should carry on their discussions at the dinner table.

Fergus had prepared risotto to go with the fish. There was a salad, too, and bread from the local Italian bakery. Annie asked Helios to uncork another bottle of wine.

"Your mother says you play in a rock-and-roll band," Caroline said, turning to him.

"Played. It's over."

"Bad Men Who Love Jesus, right? I saw you once. At the university."

It was must have been two years ago. Helios remembered not liking the crowd — student union regulars. Things hadn't gone well at all.

Sometimes he thought there was nothing worse than university students. He was glad the band had ended when it did.

Helios looked around the dining room, at the same time twisting a wooden-handled corkscrew into another bottle of Chilean red. It was like a museum. The woodwork glowed from coat after coat of orange oil. The plate racks held a dozen pieces of the Bel Fiore his mother had been collecting for as long as he could remember. The new light fixture above the dining room had been "stressed" to achieve a certain eighteenth century pre-electrical-age appearance. It's possible he'd eaten in here when he was younger. There might even be a photo or two of a birthday party with some carefully chosen friends, but it couldn't have been a pleasant experience. Just as it wasn't now. Maybe it was his imagination, but his father didn't seem to be enjoying himself either. He'd hardly said more than twenty words since they came in the door. Looked a little out of sorts, too. At least his hair was growing in. Maybe he was feeling silly with all this attention. Nobody likes being rescued, the fuss of failure.

"What was funny was the way they didn't want to be there," Annie was saying.

"He was after your bones," Fergus said.

"Don't say it like that. He wasn't."

Helios wasn't sure, but he thought his mother might be drunk. They were on their fourth bottle, and she was getting loud and pronouncing every syllable with a little too much care.

"I think it's kind of cute," Jayne said.

"Sure," Caroline said. "A little harmless fun, right?"

"Exactly," Annie said. "That's just what I told Fergus. Fun. People our age don't think a whole lot about it, but when you get down to it, the really big problem is we've forgotten how to have fun. Take those teachers, for example."

"Those guys were bored," Fergus said. "You even said so."

"That's where fun comes from," Annie said. "Kids get bored and they go and do something. Everybody knows that, Pedro."

"Yeah, Pedro," echoed Caroline.

Annie turned. "What's your kid's name, Caroline?"

"Melissa."

"I bet *she* knows how to have fun." She glared at Fergus.

"Oh, well," Caroline said.

"I told you she should've brought her, Pedro."

"I have a niece," Jayne said.

"That is so nice," Annie said.

"Stop calling me Pedro," Fergus said.

[IV]

On the day of the dinner, Fergus had spent much of his time day-dreaming. The daydreams varied in plot but the outcome was always the same. Lint in the clothes dryer had accumulated to dangerous levels and ignited spontaneously, taking out half the basement and filling the rest of the house with toxic smoke. Dinner had to be canceled. Freak tides out in the strait had backed up the sewer mains, flooding homes along the coast with untreated human waste. Dinner had to be canceled. War had broken out and all able-bodied males under fifty had to report to the front. Dinner had to be canceled. The daydreams were a variation on the wishful thinking Fergus indulged in before he traveled anywhere. They were the miracles he allowed himself to believe in just to feel the wash of relief as inevitability vanished from his skies like a cloud, if only for a second. Ever since Annie had announced the event a week or so earlier, Fergus had found himself falling into a reverie of denial. He'd be shaving or taking out the garbage or screwing the lid back onto a jar of mustard, and immediately the world was wonderful again. For a few moments, his days rolled out unencumbered before him, a blank and uncharted future, until somewhere in the house a door would slam or the sink would fill, and he'd have to shake off his new happiness like a wet dog. The daydreams followed him to work when he finally agreed he was well enough to return. He'd stop in the middle of pulling a sheet of pizza bread from the oven, and Doris would have to tap him on the shoulder or say something to get him to finish what he was doing. She told him she was worried about him. Maybe there was some damage the doctors didn't find, she said, and she wasn't being funny. Fergus almost cried when he saw the concern in her eyes.

Not that Fergus would ever do anything to sabotage the dinner. He was too fatalistic for that. Dread was one thing, action was another. Part of him was also too embarrassed to admit there was anything to worry about. This was a situation right out of high school, a party where the steady girlfriend and the new interest finally met. Fergus believed men and women remained boys and girls when it came to their affections. It was all about possession and intrigue and deceit, always had been. A combination of pouting outrage and pillow-punching grief the moment someone's hand slips away and grabs another; bad enough when the new hand is a stranger's, the stuff of rock'n' roll when it belongs to a friend. Fergus tried to imagine how he would feel if he found out later that Annie had introduced him to her latest lover, that he'd even shaken the man's hand, bought him a drink or made him dinner in complete ignorance of who he was. It was hard to imagine Annie being stupid enough to get herself into such a fix, but he decided he probably wouldn't feel very good about it if she did.

Some time ago, Fergus began to wonder if he wasn't coming down with something. All this fatigue. And recently he'd imagined some fever, too. A bit of a sniffle. There were so many diseases running around now. He hadn't thought of that, had he? No, he came from another time, a safer time. All anyone could get back then was VD. It was amazing how evil those letters had sounded once. Now they were trivial, a minor infection. What had Caroline said? Sex was a death sentence now. Lately, he'd been waking up in the night in a sweat, crazed with worry. Was he sweating because he was afraid or because he was sick? How could he tell? He'd looked up symptoms on Annie's computer, and from what he could tell, he had every one of them. Fatigue, yes. A cough, sure. Night sweats! Why hadn't he thought of asking Caroline about her "history"?

How does one do that? Ask: sleep around much? And what if it was true? He'd have to tell Annie! There was no imagining that scene. It was too terrible.

WHEN THE DOORBELL RANG that evening, and Annie went to answer it, Fergus had stayed in the kitchen poking at the fish in the oven, afraid his anxiety would compel him to blurt out the truth or that he'd walk up to Caroline and kiss her or put his hand on her breast without thinking, lead her upstairs to the bedroom and lock the door behind him. The idea appealed to him in a self-destructive kind of way, to act out the carnal drive that had got him in this mess in the first place. Or maybe he was just getting excited. If only he had the courage to admit it, but of course he hadn't. Instead, he had waited for Annie to drag him from the stove into the living room where, despite the bowel-constricting fear that threatened to paralyze him any second, he discovered he was actually pleased to see Caroline. He even managed to embrace her, give her a slight kiss on the cheek. *Remarkable,* he thought. Would she like a glass of white wine?

"So, you made it," he'd said to her, pouring, as if she'd crossed mountains, forded rivers. In fact, she was dressed as he'd never seen her dressed before, elegantly, tastefully, with an eye to the world beyond the walls of her apartment, where couples went to restaurants, to parties with friends, out for a night on the town.

"I've been here before, remember? It wasn't hard to find."

"I guess not." Fergus couldn't read Caroline. It was hard to tell if she was angry or amused. He hadn't talked to her since the accident, and even though he'd had ample opportunity during his convalescence — Annie was out most of the day, Caroline's week read like a bus schedule in Fergus' mind — he couldn't bring himself to pick up the phone. Inertia stayed his hand. Had he been too depressed to think of anything to say? Was opportunity itself a deterrent? Maybe people don't want something when it becomes easy to have. Whole hours rolled out in front of him, yet he made no effort. He wondered why she'd accepted the invitation. Was it some kind of revenge? He didn't like to think what she could do if she really wanted to make things difficult.

"I almost can't tell," she said.

Fergus must have looked alarmed, because Caroline laughed.

"Your head. It's nearly normal."

"Oh, that." Fergus felt the slight ridge of scar tissue that remained.

"What did you think I meant?" Instead of waiting for him to answer, Caroline turned to Annie and started talking to her about the accident. Fergus looked briefly around the living-room, as though he might find another person to talk to, saw instead his own face reflected in the mantelpiece mirror as well as the street behind him where, out the front window, he saw Helios and Jayne pull up to the house. He watched them get out and move toward the front yard, and for a moment he wished he could be anywhere on the planet but here. Caroline's voice brought him back.

"He'll be a good architect some day," she was saying. "This just wasn't one of his finer moments."

"I don't think Fergus has been in a church since his father's funeral. What are the chances? The day he lends God a hand, he gets beaned."

If Fergus had been sensing a diminished ability to control his life before Caroline arrived, the feeling was even worse now. This wasn't a case of losing an oar while out for a row around the lake. This was white water rapids, no paddle at all, and a hole in the hull the size of a baseball. For a moment he looked at the two women talking, and then he breathed an airy excuse about his chef's duties and escaped back to the kitchen.

Adding Helios and Jayne had been his idea. The thought of just the three of them at the dinner table had terrified him, and he told Annie how nice it would be if Caroline had someone more her own age to talk to. She'd looked at him a little strangely, as though he'd said "race" instead of age, but he could see she liked the suggestion and when he heard her on the phone a few minutes later, he felt some of the burden of the evening slipping away.

NOW, THEY WERE homing in on dessert: bananas fried in butter and cinnamon, topped with maple syrup and ice cream. It was something he had actually prepared for Caroline at her place, and he thought she might like the gesture, a nod to that day. But now he was seeing the folly of his choice. Annie would be sure to say something about how Fergus had been making this dessert for years, that it was one of their favorites, the food they turned to on special occasions. Nobody wanted to hear they were walking over old ground, that someone had already been there before them. Caroline might have guessed the truth, but it was a bit harsh to shove it in her face. Fergus had often marveled at the way he could share stories or terms of affection with Caroline that he had used for years with Annie. They fell naturally from his lips, the way his body assumed certain positions during sex, a familiar choreography but with a different partner. In the years before Caroline, he had always imagined it would be impossible to be close to someone else without resurrecting Annie in every movement, every touch, and he was right. The surprise was that it didn't matter. Here at dinner, however, where his bananas were serving double duty at one table, Fergus worried his confection would seem callous instead of cute. No matter, he thought. The end was in sight. There would be coffee, some obligatory comments on the dinner and then Fergus would yawn and plead fatigue. Goodbyes in the front hall. Clear a few dishes away. Bed. Fergus almost smiled at the thought, but when he looked up, Annie was opening another bottle of wine.

"This is just what I need. A good drunk. Things have been so curious lately."

"Apocalyptic," Jayne said.

"Yes," Annie said. "That's it exactly. The end of times. That's what it feels like. Something in the air."

The cork came free of the bottle in the way that corks sometimes do, soundlessly, and without import, and Annie waved the neck of the bottle at Caroline's glass like a gun. Caroline held it up for her.

"I don't know," Fergus said. "That's what everybody keeps saying. Time's up. The end of the world. Nothing happened at New Year. A whole new century and nothing ... no earthquakes, no comets."

Fergus covered his glass with his hand as Annie offered the bottle around the table. "The new millennium's off and running. What's changed?" He tried to look hopeful. The voice of optimism.

Annie stared back at him.

"It's not a chronological thing, Pedro." She leaned across to fill Jayne's glass, then Helios'.

"Silly Pedro," Caroline said.

"The world's ending every day," Helios said. "That's what Jayne says. She says Armageddon is a personal thing."

"That's a little grim," Caroline said.

Fergus turned to look at Jayne. Why did it seem such an impossible thing for a child to have her own ideas?

"It's no big deal," Jayne said. "I was reading some pamphlets these people dropped off at Helios'. You know the kind. Literal-minded stuff about prophecy and salvation."

"I hate Christians," Annie said.

"No, you don't," Fergus said.

"But," Jayne said, "it started me thinking about the Bible. What a pain the book is. How could any god ever expect someone to understand what it said? I mean, it's such a lousy road map to heaven."

"I do *so* hate Christians," Annie hissed at Fergus. "My mother was a Christian and I hated *her*."

"So," Jayne said, "I got the idea the Bible wasn't about getting anywhere. It was just a picture."

"A picture of what?" Caroline asked.

"Everybody."

"You're losing me," Annie said.

Fergus watched Jayne deal with the attention focused on her. She'd taken her fork between two fingers and was twisting it round and round, but her eyes remained fixed on the faces watching. He remembered a time when Helios used to pull the long strands of his hair between his teeth and chew on them, but Fergus hadn't seen him resort to that behaviour in a while. He used to do it when he was speaking to a group of people, even familiar people, and Fergus had often wondered how difficult it was for him to sing on a stage in front of an audience. Jayne, on the other hand, seemed to have no trouble at all speaking her mind, and Fergus tried his best to pretend he was interested in what she had to say.

"Obviously," Jayne started to say, "we're all born. We all have our own book of Genesis. Our time of innocence."

"I like that," Caroline said. "Our own book of Genesis."

"And we all make a leap into understanding. We get kicked out of the garden. All that stuff you hear about, over and over again. As far as I can see, the rest of the Bible is just an elaboration, the same idea only longer. First it's the Israelites, thinking they're the centre of the universe, special, and then they reach a point where they need to be saved from this idea. They have to be forced to see their common humanity. It's a salvation of sorts, but it costs. A kind of crucifixion, just the way losing the garden was. After that, it's the road to death. The universal grave. Obscurity. That's the personal Armageddon."

"I'm not up on my Bible," Caroline said.

"I wonder if the Jews would agree," Fergus said.

"Jayne's father sure doesn't," Helios said.

"It's not something that needs agreement," Jayne said. "It's just the way things are. You don't need faith to know you're alive."

Fergus didn't have a clue what to say. He always became uncomfortable whenever this line of conversation developed. Rats speculating on the existence of a maze, that's how he thought of it. Pointless, even comical. He was even less comfortable hearing someone so young talk this way. He looked at Annie, who was finishing off yet another glass of red. She wore the thoughtful look of someone who'd had far too much to drink.

"Makes sense to me," Annie said. "I'm about ready for a little salvation myself."

"Annie," Fergus said.

"You won't believe this," she said, and then stopped. She picked up her glass and looked through it at the light. "Pretty," she said.

"Believe what?" Jayne said.

"Hey," Annie said. "Let's make a toast." She stood up and raised her glass. "I'd like to make a toast to Caroline Arnaud, who single-handedly saved Fergus from bleeding to death on the floor of the ugliest building in this town."

Jayne stood up and so did Helios. Fergus followed slowly and Annie slopped a little wine into his empty glass.

"Thank you, Caroline," Annie said, bowing her head at the same time, "for keeping my husband alive. Sort of."

Fergus looked at Caroline, who was still seated. Her lips were drawn tight. The colour seemed to have drained from her face. She was the one who chose to be here, Fergus thought. I could have told her it wasn't going to be a good time.

"I didn't do anything," Caroline said. "Anything at all."

"Not much you didn't," Annie said.

There was almost a scowl on Annie's face now. It was a look Fergus had never seen before, an expression that suggested great fatigue as well as regret. Fergus and the others sat down but Annie remained standing.

"You know, a while ago," Annie said, "I thought maybe Fergus and I should call it quits. The marriage, I mean." She set her glass on the table as a kind of emphasis. "We were getting pretty stale. Two old loaves of bread. Shitty white bread. I knew every word he was going to say before he said it, and he wasn't saying anything new."

Dessert, Fergus was thinking. *I should say it's time for dessert.*

"I even told him to have an affair."

The room shrank quite noticeably after Annie said this. Jayne's eyes went to Helios, Helios' went to Fergus. Fergus' eyes went to Caroline, who looked only at Annie.

"Christ, *somebody* had to do something. We were dead. Rotting old dead bread. A sewer had more life than we did."

She waited for someone to respond, to object. Fergus thought about saying something, but he could see Annie wasn't going to let herself be talked out of this. He slumped a little lower in his chair and looked down at his plate.

"But pretty soon I said to myself, 'dead is dead.' Nothing's going to change, Annie. Nothing ever does. No matter how much voltage somebody pumps into a corpse, it isn't going to move again. Like Jayne says, the resurrection's just a fairy tale."

Annie reached for her wine. An expression rippled across her face — not a smile, certainly — a look that Fergus had seen only a few times before, the face she made when a glass slipped from her fingers and fell to the floor. Something like that. He remembered a pair of sunglasses she loved very much, ridiculous, pointy things with spots, the kind of glasses his mother might have worn when he was growing up. She was taking off her sweater in a boat they had rented for the afternoon, and the glasses became entangled in the fabric. They had both heard them as they went over the side, even caught a glimpse as they sank out of sight. That look.

"But I was wrong," Annie said, placing her glass on the table again. "Wasn't I?"

She turned to retrieve her purse, which Fergus now noticed for the first time hanging over the back of her chair. Out of it she pulled some papers, unfolded them and spread them on the table. They were receipts, bills, the kind of thing Fergus saw by the dozen in any given week. He began to feel uneasy.

"Sometimes, something will happen and a little light will go on. Click. Just like that. It doesn't take much. Like those flowers in the middle of the table. I bought those flowers. Aren't they beautiful? I think so. I bought them way on the other side of town at this place I discovered recently, a little Chinese store in Esquimalt. I think you know it, don't you, Caroline? The owner is a nice man. Really helpful. Wraps them up in two layers of paper, makes sure he tucks the receipt where I can find it. I'm careful about that sort of thing. How much I spend. Where I spend it. Business. You have to be. I've even trained Fergus. Everything he buys. Everything. And that's all it took. Click. One little receipt. Name of the store, date. Because Fergus never buys me flowers, do you, Fergus? Never. We're too old for that, aren't we?"

Fergus weighed the moment. No reply expected. He knew that much. Gears turned in his head as he built a picture of Annie going through the box she reserved for receipts, sitting at her table, itemizing the expenditures. She didn't do it often, a few times a year to keep up with things. He saw her stop when she came to those particular slips, the ones he'd tucked into his wallet mechanically, stupid creature of habit, trained monkey. How long ago had he done that? Too long. Dates that would call him a liar. They'd call him a cheat. He saw Annie's own brain coping with this coincidence. The same store, months earlier, other bits of information floating in the air before her face, coalescing into something ugly, as ugly as the obvious often is. Fergus heard Jayne shuffle in her seat, turn to Helios.

"What's she talking about?" she whispered.

Fergus felt the glimmer of a stupid hope rise within him: she didn't understand. Neither did Helios. Even with earth gaping at his feet, he was still imagining he might be able to prevent others from seeing the abyss as it yawned beneath him.

"Yes, what am I talking about, Fergus? Be a good host, won't you? Don't keep your guests in the dark."

"Bills," he said. "You're talking about bills. Slips of paper. What am I supposed to make of that? I buy things. You know I do. So what?"

"You never buy flowers. I can't remember the last time."

"So, I bought some flowers. I don't even remember it, but you say I did. What does it matter?"

"At that store? Isn't it just a little too coincidental?"

"I go to lots of stores. I don't remember them all."

"At 8:30 in the evening in March? You're buying flowers at night and you don't remember?"

"Hey," Caroline said. "Cut the drama. This isn't the end of the fucking world."

Fergus was on the edge of panic. At the same time, the film of his life rolled by in front of his eyes almost as smoothly as a play. Every word seemed scripted, every response hung in the air as the balance of power sloshed unpredictably around the room. This was exactly what he had hoped would never happen — the confrontation, the accusation, the inartistic exchange. Whenever he imagined this moment — something he had mostly avoided doing — he always pictured Annie turning away to lean on a counter, a windowsill, the room thick with disappointment. Not sarcasm, not drunken irony. Fergus stood up. He wasn't sure why he wanted to, but he felt it was a gesture he should make.

"Sit down, Fergus," Annie said. "You're not going anywhere. You're the one who wanted Jayne and Helios here, so don't start whining about their precious feelings."

"I just think it's a little cruel, that's all," Fergus said. He made a gesture toward Jayne and Helios. "Why drag them into your little 'delusion'? You could have cancelled all this. We could have talked it over in private. There was no need."

"I didn't have this 'delusion' until this morning. A little downtime before the party. Something to fill my head for a few moments. Do the bills. You know me. I didn't even imagine I'd be saying this. I didn't know what would happen."

"Is there something I should know?" Helios asked. "Because if there isn't ..."

"What you need to know," Caroline said, "is that I've been fucking your father for the last year and a half and now the shit's hit the fan."

Fergus looked at Caroline. He wanted to say they could have bluffed their way through this, that there was no need to spell it out. He could have thought of something.

"Thank you, Caroline," Annie said. "You spoke very beautifully. And you're right, this isn't Armageddon, no matter what Jayne said. No offence, Jayne. But something else is ending, that's for sure, and I think we all know what it is. Fergus Goodlake, you are way too weird for me and what's kept me with you for the last twenty-five years is a mystery I can't be bothered to solve anymore. So, thank you, Caroline Arnaud, for saving him. I'm not sure it did any good, but at least he's walking and breathing and showing up for work. Here's hoping he makes a full recovery" — and at this point she waved her glass at everyone — "but as far as I'm concerned he's on his own now and I wish him all the luck in the world. You're going to need it, Pedro."

Annie finished the wine in her glass, walked into the kitchen and out the back door. In a few moments, Fergus heard the engine of Annie's Toyota as it rumbled to life, the whine of the reverse gear as she backed down the driveway, and the acceleration once she pulled into the street and drove away. For a moment, Fergus thought someone was going to say something, but he was wrong.

"Well," Fergus said finally. "I guess nobody wants dessert now."

"You are so much stupider than I thought," Helios said.

[V]

On the morning of the dinner, Annie had worked away at her desk, combing through the stack of yellow Visa copies and invoices and other receipts. Deciphering them took time, but she was happy to do it today, a Sunday, Fergus on the mend, still a little weird, but summer well under way and the prospect of long sunlit evenings looming. Victoria in the summer was a drug. People needed only a taste, and they were hooked. Twenty years could pass, but in a person's mind some standard had been set, the bar raised to a level no place could match. The city preened itself for visitors. It lolled on the southern tip of Vancouver Island like a spoiled cat and defied people not to exclaim. Did it matter that its beaches were unswimmable? Did it matter that the condominiums overlooking its harbour resembled maximum-security prisons?

When Annie found the slips — there were two of them — from the Chinese grocery below Caroline's place, her mind slipped into neutral for a few minutes. Thoughts hung suspended like berries on a branch. She could choose them at random. Flowers. Apartment. Fergus. Caroline. Two-hour coffee breaks. Laundry she didn't remember washing, the perfume Fergus had bought for her, his insistence that she wear something new. A T-shirt she didn't recognize. Fergus never bought clothes without her. What about that whole thing with the church, for Christ's sake? The mathematics were inescapable. But Caroline was so young! Was Annie crazy to think this? Would Fergus have the nerve? She thought about what she'd said to him, her belief they needed something to shake them up, an affair. Fergus had said he wouldn't tell her if he was having one. Had he really meant it? Could he do such a thing?

She stood up and walked out into the hall. She could hear the television in the family room. Fergus was watching Sunday morning reruns on the biography channel. Canned lives. Condensed people. From cradle to grave in less than an hour. His favourite show, the same ending every time and he never got tired. Tucked up with a blanket and a pillow like an invalid. In the family room, too. What a joke. A son who lives like a vampire, a husband in his second childhood. For a moment Annie tried to get angry. She thought of the times he must have been lying to her. Those chores that took him away from the deli, the strange phone calls. How stupid she must have sounded asking him to have an affair. Annie winced as the conversation came back to her. Okay, not stupid, but stupider. She waited for the waves of indignation and hurt to roll over her, the imaginary confrontations, the schemes for retribution. But they never came. It wasn't anger she felt at all. It was relief, as though somebody had turned off a faulty fluorescent light. It wasn't until this moment that she recognized she'd been walking around for months just a little off balance, like the time she'd stepped ashore after a week on a friend's sailboat. She'd lost her land legs and everywhere she went for the next couple of days the ground rolled beneath her. She remembered again her fear and disorientation after eating Helios' cannabis by accident. He was still living at home, and she'd come in from the garden a bit hungry. In the fridge she'd found a plate of cookies, terrible cookies, most of them burnt, and bitter, but she was beyond complaining at that point and had eaten three, one after the other with a glass of juice. Fergus was still at the deli — she wondered now where he'd really been — and there was something mindless on TV she decided to watch until he got home. In a little while she found the program difficult to follow, each scene so complex and dense with unspoken assumptions about human nature that she wondered whether she had ever really watched the television seriously before. It was a sitcom from the seventies, Archie Bunker and his crew, but everything they said brought Annie near to tears with longing. Could people ever have been dearer and more naive? Oh, what she would have given to step back and live a single day from those years. The show ended after what had seemed like hours, and she found it hard to shake off the feeling of sorrow. She got up to walk around, shed the gloom, but each room she entered was a crypt of memories. They had hobbled her, dragged her to her knees. She thought she was going insane, at the very least having a nervous breakdown, and when the phone rang she embraced the earpiece as though it were the railing at the top of the Eiffel Tower, the only thing between her and a long, long fall. It had been Helios, saying he wouldn't be home tonight and that he wanted to warn her about the cookies in the fridge.

"The cookies?" she had said. "It's the cookies?"

He was there in under five minutes, and when Fergus got home an hour or so later, he'd found them watching a Christmas video together and drinking hot chocolate. She remembered it was July and there were still children playing out on the streets after dinner.

OVER THE NEXT FEW HOURS, Annie deliberated telling Fergus what she suspected. What if she were wrong? She tried mouthing the words and the result was near paralysis. Fergus, have you been having an affair? Are you sleeping with another woman? The idea sobered her for a moment. The picture that appeared in her mind of Fergus climbing out of Caroline's bed and into hers sparked a rage inside her, an anger frightening in its proportions and curious, too. Why did this one act elicit such a violent response in people? She tried the words again, this time whispering them into the still air of the upstairs bathroom, her face to mirror. She almost laughed out loud at how silly she sounded, how ridiculous she looked. Soap operas were built around sentences like these! How would she ever get the nerve to ask?

At lunch she was placing a jar of freezer jam in the microwave, and she turned toward the table as the machine counted down to zero. She imagined the computer signal erupting behind her, a kind of digital trumpet preparing the room for her announcement. But the two monotone beeps arrived, and nothing came from her mouth. She had stood there until Fergus looked up, and then she'd retrieved the jar from the oven and placed it on the table. An hour or so after that, they were pulling the dining table apart, expanding it for the dinner. Fergus insisted on this, even though they were only five. He said it was always nice to have a sense of space, some distance to allow for glasses and side plates and napkins. They were standing at either end of the table and pulling, but the space wasn't yet wide enough for the other leaf. Something was stuck. Annie had felt herself about to say something sarcastic, something about needing a third person to help them and did he know of someone, but again she let the moment pass. She decided against saying anything at all, at least for now. When she looked at him, her suspicions seemed ludicrous, the kind of paranoia she'd seen in some of her friends. Of course, these friends had ended up confirming their fears. Part of Annie believed that it was really none of her business what Fergus did. Even if she were right, it would be as though he had developed a quirky but rather personal habit that excluded her, like someone who takes up a perverse form of yoga and learns how to remove his intestines, his eyes.

She had thought about the last few weeks, how absent Fergus had been. Annie had teamed up with Doris to handle Fergus' work at the shop. She found she enjoyed spending more time at the deli and that she liked Doris, with whom she'd never had more than a passing relationship. All of Fergus' recipes were on file at the shop, and Doris and she prepared the standards, working at the long counter next to the oven. Occasionally, a customer would come in looking for some of their home-made pesto or a pound of espresso, and Doris would deal with them. But she would return and they would start talking again, and Annie was surprised to see how much she had been missing a little harmless company. In the evenings she came home and filled Fergus in on the day, asked him how he was coming along, even managing a joke or two with him about his hair, the monastic tonsure that was taking its time disappearing. These days had proved effortless, the way days do in a foreign town when there are only a few left. Whatever the flaws of the city, its rude shop owners, the inflated prices in the restaurants, one develops a fondness for it simply because of the time one has spent there. Annie took some pleasure imagining Fergus coping with the looming dinner; she saw now he couldn't possibly be looking forward to it. She remembered his protesting that she didn't need to do this, that he was sure Caroline was aware of their gratitude. *Perhaps it's a strain on her to get a babysitter. Young working mothers have so little time.*

Annie had smiled to think how she'd deflected his concern, how she'd asked if maybe he was worried about seeing her, embarrassed perhaps to be in her debt. Was there something foolish he'd done that had brought on the accident? If anything, Annie had said, a dinner like this might help jog his memory of what had happened. God, how he must have squirmed inside! He and she had been having completely different conversations. Annie wondered whether she would be able to carry on as well as Fergus, were she in the same position. She could see now that the stress had been taking its toll. She wondered what it must be like to carry such an awful secret. Could she lie? Could she slip into the same bed each night and fall asleep as he did? What a thought.

And then Fergus would shift the conversation. He wanted to discuss what he would be cooking again, how good it was that they'd invited Helios and Jayne. The days were almost nice enough to eat outside, weren't they? What about the deck? Now, Annie almost pitied his evasions. She saw the perpetual slump he carried with him, his face like a rowboat, high and dry on a sandbar, no chance of a decent tide for days. She remembered how it had been when he went back to work — the long ordeal in the morning as he pulled himself together in the bathroom, no will to jog the waterfront now. If she was right about this, stranger times were ahead and she knew it, even felt her muscles bracing for them. She thought of herself as coming to a tight turn in the road — in her mind the road was the same one she had taken out into the Highlands that day her car had broken down, the one that was all curves and switchbacks. She was behind the wheel of a car, nobody in it but her. Annie felt good.

WHEN ANNIE HAD LET Caroline in the front door, it was just after five-thirty and she was stoned. Had been for a good hour. While Fergus was busy in the kitchen, she had sat on the toilet in the upstairs bathroom with the window open and the fan on, and smoked half of what was left in her stash. Then she'd come down and spent a good half-hour arranging three bouquets of flowers: one for the living room, one for the front hall, and a third for the dining room. She used sprigs of salal and sword fern interspersed with gladioli and iris. In one, she incorporated dried blooms of hydrangea. She took her time, confident in the separate life of her hands, the way they allowed for space, proportion, without her even having to think about it. She carried the vases, one by one, through to the various rooms and placed them once and once only. They were perfect where they stood the first time, sentinels of colour, ambassadors from the world outside.

At the moment the doorbell rang, Annie was sitting in the living-room, the two casement windows ajar slightly and the sounds of a Saturday evening in their neighbourhood of Fairfield floating in from the street. She had even repeated the word to herself— "Fairfield," she'd said out loud — and was thinking about how neatly it translated into French as Beauchamp, wondering whether this wasn't just a little too coincidental that two cultures should hold fields in such high esteem as to make a surname of them. The coincidence seemed almost conspiratorial, the same way weathermen seemed conspiratorial when they reported rainfall or snowfall. Fifteen centimetres of new snow, they'd say, or thirty centimetres. Was it just coincidence that the metric measurement equated to six inches in the old imperial system? Or one foot? Was the weatherman using imperial and translating the results into metric? Why would he do that? Annie was grappling with this conundrum of meteorology when she heard a car pull up. She heard it stop in the second slot in the driveway, and then, as though the driver wasn't sure about parking there, she heard the car back out and pull up next to the curb. She heard the radio continue for a minute after the engine had stopped, and the song it was playing abruptly disappear, followed by a car door that opened and shut. She heard the crisp abrasion of leather soles against the interlocking brick of the path, rhythmic and regular like someone using a handsaw to cut a plank. She heard the leaves of the rhododendron rustle as the visitor brushed by them on her way. And though it seemed unlikely at this distance, Annie would swear she'd heard a brown paper bag, the bag's top crushed around the neck of a bottle of wine, the paper twisted and crackling like a dry autumn leaf between the hands of the person carrying it. And then the hollow thud of each of the ten front steps — the guest paused at number five to examine something, her own handiwork, perhaps.

Finally, the doorbell.

Caroline wore a long, cotton-print dress, very light, the kind of dress Annie imagined she might find in one of the India import stores downtown. The sandals on her feet were inexpensive and Indian as well. Caroline's blouse was a simple white shirt, tailored at the waist, but open and loose, untucked, the dark blue chemise underneath showing through. An outfit for a pleasant spring evening. Annie noticed Caroline was carrying a fleece vest under one arm. The pot had lifted her above her suspicions for the moment. *What a nice young woman,* Annie thought. *Maybe I want to sleep with her, too.*

"Come in," Annie said. "Let me take that." She took the wine and the vest from her.

"I'd forgotten how nice your house is." Caroline turned around to look at the hall, the refinished wooden banister that disappeared upstairs.

"We forget, too, sometimes," Annie said. She saw Caroline glance at her, a swift dart of the eye, taken back the second it was given. "You live in a place," she continued, "you don't always see it the way others do."

"Yes, that's true."

Annie showed Caroline into the living room and went to get Fergus from the kitchen.

EVER SINCE THE INCIDENT with the cookies, Helios had been selling his mother a little pot, not much, an eighth of an ounce at a time, just enough so that when she wanted to, every couple of weeks or so, she could take some time for herself to relax, walk through the streets or sit on the deck and listen to the birds. At first Helios had even made the cigarettes for her, though in the last year she had become proficient enough to roll a joint of her own. The evening with the cookies had been a mistake, a frightening one. When she woke up the next day, she was still a little bit stoned. A few of the effects lingered into the afternoon before disappearing completely. Once they'd gone, Annie found that she missed them. They gave the world a sparkle. She told Helios about the sparkle, and he said that was why he smoked it.

"Work isn't so bad after a couple of hits," he said.

Once he explained that she could control the effect of the drug, she experimented with smaller doses. Fergus didn't approve of Helios smoking pot, so she didn't tell him about her own interest in it. Sometimes, when she had smoked a little bit, she couldn't help thinking Fergus was a total stranger. She actually liked the impression. She made love with him stoned one evening and it was as though she had never made love to him before. Or to anyone.

The smoke bothered her, though. It was a continual problem. She coughed and coughed, sometimes for as long as five minutes. If only she'd been a smoker, she thought. Helios told her he'd look for a bong for her, or even a vaporizer. *For my birthday,* she told him, which was coming up in another two months.

Normally, Annie didn't drink a lot. One glass, usually; on special occasions, two. So, from the very beginning of the evening, she'd found she was having trouble maintaining her pretense of ignorance with Caroline. The pot had led her into metaphysics, and the drink kept her there. History unrolled before her. Tristan and Isolde. Eloise and Abelard. People did not behave well, she decided. She wanted to talk to Caroline, tell her that they should try and do better. She almost did, too. They were out on the deck.

"He looks a lot better," Caroline had said.

"That's funny," Annie said. "I never really think about the way he looks. He's just Fergus to me."

"Like your house."

"Like my house?"

Caroline leaned toward her.

"You forget sometimes," she said.

They both laughed at this and sat a moment to think about it. Annie remembered how, when she was young, her parents had sold her bicycle. For a long time, it had been sitting in the basement in its usual spot by the workbench, but one day after school when she had gone to look for it, it was gone. She found her mother and asked her where her bicycle was and learned that it had been sold to a second-hand cycle shop downtown.

"You weren't using it," her mother told her.

Now, Annie thought about the bicycle, and about her mother's remark. Under the influence of the pot, she believed she had discovered a connection between her current situation and the urge of all people to possess and control things — especially the things they took for granted. She was about to mention it to Caroline when a penny fell on the deck beside them. Then Helios whistled. A few minutes later, the topic seemed incredibly banal and trite, and for the rest of the evening Annie filled her glass with wine whenever she felt the urge to bring up the subject.

She hadn't planned to say anything at all. The dinner was an experiment, a study in human behaviour that she had hoped to carry off without any histrionics. Things didn't always have to end with a bang, did they? She had given no thought to confronting Fergus, to forcing him into line. She vaguely remembered saying, a long time ago, that she would kill him if he ever slept with another woman. The idea struck her as melodramatic now. She supposed another person would react differently, put up a fight. It occurred to her that if Fergus was the type of person who could allow himself to so conveniently set aside his wife, his son — in some ways she marveled that he could, even wished she had it in her, too — then ultimatums and promises and threats were probably pointless anyway. She thought of all the people she knew who had devoted years to reining in their partners; she thought of the Jensens and their therapy, their mystic counselors who promised to raise them above all breathing human passion and fuse their two souls into one single self-sufficient entity, a marriage of equals. *Better to give up and live,* Annie thought.

That things didn't work out the way she had planned wasn't entirely her fault. In fact, she could say quite truthfully that the blame lay entirely with Fergus. It was the way he had looked in the living room, at the dinner table. A sullen little boy. Laconic, too. So worried his little secret would crawl into the room and expose itself. She began to feel resentful. He was ruining a perfectly good time, sulking and saying such stupid things. It was a pity Helios was there, and Jayne was sweet. Annie knew she shouldn't really have said anything, especially when she wasn't totally sure. Even if she was. What a melodramatic scene. Caroline was right. It wasn't the end of the world. In some ways, it was the beginning.

IT WASN'T UNTIL SHE WAS in the car and backing out the driveway that she realized she had no real idea where she was going. She was just drunk enough to feel a twinge of happiness at the thought that she was going somewhere at all. *A trip,* she thought. *Just what I need.* All her clothes were back at the house. The memory of her bedroom floated in front of her as she stepped on the brake and shifted the car into drive. She didn't regret leaving her toothbrush or the expensive shampoo she had to use now that she dyed her hair. She wouldn't miss the hairbrush she had bought in Mexico at an open market in Oaxaca. The only thing she might have turned back for was on the dresser where she'd left it, the tin of Fisherman's Friends, long empty of lozenges, that she used to hold her roaches and the three or four joints Helios would roll for her. She wanted the tin. Oh, well. She could always buy another one. She turned to see her purse on the seat to her right, remembered the credit cards it contained, the rest of the cash she had withdrawn this afternoon to buy wine, those treacherous flowers. It occurred to her that she had never looked at the purse in exactly this way before.

[VI]

After Annie's exit out the back door and Caroline's near simultaneous departure out the front — where she had turned only briefly to tell Helios and Jayne she was sorry — Fergus busied himself with the dishes, reassuring himself Annie would be back soon, that they would talk it out as they always had. He even said as much to Helios, who only shook his head and ushered Jayne down the front steps.

"You shouldn't have let her go in that condition," he said over his shoulder to Fergus.

"Let her?"

Later in bed, when it was clear that Annie wouldn't return, Fergus went over the evening. He refused to believe Annie about the bills. He was sure it was Nathan who had told her about Caroline. It must have happened while he was still off work, hiding in the house with his shaved head and the remnants of a concussion. Annie always fielded the calls when she was home, and now he remembered that once around nine o'clock, a little more than a week after the accident, Annie had answered the phone. Annie seemed different for the rest of the evening, out of sorts, a little testy. Now, he concocted a scene that plagued him through to the early hours of the morning, a conversation between Annie and Nathan in which Nathan revealed his noble side, the part of him that stood up for friends in trouble, friends who didn't know they were in trouble. Fergus fabricated each line of dialogue, the shifts that occurred when information passed from Nathan to Annie. As tired as he was, he kept refining the details, editing and revising them, until crazy from sleeplessness, it seemed to him he was perhaps dreaming the event, too. He closed his eyes and saw Annie at the downstairs phone, the one in the den, surprised to hear from Nathan. She had believed Caroline when she said he was unable to come.

"Caroline said you two were having some problems," Annie said. Fergus imagined her saying that she hoped they'd managed to patch things up.

And then Fergus made Nathan speak.

"I'm not her boyfriend," Nathan responded.

"You're not?"

"No. Your husband is."

Fergus thought this last remark a clever one.

He didn't like to intrude, Nathan said. But he was worried about Caroline. She'd told him about the dinner, that she was going, and Nathan thought maybe things were getting a little out of hand. The last thing Caroline needed was a dead-end fling with a man almost twice her age — Fergus repeated this phrase a few times in his head, surprised to see in a single blunt headline the current tabloid status of his life. And then, as though he were actually reading the accompanying article, he imagined Nathan telling Annie that Caroline "certainly didn't need to make it a threesome."

Fergus wasn't quite sure what a threesome was, but he felt instinctively it was something Nathan would say.

"I keep telling her," Nathan said next, "these men never leave their wives. I mean they don't. They just don't."

"Assuming their wives don't leave them first," Annie said.

"Well, yes," Nathan said. That wasn't his intention in phoning, he insisted.

"And what does Caroline say about all this?"

"She says she's happy the way things are. But you have to know that Caroline is a bit defensive when it comes to the choices she makes."

She really is, thought Fergus. *But aren't we all?*

"How do I know you're telling the truth?" Annie asked Nathan.

Fergus knew Annie would want to check the story because that's what she thought other people would do. But he also knew she would believe Nathan the moment she heard what he had to say. Some things sound true the moment they are uttered, and what Nathan had just told her was one of these things. It made sense immediately. Just like Annie to think she owed Nathan a little resistance anyway, a touch of incredulity. After all the trouble he'd gone to.

So, in Fergus' mind, she said, "Tell me why I should believe you?"

"Fair enough. Caroline's got a little girl, Melissa." Fergus winced as his mind turned to Caroline's daughter. Children are always the best reason not to act on impulse, not to allow every urge that prods to surface. "She won't be coming to this dinner you're having, will she? That's because children aren't smart enough to shut up when they see someone they know. She and Fergus are really good friends." This last improvisation was a stretch, but Fergus felt that he and Melissa might have become closer over time.

Nathan told Annie he was sorry she had to find out. Fergus wasn't a bad guy, Nathan figured. He was just a little mixed up, and for what it was worth, Nathan said, the accident hadn't really been anybody's fault. It was just bad luck.

"I can tell you a joke, if you like," Nathan said finally. "It might cheer you up."

"I don't get jokes."

"You'll get this one."

"Sure. Fire away, bright boy."

"Why is gravity no longer necessary?"

"I don't know. Why?"

"Because the earth sucks," he said. And then Fergus made Nathan hang up.

Fergus worked at the exchange, carving it into a complete vignette, the way a playwright might, attending to each little nuance. The joke at the end seemed appropriate to him. A nice touch, one that Annie would appreciate. He tried to remember if there had been any signs that a phone call had really taken place — not the one he was imagining only now, perhaps, but something close. He remembered watching her as she came up the walk after a day at work. He listened to the door open and shut again, as if she'd just closed it. It was hard to tell what she was thinking. Just towards dawn, he decided to dismiss his fears that she had known all along. Annie wouldn't be mean enough to lead him along like that. To think that way was craziness. What did it matter, anyway? She knew now. That's what counted. Only — and he knew this was stupid — he found it annoying that he'd put the evidence right into her hand, that it wasn't some outside force like Nathan that had betrayed him. Fergus came to see that he was the author of his own undoing, a chipper little Nazi sealing his fate with paperwork.

THE NEXT MORNING, Fergus woke knowing that Annie had not come home. For a moment he tried telling himself there must be thousands of people across the continent who were in exactly the same position, their bed half-empty, a long restless night behind them, the rooms they occupied suddenly a lot larger, a lot less friendly. It was the stuff of popular songs, he told himself. My baby left me. She's gone. He could hear Eric Clapton wailing along with the rest of the Dominoes. Another of Annie's "best of" acquisitions. He sat up, shook his head, self-conscious about the ordinariness of this new development, as though somewhere a camera was running. What would he do next? Fill a basin with cold water and immerse his face? Shake the water from his head like a dog and turn to meet the day? Fergus plodded over to the window, its casement and sill covered with dust. Visible neglect. And the invisible? A spider had set up shop in one corner, husks of insects, their pointless wings, littered on the wood below. Such a messy creature. He yawned, remembered that Nathan had never phoned, that Helios was furious with him and that Caroline would probably never speak to him again. Thank goodness it was Sunday. No Doris. And tomorrow? Fergus shuddered to think he'd have to resume his life as though nothing had happened. There were catering contracts looming. He'd cancel them. The shop was all he could manage, if that. He paused in this moment of crisis management to look out at the street. A troop of children, bookended by parents? supervisors? marched in a line toward the waterfront. A day at the beach. Tide pools with bullheads and limpets. They walked with such conviction. He looked at them pass and thought: *Annie isn't returning today. Annie isn't returning at all.*

"I can't stay here," he said aloud.

Fergus went immediately to the bathroom and showered. He shaved and dressed and grabbed a coat and marched out the front door, locking the house behind him. A new purpose percolated in his bones. The pages of the local paper unfolded in his head as he walked, and he saw the classifieds in front of him: rentals, furnished. No, he told himself. Unfurnished. He walked on through his neighborhood, a June neighbourhood sitting on the peak of summer, its sleepy Sunday citizens shuffling out their French doors onto back sundecks, coffees in hand, cherries ripening on trees in front of their eyes, scarlet runners scrambling up wooden lattices, sunflowers twisting their heads as the earth turned, everybody ignoring the obvious, that the year had reached its peak and in a few days would start sliding back toward winter. Fergus could smell their dark roast, their slices of raisin bread about to pop out of the toaster, their smug trouble-free day. He walked into a corner store, grabbed the daily and filled a paper cup at one of the coffee carafes. He added some milk and walked up to the clerk to pay, but as he handed over the bill, a line of pain seemed to connect his bowels to the hand he was holding out. He almost crumpled in the wake of its passing.

"Do you have a washroom?" he asked. The clerk handed him a key and waved him to the back of the store. Fergus hurried in the direction he'd been shown, cup in hand, paper tucked under one arm. He closed the door, aware now that he hadn't peed this morning and that his bladder was screaming at him, threatening to burst, but as he turned to face the toilet, his fly open, penis poking through, nothing happened. Nothing. Not a dribble. For a long moment, Fergus thought he might die in this place, his innards ruptured in the staff washroom of a convenience store. He saw a photo of himself splayed out on the floor, head propped up against the bowl, fly agape, the coffee resting cold and undrunk on the top of the towel dispenser. He thought of Annie, wherever she was, passing a newsstand, glancing down at the photo and recognizing him, or maybe not. Someone would track her down, a reporter maybe, or the police. Are you the wife of Fergus Goodlake? they'd ask. Not anymore, she'd say, and there would be a silence while they tried to figure out what she meant.

He placed his hands on the wall in front of him and leaned over the toilet slightly to relax. In a few seconds, he could feel the pressure abating. He heard the sound of a feeble quantity of urine as it left his body and fell into the water below.

"I can't put this off much longer," he said aloud.

[VII]

A man in a 1947 Pontiac pulls over to the side of the road and gets out
of his car. Seconds earlier, he saw a boy on a bicycle cross the highway in front of him and hit the steel fence opposite. The man's family
sits in the car while he waits for a break in the traffic so he can cross to
the other side. It's the Easter weekend and in this good weather many
people have decided to go out for an afternoon drive. The man and his
family are on their way home from tea and scones at Fernie Farm, where
the two Fernie sisters serve homemade strawberry jam and Devonshire
cream along with as much tea as a person can drink and two scones each.
The two children have been looking for Volkswagens all the way home.
Whoever sees one first is allowed to hit the other, a game that annoys
the father so much that just before the top of Four Mile Hill he has to
turn around and box the ears of both of them.

Fergus is unconscious. When he hit the steel fence post, he was
traveling close to thirty miles an hour. The blow has opened up a wide
cut just above his eye that will require several stitches to close. The scar
will be hidden for the most part by his eyebrow, and because he will have
no memory of how it came to be there, he will look in the mirror for the
rest of his life and wonder if the story he was told is real or if perhaps
something more sinister took place, something which his parents have
spent their lives trying to cover up. He finds it very unlikely that he
would have biked that far by himself, and for what reason? To see his
grandmother? With all that they said he was carrying? The only other

time in his life he will lose consciousness from a blow to the head will take place when he is in his late forties. On a sorry spring morning much like this one, he will be knocked out cold by a large wooden cross.

Fergus' grandmother is no more than two hundred yards from where her grandson lies. She has just poured a pot of tea from the kettle of water she keeps at a simmer on the kitchen oil stove all day long. In a moment she'll sit down to read the flyer from the new Safeway on Esquimalt Road, a store she has never entered and will never enter for the remaining six years of her life. As she reads, she will keep an ear open for a call from her son in town, an Easter invitation to tea or a picnic tomorrow. This invitation won't come. Instead, she'll be notified by her daughter-in-law, a woman for whom she feels more pity than revulsion, that her grandson Fergus is in a coma at St. Joseph's Hospital.

"He was just here," she'll say. "We had a nice visit."

THE MAN WITH THE Pontiac crosses the road and runs to where Fergus is lying. He is a veteran of the Second World War and knows enough not to be paralyzed by the sight of blood. He knows that head wounds are often messier than they are serious, and he bends down with his handkerchief to wipe away the blood from Fergus' face. The wound is larger than he thought, and he ties the two ends of the handkerchief like a bandanna, tight enough just to stanch the bleeding. Another car has stopped behind his, and the man yells at the driver to use the phone at the drive-in around the next corner to call an ambulance. The drive-in is called the Dog and Suds, and he yells the name across to the driver, who is straining to hear him. When the other car pulls out onto the road and disappears around the bend, the man turns his attention back to Fergus. There is the bad gash in Fergus' forehead, but none of his limbs seem to be broken. He worries about damage to Fergus' spine and decides not to try to move him except to straighten one of Fergus' arms, which is tucked at an awkward angle behind his back. It's been nearly twenty years since the man fought his way up the mountain passes of Italy, but the helplessness he feels beside a broken body is as fresh as always, and he turns his attention to the business of bringing order to the scene. He picks up the ruined bicycle and places it on the gravel shoulder. Among the weeds and clumps of broom he finds a flashlight, a pair of binoculars and a khaki rucksack with some clothes and a couple of cans of beans. A copy of today's paper is starting to fly apart in the breeze, its black and white photos of yesterday's earthquake flapping against the chain link fence. *There's a story here,* the man thinks, *but I'm not seeing it.* He arranges Fergus' belongings around the bicycle and sits down to watch for signs of movement. Fergus is lying face up, the man's handkerchief wrapped around the cut on his forehead now solidly dyed with Fergus' blood. Across the road, the man's family watches through the car windows as he signals back to them to stay where they are. *If this were my son,* the man is thinking.

IN ANCHORAGE, ALASKA, a merchant has erected a sign outside his store, which now sits almost twelve feet below street level. The sign reads: "I knew making a living in Alaska would be hard, but I never thought I'd have to go in the hole." On Vancouver Island, a resident returns to his home in Zeballos, a house built on piles over the water. Mud and flood detritus cover the floor along with several inches of trapped water. He takes his '38 Winchester and blows several holes in the floorboards to allow the place to drain. "It wasn't much of a house anyway," he says.

Up in Tahsis Narrows, the incoming tidal wave has displaced thousands of bottom fish, dragging them to the surface where their swim bladders have expanded, leaving them unable to go down again. The numbers of dead fish make it hard for small boats to proceed against them. There is a story circulating in Port Alberni of a baby rescued from a house that had come adrift on the floodwaters. The baby was found, the story goes, inside the house, adrift and asleep on its very own mattress.

WHEN THE AMBULANCE ARRIVES, the man who found Fergus introduces himself as Ron. He says his name in a loud, slow breath as though it is a vital piece of information. As though the attendants are looking only for a man by this name standing next to an accident victim, as though were he not a man called Ron, they might move on, keep searching, until they found the right man beside the right injured boy. He hands one of them the wallet he has fished out of Fergus' pocket, but the attendants are all business and pay no attention, except to slip it onto the dash of the ambulance. A police car arrives a moment later and an officer takes notes as Ron tells him what happened.

"So you didn't hit the kid," the officer says, writing down the time, the day, the location, Ron's name and address.

"Christ, no!" Ron says. He tells the officer about the wallet.

Later, Ron stands with his back to the road, cars passing him slowly, their occupants staring hard at the scene, sucking up all its clues in the few seconds they have, some of them turning around in their seats and watching until they move out of sight. Ron's handkerchief has been cut from Fergus' head and replaced by gauze and Elastoplast, and the attendants are preparing to move Fergus onto a stretcher.

"What about the boy's stuff?" Ron asks as the attendants pass him on the way to the ambulance.

"Are those your kids in that car?" one of them asks.

"I could bring it to the hospital," Ron says, realizing immediately how impractical his offer is.

"The police will want you to move on now. Thanks for your help."

"Sure," Ron says.

When the ambulance doors close, Ron turns to cross the highway. Already he can see that the time has been too long for his children in the back seat. They are sitting as far away from each other as possible, their heads turned in opposite directions. His wife will have ordered them to sit that way, to be quiet and to be thankful they aren't lying bleeding at the side of the road. She will be quiet herself when he returns to the driver's seat. She will wait for him to tell her what he saw, and, when he describes Fergus' inert form, when he explains how he had to leave his handkerchief behind because it was soaked in the boy's blood, he knows she will put her arm along the back of the bench seat and squeeze his shoulder to make him stop for the children's sake. It occurs to him, as it always does when he thinks this way, that he would be disappointed if she didn't reach across to him like that.

IN THE COMING YEARS, Ron will maintain a passing interest in the life of Fergus Goodlake. For a couple of seasons, Fergus' name will catch his eye in the sports section of *The Colonist*, among the results of the Little League games. Ron will see that Fergus plays for Victoria Tire one year and for Brittania the next. The year after that he will look for Fergus' name, but fail to find it. Several years later, he will see Fergus' name again in a list of graduates from a local high school, and a little more than a decade from now he will see on the wedding page of the newspaper an announcement that Fergus Goodlake, son of Bill and Dorothy Goodlake, will marry Annie Mitton, daughter of George and Paula, at St. Matthias Church on Richardson Road, the 12th of September, 1975, at 3:00 P.M. There will be a picture beside the announcement, which will in no way match whatever memory of the younger Fergus Ron still retains. For over twenty years, Ron will make no connection between Fergus and the downtown delicatessen with which he is only dimly familiar, but he will live long enough that in 1987 he will walk in and see Fergus behind the counter, the scar above his eye now more visible, the way scars become as a person gets older. And he will order a cup of coffee and a slice of homemade rhubarb pie and sit at a table in the corner, the image of this man's scar pestering him like a mosquito until he finally puts two and two together and spends the time it takes to eat his pie and drink his coffee thinking about saying something to this man who, over the years, has come to occupy a place in his mind much the same as that occupied by an illegitimate child, the product of a chance encounter, someone who, whether he knows it or not, has been living perpetually in the conditional tense. Even as he steps up to pay his bill, Ron will be uncertain what to do, and in the end will do nothing because nothing is what he has done so far and the results of inaction are always less frightening than those of action, at least initially.

FERGUS' MOTHER IS only just beginning to become concerned about her son when the St. Joseph Emergency Ward calls to tell her Fergus has been brought in with a severe head injury. The coincidence of her sense of foreboding and the call from the hospital conspire to create a cloud of guilt around Fergus, a lingering impression that his injuries are her fault, that by thinking he was in danger she somehow caused the accident. In her mind, this is a failure of good faith, of trust, and it will colour her attitude toward her son from now on. Fergus' father is still not home from the deli, and she debates whether she will tell him the news now or later. Either way he will react badly, and she decides to call him now because he has the car, an inconvenience she has been putting up with for a couple of months, ever since he started giving the woman next door a ride downtown on his way to work. Though she doesn't like to admit it to herself, Fergus' accident is just the thing she needs to put a stop to her husband's magnanimity.

"If I had the car," she can hear herself saying.

FERGUS REGAINS CONSCIOUSNESS shortly before lunch on Monday, March 30th. He has seven stitches above his right eye. The doctor on the floor at the time tells Fergus' mother it's a good day for a resurrection. She has forgotten it's Easter, thinks he's referring to the sun outside, the sudden warm temperatures.

"I would say any day is good," she says, "as far as the dead are concerned."

Fergus undergoes another EEG. One of the nurses wheeling him down tells him he is a miracle child. The specialist suspects he may have epilepsy. Since nobody knows exactly what happened — a witness says only that Fergus swerved out of nowhere into the middle of traffic —

there is some doubt surrounding Fergus' well-being. What was he doing at his grandmother's? Why had he packed food and a flashlight? The police interview Fergus' parents, who are embarrassed to seem so ignorant of the hours leading up to the accident.

"We were all in bed by eleven-thirty," Fergus' father tells them.

"Yes, sir," the officer says. "You can see why we're confused."

On Tuesday, Fergus is given a clean bill of health and released. His mother drives him home in the car, which she has wrested back into her control. In the driver's seat, she feels awkward next to her son, tells him maybe he'd like to lie down on the back seat, just to be safe. Nobody she's ever known has lost three whole days of his life. She forgets her husband lost five years of his life in the war. She forgets her husband a lot. As she and Fergus walk up the back stairs to the kitchen, she tells him the rest of the week's his. No sense in pushing things. School can wait a few more days. The police drop off Fergus' bike, his rucksack and the rest of what they found at the site of the accident. Fergus' father dismantles the bike while Fergus watches. He removes its bent forks, the twisted front rim. He tells Fergus he'll be riding again in no time.

"You feel the earthquake?" he asks, uncertain what Fergus knows and doesn't know. "It was a big one."

"I don't remember," Fergus says.

PART V

After Goodlake's

[1]

The night she'd backed out the driveway and left Fergus and the others sitting at the dinner table, Annie had driven around for nearly an hour without any idea what she was doing. She felt like a child who'd just pulled a tantrum, condemned by her own petulant display to stay away when all she really wanted was to crawl into her bed and pull the covers up over her head. She might even have gone home and done exactly this had she not also been very, very angry. The events of the last few weeks unrolled before her — the deceit, the evasions. What had Fergus been thinking? Was sex so important to him that he had to lie to get it? She refused to allow herself to think of their own life in bed, how sometimes Fergus would decline, plead fatigue, his troubled prostate, a long day at the store. At the time, Annie had told herself all couples went through this. It was like the core of a planet cooling with age, understandable after twenty-five years of marriage.

Still a little drunk from all the wine at dinner, she was unable to place Fergus in the appropriate category of skulking liar, coward, adulterer. He was still her longtime friend, her —and here she groped for something more suitable — her companion. Yes, that's what he was. Hadn't he accompanied her all these years? Annie decided she liked the word companion, thought it more appropriate than husband or partner. So, why hadn't her companion just come and talked to her? Almost as soon as this thought crossed her mind, she saw how stupid it was. Fergus, hands behind his back, feet shuffling a little, head down, asking if Annie might be nice enough to let him fuck this new woman he'd found, this unbelievably young woman who could even be his daughter, his son's girlfriend, a waitress at his own goddamn delicatessen, for Christ's sake! Annie gripped the wheel tighter as the enormity of Fergus' infidelity became clear. Some companion! What an old fool! Okay, she thought. It's true. Men don't usually ask their wives when they want to go off and fuck someone else. And, okay, so women probably don't ask their husbands either. But do they have to act like idiots? If you're tired of living with someone, shouldn't you just say so? At the same time that she saw how difficult it would be for her to say such a thing to Fergus, she felt a huge sadness well up from deep within her, a sudden sorrow, not that Fergus might not love her anymore — such an event was inconceivable — but that Annie was no longer capable of making him happy. It was the same kind of sorrow that rose within her whenever she saw pictures of her and Fergus in their younger days, in the days just after they were married. It was the sense that something sweet had gone away forever. She thought of that stupid conversation she'd dragged him into — she should never get stoned around Fergus, not with the kinds of ideas that came to her — and wondered how she could ever have proposed such a thing. And here she was, with just what she'd asked for. How interesting was her life now? Was this progressive enough for her?

She drove the waterfront until she came to downtown. Then, she went up and down the one-ways, as though these streets with their urgent arrows and their expansive broad lanes could decide her destination for her. At one point she headed north for a few blocks and pulled into the Accent Inn. The airport shuttle was parked in front, a handful of people waiting beside the open door of the van as the driver removed their bags. A family of four stood among them but separate, their arms heavy with bags of souvenirs. Even in the lifeless glow of the overhead streetlamps, Annie could see the depth of their tans. Mexico? Hawaii?

"It's so cold here," a girl of indeterminate age was saying.

"You'll get used to it," her father said.

"But I don't want to."

Annie walked through them to the front desk, where she booked a single and arranged a five-thirty wake-up call.

"Any bags?" the clerk asked.

Annie raised her arms and twirled a little to show him she was luggage-free, then picked up the key he had pushed across the counter and walked out. It wouldn't occur to her for several days that she must have reeked of alcohol when she was talking to him, that her brief stay and minimal belongings must have raised some doubts in his mind. Hadn't she staggered a little, too? Oh, well. More than any of that, she remembered her fatigue, the urge to lie down. Her room was one of a couple dozen rooms that opened up onto an exterior corridor. She walked into the small rectangle of territory that she'd purchased for the night, with its swing-out TV and taut bed covers. The fluorescent light in the bathroom made her turn away from herself, and after fixing a cup of complimentary herbal tea in a pristine glass urn, she lay back on the bed and reached for the remote control. Tired as she was, dawn came and she was still flicking through the channels. Defeated, she showered and dressed herself again in the same clothes she'd worn the day before at dinner, a light summer dress and sandals. Without all the accessories of her own bathroom — hairbrush, curling iron, her various lotions — Annie felt a bit marginal, like some kind of suburban hooker, dressed to party, but frayed around the edges. She wanted a pair of jeans, some sturdy shoes, a decent top. At the motel office, she grabbed one of the complimentary apples, consumed it in a few bites, and left in time for the early ferry to the mainland, an annoying ride which docked late, just before nine, a frustratingly symbolic offshore wind testing her patience. Then followed a couple of dizzying hours in a shopping mall — she chose K-Mart, remembered vaguely that these stores used to be called Kresges, a name synonymous with thrift — and with a few new tapes for the car, she headed east. A bright moment occurred when she looked in her purse to discover that she hadn't left the tin of pot behind after all. She must have tucked it in there after she'd taken those few tokes before everyone arrived for dinner. Life seemed a little friendlier now. She rolled down her windows as she branched off onto Highway Ten, telling herself she was having an adventure, one that was all the more adventurous because she had no real idea where she was going. She tried to recall the date and groped automatically for her dayplanner, which usually lay on the seat beside her. When she realized it wasn't there, she felt a little happier. No days to plan. Let's improvise. It's Monday, she told herself. Yesterday was what? The eighteenth? Summer solstice coming up. The year is shifting, getting ready for a change. Me, too, she thought. I need some signs. She looked up, saw a large white arrow directing her to Hope, but refused to allow the coincidence to colour her journey. A hundred thousand cars pass this way a month, she told herself. Everybody needs hope. I'm looking for more than that.

As she drove, Annie found it tempting to believe that time had reversed itself. The usual smog of the Fraser Valley was nowhere to be seen, and the looming green of the mountains, the cornfields on either side of her, revived memories she had of summers of endless heat and blue sky. She remembered trips she had taken in her parents' car, the breeze blowing over her and her sisters in the back seat, a bowl of cherries to share among them. Perhaps just being on a highway in June was all it took to make someone Annie's age feel young again, the way the road suggested the mindless optimism of the early sixties, and even those later, more audacious years when her sisters had stuck out their thumbs and hitchhiked back through the Rockies all the way to Toronto. To travel a road and not know what was ahead of her, to dispel the certainty of tomorrow's drudgery, drudgery she had learned to accept the same way she had once accepted the inevitability of her period ... *God*, she thought, *I really need this*. The asphalt passed beneath her wheels like a long uninterrupted hiss of relief, and, unwilling to relinquish this rediscovered rush of liberty, she drove through Hope and beyond, pulling over only when the light began to fade.

OVER THE NEXT THREE WEEKS, Annie breathed the passing smells of fir and pine, open fields of blooming fireweed, the ripe manure piled up outside the barns of dairy farms. She walked the streets of small towns like Princeton and Grand Forks, making herself sandwiches for a picnic in one of the town parks, hunting down a Best Western for the night. In Osoyoos, she waded far out into the sandy lake and watched a pair of jet-skis tear up the water. Smoke hung in the air from a nearby forest fire, and in the sun's filtered light she felt she might have been witnessing a kind of post-apocalyptic joust as the two machines lunged first toward and then away from each other, twisting in the waves of their own wakes. She spent a few days in Nelson, and then worked her way up through Kaslo and New Denver and Nakusp. She avoided bed-and-breakfasts. The people who ran them wanted to talk too much. What she liked most about these days was walking into the lobby of a hotel around dusk and catching the attention of the night shift. She liked the formality of the transaction, the clear exchange of goods for money.

"Do you have a room for the night?" she always asked. Each time, Annie thought her words sounded like a line from a poem. She also liked the anonymity of this life, the deference shown to people who, for whatever reason, were not fixed to any particular address — people in transit, as Annie felt she was, from one place to another. Maids knocked politely, desk clerks breathed out their questions in a near whisper: *name? credit card? smoking?* In the hotel restaurant, guests surrounded themselves with the urgency of their own journey, no wish to find a familiar face, preoccupied with the idea of food away from home, its tricky demands.

Somewhere along the way, she'd ended up at the Quilchena Inn outside of Merritt. The inn was a nineteenth-century roadhouse with rooms above the bar and restaurant. The bartender showed her bullet holes from gunfights that had happened over a hundred years earlier. She put her finger in one and felt the ridges of wood, smooth now from the visitors who had moved instinctively, as she had, to insert themselves into history.

It was the last hotel for a while, though she didn't know it at the time. On her map, she had circled towns like Smithers and Stewart and

Dease Lake, as though she might keep drifting northward like an escaped balloon, all the way to the Arctic Circle. Helios had spent some time traveling through Central America and Mexico, and she had tried once to ask him how he'd designed his itinerary, what factors had gone into selecting the route he'd taken. He'd looked at her blankly as though she were speaking another language.

"There was no route," he told her.

She left the hotel the next day before lunch. The highway took her through Kamloops, and she tuned into a country station along the way. A woman was singing — Annie had no idea who — and it seemed the woman was missing someone or something, a place, Annie thought finally, a home she'd once had and lost, and when the chorus came on for the last time, Annie was finding it hard to keep from sinking her head onto the steering wheel and weeping. The song ended at a newsbreak and Annie never did find out the name of the song or who was singing it. In another five minutes she was standing outside the office of the real estate agent looking at photographs of houses to rent.

It was now two weeks into July. Kamloops was stoking the engine of another withering summer where walking would become more like swimming in the deep reaches of a very hot pool. Under a hopelessly inadequate awning, Annie looked at pictures of cottages, fully equipped lakeside homes, doublewide trailers, unable to remember a time when she had been alone for this long. She counted the days in her head, but they seemed too few. Time was one thing, she told herself, but distance was another. She had covered a lot of ground, too. Each day had been a day on the move, and when all the moving combined with the hours that had passed, the impression was of months, not days. She had avoided newspapers, listened only to music on the radio, and had broken herself of the habit of watching TV. The outside world — the world outside the road she followed, outside the town she chose to sleep in for the night — had evaporated, as had the world she'd left. It was amusing to think of how closely she used to read the national news, tune in to catch the leading stories. People must do this, she told herself, when their own lives are deficient in some way, less full. And she had left hers behind.

It seemed a marvel to Annie that she could have done such a thing, that she could have pulled away from her life and remained intact. Only a month ago, to walk away as she had done, to turn her back and leave in the space of a single moment, would have seemed like a kind of amputation, a messy separation that might demand tearing, some inevitable hemorrhage. Perhaps people would leave each other more frequently if they knew how easy it was — not just easy, but invigorating, too. All this land to look at. These little towns. *How much we agree to ignore when we bind our life to the life of another.* Annie supposed this was an irony, one she had never understood before.

In the heated air of a blinding afternoon, she vowed never to become so blinkered again, but, still, the vow made her think of where she'd come from, the people she'd left. What was Fergus up to? Had he taken her departure as a nod to move in with Caroline? What would Helios say about such a thing? Who was looking after the deli? She turned to the office window, its neat little itemized lists of features, the lavish use of exclamation marks — sunny deck! dishwasher! private dock! — and took her time choosing a place that would be just right for her.

[11]

Jayne told Helios that they'd be going to the oldest synagogue in western Canada, only she used the word "temple," which Helios had to ask her to clarify. "The Temple Emanu-El," she said. Jayne's nose was still a little black around the edges, and there was a line of purple under one eye.

"People are looking at me," Helios had said earlier that day when they were out walking.

"You're so vain," Jayne said.

"They think I beat you up," Helios said.

"Like to see you try," she said.

It was over a week since the strike had ended, and since then there'd been several night shifts of easy living for Helios and Jayne. They were both heroes among the brothers and sisters of Local 235. Someone had brought a bottle of tequila one night and served shots all round. The paper had run an interview. Now they were getting ready to hear Jayne's father play the mandolin. The bar mitzvah started at eleven.

"We're going to shul," Jayne said. "I think maybe you should tie your hair back."

"One thing: I don't want to know what's going on. Keep it a surprise, okay?" He wrapped an elastic around a fistful of black hair. "I want everything to be mysterious. Like the first day of school. It's better that way. You see more when nothing makes sense."

"Sense it doesn't make," Jayne said.

Helios heard the alteration in her syntax. "Shul," she'd said. Like they were traveling to another country. They headed out the door.

"You should've seen this place before the restoration," Jayne said. They were driving down Pandora.

"I don't remember it."

"Exactly. You wouldn't. That was the point. Better not to stand out. At least not back then. My father calls himself a secular Jewish humanist. That means he doesn't attend services much, but I still remember it. Like night and day. Park here."

A row of young cedars lined the north wall of the synagogue, the gift of a landscaper who had since died in a swimming accident. He wasn't even Jewish, Jayne told Helios. The restored synagogue was a monument to collaboration, she said. Everybody'd had a hand in it. They turned onto Blanshard Street and walked up the front steps into the foyer. Stairs branched off left and right to the balcony. Helios paused to look at a plaque dedicated to a Victoria man, a Dutchman who had hidden Jews in his house in Holland during the war. The dedication had been attended, the plaque said, by an Israeli foreign minister. There were other dedications and pictures, but Jayne grabbed him and led him up the narrow stairs to their seats, straight-backed wooden pews that overlooked the altar and the rows of chairs below.

Helios looked around at the semi-circle of seats and pillars and the tall multi-pane windows that let in the bright southern light. A man to his left was reading *Time* magazine, flipping through the pages quickly and then flipping through them again, as though he couldn't believe there was nothing there to read. Later this afternoon, Helios and Jayne were going to visit Fergus in the hospital. A vacancy had opened in surgery and the doctor had told Fergus he'd be a fool to pass it up. Helios hated hospitals almost as much as he hated churches. They both stank of mortality. They both had their priests. Jayne was more generous.

"Nobody knows anything," she said. "Look at it that way. People know bupkis."

If only they didn't act as though they did, Helios thought. A building like this would be a lot more beautiful if God wasn't messed up with it. He looked at the woodwork, the solid fir floors, all the tongue-in-groove, v-joint cedar the builder had used for the ceiling. He had the urge to buy some land and put a house on it, a place he could put together with his own hands.

"Want to build a house with me?" he said, turning to Jayne.

"There's the boy," she said. "The kid with the tallis. He'll introduce the reading."

"I told you not to tell me anything."

Helios listened to the boy intone the words of the Torah, the rolls of parchment spread out before him on the altar, the elders of the temple looking on proudly. The boy's family sat in the front rows below, dozens of them it looked like, cousins and uncles and grandparents. Helios tried to imagine his own family gathered for some rite of passage, but all he could think of was his grandfather walking off a cliff in Barbados, the sweet smell on the old man's breath that he later recognized on others as liquor. He thought of the silver dollars slipped into his pocket at Christmas, and the cigarettes his grandmother sent him to buy at the store, DuMaurier Kings.

"How old's he have to be?"

"Thirteen years and a day, but you didn't hear that from me."

The man to Helios' left was now going through a *Sports Illustrated.* Did Jews get bored of bar mitzvahs? Helios wondered. Kids must be turning thirteen every day. Helios didn't remember his thirteenth birthday. Or his twelfth for that matter. On his fourteenth birthday, his parents had given him a ghetto blaster with a microphone. He remembered opening the large present in the upstairs bedroom, the one he'd had before his mother had convinced him to move to the basement.

"You'll never be thirteen again," she'd said as he tugged at the wrapping. He still didn't understand what she'd meant. Of course, she was right. But her motive in saying it escaped him. When he thought of her words now, they sounded almost mean, as though she were making fun of him, another victim of time. It had been morning, and the sun had filled his bedroom (which was yellow at the time, the same colour it had been for as long as he'd been alive, and a good choice, he'd thought, considering his room faced east). He remembered sitting on his bed, still sleepy — his parents had woken him — and feeling uncomfortable with both of them sitting with him at the same time, in their pyjamas and robes. He could still see the green canvas blind over his window, the one he'd punctured with a compass point in hundreds of places to let the light in like stars, pinpricks of sunshine that expanded into constellations on the far wall. Helios could see it all quite clearly, his father supporting himself with one arm on the mattress, his mother holding onto the bedstead with both hands, a picture so detailed he was almost convinced it had taken place only a week ago. That was the thing about the past. Sometimes it seemed so real, it was hard to believe it wasn't still happening.

In the days that had followed the dinner with Caroline, he'd worried about his mother, where she had gone, what she might do. He'd worried about Fergus, too, perhaps even more. The man seemed to be crumbling before Helios' eyes. For a while, he thought Fergus might do something desperate. The sudden urge to find another place to live, his immediate refusal to stay in the house, as though he needed to atone for his crime — Helios found it hard to imagine such urges still lurked in a man his father's age — all this was as worrisome as it was comic. More and more, Helios was coming to believe that people only looked adult, that they continued to think and act as imbecilic adolescents. Jayne had been surprisingly less sympathetic. It was the first time Helios had needed to balance her criticism with a little common sense, as though Fergus' behaviour had unleashed in her a streak of pessimism that usually ran below his radar.

"What the fuck was the man thinking?" she said to Helios in the car on the way home. "She's half his age."

"Why don't you ask what *she* was thinking?" he asked. "It's not like he forced her into anything."

Jayne looked across at him. Some people's eyes rolled without actually rolling. Jayne was one of these people. She was incredulous. It was as though Helios had suddenly revealed his membership in Jehovah's Witnesses.

"She has a kid, for Christ's sake! She's in a vulnerable position. The one thing you never do in this life is take advantage of vulnerable people. It's a law, or it should be. I know what I'm talking about."

And they had driven in silence for the first time since they'd met, a long and suffocating silence that Helios couldn't bear because it seemed to suggest the wasteland of years that people like his parents found themselves in once the awful work of chipping away at each other began. The silence had continued even into the bedroom, until at last, unable to bear it any longer, they had both spontaneously curled into each other and fallen asleep. Even then, it had taken Helios awhile to convince her that Fergus was no threat to anybody, that he'd been a little stupid, maybe, but that he would never intentionally harm anyone.

Now, in the synagogue, he rubbed his eyes. He was still tired. He looked over at the bruises on Jane's face. They'd be gone completely in a couple of days. He thought about how angry he'd become, the sudden fury that had come over him, when she'd been hurt. He wondered if it was there all the time, just under his skin somewhere. He wondered if it was anxious to get out.

"THAT SHIRT UNION ISSUE?" the driver had called down to Helios from his seat in the truck cab. "You some kind of hard man? You the bad-ass that's going to keep me out of here?"

Helios had said nothing. He kept walking until he was just in front of the truck's wheels.

"That's not my Jesus you're talking about," the driver had said. "My Jesus wouldn't give a lazy prick like you the time of day."

The truck moved forward until it bumped Helios' knees. Helios staggered a bit and moved on.

"Hey!" Jayne yelled up at the cab window. "Is your Jesus a scab like you? Is he a lying whore of a scab like you? I'll bet your Jesus is a lying dickless scab!"

The driver's door caught Jayne full in the face, knocked her flat against the ground. In the disorder that followed, the driver tried to ram his truck through the line, but Helios climbed up onto the running board of the cab and grabbed the driver by the throat through the open window. The truck rolled over the curb into one of the steel gates, where the engine stalled.

"We need a medic," one of the picketers was yelling into his cell.

It was the eleventh day of the strike. Picketers had been feeling good, like maybe they were about to get a break. The union was holding a ratification vote the next day and everyone expected it to go the distance. Helios told Jayne he thought this might be their last shift. For the first time, there was some singing, a bit of life in the union line, and even Jayne led them in a few choruses of her favourite balladeer:

"He hands you a nickel, he hands you a dime.
He asks you with a grin if you're having a good time.
Then he fines you every time you slam the door.
No, I ain't going to work for Maggie's brother no more."

So they were all dumbstruck when the semi appeared just before dawn. There was nothing to identify it with Canada Post. Everybody said it was a stupid thing to do this late in the game, contract out privately like that. What was management thinking? Nothing for nearly two weeks, then a lame-ass stunt even some of the lifers had never seen before.

It took two people to pull Helios off the driver, but not before he'd broken several of the man's teeth and brought him to the brink of unconsciousness. Another striker took the keys from the ignition, and then he and a union heavy strong-armed the man out of his truck. It wasn't until someone shone a flashlight on his face that they recognized him. It was the bottle-thrower.

"This is his rig?" someone asked.

"Eat shit and die, scab," Helios yelled at the man.

The medic wasn't necessary. Jayne was more surprised than hurt, and apart from a nosebleed that lasted no more than a minute, she was up and walking almost as soon as she hit the ground. The truck blocked the entrance to the plant for several hours while the Saanich police took statements from each of the strikers. One of the night-shift administrators asked if somebody could please move the damn thing so people could go home.

"I've got my air-brakes," Jayne said, and someone threw her the keys.

Helios looked at her.

"Well, I do," she said. She was climbing into the driver's seat when the driver yelled from the back of a squad car.

"Touch my truck, cunt, I'll rip your head off and shit in it," he said. He was still yelling while the police drove him away.

"The cop said he stole it," Helios said.

THE SERVICE WAS COMING to an end. People were being asked to stay for refreshments and some music. The rattle of collapsible chairs filled the airy vault above Helios' head, joined by the percussion of dishes and cutlery and long buffet tables being pushed together, the snap of tablecloths about to cover them. Helios and Jayne made their way downstairs and joined the crowd. Jayne's father waved at them from the far wall where he and the band were setting up.

"I guess this is the wrong place to talk about Palestine," Helios whispered.

"None of these people is hard-core. But yes. Wrong time."

Jayne and Helios gave an envelope of cash to the parents of the boy. The sum remained a mystery to Helios, a figure that was some multiple of ... was it the boy's age? He couldn't remember. There were so many rituals to keep track of, and he said so to Jayne.

"You have no idea," she said. "They have a special person just to turn off the lights on shabbas. Something about electrical devices. A shabbas goy, they call him. I don't know if they have one here, but you never can tell."

Some of the food was just food, and Helios ate and drank a few glasses of wine and spent some time talking to a piano tuner. The man was a

South African who'd grown tired of apartheid and had fled to Canada with his wife in the seventies. For a while he'd taught in the public schools, but when class sizes started to tip the scale at thirty-five he apprenticed with a local piano repair business. Now, he said, he made less money and enjoyed life more.

"Do what you want," he told Helios. "Anything else will end up killing you."

"Don't be such a nebbish," the man's wife said.

Helios found out later the man had cancer, that he'd just finished a round of chemo and so far things looked good for him. This was a different crowd from the post office, a wider mix, with people he couldn't predict so easily, couldn't size up in a single glance. It still bothered him they even paid lip service to all the religious mumbo-jumbo. The subject put him to sleep most of the time, but any idiot could see the idea of a Jewish god was a contradiction from the start.

Jayne's father introduced the band and the next hour was filled with middle-eastern be-bop, a whiny, almost atonal mix of instruments Helios had never imagined together — clarinets? mandolins? — and which produced what could only be described as a kind of soulful wailing. He wondered if people were being polite or whether they really liked it. The disadvantage to growing up in any culture, he decided, was that a person lost objectivity. Or was objectivity a cultural value he'd assumed from growing up here? Helios wasn't ready for this kind of irony so early in the day and he returned to the buffet and filled his plate again. An older woman his mother's age was poking away at one of the jellied salads — at least, that's what it looked like to Helios — and she turned every once in a while to look at him. He remembered seeing her from his seat up in the balcony. She'd been sitting with the family.

"You're lucky," she said to him finally.

Helios waited.

"Such hair is a blessing on a man. So full and thick. My husband lost his early, the putz. It was like someone died or something. But I loved that about him. So passionate. The young men today, they give up too soon. I see them, heads all shaved. Life is over the day their hair starts to recede. It's a shame. What are we supposed to think? Like they're all Olympic swimmers maybe? Or cancer patients?"

Helios didn't know what to say. He was surprised that the woman had said anything at all to him. He was used to going along unnoticed despite the length of his hair, which he thought had ceased long ago to be a distinguishing feature. Possibly, he was even a bit of an anachronism. Most of the time, though, he simply felt invisible, so much so that he was startled every time Jayne picked him out of a crowd, waiting in line at the movies or walking across the shop floor at the sortation centre. The first time she did this, he realized he had always believed that, were he required to recognize himself — he imagined a police photo display or news video of some disaster — he might not be able to do it.

"Do you think they're something like that?" the woman asked him.

"I'm sorry?" Helios said.

"All those bald young men," she said.

Helios shrugged and looked over her head for Jayne.

"Or maybe they're gay," she said, walking away.

It was the sort of meaningless thought Helios had often heard his mother utter, the kind of thinking aloud she had developed over the years, which some people mistook for conversation. Helios believed everyone maintained a running silent monologue — sudden eruptions of memory or a series of almost instantaneous and often unrepeatable responses to events and people, except that his mother spoke hers aloud. She was incapable of suppressing herself. He remembered sitting in the back seat of their car when he was young, watching her nod then shake her head as she argued silently with a client or one of his father's relatives, even a politician she decided she didn't like. Even if he couldn't hear her over the noise of the engine, he knew her lips were moving. It was something he at first objected to, and then later missed when he left home.

HELIOS HAD LAST SPOKEN to his mother three days ago. She had called him from a payphone in Kamloops. Could he mail her some pot?

She wouldn't have a clue who to ask on her own, not in this town, she'd said. She'd rationed herself over the last month with what he'd sold her in the spring, and she'd never had the courage to approach someone about buying more. It seemed a dangerous thing to do in the small towns she'd been passing through, with their one hotel and their Wendy's and their tourist information booth. Hell, they'd probably throw her in jail just for asking.

"You have no idea," Helios said. "Pot is what keeps those towns alive." He told her of trimming crews that spent their winters in the Kootenays, tree planters with no work, a lot of time on their hands and snowboards to wax. They spent their days trimming the leaf from acres of bud that had been raised in grow-ops all over the Slocan Valley. "A good trimmer can make a few thousand dollars in no time."

"I didn't know," Annie said. Still, would he mind mailing her some? She'd feel silly asking around. The mornings were so fresh in the interior, she said. And the light. She couldn't remember anything quite so lovely as the light. He should think about getting away himself, with Jayne. What he needed was a good vacation.

She was disturbed to hear Fergus had gone into the hospital. Helios hadn't meant to tell her, but she had asked how he was, and he saw no real reason to keep it from her.

"He'll be happy to get this out of the way," she said after she got over her surprise. "It's been nagging at him for months. I wouldn't be surprised if he has a new lease on life. Do you think I should call him?"

Helios thought he heard in his mother's question another question, a wish to know whether a call from her was now an intrusion, unwelcome. His own feelings were not entirely clear on this issue. Mostly, he felt a murky dread that whatever he said might trigger a reaction he'd later regret. He hated this walking on tiptoe, the way his parents now listened for clues in the facts he related, gleaned them for signs, interpretations. Fergus said this; Annie said that. Finally, Helios said, "I think he'd like that. He's been a bit lonely these days." *There, she can make of that what she wants.*

"Really."

"A little down, yeah."

"This isn't punishment, Helios. I'm not doing this to get back at him. People need a reason to do what they do. Maybe I gave him one."

"She was very young."

"I liked her. How's the house?"

Helios had already told her about Fergus moving out, how he and Jayne had moved in to look after the place. "We're in my old room."

"You never liked it in the basement, did you? I'm sorry about that."

HELIOS' FATHER HAD BEEN determined not to stay in the house after Annie left. The very next day he had gone out and bought a lease on a condominium close to the deli. It was a bachelor with a loft and its own space for a kayak should he choose to buy one and recreate himself on the waters of the Inner Harbour. Helios had tried to intervene, but Fergus said he just wouldn't feel right about staying, he being the *cause célèbre* of all the fuss, and as far as leaving it empty, would he and Jayne please consider moving in together? To take care of the bills, mow the lawns, and give the place a lived-in look that would fool any of the thousands of thieves thinking of stripping the house clean. It would only be a temporary arrangement, Helios' father had said, but if it worked out that he and Jayne stayed forever, he wouldn't object, certainly not if Annie thought it was okay, and besides, he couldn't think of any better use for the house than to give it to two people who seemed as happy together as they did. Helios had developed a series of nasty foot infections since he'd moved into his basement suite — a "traveling blister show" is how he described them to the doctor — due, he had no doubt, to the rich fungal breeding ground of his bathroom and the pervasive dampness of the apartment in general. Any change was a good one, as far as he was concerned.

THE CROWD AT THE synagogue was starting to thin out. Jayne hovered close to the band. Helios knew she wanted to give her father a critique of the performance. She had written a few notes down on a napkin — which songs were successful, which needed work. The trick to klesmer, she told Helios, was improvisation. In that regard, she said, it had strong links to jazz, and her father's classical training limited him somewhat when it came time for him to let loose. She was pleased to see he had been applying himself, and she wanted to offer him some encouragement. But after a few minutes she turned around and came back to where he was standing.

"Not a good time?" he asked.

Jayne shook her head, and she and Helios walked out of the synagogue together.

Helios knew Jayne was working something out with her father, some penance she was paying or exacting, he wasn't quite sure. It was an area he had learned to avoid in his conversations with her, at least for now. He found her a contradiction, so earnest about the business of honesty and justice in her work and in the way Helios and his parents dealt with Fergus' recent indiscretion, but so tentative, cautious, whenever her own family sailed into the picture. He supposed someone else would call her a hypocrite, but Helios had seen enough of his mother's and father's eccentricities to know that Jayne was only being human. He even felt strangely hopeful when he saw her like this.

[III]

There had been a violent purge of their numbers several years earlier, but the rabbits browsing the grounds of Victoria General Hospital were as thick as ever, black-and-white lawn ornaments supplemented at intervals by a tawny member of the wild population. They carried toxoplasmosis and other viral diseases, the presence of which fueled the drive to eradicate the animals — the majority of them the progeny of abandoned pets — from the property, but sympathetic animal lovers mitigated the scope of the program so that within a short time they were crowding the patio of the commissary again and lining the boulevards on either side of the hospital's entrance drive. Some said locals came with crossbows at night, drawn by the prospect of easy prey; there was no denying that many of the rabbits had grown fat and lazy on the large expanses of lawn.

His catheter firmly strapped to his leg so there would be as little movement as possible, Fergus watched out the window of his semi-private as the pattern of rabbits against a green background changed throughout the day like a very slow screensaver. Earlier, a visiting child had forced them to regroup near the woods that bordered the parking lot, and just after lunch a hawk overhead — Fergus saw a shadow and assumed, but for all he knew it might have been a seagull — sent the smarter ones hopping for cover. They were entertainment, a change from *People* magazine and *Reader's Digest*. Fergus' roommate was drugged most of the time, a traffic victim, sporting casts on both of his legs.

Fergus had heard the nurse speak of a motorcycle, a "crotch rocket," she'd called it, how they maimed more often than they killed and guess who picked up the tab when fun turned to fracture? Fergus had assumed the patient was asleep and had taken her criticism as an invitation to contribute his own; he'd told her what a relief it was not to have to make conversation with a stranger, that he'd been fearing sharing a room with a chatty burn victim or someone with an inoperable brain tumor whose mind had started to wander. The nurse gave him a stern look, put her fingers to her lips to shush him and walked out the door. Now it seemed as if the nurses treated him like a pariah, dropping off his dinners without a word, ignoring his calls, waiting until the catheter backed up before relieving him of his "waste."

It was still better than a repeat performance at the Jubilee, Fergus told himself.

He hadn't wanted to be admitted this soon, even after the incident at the convenience store. At his doctor's appointment, he'd suggested putting off the operation until the end of summer. He'd just bought a condominium, he told the doctor. He needed a bit of time. Things weren't all that bad. "Let's wait and see," he'd said. "Maybe the selenium will kick in." Wasn't that one of the options? What had the doctor called it ... careful watching?

"Watchful waiting," the doctor said. And in Fergus' case, that option was no longer available. Retention was a serious problem now. This was no longer elective surgery. Did Fergus understand the meaning of kidney failure? This was more than a question of quality of life. This was life itself. No more questions. Time for the knife.

At least they didn't have to shave him. The catheter was a bother, but he'd be rid of it tomorrow when they discharged him. Helios and Jayne had popped in yesterday for a while. They said they'd pick him up when he was ready, but Fergus had no intention of putting them to any trouble. A city bus stopped outside once every hour. He would take one back into town. On his own again, independent, a self-sufficient man. Maybe he'd even sell his car.

The new hospital occupied a lot of land that had once been forest and field, and more land had been taken by the recent expansion and upgrading of the highway. Fergus rarely had any reason to come out this way — the last time had been to rescue Annie's car — and now as he looked out the window he tried to superimpose what he remembered of the area when he was young on top of the altered landscape that spread out before him. His grandmother had lived not far from here, and just down from her place was where he'd had the bad accident on his bicycle. This used to be country, a greenbelt around the city — not an intentional one, and more valuable now that all the easy farmland of Saanich had been bulldozed into subdivisions. Change happened so slowly in Victoria; sometimes he didn't notice it. He remembered a conversation he'd had once with Annie.

"Funny how morning slips into afternoon," she'd said. They'd been reading on the deck during a holiday weekend, completely absorbed in their books.

"Funny," he'd answered, "how youth slips into middle age."

They had both laughed — he remembered that, too — a side-splitting laugh that nearly tossed them both out of their chairs, and when they finally stopped, neither of them could say exactly what it was they had both found so hilarious.

IF SOMEBODY HAD TOLD Fergus that by pulling such and such a lever or pushing such and such a button he would be dropping Annie out of his life for good, he would have made a point of keeping his hands behind his back and staying as far away as possible from such a machine. His intention had never been to rid himself of her. He remembered a movie — he'd seen it with his parents, a film starring Jack Lemmon — with a court scene in which the main character argues that every man would get rid of his wife if he could do it painlessly and anonymously. He remembered Lemmon taking a piece of chalk and drawing a white spot on a desk and convincing the judge that just by putting his finger on it, he could be single again. By tempting the judge, Lemmon had won his case. It was a corny movie, the kind where women wore a lot of hairspray and low-cut dresses and the men were always rolling their eyes at them as though they were dumb as kitchen tile. Fergus couldn't remember how it ended, but he did remember the ride home in his parents' car.

"I wonder where I can get me a piece of chalk like that," his father had joked.

"Don't get any wise ideas," his mother said to his father. "I don't disappear so easily."

"What if I wrote you a cheque," his father said, "a nice big one you could buy yourself a ticket out of here with?"

"The day you have that kind of money," she said, "is the day you're stuck with me for good."

That was the first time Fergus had contemplated the possibility his parents might not stay together. They had fought for years — small rows, door-slamming in the worst of them, a kind of background noise he'd always taken for granted. The thought that they might actually dislike each other enough to separate came as a shock to him. They never did separate, it turned out. Instead, they resigned themselves to a truth that had become obvious to them over the years, if not to Fergus: this was the best it was going to get for either of them, and old age would be less painful and the funeral bills more manageable if they put any notions of real happiness out of mind.

So here am I, thought Fergus, almost the same age my parents were when I saw that film, out on my ear, in recovery from prostate surgery, thinking about taking a bus home to my swinger's condo downtown. Annie had always warned him against making comparisons, but sometimes it was impossible not to. Another idea for an A&E special suggested itself: "Failed Expectations — Children Who Dropped the Ball." Peter Fonda came to mind, Liza Minelli, too. Maybe Julian Lennon. At least Fergus was in good company.

Somebody phoned for Fergus after six that evening. Whoever it was reached the nursing station and no farther. The nurse didn't tell him about the call until later. It was a woman, said the nurse. She didn't leave her name.

"I could have come to the phone," he said.

"That's why people rent phones. So *we* don't have to answer them."

He thought it might have been Caroline. He hadn't seen her since the dinner. "A night like that kind of takes the wind out of your sails," she'd said, when he called her the day after Annie left. He thought he understood what she meant, but he was curious to know if the doldrums she was talking about were the permanent kind. Once, he complained to his grandmother about how cheap his parents were. It was when his father had refused for the final time to take him to the World's Fair. Fergus told her he wished he'd been born into a richer family.

"Be careful what you ask for," his grandmother said.

"Why?"

"Because you just might get it."

He hadn't understood what she meant, how there ever could be a time when he'd regret a wish he'd made. Perhaps Caroline was thinking this was one of those times.

What interested Fergus even more was how quickly his life had unraveled with just a few ill-conceived moves. Hadn't he studied this once? In "the birth of tragedy," a first-year university course, the standard introduction to the Greeks? He remembered struggling with almost everything Aristotle wrote about. A person had to be a shit from the start, as far as he'd been able to see, to do what most tragic heroes did. The best a tragic hero could hope for was to end up recognizing what a shit he'd been all his life. At least, that's all that had happened in any of the plays Fergus had read.

AFTER BARELY A MONTH in his new condo, Fergus broke the lease and moved out. He couldn't take stepping over the drunks in his door-way after dark, the screams that burst the air just outside his window when he was trying to sleep, the propositions from hookers as he walked up the street for a bite at Foo Hong's. He'd fallen down the ladder from his loft, too. He had been going to use the bathroom in the tense days after his operation. He'd been told to watch for blood in his urine, to avoid any kind of retention and to be very conscious of dribbling. His mind was preoccupied with all these and other post-op instructions, and he'd missed a rung on his way down and fallen backwards, hitting his shoulder on the corner of a bookshelf he'd picked up and put together that afternoon. For a minute he'd thought he'd broken his back, and when he finally collected himself to finish the journey, he noticed in the bright halogen glow of the bathroom that the toilet water was tinged a light pink. He had imagined something tearing inside, the wall of the urethra or what remained of the prostate itself. He had imagined his bowels filling up with blood. The next morning, he started packing.

Helios objected at first. Over the phone, Fergus could hear the exasperation in his son's voice, the incredulity, too, as though there was something intolerably ludicrous in the idea that Fergus would live in the basement while Helios and Jayne occupied the upstairs. The ceilings were too low, Helios protested. Fergus would hit his head on the beams.

"You did it for years. And you're taller than I am," Fergus said.

"I was shorter then," Helios said.

Fergus said it was ideal. He had his own bathroom, a fridge and a hotplate. Even his own private entrance. The price was right, too. This way he could come and go as he pleased without answering to anybody.

"I can take off whenever I like," he said.

"Take off?"

FERGUS HAD BEEN RIGHT about Caroline. The dinner had cut her up pretty badly. Annie couldn't have known how effective it would be in souring the way Fergus and Caroline saw each other. Or maybe she had. Annie was very smart.

"I liked her," Caroline told him. "She's a nice person. I liked Helios too. And Jayne. I liked everybody. Except I didn't like me. Or you. I especially didn't like you."

She'd told him this out near Cattle Point in Oak Bay. Fergus had just moved into his condominium and was scheduled to go into hospital in a couple of days. He'd phoned her from his new place, feeling stupidly free in his bachelor pad. There was no need now to search out a pay phone, communicate in code; he was just another single guy setting up a date with someone who was ridiculously young. He consoled himself by remembering he wasn't one of those men who had asked for this, wasn't the kind of sap who dreamed of freedom, of release from the stifling cage of his marriage, only to discover he had been happiest behind bars. No, this wasn't irony. He was a sap of a different kind. It was well into July now, almost three weeks since the dinner, since he'd last seen either Annie or Caroline, and since the first of several painful near blockages that had sent him to the doctor. He and Caroline had planned to go for a walk, but ended up sitting on the rocks that looked toward Mt. Baker. Every once in a while a truck would arrive towing a boat, and a couple of men would back a trailer down the boat ramp and head out into the strait to do some fishing. The day was a bit overcast, no actual rain, but once or twice Fergus thought he felt drizzle on his face.

"Sometimes, I get the feeling you're not all there, Fergus. I don't think you're a complete human being. You do things and you say things and you sound like you have feelings, but I don't really believe you do anymore. I think you're weird."

Fergus thought about disagreeing with her, but decided against it. Besides, he was arriving at the same conclusion himself.

"You didn't have to come to the dinner," he said. "That was pretty weird, too, if you ask me. Not many people would have done that."

"I'm glad I did. I learned a lot."

Fergus said he had, too.

"I don't want you coming to my apartment anymore. I don't think it's good for Melissa. She knows more than we think she does, and I'm not sure I like what she's been seeing."

They had left each other without kissing. Passion seemed out of place, inappropriate, the way it would between two people closing a deal on a vacuum cleaner. Fergus realized he'd been thinking about sex the entire time they'd been talking — particular sex, in Caroline's bedroom, the way she liked Italian tenors, how she played them low in the background, at least one candle burning. He liked how clothing became interesting again for a while; he liked the brief nap afterwards, the shower. He thought of her perfume on his clothes, the smell of her he tried to conceal on his way home, stopping at a gas station to fill up, splashing his hands a little, the gum he kept in the car glove box, the shirts he'd wash by hand in the laundry tub downstairs. It occurred to him he might never have sex again, and then, as though she'd heard him say this idea out loud, Caroline stopped walking.

"Don't phone me, either," she said. And then she got in her truck and drove away.

Fergus turned to leave, too, and nearly walked into two men who had just returned from fishing. One man was holding up a large salmon by its gills, his rod beside him, while the other one snapped a picture of the fish and his friend with a disposable camera.

"Smile, goddammit," the man with the camera was saying. "You know, this isn't a fucking funeral."

DORIS PHONED FERGUS at seven the next morning to say she was quitting.

"I'm going to the hospital tomorrow," Fergus told her. "I don't have time for this."

"Neither do I," she said. The work at the deli was killing her, she said. When Fergus started to explain, she told him she didn't want to know. People like Fergus and Annie would never understand what it was like to be a wage-earner.

"You expect too much," she told him. "That's your problem. You live in your own little melodrama where it's okay to do whatever you want as long as you're paying minimum wage. Like we don't have lives, too. Well, fuck you. Fuck you both."

Fergus waited an hour, and then he went down to the shop. Nothing had been cleaned properly in days. The gas burners were filthy, the oven a mess. The floor was sticky with spilt food and juice. Doris had left the dishwasher full and three bags of garbage at the back door. One of the coolers was broken. He spent an hour on the stove and another couple mopping and putting things back where they belonged. The till was empty except for Visa slips from the previous day. The flowers by the door were dead, almost dry. The water in their vase had evaporated ages ago. Somebody had thrown the tip jar against the wall and smashed it. People came by and tried the door. Most of them spent some time peering in to see if a locked door was just a mistake. A few even knocked, and one banged on the front window. Fergus ignored them all.

He made himself a cup of coffee and sat on a plastic chair in the back lot drinking it. A couple of skateboarders were throwing themselves off a set of stairs at the far end of the lot, three long steps from which they would launch into the air and land at the bottom in a crouch, struggling to stay on the board without falling. Only a tall blond boy managed to stay up consistently, quite an accomplishment, Fergus was thinking, with hair like that, the bangs long over his eyes and thick. It was a wonder he could see anything at all.

The day was sultry, almost hot, one of those doses of summer that send the people of Victoria into shock, incredulous that they, too, might walk around like tourists in their own town, sporting shorts and sandals and light cotton shirts, their cynicism evaporating, burning off like a cloud after the rains of June.

Fergus was thinking about the deli, the slog of days he saw in front of him, having to advertise for someone to replace Doris, the interviews, the time it would take to train a person who had even a little restaurant experience. A day would come, he told himself, when he wouldn't have to think about these things, when he could spend his Saturdays doing what he wanted. The idea made him pause, an unfinished thought that demanded completion, the enumeration of the hundreds of pursuits he'd been denying himself all these years. What exactly did he want to do?

It was amazing how often he had put off answering this question, and even now as it formed in his mind, he stood up instinctively and started to enter the deli, where he would invent more chores for himself, more excuses. But he wasn't opening the deli today. He'd already decided the morning was a write-off. One look at what was left in the remaining cooler told him it made sense to close for the afternoon as well. Would he open it tomorrow? Is that what he wanted to do? He should get on the phone, then, start placing a few orders. They were low on everything. He walked into the pantry and looked at the extension on the wall, the list of distributors beside it, their numbers written out in Annie's hand, a few comments scrawled beside some of them — *call Mondays; won't deliver after four.* He couldn't bring himself to pick up the phone. The thought was as repugnant as lacing up his runners to go for a run, something he hadn't done in weeks. His stamina was gone. He had no will to keep going. *There must be something wrong with me,* he thought. His grandfather had worked right up until the day he died. Thirty-three years. Fergus trembled at the thought. He'd rather shoot himself. He wondered if this was how his father had felt, if this was why he'd asked Fergus to take over. Maybe it just became too much for him. He thought of his father now, talking it over with his mother, the two of them discussing how it had passed to them, and how Fergus wasn't even full-time with the federal government, married, a young son to look after. They must have run to the phone, couldn't wait another minute, not even until Sunday dinner. What a relief that must have been for him, just to give the store away! He put himself in his father's place, imagined he was hearing his own son's voice. *Sure,* he was saying. *Why not?*

Helios, he thought. He could give it to Helios.

And then he stopped himself.

He looked around at the pantry, the brick walls that had been painted more times than he could count. He saw the ghost of his grandfather walking into the space where the meat locker used to be. He saw the greasy apron and the butcher's cap the old man always hung on the hook by the sink when he was finished for the day. He saw his father wearing the same hat, laughing about it, joking how it was one piece of clothing that had really paid for itself.

"That shirt your mother bought you?" he'd say. "Better get used to it, kid. You won't see another one for years."

Fergus imagined his father all those years later, his drinking days done, standing on a cliff in Barbados, one of a couple of dozen retired seniors who had paid to get off the cruise ship and board a bus for a tour of Sam Lord's Castle, the tour guide calling out names and Fergus' father shaking his head, telling himself it was all a mistake, that he hadn't spent his life behind a meat counter so he could listen to this jerk all day. And then Fergus saw himself, lugging cases of olive oil through the back door, sacks of onions and potatoes, the awning as it unwound each morning, and later as he rolled it back up at the end of the day. The stack of chairs, the steel cable that coiled its way among the tables outside, the local paper and the *Globe and Mail* that waited for him outside the door when he arrived.

"Enough of this crap," he said.

[IV]

J ust north of Kamloops, B.C., Paul Lake Road crossed the Yellowhead Highway and climbed east into the mountains where the air in summer was cooler and where the Kamloops Indian Band made it very clear to tourists and locals that they would exercise their historical claim to the land and close all access if they felt their rights were being abused.

It was the middle of August, and the hills were as brown as they were going to get. Tumbleweed crowded the ditches along the plateau above the canyon, and stray steers that had shouldered their way through a weak strand of barbed wire wandered along the right of way, unaware they were free. Storm clouds rolled in across Todd Mountain to the north, carrying with them the lightning that would start another half dozen fires in the area. Annie followed an RV on its way into the city, content to poke along at fifty kilometres an hour. Every once in a while a pickup or an SUV or a luridly painted Harley Davidson passed the both of them at speeds of a hundred-and-twenty or more. It was still early. The sun had not yet cleared Harper Mountain behind her. Annie had rolled down all the windows in her car to take advantage of the cool morning air before it disappeared completely. The RV's brake lights flashed on in front of her and she knew she was approaching another of the steel cattle guards that interrupted the road between Paul Lake and Kamloops. When the wheels of Annie's car passed over these grids, the chassis vibrated violently for a second. Each time it happened, Annie was surprised by the terror she felt, and she looked forward to the next one the way as a child she'd wanted to see Jack come out of his box again.

Annie was tanned from weeks of lying in the sun on a lakeside dock. She couldn't remember ever being this dark, not even when she was young. Passing her reflection in the mirror, even now, she couldn't help stopping to marvel at her arms, the darker crevices around her collarbone. *I must be rich,* she told herself. *Only the rich can afford to lie around like this. The poor are pale, like termites that never see the light of day. I'm not a termite,* she told herself. "Je réfuse," she said to the mirror.

Annie wasn't rich. She had no idea how much money she had. The bankcard went in, the money came out. She never asked for a receipt. She didn't want to know. Whatever Fergus was doing, it must be working, because there was always money there when she needed it for bottled water and groceries and propane and gas. At first she had bought wine, too, out of habit, opened it with the wooden-handled corkscrew that came with the cabin, and sat out on the porch looking over the lake, sipping from her glass. After a week, she had felt silly sitting there drinking by herself, like a travel advertisement for the recently bereaved: "When you're missing that special somebody …" The wine made her sleepy and drove her to bed early, where she spent a restless night and woke up tired.

Right around the time Fergus was getting out of the hospital, Annie had found a rental in Kamloops that looked promising — bedroom, living-room, kitchen, outdoor toilet. Right on the water, boat included. There had already been five days of solid rain, and the forecast was for more. The owner wanted a long-term lease, for the whole summer, and by that time Annie was tired of motels. The agent gave her a set of keys and a map, and she gave him three months' rent in advance. After she left the office, she went out and celebrated by buying herself dinner at a small Greek restaurant two doors down called Skipos, a whitewashed single-storey building with a patio that looked out on the main street, Tranquille Road. Annie had never seen a town quite as ugly as Kamloops. She sat in the patio looking out at the strip of thrift shops and donut emporiums, forgetting the menu in front of her, and when the waiter came with his pad, she had to ask him to come back later. When the waiter came back a third time, she knew this was a city she could grow to love. She ordered the appetizer platter and a half-carafe of retsina, and the waiter commended her choice, saying it was the restaurant's best dish. He seemed to have taken a shine to Annie, her distracted ways, and he introduced himself as Sherwin, confiding to her that he was a business student at the college. Annie listened to him talk about his courses, the girl he was seeing, all the time relieved that she would never have to invent a nickname for a boyfriend named Sherwin.

She was not driving legally when she left the restaurant. The stupor induced by the retsina made deciphering the agent's map more difficult. Twice she lost her way and had to backtrack. What she found in the end was a lake and an address carved into a plank. Beside the plank was a space to park her car. A few steps beyond the sign was a steep narrow lot and a path that led down through alders and young fir to a cedar shack built in part on piles driven into the lake bottom. The cedar siding was rough — board and batten — with holes of various sizes cut out for windows that looked as though they'd been salvaged from a house demolition. There was no insulation. A Franklin stove sat in one corner on a hearth made of used bricks. There was a three-burner gas stove and a toaster oven. The fridge was miniature. Annie lay down on the bed and didn't wake until morning.

THE WOMAN AT THE STORE called her Mrs. Goodlake. The woman's husband told Annie not to mind. She'd come around, he said. Annie had never mentioned her name to either of them. A greenhouse up the road sold Roma tomatoes and green peppers and cucumbers, and Annie spent an hour one day listening to the owner tell her about various grades of plastic and the length of time each could withstand the destructive effects of ultraviolet radiation. This last batch had lasted seven years. The fishing lodge offered cheap dinners every Friday night and sold red wine by the cup. Electric outboard motors pushed aluminum boats the length of the lake and back again while their occupants raised fishing rods to the sky, the monofilament of their lines catching the light along with stray spider threads that drifted in the breeze. Every evening the sun set behind a mountain that looked like a preposterously large pair of buttocks.

Annie thought she ought to read. She didn't feel ignorant so much as empty. There was a hollowness inside her, a chasm she had somehow failed to notice all her life. She thought of the word "fulfilling," how people used it to talk about their jobs, their family, charities they supported, as though they too had a similar hole. She brought home a pillar of books from the library on her first trip into town for supplies. The next morning, she arranged a chair on the dock, a table, an umbrella for shade. Out of her bag came *Lolita, The Sun Also Rises, Disgrace*. Out of her bag came *The Reader, Atonement,* and *Silk*. As the sun rose on her right, beyond Chase and Shuswap Lake, she opened one book after another, only to close each in turn, annoyed and confused after just a few chapters. How could she have chosen six books about love, about men and women, by chance? She pulled out *The Woman Who Walked Into Doors, The House of Mirth,* and *Child of God*. These, too, she put down. Was this what writers thought was important? She tried to remember a single book she had read that didn't have something to do with heartbreak or sex or betrayal. *Moby Dick*? Possibly. She remembered a bunch of men with harpoons, that white whale. There must be more. It bothered her to think that the antics of people who were just as self-involved and thoughtless and petty as she and Fergus were subjects worthy of literature. On her next visit to the library, she brought home the biographies of Paul Cézanne, Lord Byron and Dorothy Parker along with the history of the Suez Canal and Margaret Mead's *Growing Up in Samoa*. She suspected her objections to fiction applied to these books as well, but she found the treatment more palatable.

Annie ate, but she didn't spend a lot of time thinking about cooking. She put food in her stomach, enough to take away her hunger. Often it was a piece of fruit or a slice of bread, something that didn't require a lot of preparation. More effort than that and she lost her appetite,

as though the last fifteen years with the deli had lowered some immu-
nity she had to the business of the kitchen, the way too many bee
stings will make a person even more vulnerable to their poison. She ate
the way an animal eats, whenever she wanted to and without consideration to taste, and when she'd had enough, she stopped, no matter
what was left on her plate.

This new freedom from the drudgery of dinners thrilled her, and
whenever she was thrilled she wanted to tell Fergus of the outstanding
discovery she had made. That she couldn't do so filled her with anger, as
though Fergus had knowingly removed this particular pleasure from her
life. She wanted to call him and let him know how unfair he was being,
an idea that thrilled her even more because it meant she would hear
his voice again after two months of traveling and living alone, months
during which she hadn't succeeded once in thinking like a single person.
There was a dialogue with Fergus she couldn't shut off, even when she
was by herself. After twenty-five years, she was as much Fergus as she
was Annie, not for any spiritual reason, no conjunction of souls, but
because his was the face she had looked at for so long, and she had rarely
expressed herself or heard her own voice in a situation where Fergus
wasn't the mirror that reflected her words and ideas back to her. When
Helios was young, he had astonished her at breakfast one morning by
telling her that she would never see what he saw.

"What are you talking about?" she'd asked him.

"I see you and Dad," he said. "You'll never see that."

It was the simple truth of how people perceived the world — in the
faces of their family, their lovers. Perhaps that was why Annie was startled every time she saw a photo of herself or spied her reflection in a
store window. Her world didn't include herself.

The time she'd phoned the hospital, she hadn't got through. The
nurse had started to tell her about ward policy concerning phone calls
and Annie had hung up. These months later, it occurred to her she
didn't even know how Fergus' operation had turned out. Helios continued to mail her small packages of pot to the local post office, but he

included no note, no update on affairs at home. Annie had wanted to leave him out of things as much as possible. She'd seen several of her friends use their children as go-betweens, and the results had never been good.

THROUGHOUT THE DAY and very often at night, motorcycles rumbled along the road above her shack, their short mufflers barely dampening the loud snap of their engines as they accelerated along the straight stretches or when a rider backed off on the throttle around some turn. At the local store, Annie complained to one of the locals.

"That'd be George," the man said. "He's harmless enough, I guess."

"But noisy."

"I guess."

George had once raced for a living until an accident had left him with more steel than bone in his legs and lower back. Now he ran a garage where he customized frames and tanks and blueprinted the engines of bikers from all over the northwest. The machines these people rode were like any other machines, as far as Annie was concerned, the particulars of their make and history of no interest to her. Motorcycles, like sports and cars and computers and cameras, were just another private club, another means of exclusion.

She was picking early blackberries along the road one day when a group of motorcycles roared into the driveway just in front of her. Their sudden turn and the noise they made had frightened her into dropping her bowl, and when none of the riders walked back to help her gather the spilled berries — a gesture Annie thought was owed her — her anger got the better of her. She headed down the dirt road to the garage to give somebody a talking to. It was only ten, but already the day was hot. Long grass in the centre of the driveway was dry and tinted with crankcase oil, and hundreds of tall verbascum on either side were long past their bloom. Here and there, she saw rusting pieces of machinery disappearing into the undergrowth and, closer to the shop, the wheelless chassis of a Toyota Land Cruiser. On a level stretch of ground above the lake, a man crouched down beside a motorcycle, its engine still running, a screwdriver in his hand. He had no tattoos, no scars, no earrings, but his hair was long, as was his beard, and the T-shirt he was wearing said, "Reality is for People Who Don't Ride." Before long, another biker joined him.

"You startled me, that's all," Annie said over the noise of the engine. The two men turned to look at her.

"You should watch out for people," she said. "It's called being good neighbours. Where I come from, bikers are not generally popular. A little consideration wouldn't hurt your image."

The biker with the screwdriver stood up and approached her. For all his hair and beard, Annie could see he was barely out of his twenties. She tried to imagine a kind of deference in the way he looked at her, believing she merited some measure of respect as a person who was approaching the age of a grandmother, but there was nothing of the kind.

"This is the best chop shop outside of Vancouver," he said. "If you lived around here, you would know that."

"Maybe you should drive a little more carefully," she said, turning to leave.

"You were on the road, lady."

Annie traipsed back up the driveway, happy she had said her piece, but relieved, too, to leave the place behind. What had she been thinking? Maybe they'd apologize? Offer her a beer?

She'd looked into the garage as she passed, a red barn with a cement floor, and hundreds of motorcycle parts littered the building, hanging on the wall or suspended from beams. She'd heard that George suffered from limited flexibility after his last crash and had designed a series of hydraulically driven hoists and cherry-pickers which allowed him to work on most of his projects standing up. She saw somebody in there, and whoever it was waved at her, but she was too angry and scared to wave back.

Over the weeks, Annie became only slightly more conversant with the bikers. She was a renter without any rights, a woman on her own.

In her mind, they were like some kind of species of bird, preoccupied with the dictates of their genetics, blinkered, obsessed by speed and power, preening themselves in some extremely rare and specific manner to attract a mate that might not even exist. Their language seemed to boil down to a series of phrases, aphorisms that carried the weight of scripture.

"Cars are transportation," she heard one say once. "Bikes are a way of life."

In a rare conversation she had with one of the bikers on the roadway, she confessed to him that a little Honda might be nice. The reaction had been swift and predictable.

"Rice burners aren't motorcycles," he said.

Annie heard the racism in the man's answer but didn't push him on it. These were people, after all, not angels. It was easy to tell they enjoyed their status as mystery men, loners with dark pasts and volatile temperaments. On some days, it seemed so long since she could count anyone as her friend, Annie found herself wishing to embrace even these rough characters and their company with as few reservations as she could bear. She waved at them as they passed her car on the way into town, and once she asked one of them to carry her propane down to the shack when the forty-pounder ran out. Their number changed over time as bikes came and went, but whenever she took her boat out to do a little fishing, it gave her some comfort to see there was always someone at work on the property, a project of some sort underway. Any hint of a fairy tale ended, however, when she came home one day to find her shack had been broken into. The rental agency sent two people to repair her door and add better locks to her windows, and although she had no real proof about who was responsible, for days after that Annie kept a kitchen knife beside her bed.

TODAY, ANNIE WAS keenly aware of how the winding canyon road descended steeply on its way to Kamloops. The RV seemed to have its brakes on permanently. Annie kept a healthy distance between herself and the careening motorhome. She was in good time. Fergus' bus wasn't arriving for another hour. There might even be time to go to the liquor store and pick up a bottle of wine. He'd seemed so pleased to hear her voice on the phone the other night, she didn't have the heart to tell him she had no idea he was living in the basement, that she'd actually phoned to speak to Helios and that it was he who had suggested she might like to talk to him.

"It's for you," she'd heard Helios yell down the stairs. What a diplomat.

Not a word from Fergus about Caroline, not that Annie would have asked. His business, she'd decided long ago. She wasn't surprised to hear that he wanted to sell the deli, either. "I was wondering," she said. "It would be a lot of work on your own."

"Doris quit."

She wasn't to worry about money, Fergus told her. If the place sold, he'd put her share in a separate account. They could settle that whenever. Annie said there was no hurry. The summer seemed to go on forever up here, she said. Time disappeared.

"Nice," Fergus said.

Did he know the area?

AT THE BUS DEPOT, they circled each other at first. Fergus turned almost immediately to retrieve his luggage from the underbelly of the bus, and Annie stood on the other side of the daypack while he fiddled with the bus tags and worried the receipt for his ticket. At the car, he heaved his gear into the trunk, and when he turned back to her, they fell together into an awkward hug, which after a few seconds thawed into a familiar embrace, hanging on to each other like old friends who had suffered an unavoidable absence, a gap that even now was disappearing, the sort of trauma both their minds would choose to forget. Annie closed the lid of the trunk. He'd traveled light, she said. "Don't need much," he said. When they got to the car, she asked him if he wanted to drive.

"No, you. I'd only get us lost."

As they rose above Kamloops, the afternoon sun behind them and the high country of Paul Lake ahead, a big Harley with ape hangers came around a curve toward them, the driver waving as he passed.

"Who was that?" Fergus asked.

"You don't know him."

Annie was thinking about her bed at the shack. It would be a tight fit, she thought, but they'd manage.

[V]

Fergus has a piece missing from his life. His parents are sympathetic. They try to console him. His father shows him cancelled cheques from years earlier.

"I don't even remember who these people are anymore. You get used to it."

Fergus knows it's not as bad as giving up a finger or a toe, not crippling the way losing a single lung might be — he'd gasp for breath all the time — or even worse, one of his eyes — he'd have to wear a flesh-coloured patch to mark its absence. There are even days when his particular amputation takes on all the allure of an episode from his favourite television program, *Twilight Zone*. Perhaps he participated in a shift in time, traveled to another dimension where he had a different life, different friends, who knows, maybe even a family and job. Long after the accident, he goes to sleep believing he will dream of what happened to him. The problem, he tells himself, will be to recognize which of his dreams are true and which are false. Already, his mind is full of what people have told him about the accident, where it happened, the things they found lying beside him, and he knows he will have trouble keeping these images separate from his own memories, when and if they ever return. The task seems hopeless, but he prepares himself for these dreams anyway by lying on his back and folding his arms across his chest.

At school, he discovers that the bully has been expelled. The boy was caught breaking into the gymnasium on the long weekend and his parents have transferred him to another district. He still lives in the neighborhood, but Fergus could not be more relieved if the boy had been shot. Mr. Stringer gives Fergus the Latin prize two weeks after his return. The prize is a book about the history of the automobile. In it Fergus reads about the maker of the Rolls Royce, how, after a long illness, he lay dying in the back of one of his own cars as they sped him to a hospital for treatment. In the story, the driver tells the dying man there is another car overtaking them, despite the speed they are traveling. The old man finds the news disheartening until the driver speaks to him again as the other car passes them.

"Not to worry, sir. It's another Silver Cloud."

Fergus reads this story over and over again. He reads it to his mother while she is peeling potatoes on the back porch. He reads it to his father as he clips the edges along the driveway. For Fergus, the story is a sign of order in the world, that things happen for a reason. He imagines a similar book about his own life, the writer describing Fergus' mysterious loss of memory, the gruesome details of his discovery at the side of the road, events that will take on greater meaning later in Fergus' life. At this point in his imaginings, Fergus tries to invent the neat ironic twist that brings his memories alive again — the insignificant incident that triggers a flood of lost images that instantly take on greater meaning, as though the missing events of those days had a life of their own, a velocity, a trajectory that all this time has been leading them like that second Rolls Royce, the one that passed the dying inventor, to a moment far in the future when they will serve to console Fergus at a desperate time in his life and allow him to continue, gratified that his days upon the earth have not been in vain. Perhaps it will be a crisis on the operating table, or a tricky moment clinging to the side of a mountain face. Maybe it will be the last few seconds in the flight of a doomed plane. Fergus speculates at length about the singular event that will open his past to him, but matter how hard he tries, he can think of nothing. His imagination, he tells himself, is not up to the task, a failure that doesn't dishearten him because he believes this kind of vision is beyond the grasp of any mortal, that in fact were it possible for him to imagine such a moment, the universe would no longer be the mystery it is. Instead, Fergus invents a sort of religion for himself, an adoration of the unseen, of his lost days, a creed he practises every evening by placing the book about automobiles upright on his dresser, the cover facing toward his bed like an icon in a church. It's the last thing he looks at before going to sleep and the first thing he turns to in the morning when he wakes. But like the stairs he used to count as he went from the top floor to the main, or the sidewalk cracks he once avoided, the worship of this book is a passing exercise in whimsy. When Fergus turns thirteen, his parents sell the house and move to the far side of the bay to a more modern home with a sundeck and a dry basement. And though, for a while, Fergus continues to practise his peculiar belief, it isn't long before his faith finally wavers and dies.

[VI]

Two weeks into September, in the parking lot of a Safeway in Kamloops, Fergus leaned down to see whether the repair work on the Camry's power steering was still holding. It had been a while since he'd taken it in. The car sat between two dusty SUVs, newer models, and Fergus divided his thoughts between their lure of solid steel and power and gaping interiors, and the flyer that he had tucked into his back pocket before setting out to town. Fall giveaways were in progress, along with local harvests of late corn and beets. This far from the coast, there was a bite in the air at night. He and Annie were needing the quilt that came with the cabin, even a fire some days.

Annie had circled toilet paper and bananas. Thirty-nine cents a pound for the bananas, and tins of salmon were on sale. They talked about money, how it wasn't coming in anymore, and how they should husband their savings until the sale of the deli. Fergus and Annie shared a job mowing the lawns at the fishing lodge, weeding the beds, doing odd errands. It would end soon, but for now they spent what they made and no more.

"You just handle the upkeep," Annie told Helios over the phone one evening. He was offering to pay rent for the house in Victoria. She said, "The taxes aren't due for a while."

"What will you do?"

"Manage," she said.

The days were still hot. Sun-soaked asphalt burned Fergus' hands as he peered under the car looking for drips. He stared and stared until the lure of air conditioning and aisles of food finally pulled him to his feet and set him walking toward the automatic Safeway doors. Fruit. Some tinned fish. A carton of eggs. Fergus remembered his grandmother at the end of her life. She had lived like this. One day at a time, her kitchen table covered with coupons. She would phone Fergus' mother and tell her about the bargains she'd found, ask for a ride in the days after she'd stopped driving.

Fergus slipped a coin into a shopping buggy and unchained it from the line. He moved into the processed air of the store, linoleum muting the sound of sandals, cowboy boots, rubber wheels turning. Something Fergus had been reading nibbled at his concentration — an article, maybe, a chapter in a book about plants. Something about how people forget, about how they were forgetting things all the time. An enzyme in the brain was responsible, or a hormone. Neural transmitter, that was it. Annie had read it to him. The writer was a big fan of marijuana and how it made people forget quicker than normal. Whole conversations. The taste of a raspberry. Names. So when stoned people ate something, or spoke a thought, or sat in a chair, it was as though they were doing it for the first time.

"No wonder I like it so much," Annie had said. ·

Fergus had refrained from comment. He was saying less and less these days, even though he had the feeling he'd never talked so much in his life. This drug thing. He'd looked away the first time Annie had pulled out her pipe and lit it: the old Fergus retreating. But they were on different ground, he told himself. Different customs were required, a different language. He'd been invited here, a guest. Any welcome implied a certain level of civility, engagement. This idea amused him — that he had come calling, his shoes shined, a bouquet of flowers behind his back, his opinions banished out of courtesy. It made him think marriage was a sorry institution indeed, if it allowed gentility to pass, good manners to decay into rancor and resentment, a kind of slow-acting virus that broke down the original sweet urge to be kind, to honour, to elevate. To connect.

He had started smoking a little pot himself at Annie's urging, something he would never have done with Caroline, so conscious was he of his age, the incongruity of a man near fifty sucking in a lungful of smoke with a woman who still had friends in their twenties. The thought of sex with Caroline had never been as problematic as that of getting stoned with her, and Fergus was still trying to work out why this was so.

AT THE CHECKOUT, Fergus pushed his purchases toward the cashier, a young woman, her hair tied back, fingernails glistening from a recent manicure. It wasn't hard to see she was both beautiful and desirable, though why she should wish to appear so in such a place was a mystery to Fergus. It occurred to Fergus that some man probably loved this woman, a man who would be terribly upset if she took it into her head to sleep with someone else. Or perhaps the man who loved her was taking advantage of this time the way Fergus had so often done with Annie.

"Plastic or paper," the woman said.

"Either's fine," Fergus said.

He watched her weigh the fruit, scan the dry goods, hands passing over each item as though she were casting a spell. Or maybe she was blessing it. Fergus smiled at the thought. Enchanting, that's what she was. To sleep with a different woman was an adventure in magic. New body, signals, clues to discover. What astonished Fergus was how much less free he'd always felt after sleeping with Caroline, as though he'd slung a weighted rope around his feet. He wondered if it was the same for women. It seemed to him men lost something when they flitted from bed to bed. They became more who they really were, more earthbound than ever. Somehow, women became lighter, or so he imagined. In his head, he could hear Annie telling him he was full of shit. Caroline, too.

SHORTLY BEFORE THE accident at the church, Annie had asked Fergus to help her find her cellphone. She had lost it in the woods on the day her car had broken down, and he had driven her back to the spot the next day. It was a sunny morning just after a rain and the field was as wet as a field could be without being flooded. The trees drooped under the weight of the water that had fallen on them. Annie was having a hard time remembering exactly where she had stumbled in the fading light of the previous evening, and both he and she were soaked from walking through the knee-high salal and ferns.

"It's probably useless by now," Fergus said. "All this water."

"You give up too easily," Annie said. "You always have." She walked over to him, and at the last moment, she extended her hand. Fergus had thought she was going to hit him, but she stopped and reached down into the bag she had asked him to carry and pulled out another cellphone, his. She turned it on and dialled a number.

"Now listen," she said.

They had both stopped breathing for a few seconds. In the brush not far from where they were standing, Fergus heard an electronic chirping, and then another. Even these many months later, he could still remember the inexplicable urge he'd felt to answer it.

EPILOGUE

Out of Business

[Out of Business]

After Doris picked up the tip jar and threw it against the brick wall, she walked out of Goodlake's and followed her usual route home. On her kitchen counter lay a generic application she had been filling out, intending to send it to a restaurant that had recently opened, a hybrid Ethiopian and Middle Eastern place that had advertised for staff over the radio and in the local paper. Doris had finished the first half of the form, and when she saw it after returning from her last day at the deli, she tore it neatly into two pieces and slipped it into the blue recycling box beside her refrigerator. Then she sat at the desk beside her bed and wrote in the journal that she had been keeping since she turned twelve — now a work that occupied over a hundred spiral binders she stored in three cardboard boxes under her bed. She didn't write about the rust on the blue bridge she had just walked across, nor about the blackberry bushes that had been cut to nothing near the trestle that led into the city. She didn't write about the single Sitka spruce among a stand of fir and cedar in the park that bordered the Gorge, and she didn't write about the sound of a piece of sheet metal she'd found on a construction site, its faux-thunder that rolled into the air each time she shook it, how two people had stopped to look at her, getting off their bikes to stand with their backs to the sun, a couple of silhouettes, faceless, leaving only after she stopped making the sound. She wrote, instead, as she always did, not in her own words, but in the words of others, copying snatches of poems or novels, articles she found in magazines, words and phrases she had heard throughout the day, passages that moved her or confirmed something she believed. On this day, she chose to write out a couple of paragraphs from an essay in a periodical devoted to architecture in which the author, a retired architect from California, discussed the meaning of space. She wrote:

"People may like to believe for the sake of convenience, for the purposes of conversation, convention, clarity, that they occupy a building the way a spirit occupies a body. The analogy is pleasing to the mind, like the idea of a box that fits inside another box which itself may fit into yet another. But it is truer to say that the building occupies the person, that its bearing walls, the angled corners of its rooms, height of windowsills, thresholds, door handles, that all of these inhabit the people who live their lives walking the building's neatly established boundaries. On a moonless night, when the light from the street is too weak to penetrate the fog that has gathered just before dawn, a man might waken with the need to pee, and loath to flick a switch, to shatter the stillness behind his eyes, he chooses to walk instead across the floorboards that appear inside his mind, to make the appropriate turns and descents that lead him to the bathroom at the end of the hall. He sees everything, sightless as he is, because he has absorbed the house into himself. It is part of his understanding of measurement, of size and proportion. It informs how he sees the rest of the world.

"This is true even after the building has been abandoned or demolished. It is why we can so easily walk through the homes of our childhood in our dreams, revisit basements and attics and bedrooms, touch again the pale green coverlets on our single beds, brush our hands across rough plaster walls, feel the weight of the sash windows, their reluctance to rise in wet weather."

After reading over what she had written, Doris added a comment of her own: "People are better off without their memories is what he means to say."

Almost immediately, she grew tired of writing and lay down and slept, only to wake up in the dark and find herself wishing to sleep again.

GOODLAKE'S DELICATESSEN closed forever in July, just before Fergus bought his bus ticket to the Interior. As he was about to lock the door for the last time, he felt in his pocket for the skeleton key his grandfather had received the day he first leased the building. Then he turned the deadbolt until it hit home, noting as he always did that the doorjamb stiffened slightly with the pressure he applied. Fergus was still recovering from a chance meeting with Caroline earlier in the day, a momentary encounter that had happened on a walk through Beacon Hill Park. He had come upon a city crew on its lunch break — two men and Caroline sitting along a bench, their truck parked nearby. He had not been prepared to see her face out of context like that, simply a detail in the landscape, and when she turned to look at him, the pain of recognition almost stopped the blood in his veins. It was a peculiar feeling, strangely pleasing and repellent, as though he had run into Annie's former lover, not his own. He was astonished to remember a time at university when he had watched from the third floor of the library as Annie walked from the commons to her class with an older man he had never seen before. He remembered the sickening feeling that had passed over him when he came upon them a second time, chatting in the line at the cafeteria. The man's face had held such terror for Fergus that he could barely look at him, even when his fears turned out to be unjustified. *Which is more attractive,* he wondered in the moment he saw Caroline's face at the park: *to betray or to be betrayed?*

She had gone over to him and walked a little way with him. "This is going to happen," she said.

For a second, Fergus had been unsure of her meaning, as though she were uttering a prophecy, and not a truth about the size of the city, the inevitable coincidences.

"You'll have to get used to it," she said. And then, after a few seconds, "So will I."

"Shouldn't be a problem," he said.

"No, it shouldn't," she said.

But it is, he'd wanted to add after she'd gone.

FALL CAME, AND THEN winter. Helios and Jayne found they didn't like living in Annie and Fergus' house, not because it offended their taste, but because the temptation to stay there was too great. There was all the space, for one thing, whole rooms they never used, an entire basement that echoed their footsteps back to them. It made them uncomfortable, as though it demanded something from them, something they weren't prepared to give. For a while they worked in the garden on their days off, mowed lawns, took their coffee out on the back deck while the weather permitted. Some evenings they went for walks or rented a movie to watch on the set upstairs. They grew less comfortable instead of more. Helios discovered that he put off coming to bed, developed the habit of falling asleep on the sofa. Jayne ate anywhere but in the kitchen, took her plate and sat in the hall, the sewing room. It was as though they'd slipped ahead in time to their own retirement, and the displacement was making them ill. In December, Helios phoned his parents, who — because of their age, their apparent harmlessness — had been asked to housesit for a couple of snowbirds right through to spring. Helios told them he and Jayne had found a nice one-bedroom on the main floor of a three-storey reno near the breakwater. They needn't worry, he told them. He would arrange renters for their house, take care of the yard, box up anything valuable.

"Thanks," he told them both. "Thanks, but no thanks."

DURING THIS TIME, the man who had come to Fergus' aid so long ago died. Ron fell and broke his hip on a sidewalk outside his apartment in James Bay. It happened just after dusk during a sudden rain shower, his rubber-tipped wooden cane losing its grip as he approached the curb. He lay on the wet ground for more than fifteen minutes before someone came to help him. He was conscious all this time, but in too much pain to attempt to rise or drag himself into the bus shelter only a few yards down the street. The break in his hip was not a serious one, but the cold he caught turned into pneumonia before a week was out, and in the delirium that prefaced his death, he confused the events of his own accident with those of the day he had witnessed Fergus slam into a metal fence. In his bewildered state, he imagined he might actually be the boy he once stopped his car to help, and, in the final stages of his fever, he kept turning his head to see the family he knew to be on the far side of the road — the wife he had divorced years ago, the children in the back seat. One of those children, the one son remaining in the city, told his sister and stepbrother that he'd missed the moment his father passed away when he stepped out to make a phone call home. The truth was that he had been unable to bear the sight of his father violently twisting his neck, his eyes wildly anxious, bent on seeing something — the son assumed it was his own death. He had left the hospital and walked several blocks to a corner store where he bought a package of cigarettes.

GOODLAKE'S REMAINED VACANT and unsold for a year following Fergus' departure, its freezers agape, the coolers unplugged and emanating the scent of oxidized aluminum, while rats reclaimed the floors, counter surfaces, the dark spaces behind cupboards, stoves and sinks. The quarry tiles lost their sheen to a layer of dust. Flyers formed a messy pyramid beneath the mail slot. Without Fergus and his arsenal of solvents, thinners, wire brushes and scrapers, the exterior walls — especially the wall that bordered the alley — suffered the tags of graffiti artists. Their handiwork spread over months to include the window along the face of the building, the front door, the entire expanse of rock foundation at the rear, even the gas meter. For a while, former customers imagined Goodlake's was on holiday, that a possible renovation was in the works, an expansion, perhaps. No sign declared the owners' intentions, no rezoning notice appeared, but those who had come to rely on the place continued to walk by, sometimes stopping to peer in the window, to turn the door handle and push. Some of these people, the older ones, kept the store alive in their homes for years afterwards, referring to it in their directions to friends: *at the bottom of the street, next to where Goodlake's used to be,* they'd say. Others forgot it had closed and dialed the deli's number still listed by their phone to ask about cuts of meat, Melton Mowbray pie. Most, though, did not even register the delicatessen's demise. Or, if they did, it wasn't until much later, in the way that some people will not immediately recognize the theft of something familiar from their home — a wooden chair recruited only for Christmas dinners, for example, or a squat, serviceable pitcher — a thing that in its familiarity becomes almost invisible, and might as well not exist at all.

[Credits]

p.28. "Down in the west Texas town of El Paso" from "El Paso" sung and written by Marty Robbins on Columbia Records, released 1959.

p.75. "Hey boy ... things again" — a recording from the radio announcer R. Pate, at the radio station KHAR, who was on duty when the earthquake struck. The text was found at the following website: http://www.ce.washington.edu/~liquefaction/html/quakes/alaska/radioannouncement.htm. However, as the website acknowledges, the announcement was originally cited in the book: Bolt, Bruce. A., *Earthquakes: A primer*, pp.25-27, Publ. W.H. Freeman and Company, 1978.

p.185. "... holding the oranges they had caught minutes earlier." This particular detail comes from an account of the disaster written by Christina Ward for disasterrelief.org, which can be found at http://www.disasterrelief.org/Disasters/010326alaskaquake1964/

p. 186. Mrs. Lowell Thomas' account of the subsidence at Turnagain Heights was printed in the July 1964 issue of the *National Geographic*.

p. 197. "Genghis Khan ... when we get up to it." From "You Ain't Going Nowhere" by Bob Dylan from the Basement Tapes, 1967.

p. 226. "ALASKA RIPPED BY EARTHQUAKE" Details are taken from *The Victoria Times* issue of March 28th, 1964.

p. 227. "... a British aerialist by the name of Ann Mombray ..." This story also taken from *The Victoria Times* of the same date.

p. 315. "It wasn't much of a house anyway ... " This detail and those that follow on the next page are taken from an account given by Charles Ford which was originally published in the *Victoria Times-Colonist* and is now collected at the following website: http://www.pep.bc.ca/hazard_preparedness/zeballos_64/tidalwave.html

p. 335. "He hands you a nickel ... Maggie's brother no more." From "Maggie's Farm," 1965, words and music by Bob Dylan.

[Acknowledgements]

I WOULD LIKE to thank Bill Gaston, Mike Matthews, Jay Ruzesky and Bill Stenson for their help and encouragement with the initial draft of this book. They are gentlemen all, in fiction and in life. For the final version of *After Goodlake's*, I am deeply indebted to the fine eye and critical advice of Lynn Henry, my editor, who helped sculpt this book into its present form. Finally, I would like to acknowledge the assistance of the Canada Council and the B.C. Arts Council, and to thank them for recognizing the merit of this project in its early stages.

Part of this novel appeared in issue #86 of the *New Quarterly*, as a chapter entitled "Bad Men Who Love Jesus."

PHOTO CREDIT: PATRICIA YOUNG

TERENCE YOUNG is the author of a book of poetry, *The Island in Winter* (Vehicule, 1999), which was nominated for the Governor-General's Award, and a short fiction collection, *Rhymes with Useless* (Raincoast, 2000) which was shortlisted for the Danuta Gleed Award. Terence Young is co-editor of *The Claremont Review*, an international literary magazine for young writers, and teaches English at St Michael's University School in Victoria, BC.